# GIMME MORE

**BY THE SAME AUTHOR**

# GIMME MORE

## LIZA CODY

BLOOMSBURY

First published 2000
This paperback edition published 2001

Copyright © 2000 by Liza Cody

The moral right of the author has been asserted

Bloomsbury Publishing Plc, 38 Soho Square, London W1D 3HB

A CIP catalogue record for this book
is available from the British Library

ISBN 0 7475 5208 8

10 9 8 7 6 5 4 3 2 1

Typeset by Hewer Text Ltd, Edinburgh
Printed in England by Clays Ltd, St Ives plc

# ACKNOWLEDGEMENTS

'KIND HEARTED WOMAN BLUES'
Robert Johnson, author
© (1978) 1990, 1991 King of Spades Music
All rights reserved. Used by permission.

'SHE JUST WANTS TO DANCE'
Words and music by Kevin Moore and Georgina Graper
© 1994 Playin' Possum Music and Keb' Mo' Music, USA
Warner/Chappell Music Ltd, London, W6 8BS
Reproduced by permission of IMP Ltd.

'MEMO FROM TURNER'
Written by Mick Jagger & Keith Richards
© 1969. Renewed 1997 ABKCO Music, Inc.
All rights reserved. Reprinted by permission.

Lyrics from 'AWFUL'
(Love/Erlandson/Auf Der Maur/Schemel)
© 1998 by kind permission of Mother May I Music/
Polygram Music Publishing Ltd.

Lyrics from 'ACROSS THE BORDERLINE'
(Dickinson/Hiatt/Cooder)
© 1982 by kind permission of
MCA Music Publishing/MCA Music Ltd.

'RIGHT IN TIME'
Words and music by Lucinda Williams
© 1998 Lucy Jones Music and Nomad-Noman Music, USA
Warner/Chappell Music Ltd, London, W6 8BS
Reproduced by permission of IMP Ltd.

# Bitchcraft

'She's a kindhearted woman, she studies evil all the time.'

Robert Johnson

I am the bitch who puts her bags on the empty seat beside her. If you want to sit next to me you have to ask my permission. Even when I'm travelling scuzz-class. Especially when I'm travelling scuzz-class.

The train was hot and crowded. Coats were rolled like loft insulation in the luggage racks. Frayed and fractious children squawked. Weary travellers tried to blank them out. I had the scuzz-class blues.

We waited. It would be a few minutes before the doors closed and after the initial scramble, anxious lethargy blanketed the train.

'Um, 'scuse me.'

I looked up into a pale twitchy face.

'I'm in a jam,' he said. 'Can you help me out?'

I pulled off my headphones. 'Depends,' I said.

''Cos me an' my wife we're really in a jam,' he said. 'We've got to get to London and I ain't got any money. See, my social security cheque didn't turn up and we got on the train without a ticket.'

He was talking very fast, looking over his shoulder and sweating.

'And the ticket inspector's coming and we'll be chucked off and fined. And we've got to get to London to see our little kiddy who's in hospital. At the children's hospital. She's very sick.'

I tried to look down the carriage to see where the inspector was, but the man was blocking my view and I couldn't even see his wife.

'It's only ten quid,' he said. 'Each. Twenty quid. I wouldn't ask but I'm really desperate. You'll get it back. My social worker's meeting us at Paddington. So you'll get it back in fifteen minutes. Twenty quid for fifteen minutes. What d'you say? I'm really sorry I got to ask but the inspector's on his way and we're so desperate.'

He wasn't giving me time to think. I smiled at him slowly.

'Please,' he said, sweating, twitching. 'Can you help me?'

'OK,' I said.

'Jesus, thank you,' he said, holding his hand out. 'Only twenty quid.'

'Calm down,' I said. 'Why don't you and your wife take a seat?'

'The money,' he said, hand still outstretched, fingers shaking.

'I'll take care of the inspector when he comes. He'll take a credit card.'

'Will he?' he said. 'Oh, right. I'll fetch the wife.'

And off he went, so quickly that he didn't catch my most helpful sympathetic smile. What a waste.

I craned my head round the back of my seat and saw him approach another woman further down the carriage. He was still talking very fast, sweating, twitching, nervous. Not his wife, then.

It's none of my business how a man makes a living, but this woman was trying to keep two small children under control, and there aren't many who make the effort. She already had her hand in her handbag and I thought: effort should be rewarded, not punished. Maybe the man's effort should be rewarded too, but not by a woman with two small children who still has kindness to spare for a stranger.

I got up and walked towards them, still wearing my most helpful, sympathetic smile. I tapped the man on the shoulder.

'How're you doing?' I asked.

'Shit,' he said. 'Why don't you fuck off and mind your own business?'

I didn't say anything. I just smiled at him.

'Fuck!' he said. He ran down the carriage and jumped out on to the platform.

The shuttle lurched and started off slowly.

'What was all that about?' the mother asked.

We passed the twitchy man, still standing on the platform. He saw us watching and gave us his middle finger. Three times. Hard.

'Was he conning me?'

'Yes.'

'How do you know?'

'I offered to pay for him by plastic,' I said. 'He doesn't want a ticket. He wants cash.'

'Oh,' she said, blushing.

I went back to my seat thinking about the blush. The mother was embarrassed because a man had marked her out, seen her weakness and exploited it. Probably everyone she knew exploited her kindness – her husband, her children, her friends as well as strangers.

As for the twitchy man – well, he wasn't a very good hustler. He had some things right. Speed, not giving your mark time to think, social embarrassment, they're all good strategies. But the sick kiddy was crude. He should have worked harder on a less plausible story because a less plausible story is more likely to be believed. You have to be imaginative and articulate if you want to be a successful hustler. Or pretty and charming. You have to be able to reward your victim one way or another.

They don't call them *confidence* tricks for nothing. A good scam is based on a relationship, even if it only lasts for thirty seconds. Your mark has to *want* to give you something. And to be a good scammer you should want to give them something back.

I used to have long legs, long hair, long eyelashes and dewy youth. I was willing to share them with strangers, even for the price of a train ticket. I looked fabulous and I didn't have to pay for anything. Why? Because people wanted to be seen with me, if only for thirty seconds. I looked like a reward for a rock star. If you top the chart with your latest album you deserve someone looking like me to swish into clubs with. It's expected. I'm part of the package.

I mean I *was* part of the package. Not any more. Dewy youth, nowadays, is not what I have to offer. And when did you last see a superstar of my generation swishing into a hot club with a woman his own age on his arm?

The shuttle rolled into Paddington. The mother collected coats, bags, children, the push-chair, and unloaded them. No one stopped to help her. Not even me. I'd saved her twenty quid – that was my good deed for the day.

But as I overtook her she said, 'I should have thanked you but I was too confused.'

'That's OK,' I said, moving on, not wanting to be caught.

'No, really,' she said. 'I'd have forked out twenty pounds like a lamb and it's more than I can afford.'

'I know,' I said, backing away, suddenly distressed.

'So thank you.'

Her toddler son gave me a blindingly sweet smile and silently offered his packet of crisps.

I took one. If a man wants to give you something, take it. Even if it's a potato crisp and he's only three years old. It's what he's got to give.

That is a scammer's skill. It's a judgment you make almost instantly. What will your mark part with happily? Set the right price and you're halfway home.

Mr Twitch set my price at twenty quid; the same price he set for a harassed mother. That was the cause of my distress. It was comforting to remember that he was a very crude scammer and presumably incapable of fine judgment but it was, all the same, a bad jolt to my confidence.

Twenty pounds, Mr Twitch? That's your price, not mine. Not for this girl. Not even now. I don't live on a fixed income and I don't spend my days with only two rowdy toddlers for company. Although, sometimes, when I meet one with a blindingly sweet smile I do wonder what I missed.

But that's just sentimentality. Blindingly sweet smiles come two-a-penny. I had one myself, and I used it mercilessly.

A smile is a mask. Mr Twitch used a different mask. His was a furrowed brow, anxiety. But he was too nervous. He couldn't control the sweat, and that's because he didn't believe. You have to believe in your mask to control it – like I believe in smiles and tears and the power of a song.

Once when I was very young I was scammed myself by a song, a smile and a tear. A legendary bluesman called Dude Dexxy convinced me that he wrote 'Honey Crawl' on the spot when I walked into Crawdaddies one summer night. I'd blagged my way past the doorman – I was underage – and I was standing, uncertain, not knowing where to hide, when this deep dark voice from the stage said, 'Hey little girl. You. Yeah you. Come close. This one's for you.' Me. He noticed me. I went to the stage and literally sat at his feet while he played 'Honey Crawl' and the crowd went crazy. I was too green and ignorant to know that he wrote it ten years previously and it was his groove number for pulling dumb little chicks. I just sat there with bass and drums vibrating through my body, with Dexxy's voice seeping through my ears to my heart until I felt I'd burst.

I didn't know he'd done time in a Louisiana jail for screwing and stealing from underage girls. A lot of them. Nobody told me his European tour was as much to escape the Feds as it was to feed London's hunger for legendary bluesmen.

He told me he'd been in jail, but when he told me, later that night, I believed it was something to do with racial persecution. And so it was – in a way. A good scammer manipulates truth with a light touch; the same way Dexxy manipulated me.

The odd thing is that I still feel proud that he picked me out as his mark, that he noticed *my* weakness. Even when he'd gone, taking my heart and a fat wad of my dad's money with him, when I understood I'd fallen for a sleazy line, when I knew 'Honey Crawl' was an old song, I still felt a thrill. Because it's a great song and, one time, a legendary bluesman sang it to pull me. He set me on a path of my own, because by the time he left I was part of the legend: underage, leggy, wild child who had been touched by a god and burned. There were so many musicians, who wanted to be gods themselves, who wanted to touch the girl who'd been burned by a genuine, gold-card, legendary bluesman.

Dexxy burned me but he showed me my métier. There was no doubt that I'd sat at the feet of a master. I was his mark and I was marked by it. He showed me that anyone can be made to believe anything, and that I too *want* to believe. Nobody is immune – and that includes you, babe.

Somewhere, in my inexperienced little brain, something clicked and I asked myself – Do you want to be a mark all your life? Or do you want to wear the mask and make 'em pay? Because youth and beauty is a ready-made mask. If you are young and beautiful everyone wants a piece of you anyway. So why not make them pay? Why give away for free what time will erase? You only have it for a short while, so use it.

But that was then. This is now. What is my mask now that youth and beauty are no longer mine to use?

Let me show you. But you must attend because I'm only going to do this once and I'm going to do it fast.

Right in front of Paddington station is the Great Western Hotel. Climb a few stairs, push through glass doors, cross the lounge, slide into the ladies' room. Check the cubicles. All empty. Remove coat. Check mirror. I am wearing a simple long-sleeved, navy blue dress, low-heeled shoes, dark stockings, light make-up. I look like a respectable working woman.

I hide my coat and bag under the counter. Carrying only a magazine I leave the ladies' room and walk purposefully through the hotel lounge. I put the magazine down on one of the coffee tables, turn right again and go into the dining room.

It's lunch time and very crowded. I am looking for someone who is already there. I make that obvious, and none of the restaurant staff stops me.

I take in the whole room. I look right, left. Someone is waiting. I don't know who she is, but she's here, and she must show herself quickly because I haven't got long.

There she is – wearing the smart business suit of middle management. She's with two younger women, she's tapping her credit card on the table cloth, looking round for a server, still talking to her companions who are finishing their coffee.

I'm looking for her, I'm joining her. I smile at a waiter as I make my way over to her table. He can see I'm meeting someone. He can see I have a purpose. He doesn't stop me.

I arrive at the woman's table. I stand at her left-hand side, exactly where she expects to see me.

I say, 'Can I bring you anything else, ma'am?'

'Just the bill,' she says, hardly looking up.

'Are you in a hurry?' I say. 'Shall I take your card?'

She offers me her credit card. I remove it smoothly from her fingers and walk away – out of the dining room, through the hotel lounge, into the ladies' room. I put on my coat. I take a bright Liberty's scarf from my bag and wind it casually round my throat. I throw my bag over my shoulder. I leave the hotel. I snag a taxi.

This incident took longer to relate than it did to execute.

What sort of mask was that? In fact, there were three. When I was in the lounge carrying a magazine I was a hotel resident. When I went into the dining room I was one diner looking for another. When I spoke to the woman I was a waitress. The trick is that waitresses do not carry handbags but hotel residents do. The magazine stood in for a handbag. On an unconscious level people recognise what your function is by what you wear, how you act, what you are or are not carrying. The mask, therefore, is whatever your mark expects to see. It doesn't matter if it is glossy hair and a beautiful face or a business-like, polite demeanour – the same rules apply.

I changed my shoes in the taxi. I changed my scarf, my hairstyle, my lipstick and my polite demeanour. Little things – all of which tell you that the simple navy blue dress may be understated but it is extremely expensive. It would keep a mother and two kids in chicken nuggets for years. Or it would have done when I first took possession of it. But that was a few years ago.

I needed something hot and new for my next appointment and I don't believe in buying my own clothes – not when a bank or a credit company can buy them for me. In other words, I don't believe in using my own credit card. Spending my own money on clothes is a sign of failure. Besides, nowadays, I need to spend a lot of money to look like someone worth spending money on.

My next appointment was with a man called Barry who has a lot of money to spend. I hadn't seen him for years, and in those days he wanted me so much he dribbled.

But those were the days when I did not have mature reflection to bring to a situation. I have maturity in spades now, and reflection tells me that I should not have taken his drool personally. My mark, Barry, is an Englishman and as such he was far more interested in my lover than he was in me. He wanted me because he admired to the point of obsession the man who had me. Barry was a rich hanger-on. A sucker for talent and glamour, he was our satellite, always creeping close, like a lizard drawn to a hot rock. He needed heat but couldn't generate any for himself.

Yes, my mark is a reptile and I am the heat. He wants what he always wanted – which is to be at the centre of a charmed circle; though the charm wore out a long time ago, the magic turned against itself and a third of the magicians are now gone. Including my lover, my playmate, golden Jack.

Jack is the one everyone remembers. Jack is the one who defines me. He gives me an identity, even now. Oh yes, I owe everything to Jack. I am Jack's survivor – his rock-widow.

So I need a rock-widow's frock: something dark, mysterious and tragic. Plus shoes to show off the legs, because legs last longer than faces and should attract the attention they deserve. Unbelievable fuck-off shoes, with a hint of S-M. I want to clothe myself in mystery from head to hem, in decadence from hem to heel. A good mask, like a good hustler, should touch the truth lightly and pass on by. A good hustler should use a stolen credit card quickly and throw it away. Card, discard, and move on.

Shopping done, I checked in at the Savoy where the receptionist delivered a hand-written note. The note read, 'Dear Birdie, I do hope you'll be comfortable here. Old memories, eh? Please, *ring me as soon as you get in*. Can't wait to see you – Barry.'

I said, 'If a Mr Barry Stears rings, would you tell him that I'll meet him here at eight? I don't want to be disturbed till then.'

'I'll make a note of it,' the receptionist said.

I went upstairs. I ran a bath. I remembered Barry and his characteristic anxiety. 'Ring me as soon as you get in.' Underlined. Fat chance. I remembered Barry who had to eat his last meal of the day by 7.30 or his ulcer grumbled. I smiled. Both of us, so far, were running true to form.

I bathed. I lay down. I rested. At seven I ordered a fresh crab salad from room service. I began to dress. The salad came and I ate it. I did not want to be hungry or look hungry.

At eight, the phone rang. I ignored it. It rang again at quarter past, at half past and at a quarter to nine.

At nine I went down. Heads turned. Did you think they wouldn't? Why? It is too easy to assume when you've passed the celebrity-girlfriend stage that you're invisible. But invisibility is only a different sort of mask. If it isn't a convenience, bag it and bin it. Be Someone. Don't just enter – sweep in.

I swept. Heads turned.

Here is Barry, a plump chump in a Savile Row suit. He thinks designer spectacles will make him look hipper.

He says, 'Birdie! My God . . .' He has been expecting me to apologise for making him wait. I can see that on his face. His face changes as his expectations change. He is off-balance already.

'Hi Barry,' I say, as if I last saw him yesterday. 'Where are you taking me?'

'I thought we'd eat here.' He has obviously been keeping the *maître d'* sweet for the last hour.

'Don't you know the *good* places any more?'

He rises to the challenge and we go to the Café D'Arte.

So far so good. I can still make him want to impress me.

You have to be a bitch to force a man to impress you. Being nice does not get you a room at the Savoy or the wherewithal to look utterly cool at the Café D'Arte. It never did and it never will.

Whatever Barry was expecting, it was not a nice woman. A nice woman does not take the piss out of you to your face or even behind your back. A nice woman does not kick you in the balls when, after a couple of lines for courage, you pluck up enough spunk to dribble into her *bustier*. She does not say to her starry boyfriend, 'Hey Jack, queer Stears just tried to hit on me.'

'Kick him in the balls,' said Jack.

'Again?' I said.

'Whatever turns you on,' said Jack. He laughed but the next day he chartered a plane and we went to Antigua. 'Fuckin' rich groupies,' said Jack. 'They think they own you.'

He didn't like it. He thought I had a thing about rich men, and I let him. It kept him on his toes, kept him hungry.

As I swept into Café D'Arte, David Bowie was sweeping out. He came to a dead halt and his satellites piled up behind him.

'Birdie Walker! Jesus – I thought you were dead.'

'Dead to the world,' I said, 'exclusive, reclusive, elusive. There's a difference, you know.'

'I *do* know,' he said. 'Call me.'

I sweep on by. What a piece of luck! Barry is weeing himself – he's with a woman who knows David Bowie. That's Barry in a nutshell.

We sit. We order. Barry would like to ask for a glass of milk for his ulcer. I watch the struggle between common sense and narcissism. Narcissism wins – as it always did – and he orders wine. It is an important indicator.

I am very casual. I scope the room. Barry tries to gain my attention by pointing out the hot new writers, a sculptor, a singer, assorted socialites, a couple of MPs and bankers.

'You've been out of touch for so long,' he says.

'Being here reminds me why,' I say.

'It's changed.'

'Three times, at least.'

'Yes,' he says, 'but it's all coming back. You wouldn't believe the interest the present generation's showing in the old music. *Our* music.'

I look at him. He has enough grace to blush, but he goes on quickly, 'I told you in my letter, I've done a book, and a couple of series for the BBC and Channel 4.'

He waits for me to approve. I raise one eyebrow. Old groupies don't die. They turn into music nerds.

'They went down very well,' he says hurriedly, 'rave reviews et cetera. People can't get enough.'

Food comes: soup for him, a decorative arrangement based on an artichoke for me. He begins to gobble his soup. Good. I can spin out an artichoke for ever. I can make him ravenous.

He says, 'Of course Jack and several others of the people you – er – knew were central to my programmes. You were in there too –

12

that old footage of the Dock Concert, Live at the Hall, other stuff. And the pictures Bailey took. Birdie, you were the quintessential rock-chick.'

'Was I *really*?' I say. Does he honestly think that being called a rock-chick will appeal to my vanity? Yes, he does. He has made a career out of his own sideline association with musos so he must think we are made of the same stuff.

He has finished his soup. I suck delicately on the end of an artichoke leaf. He goes on. 'I'm a bit of a celebrity myself, now; a pundit, whatever.' He watches me eat.

'Why didn't you get in touch, Birdie?' he says. 'You knew I was looking for you two years ago. I talked to your sister and all I got was the big block.'

Always the wrong question. You shouldn't be asking why I haven't been in touch for two years, Barry, you should be asking why I'm in touch now.

'Where have you been, Birdie?'

'Fishing.'

'Fishing?' says Barry, astonished.

I nod and select another artichoke leaf.

'I thought you'd be married to a millionaire by now.'

'Why?'

'Why?' He's astonished again. He has never questioned his judgment of me. He says simply, 'Because you loved spending money.'

Now this is true but if that were all there was to it, Barry, why was I fucking Jack and not you? At the beginning, certainly, you could have bought and sold Jack and the whole band twenty times over.

'You're right,' I say. 'I still love spending money. I'm very good at it.'

'And have you got enough now?' This, to Barry, is the central element of his pitch. Because, if you haven't figured it out already, Barry is pitching to me. It is why a man I once kicked in the balls is paying for me to stay at the Savoy instead of dropping me down the deepest hole he can find.

'If I remember correctly,' he says, 'enough for you is a *lot*.'

'Absolutely correct, Barry,' I say, and I take my time choosing an artichoke leaf. It's painful for him to watch. His stomach hurts and he wants his second course. It's driving him crazy, watching me picking fastidiously at an intricate vegetable. Good. He will come to the point more quickly because he will believe that if he does, he will be controlling the situation. Hunger and impatience are my friends but his enemies.

'So, how *are* you doing these days, Birdie?'

'What you see is what you get,' I say, secure behind my obscenely expensive frock and fuck-off shoes: the frock and shoes he hadn't expected to see on someone who has been off the scene for so long.

'Shine like silver, ring like gold,' I say.

'What?'

But I shrug and don't explain. It's a song: 'Take This Hammer'. Taj Mahal used to sing it and one night I told Jack, 'Your hammer "sure 'nuff shine like silver, ring like solid gold".' He liked that. He picked out the chords till he could play it for me. I lived for those moments. God, he was good, and when he wasn't off his face, he surely did shine like silver, ring like gold. Alone, for once, and quiet, listening to old recordings by legendary bluesmen, picking out chords, riffs and fills, putting a new spin on them, making them his own. That's how the great songs pass from old to young hands, from old to young ears. Old love to new love, nothing starts from scratch. But you, Barry, you can sit and watch me eat artichoke till the angels weep and I won't tell you anything important. Because you won't understand the important things. A great song isn't safe in *your* hands.

Barry says, 'You're an expensive woman, Birdie. You cost Jack a fortune.'

'Yes,' I say. 'And worth every penny.'

'Well, Jack seemed to think so.'

Oh yes, indeed he did, Barry, and you'll never understand why.

'What I'm getting at, Birdie, is that maybe, these days, you don't have quite what you were used to.'

'That's true,' I say, scraping the flesh off another petal. 'However much there is, it's never enough.'

'I'm in a position to help you,' Barry says, smugly. 'I can put you back on the map, Birdie.'

'Where I've always longed to be,' I say. 'Another fifteen minutes of fame.'

'Don't tell me you didn't love it,' Barry says. 'You lapped up all the attention. There was a time when you couldn't open a paper or magazine without seeing your own face. Don't tell me you wouldn't want that again.'

'Even the bad bits?' I say. 'Besides, that was a different face. Who'd want to see it now?'

'You'd be surprised,' he says. 'I'm telling you, everyone's fascinated by the old rock aristocracy. Roots, genealogy – they can't get enough.'

He pauses. He's pitching but he doesn't know how to hook me. I wait, eating tiny particles of food, making his stomach rumble.

'The episode about Jack's era was a huge success. I got Teddy and Goff – they had some terrific stories. But I wish you'd responded when I tried to find you because there was something missing. In those years – those truly great years – you and Jack were joined at the hip. You were there in all the footage and all the stills. But not in person, not in the where-are-they-now section. The guys were great but . . .'

'Music's a very blokish business,' I say. 'All you need is a couple of guys.'

'Wouldn't you like to redress the balance?'

'There isn't a balance.'

He looks at me, he looks at the artichoke. It isn't even half eaten.

'There's money in it, Birdie,' he says. 'Money for old rope. I'm making a compilation programme for the anniversary. It's devoted exclusively to Jack. Maximum budget. I can get you top whack.'

'Not interested,' I say.

'A memorial,' he says. 'Aren't you interested in keeping Jack's memory alive?'

'His memory's very much alive without me making an exhibition of myself for your benefit.'

'You wouldn't be making an exhibition of yourself,' Barry says. 'And it'd be for Jack's benefit.'

'The dead don't need benefits.'

He glares at the artichoke. It's his personal enemy, and so am I. A waiter comes and asks if we're ready for the next course.

'Yes,' says Barry.

'No,' I say, because every time I say no, my price goes up, and Barry is becoming twitchy. Two Mr Twitches in one day – how lucky can a girl get?

'OK, Birdie,' he says, 'final offer: if appearance money won't do, I can negotiate production fees.'

'Oh yeah?' I say. 'What would I have to do for that?'

'Nothing. Really. You get a credit, more money. No work, no hassle. Just show up. Supply some of the material – for which you'll be paid handsomely – we do the interview . . .'

'Material,' I say.

He drags his eyes away from my plate and forces himself to meet my gaze. My eyes should be bland and blue. His aren't. I smile my sweetest smile. His cheek flickers.

'I told you I talked to Teddy and Goff,' he says. 'They say the Antigua Movie exists.'

'Do they now?'

'Everyone said the Antigua Movie was the biggest myth in rock history. But Teddy and Goff say it's no myth. They say Jack had a crew with 16 mil cameras and they filmed and taped all the sessions. Teddy told me you might have it.'

This, of course, is why I'll sleep at the Savoy tonight. This is why the man who hates me is courting me. It's why he dribbled on me years ago. It isn't me he wants, it's Jack. Creep closer to Jack. Seduce his sidemen. Maybe they'll deliver him into your frigid grasp. Buy him. Own him. Warm your chilly bones. And when you can't do that, Barry, court his chick, his bitch, his widow.

'Mmm,' I say. 'Who knows? Jack left me *so* much.'

'Bitter?' For just a second his cold dislike shows but he looks quickly at my neglected plate. I push it away. I don't need it any more. Barry's cards are on the table. All I needed to make him show his hand so soon was an artichoke.

Now he's relieved. He signals the waiter who removes the artichoke and brings us the second course. With a full plate in front of him Barry is in control again. Rich as cream, smooth as butter.

He says, 'OK, Birdie, tell me about it. You two suddenly, for no apparent reason, upped and split to Antigua. After a couple of months, Goff, Teddy and some of the others join you. You've hired some tin-pot Caribbean studio and you put down all the songs and ideas that turned into *Hard Candy* and *Hard Time*. Right?'

'That's right,' I say. 'You know all about it. So why bother me? *Hard Candy* exists. *Hard Time* exists. No one's taking them away from you.'

'They were the end product. Amazing, classic, seminal stuff. Jack's definitive statement. His finest work. But it seems to come out of nowhere.'

'The magic of rock'n'roll.'

'The albums aren't the whole story.'

No, Barry, not to you they aren't, not when you're a groupie, the monarch of music nerds – when what *you* want are the out-takes, the between-takes dialogue, the fights, the *gossip* – when you ached so badly to know what it was *really* like to be Jack you tried to fuck his chick and, for one brief spasm, be where he had been.

He says, 'Jack took the studio tapes to the record company, mainly acoustic stuff, I'm told – like a notebook full of bits and pieces. When the album was finished there was no further use for them. I've been to the record company, I've spent days in their vaults. The guys there say they were lost, cleared out, I don't know. That's what happened in those days. No one had the least idea of the value of what they were throwing away.'

'They had *no* value,' I say. 'As you say – a notebook – not Jack's "definitive statement".'

'How can you say that, Birdie?'

'Because I'm not like you, Barry. What the artist wants to give is good enough for me. I don't want what he had to do to make the gift possible. The rough cuts were not what Jack wanted anyone to hear.'

'Easy for you to say. You were there all the time. You know. You heard. What I'm hoping is that the film of those sessions in Antigua will help fill in the gaps. It would in any case be a valuable social document.'

'Why?' I ask innocently. 'The music's important, but a film of *ad hoc* sessions, work in progress, has no value at all.'

He steadies himself with forkfuls of steak and potatoes and says, 'Excuse me, Birdie, but are you the best judge of what is valuable? I've studied the work and researched it, and written articles on it for years. If I may say so, I'm the one who's, almost single-handedly, kept it alive while tastes changed again and again.'

'You've done a good job.'

He checks my eyes for sarcasm, but all he sees is bland and blue. 'Yes,' he says. 'I have.' He rewards himself with food. 'OK, Birdie, straight question. Were the sessions filmed? Yes or no?'

'Yes, you know that already. Goff or Teddy told you.'

'Then what happened? Where is the film? Was it made?'

'Sort of,' I say. 'No, not really.'

'What do you mean?'

'Look, Barry, it was just a bunch of Berkeley film students we met on a beach. It was just a couple of guys with Eclairs and another guy with a Nagra. We were all bumming around, having a good time.'

'But they were there, damn it, with film in their cameras, at the Antigua sessions. What happened to the film?'

'They took it back to the States to be developed and edited.'

'Who were they, Birdie?'

'I can't remember the names. It was years ago. We spent a load of time stoned, with people drifting in and out. What did Goff and Teddy say?'

'They didn't even remember Berkeley. I suppose that's something at least.'

'Why?'

'To help me track it down.'

'What?'

'Jesus, Birdie, haven't you been listening? The film, the film, the film.'

I pause for a moment before my precision bombing raid. I say, 'But Barry there was no film. All that happened was that these guys stung Jack for a heavy slice of bread for materials and time and what they produced was crap. He'd lost interest by that time, anyway. People were always trying to rip him off.'

I sit back and watch the explosion in Barry's head.

'Produced?' he says. Sweat pops out of his face like bubbles from a baby's mouth. 'You say they actually produced something. You've seen it? Jack saw it?'

'Of course. Jack paid for it, didn't he?'

'What did you see, what did Jack get for his money?'

'Three hours of this and that in three big film cans.'

'Three *hours*?' Barry is dribbling again. It makes me quite nostalgic.

'And all the raw stuff they didn't use. Half a roomful of cans and boxes. I'd no idea it'd take up so much space. We tiptoed around it for days before Jack took it all out to the garden and burnt it.'

Barry's face collapses. 'Jack burnt it?' he whispers.

'Of course,' I say. 'It wasn't just that he'd paid for it. He wanted it so that he could destroy it. By that time, people were already taking things, souvenirs, whatever, just to say they had something of Jack's.'

Barry's collapsed face stains red and I wonder what *he* took. I say, 'It was freaking him out. He had dreams about little pieces of himself being cut off and bleeding away. He wanted to see a shrink but he couldn't trust anyone. So he sort of destroyed the evidence. It was, like, if he had nothing, no one could steal it.'

'So *he* destroyed the film?'

Didn't I tell you? It's no use explaining anything to Barry – he has no understanding whatsoever. I sigh and get on with my job.

'He burnt all the stuff that wasn't used.'

Hope flares like a distress beacon. 'And the three hours?' he croaks.

'Oh, he kept that under the bed,' I say airily. 'He wasn't *completely* paranoid till a few months later.'

I love messing with Barry's head. It renders him so powerless that he can't ask the next question. He has even forgotten to chew.

I say, 'Look, Barry, I don't know what you want me to say. When Jack died the vultures descended. Nearly everything that wasn't burnt was stolen, even his music rights. I rescued what I could, but it wasn't much.'

'The film?' he croaks.

'Maybe,' I say.

'Maybe?'

'I never looked,' I say. 'There's stuff I haven't looked at for years. Life goes on.'

*Yours* did, he wants to say. You went off with the next brightest star as if Jack never existed. He wants to say that as far as he's concerned, I am one of the vultures. Oh he really wants to say it. Poor puppy. I smile at him. He's coming to loathe my sweet smile.

He controls himself. 'So you might have it somewhere?'

'Don't know. Possible.'

'Where?'

'Oh there's stuff all over the place.'

'Can I look?' he says.

'Certainly not,' I say. 'Anyway, it's probably not in England.'

'Not . . . ?'

'No. Look, Barry, I'm tired – I've been travelling all day. And as I'm only spending one night in London I want to get up early tomorrow. There are people I want to see before I leave.'

'But you can't leave,' he says. 'Nothing's settled.'

'That's your problem. You've been badgering me to come and talk to you. I came and talked. Now I want to go home.'

'I don't even know where you live. How can I get in touch?' He is almost wailing. 'You haven't finished dinner yet. You haven't heard my proposition.'

'Yes I have – you said "final offer" when you were talking about production fees. And the food's cold.' I reach for my handbag. There's something emblematic about a woman reaching for her bag. It frightens Barry to death.

'Wait,' he says. 'I didn't mean *final* final offer. Birdie, sit down, will you, please?'

I sit down again, sideways on the edge of my chair, where he has an intimidating view of my legs and the fuck-off shoes. Long legs, S-M shoes, ready to walk, Barry, out of here or all over you. Your choice.

'When I said, "final offer", Birdie, I just meant the programme budget. It's the *programme* which has a limited budget, Birdie, *I* don't. If that film exists, the sky's the limit as far as I'm concerned.'

'Lawd, lawd, lawdie,' I say. 'I had no idea . . .'

'You could buy a fair few frocks and take a couple of luxury cruises on what I have to offer – if the film exists.'

'Tempting,' I say. 'But I'd have to take a few cruises to find the damn thing first. It could be anywhere. For instance, after Jack died, Mick Jagger lent me an island and I left stuff there. And then I was in LA and I left stuff there too. And, who was it? – I don't remember – but he had a big house on Paxos, or was it Naxos? I got around. You know that.'

He knows that. Everyone knew about it. The paparazzi chased me all around the world – Birdie in full flight – and told everyone all about everything.

I say, 'And I'm not going to re-run that trip just to suit you, Barry.'

'Lent you an island?' Barry is appalled and impaled, as usual, on a superstar.

'Don't you believe me?' I say. 'Well, darling, you know all the old faces. Ring him up and ask him to look for your film. Maybe *he* can afford the time and trouble. I can't.'

There – message delivered, loud and clear. It reaches Barry and he sits staring at me with embarrassment, greed and social intimidation leaking from his forehead and upper lip. He's wondering why, after all these years, he still can't afford me. He should have me over a barrel: I'm an ageing broad and everyone knows they mean less than nothing. He's offered me biscuit and a little media attention, so I should be licking his hand and wagging my tail. Age should have softened me and made me malleable.

Instead, I walk, I stalk, I shimmy out of Café D'Arte and disappear into the night. Walker by name, walker by nature. I don't even need a lift.

Except that I did need a lift. My feet hurt. Pride and adrenaline don't last long these days. I was tired. I took a cab back to the Savoy, ditched the shoes, loosened the zips and straps and lay down with Memphis Slim on my Walkman. Then I rolled a joint and went to bed, hustled out. Risks taken, pitches pitched, nothing to do but wait and see how much Barry wanted to redeem himself in his own eyes. A lot? A little? Not at all?

# Part 1

# INTRODUCTIONS

'When the music starts to play, she slides out on the floor,
Dancing without a partner . . .'

Keb' Mo'

# I

## First Impressions

When George first met Linnet Walker she seemed to sail through his window like an exotic bird out of a clear blue sky. In fact, it was a grey day and she walked through the door like everyone else. She didn't perch on the edge of his desk and sing, or preen iridescent feathers – but afterwards, George could never quite lose the impression that she did.

He was not an impressionable man. His partner, Tina Cole, was, if anything, even harder-nosed than he was.

'CV?' Tina asked. 'Did she leave a CV?'

'She didn't even apply for the job,' George said, still bemused. He blinked as if adjusting his eyes back from bright to dim light. 'I think she just came to look us over.'

'She wants a job but she thinks we might not be suitable employers?' Tina said. 'Bleeding nerve!'

'She isn't exactly a school leaver spraying applications all around the neighbourhood,' George explained. 'She's a . . .'

'She's a what?'

But George didn't answer that one. He polished his glasses and said, 'How many have we interviewed, Tina? And how many of those can write a simple letter? Spell even halfway correctly? Read a spread sheet? Fill in a client form? Operate this labyrinth of a computer? Is there a single one of them you'd want answering the phone?'

'This isn't a straightforward job. We might have to do some in-house training.'

'What management manual did you find that euphemism in?'

George looked at his colleague with a mixture of affection and exasperation. 'Do me a favour and explain if by "in-house training" you mean we'll have to teach some adolescent how to spit out her gum and hide the cigarettes before telling a client to "park his arse".'

Tina snorted with laughter. 'Oh, George,' she said, 'we have interviewed some lulus.'

'And we haven't found one we'd even trust as a receptionist – never mind give access to confidential files. We're in the security business, for God's sake. We're supposed to be secure. And confidential. And tactful. And don't say, "It's early days." It's been five weeks, and we're still hanging on by our fingernails without any office help.'

It was nearly eight in the evening. Outside, the traffic was quiet and sleepy. All the other businesses in the street had packed up and gone home except for the Chinese takeaway and the pub, where trade was picking up. The street was in its night-time mode. But Cole-Adler Security still had a lot of catching up to do.

Tina sighed and said, 'Go home, love. You look shattered, and Fay will have my guts for garters. We'll sort it out in the morning, you'll see.'

For once, it was Tina who cast herself in the parental role. Usually George was the one who soothed, sorted and sustained. But methodical, calm George was tired. His comfortable flesh looked almost too heavy for him to carry.

'Go home,' Tina said again.

'You too,' George said. 'We've both reached the point of diminishing returns.'

He was right. They were both tired of running on the spot, of never getting anything done because of the time wasted answering phones, chasing invoices, buying stamps. Cole-Adler Security needed help. Cole-Adler needed a competent office manager.

On his way home, riding the rickety blind worm called the Misery Line by those who knew it best, George thought about Linnet Walker. She was not the sort of woman you'd want to meet when you'd just dropped your cheese and pickle sandwich into the laser printer. He knew what a man of his age and weight looked

26

like from behind, and he knew that the sight was not improved by bending over to scoop mature cheddar out of sensitive electronic equipment while swearing softly and repetitively. But, he reflected sadly, that was exactly what Linnet saw when she walked through the door.

He was expecting to interview a job applicant. He was also expecting a woman who wanted a burglar alarm. He was expecting, too, the accountant for the annual audit. In fact he had triple-booked himself by mistake and it was too late to put it right. Then he'd made matters worse by trying to print out the sheets of in-comings and out-goings which the accountant would need.

George was no whizz-kid. Gadgetry mystified him, and it was many, many years since he qualified as a kid. Pen and ink was his technology. Left in charge of the electronic memo system he remembered nothing, triple-booked himself, and fed his lunch to the laser printer.

He heard Linnet come in and, without straightening or turning, he said, 'Just a minute. Sorry. Bugger. Are you the job, the alarm or the money?'

A soft amused voice answered, 'Which would you like me to be?'

'A brain surgeon,' George said. 'I think I'm performing a frontal lobotomy on this printer, but I don't know where to find the front.'

'Front is my specialty. Let me look at that. My hands are smaller.'

At which point George's reading glasses slid down his nose and joined the cheese and pickle sandwich. He stood up in despair and allowed an angel to redeem him.

Later, at home, when he tried to describe the incident to Fay, he could only say, 'God, I hope she takes the job. She's like an answer to a prayer.'

'I hope so too,' Fay said. She was patting moisturiser on to her face, getting ready for bed. 'You're exhausted. You shouldn't be working like this. Not now. What's she like?'

But George, justly renowned for his careful, police-trained accuracy, couldn't seem to remember.

'She's good with gismos,' he said. 'She cleaned the printer and she figured out the bloody computer.'

'Well, that's worth a week's wages,' Fay said. 'The way you talk about that machine anyone'd think it was a landmine. What's she like with people?'

'Even better.' George was remembering that when the accountant arrived he had still been flustered and afraid he'd miss the client.

'I'll wait for the client,' Linnet said. 'Don't worry.'

And ten minutes later, with the accountant settled in his office, George returned to find that not only was the client happily leafing through brochures but the information the accountant needed was printed up and ready to take through. He felt suddenly that the placidity which was his normal response to life might one day come back to visit him.

'Maybe she won't come back,' George said, climbing wearily into bed. 'Maybe she took one look at the mess I made of the printer and decided she'd rather scrub toilets.'

But two days later, Linnet did come back for a meeting with Tina.

'Bloody hell,' Tina said afterwards, 'I only just stopped myself chaining her to the desk to prevent her leaving. Has she got a black belt in charm, or what?'

'See what I mean?' George said, happy to find out that hard-nosed Tina could be as susceptible to charm in a woman as he was.

'No CV though,' Tina said. 'And only two references. Although I suppose that's what you'd expect from someone who's been looking after her mother for the last ten years.'

'I'll check the references,' George said.

'You won't,' Tina said. 'I will. I don't trust any man as desperate as you.'

When she rang the first of the referees she found herself talking to a French restaurateur.

'Linnet?' he said. 'Oh you mean Chouette. I always call her Chouette. She is my darling of darlings.'

'Er yes,' Tina said, 'but can you tell me what capacity she was employed in, and how reliable she was?'

'She saved my life,' the extravagant voice told her. 'Without

28

Chouette I would be peeling potatoes still. I would be bankrupt. My friends would be weeping at my graveside . . .'

When she put the phone down and sorted fact from hyperbole Tina decided that Linnet had been employed as a general business manager. She must have walked into a restaurant with absolutely nothing to recommend it but a talented, flamboyant and hopelessly disorganised chef. She set up a system which allowed it to flourish, and had a pudding called the Bombe Chouette named in her honour.

'So I asked why she left,' Tina told George who was grinning from ear to ear. 'And he said, I quote, "Oh but what more could she do? Ze seestem is fulepruf. She merst fly away." '

In the end, it was George's grin which made up Tina's mind. She realised she hadn't seen it for months, and she felt responsible.

He said, 'For God's sake, Tina, let's get Linnet in here and see if she can set up a "fulepruf seestem" for us. I'm tired of being worried to death.'

'And just hope she doesn't fly away wiz ze petty cash?' Tina said. 'I'll call this other referee first, if you don't mind.'

She called and reached a freelance photographer who was equally fulsome in his praise of Linnet.

'She put him on the map,' Tina reported back to George. 'It seems she was exceptionally good at getting him work. Oh, and did you know that she's "remarkably photogenic"?'

'And did she fly away with the petty cash?'

'No,' Tina admitted. 'OK, OK, she's a saint and a genius. But I can't think of one good reason why a saint and a genius would want to work for us.'

'Can you think of a good reason why we shouldn't ask her to?' George said.

'I don't want to pay anyone who's more photogenic than I am,' Tina said. 'Oh go on, George, give her a tug. I know you're dying to.'

So Linnet Walker came to work for Cole-Adler Security, and George regained his good humour. He went back to being the kindly, placid, methodical George Tina relied on. He even looked younger. If that were the only change she noticed, Tina would have been happy to pay Linnet's wages. But the change to George came about because of changes in the office.

First, Linnet cajoled the computer into a simpler, more humane attitude towards its owners. She also kept a handwritten diary on the desk to log appointments and calls. This was specifically for George, but Tina found herself preferring it too.

Then she arranged their days for them so that they always had time to talk to each other. She made good use of their time, and she seemed to know by instinct which partner would suit which client and vice versa. The clients responded miraculously by paying up at the first time of asking and practically thanking her for the privilege.

Conversely, the suppliers seemed suddenly to become very lenient about their payments. Cole-Adler no longer had to pay for their hardware up-front or cash-on-delivery. Bills came in a leisurely fashion and at last a balance was struck in the war between income and expenses.

'I don't understand it,' Tina said. 'Last month these bastards were practically dunning us. Now they're sending us free samples and purring.'

'Don't understand,' George said. 'Enjoy and shut up.'

'It's her confidence,' Tina said. 'Have you heard her on the phone? You'd think she was sweet-talking an industrial giant – but you *know* it's only the warehouse foreman so he'll send us a gross of window locks tomorrow instead of next week. And she seems to know how to talk to *everyone* from ponce to pauper. As if she's at home in any bloody situation at all. I wonder how old she is.'

'Didn't it say on her CV?'

'No CV. Remember? Oh well, maybe I'll ask her.'

But in the end Tina didn't ask and Linnet's age remained a mystery. She was clearly a mature woman but she moved quickly and gracefully like a girl. Clothes, however cheap and simple, looked exotic on her. Her vocabulary was racy and up-to-date, but the letters she wrote were models of restrained, educated phrasing.

It's all contradictory, Tina thought, but she was busy so she didn't think about it for long. After the first week she began to relax and think that Linnet could cope with anything and everything. There was no need to watch her or check up on her, so Tina took George's advice: she shut up and enjoyed.

# II

## The Sister

My sister was up in the loft, making something from diamonds of coloured silk. Robin is always making something. She always leaves the back door open too. The crazy lady trusts people. No matter how many times she's been ripped off, she believes in the perfectibility of mankind, the essential goodness of her neighbours. Either that, or she has a memory like a lace condom. She even trusts *me*.

'Hey, Robin,' I said. 'Leaving the door unlocked is one thing, but leaving your handbag on the kitchen table as well, that's just asking for it.'

'Lin!' She turned, scissors in one hand, swatch of cloth in the other. She dropped everything and came around her work table to give me a big hug.

'You never said you were coming. You look fantastic. Are you staying? How are you?'

I put my arms around her, feeling the softness of her shoulders, the silky greying hair on my cheek. Life must be so much easier when you give up on your looks.

The warm welcome took us down to the kitchen where she made coffee and offered me home-made chocolate chip cookies. When her kids were small, she used to make chocolate chap cookies for Jimmy and chocolate chick cookies for Grace. She was that sort of mother.

The house is Victorian and it's the only one in this street which hasn't been broken up into flats and bedsits. It's much too big for Robin since her dumb husband left her and the kids went to college. But she won't move out. Jack bought this house for Mother when Dad died, and Robin would never sell anything which has the slightest connection with Jack.

Robin adored Jack. I mean truly. It made me laugh, because usually she was utterly resistant to my friends and my way of life. Usually, when she met one of my men you could see her thinking, Oh yeah – another flashy talent, another narcissist, all mouth and image but no substance. Robin was into substance. She was always looking for someone I could settle down with. She never accepted that settling down was her thing, not mine.

So when she met Jack, who was as flashy a talent as ever lived, it amused the hell out of me to watch her succumb. She could have curled up like a little mouse and existed, completely happy, in his pocket. And she wouldn't have minded if he failed to notice her, or forgot she was there. Which was just as well, because Jack, true to form, hardly noticed her at all.

There are Marys and there are Marthas. Some men go for one, some for the other. Jack was a Mary-man if ever there was one. He didn't even see Marthas.

And if you are looking for male equivalents to Mary and Martha you might find Icarus and Sisyphus. Robin was looking for Sisyphus. She respected constancy and consistency. Substance. But she was enchanted by Icarus – the high flier with unreliable wings who got burned.

She married a Sisyphus and he left her, ten years later, for a younger Martha. He left her with two small kids and a barmy mother. So much for substance. That's what happens when you give yourself up to love and family.

I never give myself up for anything. But it's very useful to have a sister who does.

I didn't eat her chocolate chip cookies. Once you start on Robin's baking you can't stop – and I don't want to look like her. She isn't fat, exactly, but she's soft and mumsy. No one would stop and wonder who the hell *she* was at the Café D'Arte.

'What're you doing in town?' she asked.

'Bit of this, bit of that,' I said. 'Remember that creep Barry?'

'You're not seeing *him*, are you? Oh Lin, he's a thief.'

'Well, yes, sort of. He's still after memorabilia. And, Robin, I need the money.'

'No!' she said. 'You can't let him have *anything*.'

'I won't if I can possibly help it. But it made me think.'

'What?' she said. 'You can't stop protecting Jack.'

'Jack's past protection.'

'No! He isn't. That bastard wants to turn him into Elvis.'

Poor Robin. She cares so deeply about someone who's long, long gone.

I say, 'But what am I going to do? It's a mean old world out there. Am I supposed to guard the flame for the rest of my life? You can't eat flames.'

'Lin, Lin, ssh,' she says. 'Here, drink your coffee. What's happened? Tell me.'

She's so soft. This won't take long.

'Nothing,' I say. 'Nothing new. Just people hassling me. I'm supposed to be writing but they're messing with my head.'

I allow her to comfort me because that's how she comforts herself. Then I say, 'I wish I had something solid: a job to go to; someone to tell me what to do.' This is precisely what she wants to hear because it's what she thinks herself.

She says, 'Stay here, Lin. I'll keep everyone off your back while you sort yourself out.'

'But people know you're my sister. They'll call here.'

'They do anyway,' she says. 'There's a pile of mail for you in the hall cupboard. I'll just keep on saying what I always say: I haven't heard from you, I don't know where you are.'

I say, 'Robin, you're too sweet. I can't ask you to do that. These are real hassles – I've maxxed out on my credit card and I've run up some debts. I'll have to get a job – it may take some time to sort myself out.'

'Stay as long as you like,' she says. She looks anxious. Debt gives her the shakes. It reminds her too much of the past.

'You'll straighten yourself out,' she says bravely. 'You have before, you will again.

'I'll help,' says poor deluded Robin. 'What sort of debts?'

Now this is an interesting one. Again, I must get the price right.

But this time I have to find an amount which is outside her range or she will be tempted to help me out. It must be beyond her ability to bank-roll me but it must be possible for me – with hard work and application – to pay off in stages.

'Shit a coalpit,' she says, when I tell her. She falls silent and chews the knuckle of her ring finger – a sure sign of high anxiety.

I'm such a bitch, and it's time to pull back a bit.

I say, 'I'm owed money too. That's what caused the problem. Dog Records owes me for work I did with one of their new signings. And they've asked me to look at some raw talent in Oxford next week. They pay slowly, but they do pay in the end. The trouble is it's all a bit hand-to-mouth. I'll have to figure something out while I wait.'

She says, 'You can stay here. It'll hardly cost you anything. If you *could* find some sort of job . . .' Her voice dies under a justifiable weight of uncertainty. It is not simply rich living I am renowned for, it is also a contempt for sustained effort. I get bored and bolt. In short, I am flighty.

'Oh Lin,' she says, 'you could make a success of anything if only you . . .'

'Put my mind to it? Hung in?' I smile. Because it's funny how sisters define themselves in comparison to each other rather than by an objective standard. Thus, hanging in is Robin's thing. Bolting is Lin's. There are times, of course, when Robin bolts and Lin hangs in but those, according to family lore, are exceptions. Robin is the peat fire, Lin is the firecracker – that's how we are stereotyped. And very useful it is too.

We decide that I will stay with Robin, however reluctant I am to take advantage, and that she will filter all calls and act as my early warning system. While I take on the terrible task of 'sorting myself out'.

Perfect. Job done.

It was hardly worth the effort. I could have just turned up with my bags – she would have taken me in anyway. But I wanted her invitation. I want her to feel she is actively protecting her little sister.

I could have told her that I'd already lucked into a job, but I want her to feel that she has a stake in putting me on the right track. If you want someone to do a good job for you, you should build in job satisfaction, build in a degree of achievable success. Make her a shareholder.

She sat at the kitchen table nibbling a cookie, her eyes vacant. She looked thick. She isn't thick, but she dreams her way through problems. She doesn't analyse – she tries on scenarios, like clothes, until she finds one she's comfortable with. Just then she was dreaming her way through what she imagined was my problem. And if what she imagined was true, eventually she would solve it for me. Unfortunately, I misled her.

I said, 'Robin, sweetie, let me put a rinse on your hair.'

'A rinse? Why?'

'Grey hair is so ageing. It makes you look ten years older than you really are.'

She laughed, distracted from my problem, and dismissed the subject without a second's thought.

'Remember Auntie May?' she said.

I laughed too. Auntie May was our mother's sister. She lived in Weston-super-Mare and worked as a waitress-cum-chamber maid at a hotel there. She had preposterously red hair and when we were kids she convinced us that it was natural. She said that redheads never went grey. Redheads, she made us believe, had the secret of eternal youth. We were far too young to be interested in eternal youth and in any case we wondered why she bothered to be vain about her hair when her face was so old.

Robin said, 'Funny. Auntie May was younger then than we are now. And weren't we little snots? We mistook panic for vanity.'

'Weston-super-*Merde*!' I said.

'Snob,' said Robin.

Something happened at home the summer Robin was twelve and I was ten. We never found out what. We were packed off one morning in August and Auntie May picked us up at the coach station at the other end. No explanation. All Auntie May ever said was, 'Your dad's gone and Done Something.'

'What?' Robin asked, chewing her knuckle.

'Never you mind,' said Auntie May. But Robin did mind, and

when she wasn't chewing her knuckle, she chewed the ends of her hair. I was excited: my dad had Done Something worthy of high secrecy, a hushed voice and a pursed mouth. As far as I knew neither my mother nor father Did anything. But the Something he did was big enough to send Robin and me away alone for the first time in our lives; and to bring our girlish hopes and fears face-to-face with a grown woman's delusions and disappointments.

May was never married. She had no children. In another age she would have been the spinster doomed to live with one married relative after another. She might have been happier for that. Because although spinsterhood was by then an archaic concept, singularity was not yet accepted as it is now. The single woman was neither an economic force nor was she a political entity. She was still considered an unfulfilled creature. She had an impoverished independence but no dignity or respect.

Yes indeed, poor Auntie May. She had a string of what she called gentlemen friends. These gentlemen friends bewildered the shit out of Robin and me. Clearly they were too old and seedy and unattractive to be boyfriends. Clearly Auntie May was too old to have boyfriends. But they could reduce Auntie May to tears by being half an hour late for a walk along the sea front.

Watching her get ready for a date was a revelation. Off came the plain black dress with the white Peter Pan collar. Off with the white nylon slip, the Marks and Spencer cotton underwear, the thick stockings and flat shoes. On went Mum Rollette and a squirt of Diorissima. And the running commentary began: 'Always apply perfume to the pulse points. See these veins in the crook of my arms. Well, my skin's very thin there. I'm famous for my thin skin. Never call it scent, dear, it's perfume. My skin is so delicate some of the perfume seeps into my blood. It even finds its way into my hair.'

On went the lacy underwear. 'White is for purity, black is for sin. Red is too crude for words, children. If you want my advice – stick to coffee colour or ashes of roses. No, it isn't pink, Lin dear, it's ashes of roses. No, that isn't pink either, it's cyclamen. It enhances the colour of my skin – makes it pearly. Redheads have very pearly skin.'

There I was in my ten-year-old skin watching, horrified, and wondering if the seriously demented lace contraptions May wore were an obligatory part of becoming a woman. I could not imagine what process would give me a body which would need such preparation, such lifting and separating, tucking and tweaking. I thought of it happening all at once, like in the horror movies. I could see myself walking into a mad scientist's transformation capsule. He would flick a switch, laser lights would flash, I would writhe in pain as, before my eyes, flesh bulged and wobbled, coarse hair sprouted, breasts extruded like sausages from a sausage machine. Then I would walk out of the capsule slowly on feet which hurt because my toes were bent and bunioned. I was a woman and it only took two minutes.

Now, of course, I know that the mad scientist is Father Time. But then ageing and womanhood looked like a dirty trick played on an innocent victim to turn her into a disappointed idiot. Demented underwear, it seemed, was the badge worn by a grown-up woman to set her apart from the rest of the human race.

Oh, it was a formative experience all right. Only five years later, sitting at the feet of a legendary blues man, in torn jeans and a skinny sweater, I remember the sudden pang of acute doubt about my cotton briefs and no bra. I should not be in adult company – not because of my age and the licensing laws, but because I was wearing the wrong underwear. Or, more specifically, hardly any at all. Would Dexxy be singing *Honey Crawl* for me if he knew? Answer: yes, of course he would – extreme youth and inexperience were part of the attraction. If not the *only* attraction. I thought it was me, but it wasn't. It was only young skin. One is never too old or too young to be deluded.

'You can come with me as far as the beach,' said Auntie May, 'but I'm not introducing you to my gentleman friend. He thinks I'm too young to be an auntie.'

Robin and I were too young to understand what she really meant. What we puzzled over was how she could be too young to be an aunt when she was three years older than our mother.

'Your Auntie May has a heart of gold,' Dad said when we got home, 'but she's a very silly woman.' And we accepted his judgment. We had, as Robin said, mistaken blind panic for vanity.

# III

## The Band

InnerVersions is a clever-dick band from Oxford. Sapper, lead vocals and rhythm guitar, spent a year at Exeter College before dropping out. He likes to give the impression that he barely made it to the tech. He doesn't want to be thought of as an elitist bastard. Dram, lead guitar and back-up vocals, studied art at St Martin's. He's less shy about his education and talent. Corky, bass, actually did go to Oxford Tech and he has a qualification in psychology. He never mentions it. Flambo, drums, did two years Eng Lit at St Katherine's. InnerVersions is Flambo's brainchild. He can't sing, he can't write songs, but he knows, absolutely knows, what the band ought to sound like. Karen, keyboards and back-up vocals, went to the Guildhall School of Music. She doesn't know how the band should sound but she shags Flambo so she agrees with him.

Each member of InnerVersions has learned something about the craft of music-making. Each has a little talent. All are hugely ambitious. All would deny it. Together, they are constantly at war. Separate they are nothing. They are intelligent enough to know this, but they are dumb enough to hide their intelligence.

They want to look like an inner-city warehouse band but they want to sound like Cream if Cream were playing today. They want to be more famous than the Beatles. They want to be richer than the Stones. Cream, the Beatles and the Stones were making their names before the members of InnerVersions were born. But Sapper, Dram, Corky, Flambo and Karen know the legends. The legends serve to feed them and keep them hungry.

After a couple of years playing the pub, club, college circuit on a mixed repertoire of original songs and covers, InnerVersions were taken up in a lukewarm way by a record company called Dog. It wasn't what the band had been dreaming of, but shit, you've got to start somewhere.

The trouble is that they know, know, *know* that they're more talented and prettier than bands who are doing a lot better than they are.

They need a little bit of luck – a little bit of magic. That's all.

And when it is offered to them, they need the wit to recognise it for what it is.

Karen recognises it almost from the beginning. The others are sceptical. Flambo is dismissive. He says, 'You *are* shitting us, aren't you? The deal is, we sign, you pay, we get studio time. That's the deal. We do not get a make-over from an old tart everyone's forgotten. That *ain't* the deal.'

'Well . . .' says the A&R man.

'Come *on*,' says Flambo.

'I'm bringing her to the Cellar Club tonight,' says the A&R man, who may look like a limp rhubarb stalk but who has an implacable side to his nature. 'Talk to her afterwards.'

'Fuck off,' Flambo says. 'We're staying the way we are. If you don't like us, why sign us?'

'We haven't yet,' says the A&R man.

'Like, listen to the man,' Sapper says.

'Who else has she worked with?' Karen asks.

'Recently?' the A&R man says. 'Dream Therapy. You know "On Your Toes"? Six weeks in the charts. That was one of her co-writes.'

'Six weeks in the charts.' Sapper repeats the phrase like a mantra.

'I didn't know that,' says Karen.

'Industrial secret,' says the A&R man. 'Bands want to do their own songs but sometimes they need help with writing and arranging. People who spin-doctor songs and don't get credited are usually called producers. But there are a few who do it just for the money.'

'Fuck off,' says Flambo.

'Six weeks in the charts,' says Sapper.

'In your dreams,' says Corky.

'Suck it and see,' says Dram.

'Birdie Walker,' says Karen, who has read some of the books and seen photos of Birdie in a coffee-table volume called *Chelsea Chicks – Faces in Film and Fashion (1965–85)*.

'I thought she was just a rock'n'roll mattress,' Corky says.

'You mind your fucking manners,' says the A&R man. Up to now he's sounded like a public school type. InnerVersions stare at him in surprise: there's more than a touch of Rottweiler in this limp rhubarb stalk.

A typical InnerVersions gig goes like this: there is a smallish venue, like the Cellar Club. There are two bands. One band is trying out: it's new, maybe a college band. It opens while people are coming in, buying drinks, horsing around. No one dances. Then Inner-Versions come on for their first set. They have better equipment, a better sound. They are known to the audience because they've been doing the local circuit for two years. Some of their numbers are danceable and, if enough beer or pills have been swallowed, people will dance. InnerVersions call these people their Following.

They know what it's like to be the opening band. They know how depressing it is to perform for people who aren't there for them, who aren't listening, aren't responding. They know how crucial it is to have a bunch of people, even a small one, who will show up because InnerVersions are on. Their Following is very important.

Between sets, the band goes to the bar. They mix with their Following. Drinks are bought, pills popped. And why not? The band and the Following are contemporary. There is no distance between them.

It's a democratic, friendly scene which InnerVersions would sell their souls to escape. Given half a chance, they would be behind crowd-control barriers, in limos, holed up in luxury hotels, recording in LA studios. Friendly, democratic scenes are what you leave behind when you succeed big-time. They are what you return to when you fail. If, that is, you don't self-destruct first and never return at all. Heroic failure is also a romantic option. There are mythical burn-outs.

Tonight, Karen is thinking about one mythical burn-out. She knows Birdie Walker will be somewhere in the audience, watching and listening, so she is thinking about Jack and the nature of heat. There's the heat of animal magnetism. Jack had buckets of that. Talent's hot too. Jack had loads of that as well. Luck? Timing? Yes. Yes. Shake them all together and you get a chain reaction. Magnetism and talent rubbing together, igniting a spark, a series of small explosions, which generate publicity, which flows along invisible wires, which in the end light the big fire called fame. Jack's fame eventually became too hot even for Jack to handle. It burnt him to death – fame and flame.

To Karen, it seems emblematic. Life and death were in cahoots, producing something dangerous and symbolic. Almost like art, Karen thinks, because she is romantic about art.

She is in no danger, herself. She's stuck behind her keyboards, way behind the three guitarists. There's supposed to be a baby spotlight on her, but it isn't working so she's doing her thing, supporting the guys, almost invisible. Which, she thinks, is just as well. She's getting some annoying feedback and between numbers she's fiddling with the amps. If InnerVersions were a name band there'd be engineers and roadies to do it for her. If they were a name band she wouldn't be using knackered amps. She'd have state-of-the-art hardware and someone to carry and maintain it for her.

She looks across at Flambo. He's the only one who's noticed her difficulty. The others aren't listening. Flambo's arms are shiny wet blurs. He's whacking out a complicated pattern but he turns his head towards her and frowns. She gives him a despairing shrug. They are playing a number called 'More and More'. It's eight minutes and forty-five seconds long. Karen wishes it was three minutes long and called 'Less and Less'. Then the set would be over and she could get help with her amps. But 'More and More' is one of their groove numbers and the Following are on their feet. She switches from the Roland to the Korg because the Korg feeds through a different amp. It's the wrong voice and some of the extra sounds are missing but at least she can play without her ears being blitzed.

Flambo scowls ferociously. She tries to ignore him. In a minute there'll be a thirty-two-bar drum break which will cheer him up and give him something else to think about. She doesn't usually look forward to drum breaks, but now she can hardly wait. Dram's lower E string has gone flat and that's annoying her too.

For a moment she wishes she were at home eating chocolate and watching TV. With her qualifications she could teach music at a school, never have to get up in front of a live audience. Chocolate and TV. Chocolate to rot the teeth, TV to rot the mind. No hard-edged, glittering ambition, no knife-edged teeter between success and failure. At the moment she would give up anything for the chance to sit at home in the dark and not be judged in public. At the moment she thinks 'More And More' is trite and repetitive. She doesn't want to play it here, with everyone listening and watching. It doesn't represent her. It's just a long, loud, pointless wank.

To make matters worse, out there, somewhere behind the lights, behind the Following, is Birdie Walker. To Karen, Birdie Walker is a woman who *knows*. What does she know? Karen can't say, but it has something to do with how to *be* a woman – something alien and dangerous, to do with glamour, collective desire, spells. She has been somewhere Karen has never been and isn't sure she wants to go. She has been the woman every man wanted and every woman wanted to be. She has had the men every woman wanted and every man wanted to be. She was close to the music everyone wanted to make. She was close to unbelievable success and tragedy.

No unbelievable anything for me, Karen thinks dimly, standing there in a nothing club in Maidenhead, about to endure another one of Flambo's thirty-two-bar drum solos. She wants to switch off the Korg and go home. Switch off and fuck off.

Four bars into the drum break, without even thinking about it, Karen hits a button. The LCD screen on top of the keyboard flashes 'harpsi', and Karen begins to play a left-hand pattern which runs counter to the drum pattern. Down low, fast, staccato, the harpsi voice sounds like someone grunting – uh-uh-uhn-erh.

Flambo is so surprised he nearly falls out of his pattern. He throws Karen a look of pure hatred. He grits his teeth, steadies and sticks with it.

The next twenty-eight bars are like a skirmish in a war. Flambo digs in behind his battery. Karen flashes in and out with guerrilla raids. She assaults his steady, heavy barrage with a light, sharp, almost Cuban cross-rhythm.

Sweat flies from Flambo's hair. Karen looks up and sees Corky grinning at her. Corky enjoys friction. She closes her eyes and concentrates.

Afterwards, Flambo says, 'What the fuck do you think you're playing at? Don't you *ever* do that again.'

Karen says nothing. She walks offstage and threads her way through the Following at the bar. She's frightened and elated.

She feels as if she has blurted out the first thing to come into her head – it might be inane or obscene. She doesn't know. One thing is certain though – there will be a very nasty row when Flambo gets her home. By the time it's over, she may not have a home. Or a band.

She sees the A&R man waiting, so she turns and ducks into the cloakroom. Elation shrivels. She slips into an empty cubicle and locks the door. There's wet tissue on the floor. Some sad woman has scrawled the words 'He beats me' on the wall. Underneath, someone even sadder has written, 'Do you like it?'

Karen grabs a fistful of bog paper and blows her nose. She doesn't want to cry, but there's a hot ache behind her eyes. Life is spent hiding your feelings in tiny, smelly places.

'Sick,' Karen says out loud. She waits till she thinks there's no one around and then she leaves the cubicle to wash her hands.

There is a woman leaning casually against the door; gold blonde hair, black Levis, a man's jacket.

'Oh shit,' says Karen, 'you're Birdie.' And instantly, she's positive the Cuban cross-rhythm was inane. Inane is all she's capable of tonight. Or ever.

She says, 'Don't worry, I'm giving it all up. I don't want it. I can't do it.'

Birdie says, 'Wash your face. Don't let them see you cry.'

Birdie says, 'If you want to give up, by all means give up. But don't do it from a position of weakness.'

Birdie says, 'Don't run away. Flounce.'

Birdie says, 'Never flounce without lipstick.' She adds, 'Lipstick is a metaphor.' And Karen starts to laugh.

She borrows Birdie's lipstick. Birdie backcombs her hair into an aggressive, tousled mass. Karen stares into the mirror and watches her own dim image morph into lioness.

'What're you thinking?' says Birdie.

' "He beats me", ' says Karen. ' "Do you like it?" It's on the bog wall.'

'I saw,' says Birdie. She chants, 'He *beats* me. Do you *like* it?' Call and response.

Karen: 'Lipstick is a meta*phor*.'

Birdie: 'I *saw* it on the *bath*room wall.'

'Way to go,' says Birdie. 'Your first bog wall song.'

'The guys won't do anything with lipstick in it. Except maybe "Paint lipstick on your nipples." '

'Banal,' says Birdie.

'Yeah,' says Karen, who has never painted lipstick on her nipples. She may be in a band but suburban repression still has her chained to her parents' garden gate.

'OK?' says Birdie, and they leave the cloakroom and go to the bar.

'She fucking seduced you,' Flambo says later. 'I know her type: divide and conquer. You let her walk all over you.'

'She can seduce me any day of the week,' murmurs Sapper. 'Is she gay?'

'Banal,' says Karen.

'I dunno,' says Dram. 'I reckon she could swing whatever way suited her. There's something *fleurs-du-mal* there.'

Karen does not go home with Flambo. For once, she takes the initiative and a taxi she can't really afford. She disappears without explanation.

'Watch it,' Corky says to Flambo. 'You could lose your grip. *And* your block vote.'

Corky is excited. He sniffs change on the wind like a hound scents a fox. In the politics of the band, the block vote, Flambo and Karen together, gives Flambo more power than Corky thinks he should have. If Flambo lost his grip and Karen's vote was up for grabs, Corky might grab her.

He doesn't exactly want her, he's never seen her as anything but an extension of Flambo, but she has more music theory than the rest of them put together and he needs someone to shape his ideas. At the moment it's Flambo's ideas she's shaping.

It doesn't occur to Corky that Karen might have ideas of her own. Rock'n'roll, after all, is a dick thing – a young dick thing – and Corky is a young dick. He has ideas but no imagination.

He says, 'Hey guys, what d'you call a drummer who's just broken up with his girlfriend?'

'Homeless,' says Dram.

'A wanker,' says Sapper.

'Ha-fucking-ha,' says Flambo. 'Here's one for you – what do you call a sad fuck who hangs around with musicians?'

'What?'

'A bass player,' says Flambo. 'Thank you and good night.' He wishes he could walk away like Karen, but at the moment he's driving the van with all the gear and the others squeezed in around him. It's another thing he plans to criticise Karen for – she walked off without helping to load the van.

But, of course, when he gets home, the flat is dark and silent. He sits. He waits. His grievances breed like rodents. Karen has fucked up. Karen *is* a fuck-up. She isn't even pretty. Where does she think she gets off – acting like a bleeding girl? She *always* helps hump the gear. Carry your own bags, Karen, open your own doors. If you want to play with the boys, don't expect any special treatment. That's the arrangement. And speaking of arrangements, what the fuck was that harpsi riff? Who told her she could do that? Arrangements are Flambo's thing. He's the one who knows what InnerVersions should sound like. He's the man who makes the decisions.

Flambo drinks from the neck of a cheap wine bottle. Clumsily, he rolls a joint. A guy's got to come down after a gig. Normally, Karen would roll the joint with her fast little fingers. Good with her hands, our Karen.

Flambo stirs restlessly. He has after-gig jitters and no one to soothe him with bacon and eggs. Restlessness segues into scratchy irritability, and from there it changes tempo and becomes randy anger. He watches the door and waits. He imagines Karen in a bath with Birdie; they are soaping each other. Later they sprawl in his bed doing a sixty-niner. This is going to be good. But first he unzips his fly and pisses on them. They like that. Oh yes they do.

But Flambo does not have fast little fingers and, unlike Karen, he isn't good with his hands. So, afterwards, he feels almost as raw and empty as he did before. He sleeps in his chair, facing the door, head lolling.

Karen, at her parents' house, goes to sleep in her old bedroom, under her old Wonder Woman duvet, and here she dreams one of her fear-of-failure dreams. She dreams that she is on stage with a superstar who might or might not be Sting. She is playing the Korg, but it is perched on top of an upright acoustic piano. She can't reach without stretching. As she plays, the Korg starts to heat up and melt. It drips and oozes down on to the acoustic piano until there is nothing left of it to play. The superstar who might or might not be Sting watches contemptuously. 'Stir it with a wooden spoon,' he says, 'or stay out of my kitchen.' Karen looks down at her hands and sees that she is trying to play a large pot of soup.

Sometimes, late at night, when she looks at the linear beauty of a piano keyboard, she thinks of the clean, logical progression of semitones which walk, step by step, ineluctably from low A in the bass across seven octaves to high C. Cool reason and symmetry. Each scale doing the same thing yet feeling so different to the fingers. The relationship of chords, inevitable, bound together in groups by a chain made of numbers. It's all too perfect. It excludes her. She can't imagine who invented this ultimate music machine. A mathematical genius? An acoustition? A nerd? She doesn't think it could possibly have been a musician.

She imagines the kind of musician she knows rolling a spliff one night and saying, 'Yeah. I think what we need is a machine which will render the precise tonal relationship between eighty-eight notes at the touch of a finger. Yeah – but I can't get my head around it tonight, man.'

Now, here she is, playing a computer which looks like a piano keyboard but which can sound like a horn, a violin, a clavichord, marimbas, percussion or raindrops. It can remember sequences. It can split. It can do just about anything short of climb on a table and dance. In fact, it can do more than Karen can think of to tell it to do.

And here is InnerVersions in a scraggy little rehearsal room in Fulham. They are fooling around with a number called 'Howl'. Birdie Walker looks up from her notes and says, 'Drop in a minor chord there.'

Flambo says, 'Fuck off, you can't because . . .'

Karen drops in the relative minor and it sounds right. It leaves more space for the lyrics which were always too dense. And Karen wonders, 'It's obvious. Why didn't I think of that?'

But she didn't. Birdie did.

Birdie takes Karen to a voice coach, which alarms the shit out of Sapper and Dram.

Birdie takes Karen to a terrifyingly cool hairdresser in Mayfair, which alarms the shit out of Flambo.

'What's she doing to you?' he says. 'More to the point – *why*? Are you being groomed for fucking *stardom*? Is that your game? Because if it is, I'm telling you right now, this ain't a girl band. Never was, never will be.'

Corky says, 'We need a bit of colour.'

'Then Sapper can dress up like a drag queen for all I care. He's the singer.'

Sapper doesn't say anything. In the last few weeks he's noticed that Karen is singing a lot more harmonies than Dram. He's noticed that whereas Dram's harmonies are there or thereabouts, Karen's are accurate. It makes him think he should be more accurate with the melody line. It's an unnerving thought because he's already turned down the offer of a voice coach and cut himself off from a chance of immediate and quick improvement.

It seems as if two camps have formed, with Sapper and Dram supporting Flambo, while Karen and Corky support Birdie. Sapper is beginning to wonder if he chose the wrong camp.

To begin with it was obvious: Flambo is a mate, Flambo likes Sapper's voice, and his ideas. Flambo is the drummer and he isn't in competition with Sapper. That threat always came from Dram. But

Flambo said it was creative to have artistic tension between singer and lead guitarist – look at Aerosmith, look at Oasis. There were a million examples. And Sapper agreed.

Now, though, Sapper is confused. Yesterday he had a sudden insight, and he is often confused by his own insight.

They were working on one of his songs – a song that neither he, Flambo nor Dram thought needed work. It just needed recording. But Birdie said it could do with a change of perspective.

Why? It's a song called, 'Won't Go Home With You', and it's about a rude waitress. It's based on a real-life encounter Sapper had with a woman in an Italian restaurant. In it he notices the smear of her lipstick and a scar on her hand. She puts him down but takes his money.

'OK,' Birdie says, 'but the verse is too long and wordy. Cut to the chorus more quickly. Give the chorus a different voice.'

Sapper doesn't want to, but Birdie keeps coming back to it. She fixates on the scarred hand.

'It's only a detail,' Sapper says in exasperation. 'It doesn't matter.'

'It does to her,' says Birdie.

Whose song is this? Sapper wants to say. Is it mine or yours? But he says, 'Is it mine or the waitress's?'

'Both – if you want it to be interesting,' she says. 'Yours if you want it boring.'

So, reluctantly Sapper starts to work with Birdie and the chorus becomes the waitress telling the singer about the scar on her hand. She says, 'Thirty-nine stitches, those sons of bitches, God how it hurt. They made me eat dirt. Don't you ever tell Mama, Don't cry.'

When Sapper sings it, Birdie gets him to growl in a mocking way. She puts the harmony a fifth above to give it a harsher sound. Karen isn't around so Birdie sings it herself. What emerges is a tired, hurt woman who won't take any crap from an attractive young man.

Sapper would never have written a song like that by himself. But when he listens to the playback he realises that the chorus now defines the song and that the song is dark and much stronger.

The A&R man drops in and hears some of it. 'Better,' he says. 'Way more punch. Could be a single.'

And Sapper feels proud.

'I don't think you guys understand what proper A&R is,' the A&R man adds. 'A&R is whatever it takes. And sometimes what it takes is a song doctor.'

And Sapper feels humiliated.

Proud. Humiliated. Confused.

The A&R man takes Birdie aside and Sapper watches their private conversation through an open door. He can't hear what they're saying but he's sure they are talking about him and his song. He hopes Birdie isn't reporting that he gave her a hard time, that he thought the song was perfect and didn't want to work on it. His dim little insight is that there might be people around who know more about stuff than he does. Well, anyway, different stuff.

In fact, the A&R man is worried about his job. Dog Records has a new boss and the company is cutting some of his bands. Others have been in preproduction far too long. Is Dog edging him out? He thinks Birdie has friends in high places and perhaps she'll put in a word for him.

Sapper, watching through the open door, sees Birdie pull her sweater down over her fingers as if her hands are cold. He can't see her face but her pose is defensive. She looks like something out of an old French movie – the faulty strip lighting in the corridor is stammering and her hair flares in staccato bursts. The A&R man has more to say. Then he stoops and kisses her on both cheeks. He turns and walks away. Birdie, starring in an old French movie, remains. She doesn't watch him go. She stands, head lowered, thinking.

When she returns to the rehearsal room, Sapper feels her absence more than her presence. During her talk with the A&R man she has become detached from Sapper and he misses the warmth.

# IV

## Dancing for Daddy

Before he met me, Jack was managed by a man called Sasson Freel. Sasson and Jack went to the same school and Sasson got Jack's first band its first ever gig at his sister's birthday party. Sometimes it happens like that – a bunch of fifteen-year-old kids banging away in their dads' garages or school music rooms become hot property. And the first kid to pass his driving test and acquire wheels *can* find himself with hot property on his hands.

But not for long. As they say, rock'n'roll is here to pay, and where big money is involved amateur management is about as much use as shoes are to a mermaid.

People say I came between Jack and Sasson. They say I was the greedy bitch who intercepted Jack on his way to stardom; that I attached myself to him, rendered him fuck-struck and pushed him towards fame and the highlife. They say that I was so impatient for Jack to become a gourmet meal ticket that I separated him from his old friends, corrupted him and introduced him to the professional sharks of the music biz. Oh what power I had.

It simply isn't true. Well, true and simple aren't words which sit comfortably side by side, but apart from that – it didn't happen that way.

None the less, some things get said so often that even the participants in a story come to believe them. You wouldn't think that either Jack or Sasson would accept alien versions of their own story, would you? But it was convenient to both of them for Jack to forget about his ambition and for Sasson to forget his incompetence. If they wanted to forget those critical facts they had to replace them with fiction. And why go to all the bother of inventing a fiction when fans and critics had already done the job for them?

Well, who cares how it happened? The important thing was that I hadn't spoken to Sasson in years. And now I am going to meet him for lunch at that Hyde Park Corner hotel which used to be a hospital. Not my choice of venue.

As a matter of policy, I am always late for an important meeting, but judging just how late to be is a fine art. It's easy with people like Barry because what you are demonstrating is indifference and contempt. With others, it's a question of reminding them that you're worth waiting for. Sometimes you do it to demonstrate how important and busy you are.

What I wanted to show Sasson was not indifference for *him*, but indifference for time itself. I wanted to show him my arty side. He knows it exists because, at several steps removed, he pays me for it. He has recently become Managing Director of Dog Records. And, whatever he thinks of me personally, he also thinks that I'm capable of giving some of his baby bands, and their baby songs, a bit of spin and polish.

To give him credit, when he was frozen out of Jack's charmed circle, Sasson must've admitted to his own shortcoming. Because after wasting a few months ranting about ingratitude and betrayal he got a job with Wild Management and later became part of a consortium which set up an independent label. In other words, he learnt the business and understood that there was more to it than the blind luck of being at school with a major talent.

He came to understand that the music business is business, not music. True, he made quite a nice chunk of change for a few musicians, but he made a fortune for himself. He became a serious player in a dirty game. How serious and how dirty? I'm beginning to find out, thanks to a small South London security firm with a good computer and an extensive network of contacts.

Now that I can research Sasson Freel I've come to admire and despise him in equal measure. What I've found out makes me a little afraid of him.

Working for a security firm would be a truly unprofitable use of my time if I didn't have an agenda of my own. But I always do have an agenda of my own, and I don't work for peanuts unless my employers can supply me with the facilities I need to make a bigger score. Cole-Adler provides me with research facilities. The score is information.

There is a problem though: if you want, successfully, to pose as a good employee, a reliable office manager, a loyal wage-slave, you have to think like one. And after a while you begin to feel like one. Feeling like a good employee is death to the entrepreneurial soul. The fox, posing as a rabbit, feels like a rabbit. And, believe me, it's dangerous to go to lunch with another fox if you happen to be feeling like a rabbit.

I caught myself walking up Sloane Street, looking at expensive shop windows like an obedient office worker who has asked for and been granted time off. Obviously I wasn't ready for Sasson.

I turned into the Connaught Hotel to steady myself and adjust my mask. I was angry with myself. I used to be able to switch characters at the speed of light. It isn't just your skin which loses elasticity as you get older.

I followed two well-heeled American women into the cloak-room. There's something reassuring about cloakrooms in big hotels: they're designed to make you feel worth pampering. Even the tint and tilt of the mirrors give you a rosy view of yourself and your place in the world. You're valued.

I checked my reflection for weakness, spiritual flab and lumpy mascara. I found a hint of doubt in my eyes. Bad, very bad. I thought, I've been in this cold, cramped, soggy, snobby little country too long. I'm beginning to look as if I know my place.

Behind me, the American women smoothed their non-iron garments and blotted their lipstick. I gathered that they were off to tour the public wing of Buckingham Palace, to trot through royal halls fast enough so that they could hit the stores afterwards and still manage tea at Brown's. They wore energy and confidence like I wore *L'Air du Temps*.

In the mirror my eyes seemed to flinch. I envied the Americans their certainty and I knew I couldn't meet Sasson with docile eyes. I turned my back on myself.

'Buckingham Palace?' I say. 'How lovely. Have you any connections there, or are you just doing the *public* tour?'

The mark I pick is the taller of the two. She has honey beige hair to match her foundation. She stands securely on tennis player's legs.

'Excuse me?'

'Oh, I'm sorry,' I say. Very English. 'I shouldn't have butted in. But I was there only a few weeks ago – sublime, of course. I just wondered if you . . . But I shouldn't have mentioned . . .' I am playing with my own trepidation.

'No, go on,' the beige mark says. 'I didn't know there was anything but the public tour.'

'Well, you have to make a special appointment,' I say. 'And it is quite expensive.'

The other woman says, 'I'm surprised my travel agent didn't put me down for it. This is supposed to be a deluxe vacation.' She is wearing sage green silk, a lot of gold and an avid expression. Whatever's happening, *this* one won't want to miss out.

'Well, never mind,' I say. 'Perhaps another time. It's a shame though – it's nice, occasionally, to be able to do something not everyone gets to do.'

'What should we ask for?' the sage-and-gold woman says. 'I mean, we're going there anyway. We could get an upgrade.'

'It doesn't work like that,' I say regretfully. 'You see, your guide would be a Royal Equerry.'

'A Royal Equerry,' breathes sage-and-gold, a sturdy, gleaming fish nibbling my bait.

'So, you'll understand that it isn't simply a question of renegotiating at the box office.' I return to the mirror and take a small gold powder compact from my bag. Delicately, I touch my face with the tiny puff. It is exact mimicry of what these American women were doing five minutes ago. I'm just like them except that I am English and, therefore, infinitely foreign.

'In fact,' I say, smiling through the mirror at my beige mark, 'the box office doesn't come into it at all.' I give the words 'box office' a little extra flick so that the bait will fly out into deeper water. I'm wondering why I've picked the beige one as my mark. I did it instinctively. She *is* the taller, slimmer one, but it isn't always true that physical characteristics are a clue to social status. However, we are all animals and animal judgments can prove to be useful.

I smile at her again, humorous, rueful. 'Oh it's all so boringly British. You can't get a thing done in this country without introductions and connections.'

She smiles back at me. She is making an inventory of her own. My accent, naturally, is impeccable and intimidating – it whispers 'culture'. The venue, an expensive hotel cloakroom, is reassuring. She cannot place my clothes. But my hair has a shining insouciance which, she probably estimates, cost the earth. But am I sound? Would I pass muster at her club? She isn't stupid, but she is in a foreign country, which can have the same effect.

She comes to a decision. She extends a beautifully maintained hand and says, 'Sylvie Glick.'

Yes! I was right, beige is the social leader.

'Diana Beresford,' I reply, noting an unexpected pang at my impromptu choice of *nom de guerre*. Mr John Beresford was a name Jack used when he wanted to make anonymous travel plans or reservations.

Margaret, the sage-and-gold one, comes directly to the point. 'So,' she says, 'what do you get to see that other people don't?'

'It's a suite of quite small rooms,' I say. 'I believe they were used most particularly by Edward VII for his more private assignations. The, er, family still occasionally employs them for the same purpose. But the art and antiques are exquisite.'

'What do we have to do to get in?' Margaret says. She is quite transparent: the tour of Buckingham Palace is already ruined for her. Behind the tapestries and security guards is another world that Joe Public does not have access to, and of course it's more wonderful than what she's been offered. This is the story of her life – what she already has, by its very nature, is not special. What she has is always spoiled by what she doesn't have.

'Well,' she says, defending herself from Sylvie's scolding glance, 'she, I mean, Diana, she's been there. She must know somebody.' She turns her disappointed gaze on me and goes on, 'Tomorrow we're flying up to Scotland. The guys are crazy to play at St

Andrews. A coupla days in London is all we're getting. I might've guessed we'd be fobbed off, even though we paid top dollar.'

'What a shame,' I sympathise.

'So we really wanted these two days to be something to remember,' Margaret goes on. A disappointed, middle-aged child.

'We-ell,' I say. I raise an eyebrow in the direction of the social leader. Her decision. Her responsibility.

'We can't ask you to put yourself out,' she says, 'but if you have a number we can call?'

'I do have a number,' I say. 'It's a personal contact. I could just enquire, if you like. But I should warn you, it's expensive.'

'How much?' says Sylvie.

'I'm not sure,' I say. 'I'll enquire about that too. It's unlikely to be less than a hundred pounds a head. If that's too steep for you, please tell me now because I don't want to waste my friend's time.'

'What's that in dollars?' asks Margaret.

'I don't know.' I'm cool. No pressure. These women are hooked. I don't have to go any further. I can meet Sasson feeling like a fox. This one, you see, was for laughs, for ego, a practice hit. It wasn't for money.

But sometimes, as in the past, my detachment acts as a come-on. And now I had two very hot-to-trot American women on my hands.

We left the cloakroom and went to consult the husbands. Sylvie's was a man who knew beyond any question that he was an Alpha male. Sylvie might be the queen of the women's cloakroom, but he was king of everything else.

The women make their pitch. I sit, nonchalant, on a fake regency sofa, uninvolved. I look at my watch. Time *is* passing. Sasson is ten minutes' walk away. If I leave now I will be five minutes late. I watch Sylvie's husband, and without warning I find myself imagining lying in bed with him, playing the whore for him in a way that Sylvie, with her tennis player's legs, would find impossible. I can imagine his prudent passion, his puritan porno-graphy. A few years ago I would have bet on myself to make him part with a Central Park apartment within a week. I stop the thought dead and look at my watch again.

Sylvie's husband is The Banker. All decisions depend on his indulgence. His. Money, time, all his to dole out or deny.

Suddenly, I hate the prick. I get to my feet. I say, 'Sorry, I should be on my way.'

'Oh, Diana,' Sylvie says, 'I didn't realise . . . But my husband says . . .'

'Don't worry,' I say, looking at my watch again. 'No harm done. It was a pleasure to make your acquaintance, but now I really must go. I hate to be late.' I nail her husband with a smile of pure charm and regret.

'Wait,' says The Banker. 'Can't I persuade you to stay for a few minutes longer? Sylvie was just explaining the deal.'

'There's no deal,' I say, taking offence. 'You've misunderstood.'

'I used the wrong word,' he says smoothly. He detaches himself from his wife and isolates me a few steps away. A practised power move. 'The girls are very keen on this palace tour thing and I hear that you know a Royal Equerry.'

'Let me explain,' I say. 'It was just friendly chit-chat, and all I was offering was an exploratory phone call. Your wife is a very charming woman.'

'It takes one to know one,' he says, eyes warm and focused. 'Would you like to use my phone?'

'I'll use my own,' I say. And then, to punish him for the warm focused eyes, which probably worked on his secretary but which he should never have used on me within two paces of Sylvie, I add, 'If I do get through, and if my friend is willing, would you be interested in the *Private* Portfolio?' Always dress a punishment in a reward's clothing. 'Just the *men*,' I say softly, and my smile is full of dare, amusement and complicity. I know you're flirting, my smile says, but how far will you go?

The words may not have registered, but the smile certainly has. 'My god!' he says. 'They keep that sort of thing at the palace?'

'What sort of thing?' I say, with just the hint of a dimple.

He laughs. Naughty boy.

'It's amazing.' I let my lashes tremble. 'Raphael, Leonardo, Rubens, Michelangelo. Well, Michelangelo you might expect, but *Fra Angelico*?'

'Good grief,' he says.

'And hardly anyone has ever seen them. Only the cognoscenti even know they exist. It'll cost a little extra, of course.'

'Make the call,' he says.

I move off a few paces. I produce my phone book. I look up a number. I punch buttons. Reception is poor. I go to the hotel door. I have a two-minute conversation with my sister. The Banker hovers.

'Well?' he says, as I snap the phone back in my bag.

'Well, you're in luck,' I say. 'But can we solve the money problem? You can't hand traveller's cheques to a Royal Equerry. You can't be seen paying him at all. It's etiquette or protocol or something.'

The Banker is good at solving money problems. And so am I. He can lay his hands on a lot of cash and I can relieve him of it. We both do what we're good at. Dance for Daddy, little girl, and make him pay.

My reflection in the window of Harvey Nick's didn't flinch at all so I dropped in and bought an extraordinary velvet jacket. A prize. The velvet was dark, dark green, crushed and antiqued. The soft fabric caught the light and glowed. It draped and floated. The design was so clever that you couldn't tell whether it was brand-new or a rare art-deco hand-me-down. Exactly right for Sasson, and the best part of all – it was a present from The Banker. I saw it, I wanted it, The Banker bought it instantly. And now I was half an hour late for lunch, which, in the circumstances, seemed exactly right too.

The walk into the hotel was a walk into parallel time. Walking beside me was baby Birdie, bleeding from a wound in my shoulder when one of Jack's fans stabbed me with a pair of hairdresser's scissors. Another Birdie was carried in – miscarried, actually, after Jack, wired beyond sanity, beat me up. Yes, Saint Jack could be hard to handle after a concert and so could his fans.

It looked like a hotel, it smelled and sounded like a hotel, but it will always be St George's hospital to me. I even met Sasson here once, when Jack OD'd on goof-balls and Southern Comfort. Happy days!

The Sasson I knew then and the Sasson I met today were also as different as hospital and hotel. Yesterday's Sasson wore jeans and a sloppy sweater. He did the I Ching, bet on no-hopers in the Grand National, watched Grand Prix motor racing on TV with a tab of acid under his tongue and was always in love with some pretty girl or boy who had problems but never, ever wanted to go to bed with him. Yesterday's Sasson was permanently eager and always disappointed. His hair was Spanish black, his eyebrows met in the middle and he would've died rather than wear a collar and tie. No suits for yesterday's Sasson.

Today's Sasson *was* a suit. His tailor had constructed him. His eyebrows were plucked and the Spanish black hair was steel grey. Poor, rumpled, dark Sasson was gone.

I said, 'Remember visiting Jack here?'

'Here?' he said. 'Birdie, you're late. Whatever are you talking about?' Even his voice had grown richer. His accent was now patrician.

'EMI were sniffing around, waving a contract and I was totally panicked and rang you. You came running and we schemed all night about a food-poisoning story and how to get Jack up for the London Uni gig so that they'd never know. And then, after we'd spent all night in a state of advanced paranoia, Jack woke up, bright as a newborn chick, and we all went next door to the Pizza Express for American Hots.'

'Good God,' Sasson said. 'I haven't thought about that for years. Was that here? I remember the EMI deal fizzled out – which was probably just as well, in the long run.'

'Well, well, well,' I sighed. 'You remember the paper; I remember the pizza. No wonder you're so prosperous and I'm so broke.'

He scopes the jacket and smiles. 'Word games, Birdie,' he said. 'You always were good at those.' But his smile was smug. He's up. I'm down. As far as he's concerned the seesaw has come to rest in its proper position.

'Let's go through to the restaurant,' he said. 'They've been keeping our table too long.' He led the way.

'Why did you pick this place?' I asked. I know the answer but I don't want him to know I know.

'I live just around the corner,' he said. Belgrave Square, to be exact – as up-market a slice of property as a sloppy young London lad could ever have hoped for.

'Mmm,' I say with a barely concealed little shiver.

'What?' he says, poised in the entrance to the restaurant. The *maître'd* is on his way over. I touch his arm with two fingers. I want to know how much room I have to manoeuvre in.

'Memories,' I say. I remove my light fingers and clasp my own arms, feeling the silky velvet. Hesitant, reluctant posture. I wince ever so slightly at a convenient clash of cutlery.

'Did you know?' I say, so softly that he has to bend towards me to hear.

'What?'

'I lost a baby here.'

'No,' he says. But he did know. He treated me with embarrassed care for weeks afterwards. Jack told him, even though he promised he'd never tell a soul. That was Jack's way: when he was ashamed he always tried to spread the load and redistribute the blame. And Sasson would have been scared. It was A Woman Thing. We were all so young. None of us knew anything about miscarriages. Hell, I hadn't even known I was pregnant till the doctor told me I'd lost it. As for the post-gig violence – well, Sasson would have seen that from Jack's point of view. It was just speeding, out of control. It was just Jack, strung to snapping point. Understandable. Boys identify with boys. Consequences come as a nasty shock.

'What do you want to do, Birdie?' Sasson says. He shows no annoyance whatsoever, just the same embarrassed concern he'd shown years ago. He remembers.

I turn my head away. 'It's all right,' I whisper. 'But I'd be much more comfortable next door.'

'Let's do that then,' Sasson says and takes charge.

I stood back and watched him explain and apologise to the *maître'd*. He was firm, quick and polite. No fuss. I wondered what he thought about violence against girlfriends nowadays. Had he understood the reality or was this patrician *noblesse oblige*?

We went outside and I felt the wind blow the velvet against my body. My hair flowed like water across my face.

'Just like that *Rolling Stone* cover picture,' Sasson said suddenly.

'Hah!' I said. 'Never kid a kidder, but thank you.'

'You look well,' he said, returning to formality.

Inside the Pizza Express, neither he nor I ordered an American Hot. Instead we ate salads and he began by asking after Robin. I was surprised he remembered her name but maybe he'd prepared for this meeting too.

Then he asked about InnerVersions.

'What do you think?' he said. 'The A&R report was equivocal.'

'Hmm,' I said. 'Could be something in the mid-list if current trends persist for a year or two. Could be not. Depends what Dog has in mind.'

Sasson didn't take the bait so I went on, 'The frontman's quite pretty. He has a goodish voice which could come up with polishing, but he has a lot to learn. There's a girl with a lot of musical talent but very little in the pretty department. The others are betwixt and between.'

'Meaning?'

'Meaning, unless Dog wants to invest more development money, at the moment there isn't enough shaggability to compensate for naïve musical ideas.'

'Brutal,' he said, 'but succinct.'

'But they're improving rapidly and would improve even more if the label is willing to commit time and money. You *could* have a nice little earner if you're at all interested in your mid-list.'

'We put *you* with them.'

'Peanuts, Sasson, and you know it. Dog always puts me with bands that aren't ready for a big commitment.'

'We trust your judgment, Birdie.'

I smiled sweetly.

'Damn it, Birdie,' Sasson said, 'I know that smile. It means you think I'm talking through my underpants.'

'It means, what's your interest, all of a sudden? The Managing Director doesn't usually ask me for an interim report. In fact, I've worked with several Dog acts in the last few years and this is the first time I've met a top exec. And how long has it been since *we* met?'

'Too long,' he admitted. 'I just wanted to know how you were doing.'

'Fine,' I said. 'Fine and sweet as sugar candy.'

'Good.'

My bland blue stare met his bland brown one across the table. We both smiled.

'So is it true?' I say.

'Is what true?'

'That you are Dog's new hit man.'

'Is that what they're saying?'

'They're saying that you're cutting the dead wood, redefining Dog in order to make it attractive for a big buy-out. Or it's going belly up.'

'Amazing,' says Sasson. 'Where *do* these stories come from?'

'Paranoia in the record industry – amazing indeed,' I say.

'Are *you* paranoid, Birdie?' Neat little sidestep there, Sasson. I laugh.

'Have some wine,' Sasson says, 'and don't worry.' He fills my glass. 'I believe', he goes on, 'that every now and then, there is a minor clear-out on the ground floor. You needn't take it as anything more dramatic than prudent housekeeping.'

Needn't I, Sasson? Well, that's nice to know.

I sip the wine. It's simple and tasty.

He says, 'Really, Birdie, you mustn't worry. Your instinct for trends will always be useful, whatever happens.'

The sum of all my experience, experiences and experiments – the net weight of my talents is reduced to an 'instinct for trends'.

I put my glass down and closed my eyes. Lunch with Sasson was beginning to feel like an unsuccessful fishing trip. I could feel a boat rocking under my feet, wind in my face. The dark red ball of a setting sun tells me it's time to gun the motor and go home, but I flick my wrist and send the hook and line sailing out into a pool of still water between the writhing mangrove roots. One more time, just one more time. There's slim silver snook in there.

What's fascinating about fishing is the uncertainty. If you *knew* you could always catch a fish, it'd be called catching. But you don't know, so it's called fishing.

★   ★   ★

'Birdie?' Sasson said. 'You aren't listening.'

'What did you say?'

'I was wondering if you'd like to have coffee at my place. I have a wonderful new espresso machine and I can make it much better than they can here.'

One more time? 'Why not?' I said. But I picked up my wine glass again. The Pizza Express was safe and cheerful. Conversation clattered around us, echoing off the marble surfaces. I was in no hurry to move. Maybe getting in here would be my only victory. Such a small thing – to make Sasson change the venue of a meal – in other ways his well-kept exterior remained impregnable. He was regarding me with amused dark eyes, not giving anything away.

Yesterday's Sasson had been such a transparent, eager fish. And yet power and money suited him. The extra weight seemed like substance rather than fat. Old, sloppy Sasson dithered whereas this strange familiar man lurked with quiet confidence.

He emptied the wine bottle into my glass and said, 'What're you thinking, Birdie?'

'Not thinking – listening to the reverb in this restaurant,' I said promptly. Because when a man says he wants to know what you're thinking, the odds are fifteen to one he's lying. I went on, 'Remember "Going Down in the Diner"? The diner reverb we dubbed on to the coda?'

'Good lord, Birdie,' he said, sitting back in his chair and looking at me with narrowed eyes as if trying to read someone else's paper from a distance. 'You *do* have an eidetic memory, don't you? It's odd. You never struck me as someone who lived in the past.'

'I didn't have much past to live in years ago.'

'I remember some things,' Sasson said, 'but they're just facts, like old newspaper articles. They don't *live*.'

'How grey,' I said. 'As a matter of interest, Sasson, doesn't the word "eidetic" refer to visual memory? I was talking about a sound. What's the word for that? Ear-detic as opposed to eye-detic?'

'Aural,' Sasson said flatly.

'Boring,' I said.

He shook his head. 'What is it with you, Birdie? Games, games, games. You haven't changed at all.'

'Why should I?'

'Age,' he said. 'Real life. No money. Aren't they humbling experiences?'

A slap in the face, no less.

'Humbling to whom?' I said sweetly. 'Are you *humbled* by your age or your real life?'

'But I'm not you,' he said. 'I never had it all and lost it. No peaks to tumble from.'

'And you were never a woman. So youth and beauty don't matter. You aren't "humbled" by grey hair and a paunch. You never made anything except money so your work will never go out of style. You were never stylish. You were never judged for the way you looked or your shaggability or your "instinct for trends". You just sell what stylish shaggable people produce.'

'Birdie, I . . .' He was flustered and dithering now. I was relieved to see it because letting myself go has no place in my scheme. It's indistinguishable from letting myself down.

'Games!' I said in disgust. 'You think of games as winning and losing. Why can't games be merely playful?'

'Because yours, yours and Jack's, were always designed for the bright and beautiful. You never gave the rest of us a chance.'

Aha, I thought. An old wound. It went some way to explaining his surprising outburst.

I said, '*Now* who's tripped over memory? I make a bad pun and young Sasson cries "foul". Were you "humbled" by your youth, Sasson, the way I'm supposed to be "humbled" by my age?'

'Yes,' he said, vehemently. 'That was the wrong word. I apologise for it. But yes. I could never keep up.'

'With what?'

'With Jack. And you, when you came along. You made matters infinitely worse. At least, before you turned up, I was part of the team. At least I was useful. You changed the game. The team became you and Jack. Everyone else excluded. Everyone else made to feel dull and plodding.'

I said, 'Couples are like that. All couples exclude.'

'Yes,' he said, 'but . . .' It seemed as if he was going to go on but he restrained himself. I'm sure he would've said, 'But Jack was different. Jack was special. Every piece of Jack you took was a piece I couldn't keep for myself.'

Picture. A young guy with Spanish black hair picks up the phone. An agent is offering his talent a soon-to-be-very-famous photographer for his new album cover. When he puts down the receiver he rushes to tell his talented friend. Without knocking, he opens a door and sees the golden body of his talented friend asleep naked on indigo satin sheets. A golden girl sprawls like an exhausted kitten across his belly. The talent opens a sleepy, sensual eye and says, 'Fuck off, Sasson.'

Picture. A young guy with eyebrows that meet in the middle knocks at a door he would have previously walked through without thought. There is no reply, but he can hear a piano being played so he thinks it's all right. He opens the door and sees his golden friend sharing a piano stool with the golden girl. He has his left arm around her shoulders. She has her right arm round his waist. He is playing chords with his right hand. She is playing a skipping bass line with her left. He is singing nonsense words. She is harmonising with a shoo-wa line. They are both trying not to giggle. The young guy with the single eyebrow says, 'Sorry, Jack, but . . .' The music stops. The giggling voices shut up. Two heads turn simultaneously. Two pairs of Siamese cats' eyes blink. Jack says, 'Fuck off, Sasson.'

Sorry, Sasson, but it was a romance. You wouldn't expect to break in on Jack and Jill's honeymoon, would you? So why were you so hurt by Jack and Birdie's? Why was *everyone* so furious when they were excluded? Answer that one honestly, Sasson, and see what it tells you. It won't tell you anything about love that you don't already know. But it might tell you a little something about your attitude to a star.

Now, that's a sorry nest of snakes to uncover in the Pizza Express at Hyde Park Corner. It wasn't my intention. It wasn't Sasson's either. But, whatever he says about memory, he's as much a victim of it as I am. I intended to use it but, instead, it used me. He wanted to keep memory and me at arm's length. But it seems we both jumped out and bit him.

Lunch is a bust.

It was time to fold my hand and pass.

I put the wine glass down and say, 'Thank you so much for lunch.' Good little girl. I say, 'And thanks so much for your offer of coffee but I'm afraid I have to blow.'

'Please don't go,' he says, without meeting my eyes.

This was unexpected. I thought he would be relieved. No one likes a witness to a lapse of control. And, if I'd read him right, his control was something he prized.

I watched while he composed himself. Which is to say, I watched him put the table straight. He folded his paper napkin, tidied the cutlery, rearranged the salt, the pepper, the flowers, as if they were on an office desk. When he was satisfied, he turned in his chair and beckoned a waiter. The waiter came immediately and, calmed by obedience, Sasson's rich patrician manner returned. He asked for the bill.

Only then did he make eye contact. 'That was stupid,' he said. 'You must be right about memory. But I didn't come to pick at old scars and I certainly didn't mean to be insulting. I don't know what happened. But I do hope you'll come to my flat for coffee. I promised an old friend we'd meet him there.'

An executive apology: the apology of a man or woman who would not apologise if it weren't tactically necessary.

I raised one brow and gave him my blue Siamese stare.

'Barry Stears,' he said smoothly. 'I believe you had dinner with him a few weeks ago.'

So that was what lunch was about. Not a meeting between old friends. Not my baby band. Bloody Barry. I put my elbow on the table and rest my chin on the heel of my hand. It's a pose which does wonders for your jaw line. You can also hide any expression of distaste which might twist your perfect lipstick.

Oh yeah, summon the tricky little lady, soothe her with lunch and small talk. Keep filling her glass and then lure her to your apartment with promises of a slick new espresso machine. She'll fall for that, won't she? Then you can spring Fat Barry. And the big bad wolf will eat her all up.

'Look,' Sasson says, 'I know you don't take Barry seriously but he's become a media heavyweight and you'd be wise to listen to him.'

'Forgive a crude question,' I say, 'but what's it to you?'

'Well, you don't answer his letters or his e-mail. You don't return his calls. Your sister won't let him in the house. Why? He's harmless enough.'

The waiter interrupts by placing the bill in front of him. He snaps his platinum card down and waves it away without looking. Careful, Sasson, that might have been me.

I say, 'Sorry, but I don't want to meet Barry.'

'Why?'

'Because he's a grave robber, a body snatcher.'

'Come now, Birdie,' says Barry's ambassador, 'there's no need to get emotional about it. He isn't as bad as all that.'

'You *know* he's as bad as all that,' I say. 'And I repeat, what's it to you? When did you become Barry's messenger boy?'

He looks at me. 'There's mutual interest here. Dog owns the rights to *Hard Candy* and *Hard Time*. What Barry has in mind – the definitive appraisal of Jack, the life and work – will stimulate sales. Mo'Zee has all the previous product. They're enthusiastic. In fact they're putting up preproduction money. They'll publish the book too. It's a neat little package, Birdie, and it's all ready to go.'

'So go,' I say.

'It won't be definitive without you.'

'Then it won't be definitive.'

'In which case, both the BBC and VH1 will pull out.'

'Good,' I say. 'I'm tired of myths and legends.'

'No one else is,' Sasson said. 'Barry tells me you have the Antigua Movie. And I know there was a whole raft of stuff in Jack's collection – photos, audio tape.'

'Barry's probably got most of that already. He was thieving from us even before Jack died.'

'Oh Birdie,' Sasson says, 'I'm sure you exaggerate.'

'Do I?' I say. 'Everyone was at it. They'd say it didn't matter – like nicking towels or ashtrays from a hotel – just a little souvenir. Jack won't notice – he's got plenty. He won't miss a little photo, he won't mind if private letters disappear or personal conversations are taped secretly.'

'Yes, I know,' he says. 'It can be very trying. But Barry was a friend.'

'Barry was a groupie. He still is.'

'Nevertheless, he's a groupie with a big fat chequebook who can pay a big fat fee. In fact,' he adds, as if he's only just thought of it, 'I can arrange things so that you don't have to deal with Barry at all.'

'You can?' I say, with a cute little flutter of surprise.

'Why not? Dog has an interest. I know things have been tough for you lately. But we can turn that around.'

I sigh, pure longing and nostalgia.

'Of course you're right about Barry,' Sasson says sympathetically, 'but he does talk a good game. Maybe he hasn't changed though.'

Yeah, Sasson, maybe he hasn't. But you have. You seem to be making a bid which could cut Barry out of the deal. I can still get to you, babe.

I gather my purloined velvet around me as if I'm cold, and say, 'I'm so tired, Sasson. This thing follows me everywhere I go like a long shadow. I used to have some protection . . . I really miss that.'

'Are you on your own now?' He leans forward, interested. He really, truly doesn't know a thing about me. Dog's accounts department and a few commissioning producers know more than he does. And all they have are my sister's address and one of my e-mails.

I shrug my shoulders and say wistfully, 'Nothing lasts.' Poor Birdie – she's had the best and now nothing less can ever match up. She's softened by nostalgia.

Sasson leans across the table and takes my hand. He says, 'We have a history, don't we? Not an easy one, admittedly. But wasn't I always pretty straight with you?'

Yeah, you were, Sasson. You resented me in a pretty straight way. It's true, I always knew where I was with young Sasson.

'Yes,' I agree. 'You were pretty straight. But Dog wasn't.'

'That's contractual, Birdie. That's to do with accounting periods and lawyers. Besides, back then, it wasn't even Dog.'

'Copyrights and title,' I say. 'I was cut out every which way.' I don't withdraw my hand and nor does Sasson. It's a warm clasp. Forgiving. He will forgive me for being a greedy bitch if I'll play nicely now.

'Maybe it's time we looked at all that again,' he says. He strokes my knuckles with his thumb. It's a nice hand, warm and smooth. Yes, he has a good hand. All the cards, where contracts, royalties and deductions are concerned, are in his hand. All the lawyers are in the palm of that hand too.

I say, 'I'm tired of fighting. I just want to know that, if I supply any new materials to you, they belong to me. I want to be accepted as the owner of my own image for a change. I want to be paid for my own work.'

'If there are any new materials, we'll sort it out,' Sasson says, dismissing the crux of the matter with a reassuring squeeze. Does he have any idea how many reassuring squeezes this old hand of mine's endured? How quickly the reassuring squeeze turns into a stranglehold?

He goes on, 'It all depends on what you have. What's on the film, Birdie?'

'Music and memories,' I say. 'A lot of beach stuff, as far as I can recall. But the bit Barry wants is the recording work. I don't know – it was a long time ago.'

Sasson has his reactions well in hand now. He shows no particular interest. He says, 'We'll have to show it to the lawyers. But I promise you that if you give it to Dog you'll be fairly compensated.'

Now's the time to withdraw my hand.

I say, 'It's not just the film. It's the music rights, the publishing, copyrights, authorship . . . That whole can of worms.'

'We'll look at all that again,' Sasson says. 'Just show us what you've got.'

'Oh Sasson,' I sigh. 'Give me a break, man. I don't even know where next month's rent's coming from. If you cut my baby band I'll be out of work again.'

'Your baby what?'

'InnerVersions. The band I'm working with.'

'Never mind that,' says Dog's Managing Director. 'We've got much more important things to think about. What we're talking about is nothing short of a multi-media event.'

'I know,' I say. 'But I don't want to rake up the past. What

68

concerns me is making a living in the here and now. Making music, working with a young band which needs a commitment from you.'

'But compared with Jack they're nothing,' he says, looking puzzled. 'What was it you said? Not good enough musically to make up for . . . what was it . . . shaggability?'

'They need help,' I admit. 'I was trying to find out how committed Dog was to its could–do–a–lot–better–with–a–little–help bands. And you wouldn't answer. I did not say they were "nothing". It's not up to me to dismiss them or sign them. That's up to you. And you'll probably never hear them.'

'I'll come and listen to them if you like.' He lets a little of his irritation show. He nearly had me, and now, for some whimsical reason, I've changed the subject.

'They aren't ready,' I say. 'If you want to show some interest, give them a few months' more development – enough to polish up a tight set list. Let them record it. And then send them out to open for one of your name bands. Let the punters choose. That's the fair way. That gives them a chance to make something slowly and test it against a live audience.'

'That seems fair.' Sasson pretends to think about it. 'But I don't know what the bean-counters'll say.'

'Just give them something to sell – could be two or three numbers on a single. Count units sold at live performances. Also, and this is important, ask a producer to persuade the frontman into voice coaching. He's okay, nice natural voice, but imprecise. And there's a nasty gap between his head and chest voices which exercises could fill in fine.'

Sasson stares at me. He says, 'You never used to be this analytical, Birdie.'

Did I not, Sasson, babe? I used to wear a T-shirt which said, 'Speak slowly, I'm a blonde.' Nobody but me saw the joke. I used to be very young, very pretty and very fanciable. Everyone looked. My God, how they looked. But no one listened.

Sasson says, 'This front man – this singer – is there something going on that I should know about?' He's smiling, intimate, sharing what he thinks is a pleasantry.

Abruptly, I rise to my feet. I walk.

Head high, long easy strides, velvet swinging, I walk out on Sasson Freel – every inch of me a wounded queen. An immaculate exit. Eye-catching too. Several heads turn to watch my passing.

Outside, moving as fast as I can without actually sprinting, I turn east and disappear down the underpass. Not bad for an old broad.

Sasson would try to make a dignified departure from the Pizza Express. He would reason that when he got outside I would be somewhere in sight. He would think that I wanted to be caught, mollified, petted and stroked because, otherwise, why did I walk? Women want to be caught. Women want to kiss and make up, be reassured. Women always give you a second chance, don't they, Sasson?

Not this one. And anyway, it was time to go. Time to let him think or stew a little. He just gave me a good excuse.

I walked along Piccadilly, mingling with the tourists, thinking, yes, it *is* time to go. I was tired of juggling two jobs and sorting out other people's lives for them. I'd been reliable for weeks, and being reliable is boring and exhausting.

I stopped at a public phone and called the office. The sweet old man answered the phone. I tell him that my niece has been involved in a motor accident in Paris.

'Of course you must go,' he says. 'How very worrying.'

I say, 'I'm the only one in the family who speaks half-way decent French.'

'Don't bother about us,' says Mr Adler. 'Just tell us if there's anything we can do.'

'You're very kind,' I say. And it's true. The lie was especially chosen for a kind man.

'I shouldn't be gone for more than a week,' I say, anxious and regretful.

I took a taxi to Maida Vale and an address nobody knows. After that, with a sizable slice of fuck-you money, I went back to Robin's house.

The next morning I was on a plane to the States. I even wangled myself an upgrade. Birdie flew away. Club Class.

Stretched out, ankles crossed, sipping complimentary wine, I breathed out slowly. Yes! It was time to bask in the sun, to go fishing for real fish, to let the mud I'd stirred up in that cold English pool settle. I get restless and claustrophobic in England. It's all too tight for me, and reliability just isn't my thing. When I got back, one way or another, things would be clearer. Sometimes success depends on knowing when to take yourself out of the game.

I wanted to empty my mind, to feel loose, but images of Sasson leaked in. In the old days, I wouldn't have given him a second thought. But somewhere, in the intervening years, he had muscled up. He now had power, status and money. I'm almost Darwinian about that. A man or woman with power and status is far more useful to me than one without.

But along with the benefits comes the danger. A man or woman with power and status should be manipulated with caution. They are strong, often at the expense of people like me.

# V

## Victim of Comfort

When Junior Moline's career stalled there was no one to blame but Junior, and he was too laidback even to do that. On his business card, if he could find one, it said: 'Producer/Engineer', and it's true that he'd had his moments. Years ago he'd worked with some very big names. Years ago he'd been going places. He'd travelled all over the world, on tour with bands, in studios with bands. And then, one day, he found himself in New Orleans.

What he always said was, 'They don't call New Orleans the Big Easy for nothing. Well, I'm big and easy myself, where else should I go? My feet got stuck in the Mississippi mud.'

It could be said too that his mouth got stuck to the business end of a chillum, and his arse got stuck to the cane chair on his lady's balcony, and his ears and heart got stuck to the throb of Delta blues.

It wasn't that he didn't work. He did work. Regularly. Seven days a year. On the last weekend of April and the first weekend of May during the Jazz Festival anyone could find him out at the Fairground wearing a sweat-stained Stage Krewe T-shirt decked with backstage passes. Happy as Larry, balancing instruments, monitors and microphones.

'One-one, two-two. One-one, tsu-tsu. One-one, chu-chu. Little more off the top there . . . One-one, tsu-tsu. Yeah, got it.' Seven acts a day with only thirty minutes between them to break down one set and then sound-check for the next lot.

Yes, he worked hard then, his big feet slapping across the boards in open-toed sandals, and as the day wore on, his outsize jeans slipped lower and lower and his T-shirt slid higher until everyone in the crowd below could see what he called his double bass. Sometimes, friends and acquaintances, partying out there on the other side of the crush barrier, would call up rude remarks about his increasing girth. And he would call back, 'Do you mind? I'm proud of this – I built it myself. Brick by brick.'

Then, laughing, a friend might lob a can of Miller Lite over, and later, backstage, Junior Moline would sit back replacing fluid lost in the thirty-minute scramble. He would feel the beer vibrating in the can to the beat of bass and drums. He'd know that everyone in front of the giant stacks of speakers would be feeling something close to cardiac massage from the sound he'd helped to produce. Sound waves, punching through the hot, humid air, rattling your ribs, nudging your lungs and hammering on your heart. Exactly how live music ought to be felt out there in the sun.

Junior Moline loved the Festival. Once a year all the talent spawned and nurtured around the Delta crawled out into the sunshine and made sweet music for New Orleans to dance to. Jazz, blues, cajun, zydeco, R&B, rock, latin, reggae, country, with a dash of hip-hop, African and Native American for seasoning. There was a gig for everyone. No matter what you played, there was always someone to dance. No matter how badly you danced there was always someone to play for you. And there would always be people like Junior EQing the sound.

In the beginning it was the Festival that brought him to New Orleans. He first came with an American band he'd been recording with in London – out of England's tight grey fist into the hot wet light. A climate he fell into, relaxed into, like a warm bath on a cold night.

The band was Thieves Like Us, long ago split and divorced. But the lead singer and guitarist was Cy Fuentes whose solo career became the stuff of music fairy tales – or cautionary tales – depending on your point of view.

Sound engineering for Thieves Like Us had been, at that time, a significant step for Junior. It was one of those steps from which his own career might have taken off, had he not been seduced by the Big Easy. But, more significant in the long run, was his meeting with Birdie Walker. Sometimes, lounging on his lady's balcony, he remembered the first meeting. She was ushered into the sound booth, like so many celebrity girlfriends, with a mixture of indifference and curiosity – another pretty chick there to admire the talent on the studio floor. She was there, he thought, to be impressed and also because while she was there she couldn't be with anyone else and she couldn't be out spending the star's money. The usual thing.

The half-glance he gave her took in a jail-bait adolescent body, long blonde hair and coltish grace. Cy's new babe was a baby, and Junior might have felt sorry for her except that he was too busy, and in those days even baby chicks didn't merit any sympathy: they were part of the furniture.

As the night wore on though he noticed something else: unlike the other chicks he'd seen come and go, she didn't get bored or read magazines or whine. Nor did she run around rolling joints and fetching refreshment for the band. She paid attention. She didn't chat or ask questions or in any way interrupt, but he became increasingly aware that she was watching every move he made. At one point, when a discussion between the band and the producer turned into a slanging match, she sat on the floor as if the dramatic interlude was too boring to witness. Junior's feelings were similar. He said, too quietly to be heard by anyone else in the booth, 'If it was me, I'd put in some silly brass.'

'What?' she asked, just as quietly.

'They're fighting about strings,' he said. 'Stupid idea. But they do need something, and if it was me . . .'

'What do you mean "silly brass"?'

'Well, like a bass tuba or a sousaphone – a bit of deep-down oompah for extra beat and texture.'

She considered this for a moment, smiling dreamily. Nothing else was said.

But the next day, late in the evening, a bewildered spotty young man with a bass tuba was shown into the studio. Cy's explanation to the producer even recycled Junior's description, silly brass. Junior, of course, got no credit, either for the idea or the description. Nor did Birdie. Cy took that. All Junior got was a long slow wink from Birdie.

The real payoff came later when he was hired to produce Wild Jack's second album and found that he'd been hyped as a sound man with imagination. And who should turn up with Jack to the first meeting? She was a little taller perhaps and more polished, but the long blonde hair and the lazy wink were the same.

The wink, Junior thought, was absolutely something to write home about. Birdie turned her head so that no one but Junior could see the winking eye. Then, without moving any other facial muscle, she slowly dropped one eyelid. It was like an illusion: one half of her face went to sleep while the other remained sweetly attentive. Everyone else in the room saw only her perfect profile. It was the first hint Junior had that with Birdie what you saw was *not* what you got. What you saw, of course, was so beautiful that it was hard to respond to her as anything but a visual feast. 'Blinded by beauty,' Junior said, ruefully explaining why even he had been slow to take her seriously.

'If she'd been a guy or a bit uglier,' Junior said, 'who knows what she might have achieved.'

He once heard Jack say to her, 'Jesus, babe, you don't have to *do* anything. You just gotta *be*. Sit there with your mouth shut and you're perfect. I love you.'

With half the world, as it seemed then, aching for Jack to love them too that sounded like a compliment. You're perfect. Jack loves you. Stay that way and shut up. What a trap, what an insult, Junior thought later. But only years later, and only after years of being looked after by a short string of independent women – the sort of women a lazy, easy-going man is attracted to. Because if a lazy, easy-going man wants the support of an independent woman he learns to listen to her. If you don't pay the piper, you don't call the tune. But you really should listen to it sometimes or you'll end up a lonely, lazy man.

What surprised Junior was the way his acquaintanceship with Birdie slowly turned into an on-again-off-again friendship. He was surprised that he still knew her, and even more surprised because it was she who kept in touch. At first he thought that her interest in his job was because he was useful to her. If she studied his working practices and his vocabulary, he thought, she would look less like the gorgeous idiot everyone thought her to be, and she could stay one step ahead of the competition. But then he noticed that what she knew was of no importance whatsoever. Because no one listened to her. Even Jack, even when he was using her as a co-writer, back-up singer or piano player, behaved as if he was indulging a pretty child. Jack might come in with a rough track to show the band. It would be clear that the harmony voice was hers and that she was playing the electric piano pad which under-pinned his guitar riffs, and that half the lyrical ideas could only be hers. And even though that rough guide was what the whole studio used to build a polished song, the most Jack would say was, 'Ah well, got to keep the girl amused – can't let the girl get bored.'

Music was man stuff – unless you had a voice like Etta James or Aretha Franklin, in which case you would be allowed to sing.

Birdie did not have a big black voice. What she had was soft, white and, worse, English. She could not even be a respectable harmony singer. Her growing feel for melody and harmony was not something she could use herself. She could only give it away to people who would make it sound right.

At one time Junior thought she might want to use his expertise to give herself credibility. And it was true that she did. But even now, when he hadn't recorded with a Name for years, she still played him tapes of what her 'baby bands' were doing and listened to his comments and suggestions. He knew that nowadays there were other, more useful, people to use as sounding-boards. He was out of it. The big time had ticked away.

But still she kept in touch. Even when he was flat broke and couldn't offer her so much as a sofa to sleep on when she showed up and hung out. Then, it was her turn to offer him notions – money-making schemes to tide him over. Schemes which were actually scams: how to blag a free meal, how to con the bank into giving him more credit, how to fake references for a suspicious landlady. In other words, she taught him how to get by in an expensive place without a penny in his pocket.

'Swimming under water,' she called it. 'Survival techniques, so's you can hold out till the next breath.'

Eventually it occurred to Junior that this was, quite simply, how

Birdie lived: someone else paid the bills. What was more, people seemed to fall all over themselves for the privilege. He knew he should have despised her. He knew that he should despise himself, but he could never quite summon up the energy. Drifting, as he did, between boom and bust, what he felt was a kind of kinship.

Maybe she just fuckin' likes me, he thought, when he thought about it. Maybe it's because I never hit on her. Maybe with so many sweaty erks pawing her all the time she could relax with a lazy technician who considered her out of his league.

Birdie, he thought, used to be the most beautiful woman he'd ever seen. And both men and women couldn't seem to keep their hands off her.

He remembered once leaving a restaurant with Jack. What were they doing? Probably having a preproduction meeting about *Hard Candy*. After about two hours Jack called his car. Jack would never leave anywhere until he knew his transport and security were in place. Even so, on this occasion, word got out and Jack, Birdie and Junior had to wade through a boiling crowd of photographers and fans to get into the car.

Junior, in those few violent moments, had a confused nightmare impression of grabbing hands and flashing lights before he was bashed on the head and dragged into the car. The car lurched slowly away, covered in kids. Kids on the roof, kids clinging to the hood, kids spraying hearts in shaving cream or Miracle Whip on the windscreen. Kids writing 'Screw me!', names, phone numbers, in lipstick on the windows.

Inside Jack was screaming furiously at the chauffeur and the security man. Birdie was trying to make herself decent. Her shirt had been yanked so violently that there were no buttons left and her skirt was torn to the waist. Even her lacy black underwear was in tatters.

Junior, who was feeling shocked and stupid, said, 'Ain't stardom just peachy?'

Jack sat back adjusting his own vandalised clothing and said, 'I reckon I must be one of the few men in the world who knows what it's like to be a beautiful woman. Junior, give the girl your jacket.'

Junior struggled out of his jacket and Birdie put it on without a word. It was big enough, even in those days, to cover her to mid-thigh. She wrapped it around her like a dressing gown and sat with her arms folded across her chest.

All legs and eyes, Junior thought, trying not to stare.

'Yeah,' Jack said, reading his mind, 'she'd look like a doll if she was wearing a brown paper bag. They try, but they can't seem to ruin her.'

Birdie said nothing. Of the three, she appeared to be the calmest.

'You look like a rape victim,' Jack said. 'Battered and beautiful. Want a fuck?' His hands were shaking and his eyes were raw and angry.

'Do *you*?' asked Birdie.

'Yeah,' said Jack.

'Then go fuck yourself,' said Birdie, in her soft, white English voice.

'I could throw you out there to the wolves,' Jack said.

'You could,' she agreed. She searched in the small bag she always carried and produced a gold powder compact. Inside were a few capsules wrapped in tinfoil. She gave two to Jack and offered one to Junior.

'What are they?' he asked.

'Peace,' Jack replied, stuffing the capsules into his mouth. 'Time out of war. Cessation of hostilities. Surrender.'

'Jelly babies,' said Birdie.

Junior shook his head. For the rest of the trip he remained as shocked and stupid as he had been at the beginning.

What had Junior seen that day? He replayed the incident in his mind many times, especially after Jack's death. Because rumours surfaced in the press, persistent rumours which even now floated around on the Internet. They claimed that Birdie was Jack's murderess – that she had set the fatal fire, that she had drugged Jack so that he couldn't respond to the emergency, that she had supplied him with enough scag to kill six horses and then burnt him and his house to destroy the evidence.

What had he seen? Two young people under great pressure? Jack's unexpected thuggish side? Birdie controlling Jack with drugs?

Surely not that. Junior knew, better than most, that the Name, unless he's desperate or a moron, never carries his own stash. That's the roadie's job, or the friend's, or the girlfriend's. At a pinch, it might even be the sound engineer's. No one wants the Name to be busted. So, while it might look as though Jack's girl was supplying, it was more probable that she was simply carrying. Even so, when Jack died and was sanctified – as is the custom with beautiful young rock stars – Birdie was demonised. And the underground rumble was so hostile to her, so full of conspiracy whisperings, that Junior himself wondered if a small percentage might be true. Lost in Louisiana, away from the action, he read stories about mythic strangers called Jack and Birdie the way a child might read stories about Snow White and the murderous wicked stepmother. The stories, he felt, had more to do with folklore than fact, but they were as infectious as germs and, like germs, they multiplied.

Every objection was countered: why would Birdie do away with her meal ticket? Well, said the anonymous accusing voices, Jack was already fed up with her. He was going to dump her. He was seeing someone else. She was about to be publicly humiliated.

No, said others. She wanted his money. She had secretly forced Jack to marry her. In Vegas. In Mexico. In Tahiti. In Cuba. He was furious with her for her extravagance. He was going to cut off her funds. He was going to divorce her.

Wrong. She was a member of a coven. The Sisterhood of Ishtar. An extreme right-wing/left-wing sect. She was a hypnotist. She involved him in satanism. When he woke up and wised up she had to kill him.

That's stupid, said others. Why ignore the obvious? Birdie was seeing someone else. Jack caught them together. There was a fight. Jack was killed. Birdie torched the house to protect her reputation and her lover.

Who was her lover? Ah, now *there's* a loaded question. He had to be big. Someone worth protection. So let's begin with the British Royal family. The long list of possibilities began with Prince Charles and worked its way through sheikhs and kings. It included any of the fifty richest men in the world who were not gay. Industrialists. Politicians. Film stars.

And so on, and so on. It was enough to make a lazy man's head spin. And, being a lazy man, Junior simply turned his back on it as he did with anything that caused him hassle. It was easier not to think about it. If he thought about it, he might have to do something about it.

He might have to leave New Orleans and find out for himself what the truth was. He might have to accuse Birdie himself. Or he might have to defend her.

It is best to know nothing if you plan to do nothing.

Besides, Birdie never defended herself. Perhaps that was her greatest crime. She spoke to no one. She gave no interviews. Even Jack's funeral was a secret affair – the cremation, wags said, had already taken place and no one could find a grave to desecrate. Birdie was never seen in mourning. If she wore black it was because black was stylish and it suited her.

'Why don't you set the record straight?' Junior once asked her.

'Which record?' sighed Birdie. 'To whom? People think what they want to think. They aren't interested in the truth. They only want a good story. With pictures. If I so much as open my mouth I'll only be giving them weapons to use against me.'

Ambiguous, Junior thought. And then remembered how experienced she was with journalists and photographers. Experienced enough to be for ever on guard. He'd often wondered why the famous or notorious didn't simply keep their mouths shut more often, since they were made to look such idiots when they opened them. Damned if you do, damned if you don't, he mused. He himself would surely be damned for what he didn't do if there was any choice in the matter. So his feeling of kinship with Birdie strengthened.

He was glad she didn't want to talk about it because, deep down, he didn't want to know. That was heavy stuff. Heavy feelings. Hassle. Better to smoke a little herbal and chill. Don't let it get to you, man. Who needs it?

That's eventually what he said to Teddy when Teddy unexpectedly came knocking at his door. At first it was, 'Hey, man! God! Shit – how long's it been?' Thinking, fuck, if he hadn't said his name I'd never've recognised him. Bald, for fuck's sake. What happened to all the hair?

Teddy used to have authentic rocker's hair which he waved like a banner for the cameras. In all the pictures of Jack on stage, somewhere behind or off to the side, you'd see Teddy with those streamers of rocker's hair. Or Teddy, the typical autistic axeman, curled over his guitar, hiding behind his own tangled vines. That was one of his favourite poses – the recluse in the spotlight. Especially after a solo. Camera-shy, and modest with it. Wanker, Junior thought. Because nothing could have been further from the truth – every scrap of tension between Jack and Teddy could be put down to the perpetual war waged between frontman and sideman.

'Those were the days,' Teddy said, from the prison of Junior's woman's armchair. 'Don't you miss it?'

'Dunno 'bout that,' Junior said. 'I don't miss the friction or the nerves. I was fuckin' getting ulcers back then. Everyone on your case all the time. No, I was glad I got out of it when things got *really* brutal.'

'But not before Madison Square Garden.' Teddy really did sigh then. Because Madison Square Garden was the venue of the famous axe'n'sax thrash which Junior captured for all time on *Jack's Back Live in the USA*. It was one of those rare occasions when Jack was forced to step away and let Teddy take centre stage – a time when they'd asked Al McQueen, sax maestro, to sit in, and Teddy's solo on 'Packet of Ten' turned into an extraordinary exchange between guitar and sax. A battle in which neither was prepared to yield. Lunge, parry, riposte. Hit and run. Trading bar for bar, blow for blow, it was a passage of pure musical aggression fuelled by pure adrenaline. It was a spontaneous event which usually only works live. But Junior, going mental at the mixing desk, caught it and preserved it, as if he knew it would be special even before it happened.

Both Junior and Teddy were justifiably proud of what they did at Madison Square Garden all those years ago. The ephemeral made permanent.

'Man, you were the best,' Teddy said.

'Oh yeah,' Junior said, sceptical, remembering all the mixing wars. If for some reason you wanted to mix Goff or Wills up at Teddy's expense you had a fight on your hands. It was all like that.

Every band member wanting to be heard loud and clear. No one satisfied. No one wanting to be the texture behind. Every silly sod a soloist, Junior thought. All at the same time. Then Junior was the ignorant bastard who was paid exorbitant sums to wreck their careers.

'I was working with Wills in New York only last week,' Teddy said. 'Do you see any of the old faces these days?'

'People drift through,' Junior said. 'Like *everyone* comes around April, May.'

'I mean us,' Teddy said. 'Jack's people.'

'Anyone comes to N.O. and looks me up, I see 'em.' Junior snapped open a couple of cans of Bud and passed one to Teddy. Outside, dusty afternoon sun fought its way through the hanging jungle on the balcony and began to creep into the room. Time to pull the blinds. Junior thought about it but tipped a little beer down his throat instead. Having company was hard work when you didn't know what the company wanted after all this time.

'Goff told me you kept in touch with Birdie,' Teddy said, looking round for a glass. There wasn't one.

Uh-oh, Junior thought, time for the blinds, and he heaved his bulk off the sofa. While he threaded his way through his woman's delicate knick-knacks he said, 'She's still in the business, you know.'

'As much as she ever was,' Teddy said. 'I'm surprised anyone wants to know. How old is she now?'

'Never asked.' Junior busied himself at the window. It was a precise operation. His woman liked the blinds closed enough so that direct sunlight was blocked from her paintings, carpet and soft furnishings, but open enough to air the room. He didn't usually give it as much attention as he was giving it now.

'She's still a full-on bread-head,' Teddy said. 'You know she's always fighting the labels to give her half Jack's royalties?'

'Yeah?' said Junior, padding back to the sofa. 'Well, that ain't nobody's business but hers.'

'You might as well say I co-wrote,' Teddy said. 'Which I did. Or even you. Think of what *you* put in. Jack would've stayed a fucking pub player without us.'

'Improbable.' Junior lowered himself into the cushions. 'Jack had the magic from very early on.'

'Oh he was the best frontman in the business, I'll grant you that. No one could sell a song better than him. But whose song was it? That's the question.'

Junior looked at Teddy over the rim of his beer can. Confrontation, he thought. Hassle.

'Well?' Teddy asked, leaning forward.

'I don't think about it, man,' Junior said. 'I got well paid for what I did. So did you.'

'That's open to question too. How much did *you* make when the albums were re-released on CD?'

Junior didn't answer. This was what he didn't need. This murky, dirty music-business talk – resentful victim-speak. It got you in a bean-counting mood and you ended up feeling you'd been shafted all your life. Everyone else was getting rich off your creative input. Only the stars could fight and win. Nobody else even fought. They just gathered in small rooms and bitched. About money. About recognition. About contracts, credits and Christ knows what-all else.

What the fuck, Junior thought, everyone knew it was a dirty business, and everyone still wanted to be in it. So you signed an agreement and you were happy to get the gig. But when the gig turned out to be a money-maker and you weren't cut in . . . When there were big-time winners on the music lottery and you were never one of them . . . Bitch, bitch, bitch.

But it was justifiable bitching. You *were* shafted. The fat cats *were* blowing smoke up your arse. You thought about it. You started bitching. You got hassle. You got ulcers. And, if you were called Junior Moline, you got out. You sucked on your beer can, you sucked on your chillum and went back to loving the music. Forget about hating the business – that takes too much energy, man, that just fucks with your head. Listen to the sounds and kick back.

New Orleans was the place to do that. There was a pair of buskers under Junior's window right now noodling on 'A Place in the Sun' and doing it more than justice. This was a town where buskers could sound better than Eric Clapton. Junior tuned Teddy out and tuned the buskers in. Yes. One voice. Two acoustic guitars. Pick ups, amplifier, two small speakers. He could imagine two old guys on folding chairs, guitar case open at their feet to catch a few thrown dollars. Crap equipment – all of it beat-up and warped by the wet heat. Ah, but that voice, man, those finger-licking riffs.

God bless their golden hearts, Junior thought. Better to have your guitar warped by the sun than to have your heart warped by a dirty business.

Teddy was saying, 'C'mon, June, don't you want to claw some back? It won't cost you nothing, all you got to do is talk to Birdie.'

'And tell her what, man?'

'Tell her to release the materials. All the Antigua stuff. I mean, you could help with the re-mix. We could all come away with another slice of the pie.'

'Not me, man,' Junior said, slowly. 'I don't want any more of Jack's shit. Dead or alive, if it's anything to do with Jack, it's always a heavy scene. Everyone fussing and fighting. Bad karma, man.'

'That's bullshit, June, and you know it. Don't hide behind that karma crap. This is a big deal. They're making a telly programme. There's going to be a book. The full package. It's like our time came round again. All the old stuff's cool.'

Unbelievable, Junior thought. Bald and still hungry. Still aching for the super-trooper and the big car. Whatever happened to counter-culture? Did it go under the counter when the bean-counters took over the world?

'I don't know about you,' Teddy said, 'but I could do with the extra moolah. I got three kids and four mortgages to service. You never had any kids?'

'Not that anyone told me,' Junior answered.

'Birdie didn't either. Too busy looking after number one. But they say she's hit hard times now.'

'We all have our ups and downs,' Junior said.

'More downs that ups these days.' Teddy eyed the sagging furniture. 'What I'm saying is that Birdie's got access to stuff that could make us a lot of bread. If you don't want to be involved, well, cool. But I do. I think I'm owed, man. I was there on the film. I was playing in the studio. That stuff's as much mine as it is hers.'

'Maybe,' said Junior, who would say anything to avoid an argument, 'but what am I supposed to do about it?'

'You don't have to do anything,' Teddy said, to Junior's great relief. 'But didn't she, like, come to see you after Jack died? I mean, she did one of her disappearing tricks, so did she ever turn up here with stuff to store in your cellar?'

'There aren't any cellars in New Orleans,' Junior said.

'The attic, then.'

'Why would she do that? What stuff?'

'I don't know,' Teddy said. 'Who knows what women keep. They say she rescued everything of value after the fire. Pity she didn't rescue Jack, eh? They say she grabbed everything – stuff that wasn't hers – and took it out of the country. She'd have to store it somewhere.'

'Not here, man,' Junior said. 'I've only lived here eighteen months myself. This is my woman's place.'

'Oh well,' Teddy said, losing interest.

'What're you looking for?'

'Nothing,' Teddy said. 'Her, actually. Thought I could persuade her to co-operate. Appeal to her better nature, if she's got one. I was Jack's best friend, after all.'

You and whose army? Junior thought. It was amazing how many best friends Jack had after all these years. He said, 'Can't help you there, man. I don't know where she's at.'

'You must have an address.'

'E-mail address,' Junior said, vaguely slapping his pockets. 'I only see her when she shows up. But I can give you the e.'

'Got it. She isn't responding. C'mon, man, where do you send the Christmas card?'

'Christmas card?' Junior laughed. 'Look, Ted, as far as I know she's been in L.A., Geneva, Kingston Jamaica, Kingston England, Kingston Ontario, Sydney, Berlin and Tunis. All in the last couple of years. Oh, and Kuala Lumpur. She ain't what you'd call a home body.'

'Shit,' Teddy said. 'When did you see her last?'

'Dunno. Oh, must've been May. Festival. She was scouting acts for a night-club owner in Malaysia. That's how I remember Kuala

Lumpur. He was even fatter than me and a damn sight richer, man. Best hotel in town. Three secretaries. If you want to know who's paying the bills, try Kuala Lumpur. Or better still, try her sister.'

'Done that,' Teddy said, standing up. 'She was in London up to two weeks ago and then she took off. The sister doesn't know where to.'

'Where are you staying?' Junior stood up too. 'I might think of something.'

'The Sheraton on Canal. Just the one night. Yeah, if you think of something, let me know.'

'I'll look in my files,' Junior promised. He padded barefoot to the door and watched Teddy go down the narrow staircase to the courtyard. Sharp shoes, he thought, but it's too damn hot for socks, even silk ones. Teddy slid a pair of celebrity shades on to his nose, raised a hand in farewell and walked away into the dense, wet heat.

What, no limo? Junior thought and shut the door.

When he got back to the lounge, he saw, without surprise that Birdie was coiled in the deep armchair Teddy had just left.

'How the fuck did he find me?' Junior asked, flopping down on the sofa. 'You could've struck a flint off me when he said who he was on the door phone.'

'I thought you were superb,' Birdie said. 'Super cool.'

'Yeah, well – I was having caniptions.'

'Poor baby,' Birdie said.

'You can laugh,' Junior said, 'but my shoulders hurt.'

'How about some ice cream and a back rub?'

'Yes and yes.'

'And then a game of cribbage,' Birdie said, gliding away to the kitchen. 'I've got to think fast.'

'OK,' Junior said, with less enthusiasm. He owed her four thousand, seven hundred and twenty-nine dollars from cribbage games over the years. At a hundred dollars a win and a dollar a point, that represented a fair number of losses.

He remembered his own astonishment at seeing her play with Jack the first time he travelled with them. First-class on Concorde from London to New York, the compartment full of musicians and tour bigwigs. Ignoring them all, at the front of the plane sat Jack and Birdie with a deck of cards and a cribbage board, deadly serious. Rock stars don't play cribbage, he thought. But Jack did. When he was feeling unsociable he played obsessively, game after game, dragging himself through the dead hours of travel.

Junior sat with his back to Birdie, digging Cherry Garcia out of a tub and licking it off a long spoon while she dug her thumbs into his shoulder muscles, loosening the kinks. Nothing was said until halfway through the first game of crib when he was already trailing by seventeen points. Then she said, 'Well, my guess is that Barry Stears sent Teddy to find you. It's the sort of thing he'd do. If it were Sasson . . . I think Sasson would do something more sensible.'

'What's going down?' Junior asked reluctantly.

'I don't think you want to know,' she said. 'But Teddy's right. There *is* a Jack-package on the burner and they're turning up the heat. You *could* make some money.'

'Nah,' Junior said. 'Let it be.'

'Why? Suppose they show up here with a film crew and want an interview. Suppose Barry asks a load of silly questions about the making of *Hard Candy*. You could ask for whatever you wanted.'

'You wouldn't like that.'

'Why not? They're going to do it anyway, and if they're interested in the production side you're The Man. At least you'd give them straight dope. I'd rather it was you than some ignorant ligger.'

'What if they want personal stories?'

'That's not your scene,' Birdie said, turning over the cards in the crib and displaying a nice double run for another eight points. She grinned and said, 'Anyway, if it's stories they want, we could cook up a couple of dillies. I think you should ring Teddy and maybe take him out tonight. When's Sandrine coming home?'

'Sevenish. But I don't want to spend any more time with that son of a bitch.'

'Who's in town? Anyone good playing at Tips or The House of Blues? You could take them both there. Sandrine likes a night out, doesn't she?'

'I'm broke,' Junior said, feeling like a paper boat approaching Niagara Falls.

'My treat,' said Birdie.

'Oh shit,' said Junior. 'What d'you want me to say?'

'I'll think of something. Don't worry. Just have a good time. Enjoy yourself. Sandrine didn't know I was coming, did she?'

'How could she?' Junior said ruefully. 'I didn't know myself. And Teddy was quite a shock – he hasn't spoken two words to me in the last ten years.'

'Yes, that was awkward, but you were terrific and I think we can turn it all round.'

'We?' said Junior with foreboding.

Afterwards, when Teddy rang the next day and complained that his hotel room had been broken into and that traveller's cheques, personal stereo, laptop and shaver had been stolen, Junior felt dismay but no surprise.

'Bummer, man,' he said. 'This town, eh?'

'All electrical goods,' Teddy told him. 'Good thing I didn't bring a guitar.'

'While we were out dancing?' Sandrine said. 'That's a shame.' She was what Junior called a jolly dancer – plenty of bounce and footwork. It was the bounce that had caught his eye in the first place. Bounce and a D-cup. Junior liked Sandrine a lot. She had a good, steady job, and that was a turn-on too.

She said, 'Tell him to give our number to the police in case they recover any of his stuff.'

She was generous too, Junior thought as he relayed the message into the telephone.

'Fat chance of that,' Teddy said. 'Neither the police nor the hotel seem interested and I'm leaving in an hour.'

'Where're you going, man?' Junior asked. 'In case we hear anything.'

'Thought I'd give LA a shot. Thanks for the tip.'

The tip, of course, was Birdie's, so Teddy was about to take off on another fruitless journey.

'Well, good luck, man,' Junior said, and hung up thinking that Birdie was probably right: Teddy must be travelling at someone else's expense. If he was flying to the West Coast to look for a Chinese-American she-male who might or might not still have a house near Venice Beach, he was unlikely to pay for the ticket himself.

At dinner the previous night, when Junior, Sandrine and Teddy were sitting round a courtyard table, Junior said, 'If I was you, Ted, I'd look for Renée-Ronny Pang.'

Teddy almost choked on his French onion soup. 'That fuckin' pervert!' he said.

'Who's Renée-Ronny?' asked Sandrine, who was interested in the lives of the rich and famous.

'Never met her myself,' Junior said. 'But Birdie said she was a masseuse, an astrologer and sometimes a sort of cabaret bandit. She was about as androgynous as you can get. One of those West Coast bands introduced her to Jack.'

'He had a sore neck,' Teddy said, 'an old whiplash injury. The Thing treated it and then just stuck around. It was Birdie's friend really. It was Birdie who was into all that freaky stuff. Not Jack. He was just trying to fuck with my mind. One gig, he even had her-him come on stage and try to smooch me. Shit!'

Now Teddy was flying off to see The Thing who made his skin crawl, exactly as Birdie predicted he would.

'Give them what they want,' she'd said. 'The trick is to know who wants what. Like the *National Enquirer* knows what its readers want. And Renée-Ronny certainly knew what the *National Enquirer* wanted.'

'She really let you down,' Junior said.

'Yes, those stories caused a lot of trouble.'

'So why resurrect them?'

'They never died,' Birdie said with a shrug. 'You can't resurrect something which isn't dead. Anyway, the stories don't matter. All we want to do is remind Teddy and Barry that I stayed with Renée-Ronny after the fire. That I confided in her. Nudge Teddy in that direction.'

Nudged, Teddy said, 'Oh shit, yes – that crap: "Jack Feared for His Life" and "Beware the Blonde Bride – I saw it in the stars".'

'Hey, I remember that,' Sandrine cried. 'I was just a kid, but my big brother had all of Jack's records. I remember seeing that headline at the check-out with my mom. There was a picture and the caption said, "The smile of an angel, the heart of a demon", and I thought it was so cool, you know, to be bad and beautiful, when I didn't even need a brassière or have a boyfriend yet.'

'You're not saying all that tabloid stuff's true, are you?' Teddy said.

''Course not,' Junior said, 'it's garbage. But Birdie did tell me about going to see Renée-Ronny. Turned out she wasn't the friend Birdie thought she was.'

'Surprise, surprise,' Teddy said.

'She was looking for a port in a storm, only Renée-Ronny wanted to be Birdie's publicity agent – a real twenty-percenter, while Birdie just wanted a friend and as little publicity as possible.'

'Poor Birdie,' Sandrine said.

'They had a bust up,' Junior said, 'and when Birdie got up the next morning she found half the world's press camped out on Renée-Ronny's doorstep, and the other half in the living room. She told me she had to escape in just the clothes she was standing up in at the time, and she never went back for the rest of her stuff.'

'What did she leave behind?' Teddy asked.

'Dunno, man,' Junior said. 'What she told me was, "I hardly had time to grab my passport. I had to climb out the bathroom window and run across the garage roof." I think she regretted it later.'

'Regretted what?'

'Leaving things behind. She said once she wished she hadn't lost so much.' Message delivered, Junior thought. The warm air trapped in the courtyard was making him sweat.

But Teddy wouldn't leave it alone. 'I could've told her,' he said, 'but she wouldn't have listened. That pervert was toxic. But Birdie thought it was all *interesting* and *exotic*. She wanted Jack to be more androgynous. If you ask me, she had her eye on the gay market.'

'You make her sound so cynical,' Sandrine said. 'She doesn't strike me that way at all.'

'You've met her?' Teddy's eyes flicked from Sandrine to Junior and back again.

'Sure,' said Sandrine. 'She was here for the Festival. We had a party.'

Junior laughed. The Festival *was* a party as far as she was concerned.

'I was really fascinated to meet her,' Sandrine said, "cos you hear so many stories. She's like, a living legend, but there she was – she was working for some millionaire but she still had time to hang out with us. She seemed, you know, just like one of us.'

'She *is* one of us,' said Junior, lying. She was never one of us, he thought. Fame, he thought, notoriety. It does something irreversible. No matter how old or how broke Birdie became it would always surprise him to see her in Sandrine's kitchen making a cup of coffee. She'll never be one of us, he thought. And it's not her fault. Because people like Sandrine were always amazed when she acted like regular folks, it was impossible for her to *be* regular folks.

And now it was a day later. Sandrine left the apartment to go shopping with friends and Junior was alone. Beneath his window a new set of buskers was doing a witty, raunchy version of 'Frankie and Johnny'. This lot were definitely into narrative songs. They'd already done 'Stagger Lee' and the woman who sang gave it all the attitude it needed.

He looked around vaguely but couldn't place his chillum, so he sat and rolled a fat and ragged spliff. Then, with his lips tingling and his ears buzzing, he turned on his computer and, on a stoned whim, called up Birdie's name on the web. He wasn't focusing too well, because the first site to come his way was a porno page, and he tilted his head this way and that until he realised that he was staring at a picture of a very young Birdie being fucked from behind by a creature with the head of Bill Clinton and the body of a goat. He was invited to interact.

'I don't think so,' he mumbled, out loud. 'But now that you've reminded me, I did say I'd call.'

He exhaled slowly, blowing sweet smoke at the computer. What time was it in London? Ahead or behind?

'Who cares?' he said to the abused image on his screen. 'Now is now, wherever you are.'

He dialled a London number. A soft voice said hello.

'Birdie?' he said.

'Birdie isn't here,' said the voice.

'Oh,' Junior said, stumped. 'You sound like Birdie.'

'Everyone says that.'

'Do you look like her?' Junior was still staring at his computer, his head at an impossible angle. 'Have you ever met President Clinton?'

'I beg your pardon?'

'Robin!' Junior shouted, a lightbulb flashing on in his brain. 'Don't hang up.' He switched off the computer. Boy, was that a relief! 'It's Junior Moline. We met years ago. Birdie asked me to call this number.'

A moment later, Birdie was on the line.

'Mad axeman flew to LA this afternoon.' That was the message, wasn't it?

'Interesting,' she said. 'Thank you.'

'Hostile,' he said, 'very hostile.'

'Yep,' she said breezily. 'That's why I'm so grateful. I didn't want him on my tail.'

Junior put the receiver down wishing she'd chosen a different word. Then he thought about Robin. The serious one with the babies – that was her, wasn't it? No, not serious, he thought, just not blonde.

He found that he was sitting on his chillum, but by that time he didn't care any more. And he'd forgotten to tell Birdie about the break-in at Teddy's hotel room. Except, of course, he'd put money on the fact that she already knew – if he had any money, if he were a betting man.

'Birdie, Birdie, Birdie,' he sighed, looking at the phone. 'Better look out for that pretty tail of yours. Hassle comin' down.'

# Part 2

# PAY THE MAN

'You're the man who squats behind the man who works the soft machine.'

Jagger, Richards

# I

## Big in Brazil

You want a rock'n'roll story? Well, here's one. It isn't about music, or drugs, or sex. It's about money and accounting. Still interested?

Early on, when I'd only just met Jack and he didn't have much more than a cult following, he wrote a song called 'Dance for Daddy'. It was supposed to be a slowish filler for the second album. A ballad – Jack didn't write many ballads. It was pretty but ordinary. And then, talking about it, we decided to give it a sort of bossa nova spin. We upped the tempo a bit and brought in congas and a bunch of South American stuff. Even so, it was an unremarkable track on an album which didn't get many plays in the UK. Jack was not on the Radio One playlist at that time so he didn't have a UK hit.

The album was released, sold slowly and died. But a few months later we got a call from a distributor who said, 'Congratulations, you're number one in Brazil.'

'Dance for Daddy' was a huge hit in South America, and the whole album went platinum in Brazil, gold in Argentina and Colombia.

Number one in Brazil, unknown in the UK.

Even so, Jack was thrilled. He'd never been number one anywhere. 'It's coming, babe,' he said. 'It's on its way – I can feel it. Let's buy a house.'

Because you'd think, wouldn't you, that a hit record anywhere in the world would make you some serious bread. Jack thought so. Me too. But that was before we found out about the now-you-see-it-now-you-don't nature of accounting for foreign earnings. Put it this way: we saw that Jack had earned a packet in South America but we never saw a penny of it.

Here's how it went. At the time Jack was recording for a little indie label called Cutz. Cutz did not have a foreign distribution arm, so for South America they sublicensed Jack's album to a record company whose head office was in Belize. There were other similar deals for the US, South-east Asia and Australia, but that's another story.

So, unknown to Jack, 'Dance for Daddy' and the rest of the album was sublicensed to a company in Belize which was collecting his earnings, taking a hefty cut, and presumably paying some tax.

Cutz might not have had a foreign distribution arm, but it did have an off-shore account in the Cayman Islands. Eventually, money filtered out of Brazil, Argentina and Colombia, to Belize, and from there it went to the Cayman Islands where it was held in Cutz's account.

At first, when Jack told Cutz he wanted money to buy a house, he was informed that the company in Belize hadn't passed it on yet. They had a twelve-month accounting period and no money was expected until March. Cutz offered to loan him the money or set up the mortgage for him in the meantime. Alarm bells went off in my head. I told Jack to say no. Sasson Freel told Jack to say yes. Jack said yes and he bought a nice house on Camden Hill.

March came and went without Jack's bank balance growing noticeably fatter. I asked Sasson to find out what was going on. After all, he was Jack's manager and it was his job to find out. Sasson disappeared for three whole days and nights. He missed a gig in Plymouth. He never missed gigs. The boys in the band were furious, but Jack was worried.

Sasson came back unshaven, dirty, shaky and with a dose of clap. He'd been in Brighton and he couldn't remember how he got there.

'I went to the meeting with Cutz,' he said. 'And then I had to get drunk. Jack, I'm so sorry.'

So what happened to make Sasson go on a three-day bender? Poor young Sasson. Well, in the simplest possible terms, he discovered that he had helped Cutz to stitch Jack up. When signing agreements and consents on Jack's behalf he only had his eyes on the US and UK sides of the deal. Like a lot of ingénues in the rock trade he thought that everything began and ended with fame and fortune in the States or at home. You can't blame him exactly. Nearly everyone thinks the same. The rest of the world doesn't quite count. And no one expected Jack to be big in Brazil.

Cutz didn't expect it either, but they did have the means to exploit it. What Sasson failed to notice, while signing agreements on Jack's behalf, was that there were two separate companies: Cutz UK and Cutz Cayman. Cutz UK dealt with the home market – which was pitiful. But Cutz Cayman dealt with the South American market which turned out to be surprisingly lucrative.

'OK,' says Sasson. 'But it's still Cutz, so where's the money?'

Not so fast, young Sasson. Didn't you notice that you gave Cutz UK permission to sublicense Jack's work to subsidiaries?

'Yes, but . . .'

No buts, young man, it's right here in black and white. Cutz UK has your permission to sublicense. And so, *with your permission*, Cutz UK sublicensed to Cutz Cayman, who in turn sublicensed to a company with offices in Belize.

'OK,' Sasson says. 'But we're making money out there. Where is it?'

In the Cayman Islands, young Sasson, can't you read? Cutz Cayman is a holding company. It is holding Jack's money. You agreed to this, and here is your signature to prove it.

'So transfer the money to the UK.'

You aren't listening, young man. We can't transfer any money. It's not ours to transfer. It's Cutz Cayman's. We aren't Cutz Cayman. We're Cutz UK. Separate companies. Don't you read what you sign?

'But,' says Sasson, thinking fast, 'surely Cutz Cayman has to account to Cutz UK?'

Of course it does, you pathetic excuse for a rock manager, but only at the end of the accounting period. And it isn't up for another nineteen years.

'*Nineteen years?*' Sasson shouts.

Keep your voice down, silly boy. You weren't shouting when

you signed these contracts. You were only too willing to sign whatever we put in front of you. You practically tore our hands off to get to the pen . . .

No wonder poor young Sasson had to go on a three-day bender before he could pluck up enough courage to tell Jack – 'Sorry, Jack, there's not going to be any money for nineteen years, and what's more, Cutz UK owns your new house. Because of my advice, Jack, you owe Cutz real money, but they don't owe you diddly-squat. Like it, Jack?'

Oh yes. Jack liked it enough to fire Sasson on the spot and to make his next album with a different label.

Isn't that a nice little rock'n'roll story? All about a silly little song called 'Dance for Daddy'.

Well, it taught me to dance all right. And I'm still dancing, because it didn't end there. What goes around in this business comes around. Sometimes more than once. And every time it comes around it gets better.

# II

## Hopelessly Devoted

There was a photograph of Jack in Robin's bedroom. It was the first image she saw in the morning and the last image she saw at night. He was sitting on a stone wall, wearing a loose white shirt open over his bare chest. The breeze swung through his sun-bleached hair, ruffling it into a halo around his head. He looked at her with a half smile, relaxed and amused. Behind him, the sky was blue, blue, blue as an angel's eyes. Blue as Jack's eyes.

When Robin took the picture she was standing on the patio at Villa Verte and Jack was talking about how nice it was to be able to let his chest hair grow for a couple of weeks. No public appearances, no photographers. He didn't have to look like a hairless boy for the fanzines. So Robin pointed her camera at him and said, 'So show us your tits.'

There was very little chest hair anyway, and it didn't show in the picture even when she had it enlarged. He looked angelic, and you can't imagine an angel with chest hair.

He laughed at my joke, she thought with pride, even now. I could make him laugh. Everyone enjoys laughter. So I contributed something.

But it was a very small contribution and it didn't make up for the fact that Jack flew her and little Grace down to the South of France and that they were staying in a luxury villa with its own pool and games room. It didn't repay Jack for the car and chauffeur or the horribly expensive restaurants. Robin felt the debt keenly. Being the poor relation wasn't comfortable.

Robin cooked for him when she was allowed to. But even that wasn't necessary because of the chef. Her strengths were invisible, her weakness on display.

'Just relax, sweetie,' Lin said. 'Get a tan. You don't have to do anything.' Lin had a tan like clover honey. Lin did not have a seventeen-month-old baby to look after. She could wear tiny sundresses and tinier swimsuits. Robin was already pregnant with Jimmy. She was heavy and clumsy.

'Doesn't matter,' Lin said. 'You're lovely pregnant. And you've had a hard year. Let it all go.'

Robin didn't want to let anything go, and sometimes on a chilly English morning she'd look at the sun shining on Jack's angel face and try to remember every minute of one month in the South of France. One month under the same sun. Jack and Lin. Twins. Children playing. Irresponsible. Infectious. The only way Robin could match their lightness was to float in the pool, an extra-large T-shirt billowing in the water to cover her bulge. Mercifully weightless, but never irresponsible.

It was a floaty feeling she could only relive in the early morning, half awake, or at night, half asleep, before her weight caught up with her. The weight of years and loss.

Jack was dead. Mum and Dad were dead. She was a middle-aged woman. Her babies were not babies. Everything passes except for responsibility.

Sometimes she felt that age was simply a wrinkled mask you wore over a young face. Or an adult mask over a baby face. Jimmy and Grace, she felt, wore translucent masks, their baby features showing through like double exposures.

Robin collected masks. They hung in pairs, trios or singly, from nails, over picture frames, hooks, mirrors, hatstands. They propped each other up on the mantelshelf, the desk, the piano. They came from every continent and every culture. Even paper or plastic faces which caught her eye at a fair or a market would be given a place, sometimes a name. Occasionally she thought that her masks had clearer identities than the people she knew. At least she knew they were masks. Whereas people . . . How could you tell what people were hiding – with or without masks?

'A mask doesn't hide a face,' Lin told her once. 'A mask *is* a face. Everybody has more than one.'

Robin had hundreds. Lin didn't have any. Or did Lin have hundreds and Robin only one? Were masks for protection, deception or fun? All of the above? Or none of the above?

She dragged her gaze away from Jack's smiling face and got out of bed. Immediately, the phone started to ring. She didn't answer. The machine took the call. She pulled a flannel shirt on over her nightgown and padded barefoot down to the kitchen to make coffee.

She squeezed two sweet Florida oranges while coffee was brewing and drank the juice, staring out of the window into the garden. Persistent rain was making the pink and white mallows droop and drip.

Upstairs again, she showered and dressed. Two more calls came in. She ignored them. Before climbing up to the attic, she went to Grace's bedroom to check that there were clean sheets on her bed. Clean sheets, fresh towels. Grace was coming home today. Robin smiled and started work – fabric in her fingers, fabric feeding through under the punching needle. Real stuff she could cut and shape and sew. A garment which would turn out more or less as planned. A process she had some control over. Unlike life. Unlike people.

Two hours later she raised her head and saw Lin standing in the doorway watching her. She was so startled she nearly sewed through her finger.

'Hi, dreamer,' Lin said.

'When did you get back?'

'Last night. The lights were out, so I didn't wake you.'

Even the house told Robin nothing. She had slept, awakened, got up and worked, thinking she was alone. And all the time her house was sheltering another occupant, hiding Lin in silence.

She said, 'You might have left a note.'

'I was tired. I just crashed.'

'And another thing,' Robin said, unexpectedly cross, 'when you lie to your boss, I wish you wouldn't use one of the children as an excuse. You told that nice man that Grace had an accident. It was almost like ill-wishing her.'

'Oh baby,' Lin said, instantly contrite. 'I'm sorry. It was the first thing to come into my head. I didn't think.'

Robin could feel Lin eyeing her curiously. She ducked her head and switched off the sewing machine. She wasn't ready to be charmed or mollified. She said, 'I don't understand. You seemed to like that job, but then you just split and lie, and all you leave me is a garbled message on the answering machine. So I can't do anything but pass on the lie, or stone-wall.'

'Oh sweetie, I'm so sorry . . .'

'*And*,' Robin ploughed on, '*and* the phone's been going crazy. Day and night. I can't answer it any more. What if it was one of the children? An emergency?'

'I knew this wasn't fair,' Lin said. 'I knew it'd be too much for you. Look, love, I'll pack. I can be out of here in twenty minutes.'

'I'm not asking you to go.' Robin, all of a sudden, felt her attic was empty and hollow. Lin was her little sister, her third child.

'I've got to stand on my own two feet,' Lin said. 'I can get a room nearer my job. It'd be more convenient. And, for a while at least, no one'll know where I am. You'll see – it'll be all right.'

'Lin, just shut up,' Robin cried. 'Why must you be so extreme? I don't want you to leave. It's just that when this began, you were going to get a job and pay your debts. You were doing so well. It was nice. We were a team. And then you just bugger off, and everything goes crazy.'

'I didn't "just bugger off",' Lin said sadly. 'It's the other way round. Things go crazy, and then I'm forced to bugger off. It's the same old story. Only this time it's worse because of the *zeitgeist*. Everyone's hunting me. Except it isn't really me they're hunting. It's Jack.'

'Oh Lin,' Robin said, just as sadly. 'What're we going to do?'

They went downstairs and Robin sat her little sister at the kitchen table while she made scrambled eggs, a green salad and a big pot of tea.

She said, 'I'm sorry I freaked. Don't take any notice.' Lin looked so slight and alone. Why hadn't she put on more weight, Robin wondered. It was as if she'd been caught in a drop of amber by the trauma of her past life and condemned to be forever girlish, forever Birdie the Ultimate Chick.

Robin heaped the lion's share of scrambled egg on to Lin's plate with two slices of wholegrain toast, as if all her problems could be solved by a decent lunch. She thought, as she often thought, how sad it was to be the golden girl when you were too young. Everything she'd envied Lin for when they were both young – her looks, her wit, her freedom, her lover – had all come back as nightmares to haunt her. All the blessings morphed into curses.

They ate in silence for a while and then Robin asked, 'So where did you go? What did you do?'

'Devon,' Lin said. 'You know – Homer. It was fine. I wanted his advice about a song anyway. But I couldn't stay for ever. Like you said, I've got a job now.'

'Will they take you back?'

'I hope so.'

Robin was about to give Lin some good advice about how to placate employers when the doorbell rang and they both jumped.

Outside in the light rain stood Grace, saying, 'Why did you leave the chain on, Mum?' Behind her, a little off to one side, was a young man with a self-depreciating grin on his face.

Oh God, Robin thought, she's brought a boyfriend home. She didn't tell me about a boyfriend. She opened the door and the two young people came in dragging backpacks and carrier bags.

Robin hugged her daughter, automatically gauging her height and weight. She seemed to have been looking after herself. Her cheek against Robin's lips was smooth and rosy. She smelled of shampoo and urban rain.

'This is Alec,' Grace said. 'Is there anything for lunch? I'm starving.' She detached herself from Robin's embrace. She had her own priorities.

'Hi, Mrs Emerson,' Alec said, still wearing the lopsided love-me-do grin.

'Hi,' said Robin, thinking, and who the hell are you? 'We were eating scrambled eggs in the kitchen.'

'We? Is Jimmy home?'

'No. It's Lin . . .'

'Lin!' Grace shouted. 'Lin, Lin, Lin. Alec, come and meet my Auntie Lin.'

Meeting Auntie Lin was an event. Meeting Mother Robin was not, Robin thought, moving a bag out of the way with one foot and following along to the kitchen where she found Lin and Grace doing a short Lindy-hop routine by way of greeting – a couple of spins, a couple of slides. It was something Lin had shown Grace when she was nine and recovering from chicken pox. Lin was fun, fun, fun. Lin Lindy-hopped. No one else's aunt did that.

'Wow!' said Alec. 'You guys really *move*.'

Robin slid past the dancers and took eggs, bacon, tomatoes and mushrooms out of the fridge. There was a bowl of Grace's favourite king prawns marinating in ginger and garlic on the middle shelf but she wouldn't cook those until she knew whether Alec was a fixture or a fitting. Temporary food till then.

She listened while Lin effortlessly asked all the right questions and provoked Grace into a stream of chatter about her new job, her friends, her shared house. Grace, within minutes, was feeling like the most fascinating creature in the world and showing off. Robin, quietly cooking, hung on every word. Why wasn't it a conversation a mother could have with her daughter? Stories, jokes. No defences. Robin, the cook, was like a beggar at the feast, snacking on leftovers. And grateful. She didn't have to ask any direct questions and watch Grace clam up. She didn't have to feel intrusive and hear the dreadful, 'Don't worry about it, Mum,' which was supposed to be the all-inclusive answer to each and every question. Thank you Lin, but why do I need you? I should be able to do this for myself.

She sighed and laid plates of food in front of the kids.

'Thanks, Mrs Emerson,' Alec said, dutifully, hardly daring to take his eyes off Lin and Grace, afraid of missing any sparkle.

And then, 'Mum, can Alec stay in Jimmy's room for a couple of nights? When's he coming home? Next week? There's a party in Camden Town we want to go to.'

All the questions she should ask, like, 'Who the hell is Alec? Where's he from? Does he suffer from any communicable diseases?' All those sounded like clunkers and she didn't ask them.

She said, 'I suppose so,' and watched Grace slip from her chair and run out to show Alec his new quarters.

Lin said, 'Who the hell is Alec?'

'I don't know.'

'Boyfriend?'

'Don't know.'

'Hasn't Grace mentioned him before?'

'Not that I remember. Why?'

'I don't know,' Lin said. 'Something's wrong. They don't seem to know each other at all.'

'Do they have to?' Robin asked. 'At that age . . .'

The sisters looked at each other. Two women of the same generation now, Robin thought. Two old broads fretting about the youngsters. She smiled. 'We'll sort them out. He'll be no match for us.'

'I should bloody well hope not.' Lin smiled too. 'Grace seems to be doing all right, doesn't she? You're not worried, are you?'

'Not really. She's settling in, getting used to real life.'

'Well, then?'

'No worries.'

'Mama's little baby?'

'Oh, I'll get over it,' Robin said. 'I just wish she'd tell me more.'

'Don't be absurd,' Lin said. 'How much did *you* tell?'

'A damn sight more than you did.'

'So will she – you'll see. Give her time. You're the best friend she'll ever have.'

'Oh Lin,' Robin wailed, 'I feel so old and impotent.'

'Well, you're not, kid. It's her. She's big and bouncy and feeling her oats. Making her mother feel like an old mare is part of the thrill.'

'She must be thrilled to bits,' said Robin.

'All the same, let's check Alec out, mmm?'

Robin got to her feet and said, 'I'll go up and be the mother from hell, shall I? Embarrass the shit out of both of 'em.'

'Whoa,' Lin said, catching her hand. 'I had something a little more oblique in mind. Let's just see if there's anything to embarrass them for.'

'You're not going to . . . ?'

'Leave it to me, Ms Clean,' Lin said, and wandered away to read her mail and go through the phone messages.

Robin, alone in the kitchen, cleared up, rinsing pans and stacking dishes in the washer. She made another pot of tea, but she didn't go back to the attic to drink it. She stayed at the kitchen table. She wanted to be at the hub of the house in case Grace decided to come down and talk. Fat chance, she thought, but you have to make yourself available.

Paralysed at the hub of the house but on the rim of her own life, waiting, watching, listening. Like when the children were small. Or when her mother was going doolally. Always reactive, never active. I'm a counter-puncher. I'm the girl who can't get out on the floor and dance. I have to wait to be asked. Why?

This was the house Jack gave her mother when her father died. This was the house she moved into when her mother began to need care and her man left her. She wore it like a coat against the weather. It represented shelter and defeat – almost as if she'd come into the world unprepared and Jack had lent her his coat. She sat in it, perpetually wondering what would happen next.

At last she heard footsteps on the stairs. But no one came to the kitchen. The front door opened and shut, and then there was silence. Grace? Grace and Alec? Lin?

Once, years ago, when the twin forces of her children and her mother were keeping her prisoner in the house, Lin came to stay. Out of the blue, she turned up with a single bag and camped out in the attic.

'Why?' Robin asked. 'Where's Jack?'

'In the States,' Lin said, answering the second question first, and the first one not at all.

For nearly a week it was as if the doors and windows had been left open. Lin came and went. Sometimes she went alone. Sometimes she took one or both of the children. She even took their barmy mother to buy hats and handbags. She made Robin go to the movies or to visit friends. It could have been a holiday for Robin except that, for the whole time, she felt as if she were holding her breath. She was in suspense, tied by a skein of silk threads to the phone and the doorbell, waiting.

For what? For Jack to call? For Jack to come? Why? He wasn't going to call *her*. He wasn't going to visit her. It was as if she were waiting on Lin's behalf. Which was a complete waste of her emotional energy because Lin didn't seem to be waiting at all.

It was clear to Robin that something had gone badly wrong between Lin and Jack. But Lin never said what it was. And Robin was afraid.

Lin wasn't waiting, she wasn't afraid. She stepped out and danced. She didn't seem to give a damn if Jack phoned or if he didn't. It was Robin who cared desperately that he didn't. And when at last he did, Lin was out and she didn't ring him back.

Then a long white car arrived at the door and the driver came in with a letter. Lin was out then too. Robin, aching with tension, gave the driver lunch. The letter sat on the table between them like an unexploded bomb.

Lin came home three hours later. She said, 'Hi, Mr Peters,' to the driver, and took the letter up to the attic. She came down again a few minutes later and said, 'Thanks, Mr Peters. There's no reply. Would you like another cup of tea?'

Mr Peters declined the tea, but used the phone and then left.

Robin said, 'What's happening, Lin? I don't understand. Are you breaking up with Jack?'

'Maybe,' Lin said.

'Maybe?' Robin asked pathetically. 'Don't you know? Mr Peters said he had instructions to take you with him.'

'Instructions,' Lin said. 'My, my. Look, Robin, do you want me out of your hair? Are there too many people here? Is that the problem? Because I can easily find somewhere else. I can go if you want.'

'No,' Robin said. 'It isn't that.' But there she was, wanting Lin to go running to Jack as if her own life, freedom and happiness depended on it. Waiting, holding her breath for Lin to make the right move, or for Jack to say the right thing. Wanting to say, for Christ's sake Lin, resolve this so that *I* can breathe again. Lin, it seemed, was on the brink of throwing away something which was crucial to Robin. And Robin couldn't even begin to explain it. It wasn't her life – Jack wasn't her man.

'It's *my* life,' Lin would have said, had she known. 'Am I supposed to live it by your criteria?'

'Yes!' Robin would have howled. 'Don't leave Jack. Be faithful, honest and true. Put up with anything he does, but *keep* him.' Because that's what Robin would've done if she'd been given the chance. Oh yes she would. Without question. Then maybe things would have turned out differently.

Jack arrived in the dead of night when Robin was already in bed. He was tired, his eyes were ringed and sunken – not the angel boy in her photograph. He asked for Birdie, and Robin realised with horror that Lin had not come home from a date with someone almost as beautiful as Jack. Someone, Robin realised, she ought to have recognised from the glimpse she had of him through a Porsche windscreen.

She couldn't tell Jack that, so she asked him in and sat him in the living room, offering him tea, coffee, alcohol, whatever she could think of, chattering uncontrollably. Finally he asked for hot chocolate, more to shut her up, she thought, than because he wanted anything. And when she came back with it, she found him asleep on the sofa. So young, too young to be so weary. It nearly made her cry to see the drooping head and long eyelashes. She covered him with her patchwork quilt as if he were an orphan she'd taken in from the street. And yes, she would have kissed his eyelids if she hadn't been afraid to wake him. Because if she woke him she'd have to talk to him and she never knew what to say. She didn't know what interested him – or rather she didn't know what didn't bore him, and she suspected that she was boring.

So she crept out of the living room and went to sit at the bottom of the stairs waiting to warn Lin. At first she was angry with Lin. How could she go off with someone else? Then she was angry with Jack. Who did he think he was – turning up unannounced and putting her in this embarrassing situation? Last, she was angry with herself. Why was she getting in a state about her sister's boyfriend? That's all it was – her sister and her boyfriend had a row. It wasn't the end of the world. Lin going out with another guy wasn't high treason.

But it *was* the end of the world. It *was* high treason. Because it was Jack. That was the last unreasonable thought Robin had before she too nodded off.

Much later something disturbed her, and she woke cold, stiff and gummy-eyed. It was after five in the morning. She got up and peeped round the living room door. Jack was gone.

She tiptoed up to the attic. The attic was empty. Lin's bed was unslept in. Her bag was gone. Downstairs in the kitchen she found a note on the draining board. It said, 'Thanks for everything. Talk to you soon. Love, L.'

Desolate, Robin went into the living room. The quilt was half on the sofa, half on the floor, like a sloughed snakeskin. The sofa was dented and rumpled. The mug of hot chocolate had been left where she put it, untouched, cold. She picked up the quilt, meaning to fold it, but it felt a little warm. A little heat was all that remained of Jack's visit. She wrapped herself in it and lay down where he had lain. She buried her face in the cushion on which he'd rested his head. And smelled her sister's perfume.

Sitting bolt upright she said aloud, 'You stupid, stupid cow.' And then she went to bed. Something important had happened under her roof – under her nose – and she had missed it.

Always losing the thread, Robin thought, always missing the punchline. Enough. There was work to be done, so do it.

She went slowly upstairs and walked quietly past closed doors. She wouldn't intrude. Lin was in her mother's old room. Alec was in Jimmy's. Grace was in her own. Maybe. The only open bedroom door was Robin's. Was she really the only one in the house with nothing to hide or no one to hide from?

As she passed her room she caught sight of an alien shape. She turned quickly and saw Alec in her bedroom.

'Hello,' she said. 'What're you doing in here?'

'Oh, sorry,' he said. 'I was looking for Grace.' He smiled at her, apologetic, but not guilty. 'Love your masks. Is that a picture of The Legend? His music's incredible. I only got into it recently but I'm hooked.'

'Yes, that's Jack,' Robin said, warming to him. She sat on the edge of her bed. 'Do you live in Bristol like Grace?' Alec might have been looking for Grace, but he'd found her, so he was going to have to put up with a few questions.

'Actually, no,' Alec said. 'And, before you ask, we met on the Net. We've been corresponding for months.'

'No. Really?' she said, alarmed and fascinated. No sex yet, she thought. Is that good or bad?

'She signs on as g.ace, so it was a long time before I found out if she was male or female. We just hit it off, if you know what I mean. I suppose, in your day, it would've been a pen-pal thing.'

In my day? Robin thought. Cheeky bugger. But Alec seemed to be too young to know he was insulting her.

She smiled and said, 'So, this is the first time you've met? In person?'

'We decided that I'd meet her train and we'd let an element of chance take over. She'd described herself to me and I'd described myself to her. And we thought, if we recognised each other from the descriptions – like, if neither of us had been telling porkies – we'd be off to a good start.'

He was laughing now, and blushing. Good, healthy teeth, Robin thought. Well, if they met on the Net, at least it means he can write.

He said, 'I know it's a risk, Mrs Emerson. People can say any old thing and you never know if it's true or not. But I recognised Grace straight away, so I reckon she's the honest type.'

'Oh, she is,' Robin said. When she actually tells you anything.

'So I guess we both thought, like, OK. We can go to a party together and see how it goes from there. I don't know about you, Mrs Emerson, but I like to get to know people slowly.'

'We-ell,' Robin said, pretending to think about it, 'there's no point in rushing things, but you *are* in my bedroom and I don't even know your last name.'

Alec looked mortified. He even squirmed. 'Parry,' he said. 'Alec Parry. I'm such an idiot. Sorry.'

He's a puppy, she thought, all wriggly and waggy. Odd how much more mature Grace seems. Perhaps she feels most comfortable with men she can control. Well, it's as good a way of finding out about men as any. Better than finding out about them from the ones who can control her.

She said, 'Don't worry about it.'

'But, in the same situation, my mother'd go potty. You're so cool, Mrs Emerson. Your whole family's so cool.'

'Wait till you meet Jimmy,' Robin said, laughing. 'Now, I must go and do some work. Grace's room is next to yours on the other side.'

'Right,' he said, 'but I'm really glad I had the chance to talk to you.'

'Me too,' she said. A happy accident, she thought. It would've taken ages to learn as much from Grace. She hoped he liked garlic and ginger prawns.

She sat for a moment, after he left, staring absently at Jack's young smile. So, so long ago, Jack, what would you look like now? Would you be fat or thin? Would your hair be grey, like mine, or would you touch it up, like Lin? Would you *have* any hair? Would you be famous or forgotten? Would you have dumped Lin or would she have dumped you? Would I have ever really got to know you or would you still be an icon on my wall? If you were alive, Jack, would you still be a memory? After all, there are many more ways to lose people than by death.

Upstairs in the attic she picked up the work Lin had interrupted. She was making an old-fashioned frock coat for a fat actor and she was taking pains over the detail because she knew he'd buy it from wardrobe when the production was over. He always did. But the cloth was heavy and dull, so after a while she put it aside and took up a riot of colour – something she was making for a private client out of hundreds of pieces of off-cut silk. This was what she enjoyed most – making the fabric from which the garment would be shaped – holistic dressmaking. Very slow. Very expensive. Thank God for private clients.

And there, blinded by colour, soothed by silk, Robin lost herself for a few hours.

'That's beautiful,' Lin said, putting two glasses of white wine on her work table. 'Who's it for?'

Robin blinked, slowly refocusing her eyes. She slid her reading glasses up on to her hair and said, 'Rich old lady. It'd suit you better. Where've you been?'

'Out. Trying to mend bridges, but . . .'

'Oh no.'

'Sorry, darlin', I've been replaced – no more Cole-Adler pay packets. Don't look like that – it isn't the end of the world. I'll find something else. They're giving me a great reference.'

'I suppose that's better than nothing.' Robin stretched and then took a sip of chilled white wine. 'Where are the kids?'

'Movies,' Lin said.

'Well, I'm not worried about Alec any more. He's a puppy.' And she told Lin the story of Grace and Alec meeting on the Net.

'Which site?' Lin asked immediately.

'Huh?'

'Never mind, sweetie. I'll find out.'

'Does it matter?'

'It might,' Lin said. 'This is a guy who travels with a locked camera case hidden in a studenty backpack. For your information, he also has a big box of gossamer condoms and half a pint of lubrication gel which he's carrying quite openly. And an ounce or two of very nice grass and some sweet little white tablets with doves stamped on them. He's not bothering to keep *them* hidden. Makes you wonder what he'd lock up, doesn't it?'

'Oh *Lin*,' Robin said.

'Well, he's got the sex and drugs bit covered, hasn't he? So what's he doing for rock'n'roll?'

'Shit, shit, shit, Lin. I thought butter wouldn't melt.'

'Well, they're going to a party.' Lin shrugged. 'Which bit upsets you most? You've got to assume Grace is doing all the usual stuff.'

'Yes, but not under her own roof, my roof, with a stranger.' With a sudden gut-lurch, Robin felt herself sliding into a knot of linear time. The thread of her life wove over and under itself in a pattern which had no end and no beginning. She was a responsible, experienced adult who felt like a mystified, frightened teenager. She was conversing with a responsible, experienced woman who was, at the same time, her little sister – the one who ran wild and took appalling risks, and yet always seemed to come up smelling of roses.

She, Robin, was the sister who stayed home, stayed in school and studied hopelessly for the exams she only just scraped through. She had to keep trying. Because there must be one good sister, one good daughter, mustn't there? Above all, Robin hated conflict. Anger scared her. How many screaming rows could a kid endure?

Then, one day, it stopped. 'I can't do this any more,' said Lin, sitting on Robin's bed, skinny legs tucked under her. 'Fighting's crap.'

'So don't fight,' Robin said. 'You're never going to win. Parents hold all the cards. And I'm fed up with it.'

'So'm I. But it's like being in prison. Parents control everything. Nothing's mine. Not even my time.'

'We could go away to university. Somewhere like Edinburgh.'

'That's years away. And that's the other thing – it'd be just like school. And school is as bad as parents. "One fist of iron, the other of steel. If the right one don't get you, then the left one will." Sing it, Robin.'

They sat on the bed, two kids, singing 'Sixteen Tons', Lin trying to harmonise a third above the melody and getting it wrong. Giggling miserably. Because Robin knew that realistically she didn't have a snowball's hope in hell of getting into university, and she didn't think Lin would even try. All she could see ahead of her were years of the same old same old.

Now, she had a son and daughter and she was supposed to be the one fist of iron. She was supposed to be contemplating the control of her daughter – how to stop her doing what Lin so carelessly described as 'the usual stuff'.

The trouble was, she didn't have a clue. She was so busy avoiding confrontation that she rarely confronted Grace. So quite how much of the usual stuff there was in Grace's life was a mystery to her. Maybe Grace was simply getting away with it. Just like Lin did when, at the age of thirteen, she decided fighting was crap. Everyone was so relieved when Lin stopped needling and demanding that they failed to notice that she hadn't changed at all. She merely talked sweet, looked sweet and appeared with clean hands at meal times. Precocious in the art of man-management.

Is Grace a good, sensible kid, she asked herself, or is she managing me? Am I skilled at avoiding rows, or am I a neglectful parent?

She said, 'Lin, do you think Grace is like me? Or is she like you?'

'Grace is like Grace,' Lin said, with her silly-question expression.

'Do you think she knows what she's doing?'

'Not for a moment,' Lin said. 'Who does? But she probably thinks she does.'

'Then she's more like you,' Robin decided. 'I never even thought I knew what I was doing.'

'Bollocks,' said Lin. 'You had it all mapped out.'

'Did not.'

'Did.'

'It was a screwy old map then,' Robin sighed. 'Nothing turns out the way you plan.'

'Let's hope that's true for Alec as well. Some plans deserve a good trashing.'

'Do I kick him out? Or keep an eye on him?'

'Oh, definitely keep him.'

'But I really don't want drugs in the house.'

'Mmm,' said Lin. 'We could probably sabotage those without being rumbled. If you want.'

'The condoms are a symbol of social responsibility, don't you think?' Robin asked hopefully.

'We don't want to damage those.'

'OK,' Robin said, 'let's do it.' She was thrilled. Years of passivity and ignorance fell away.

In Jimmy's room, under the eyes of famous footballers and Nobel prize winners, Robin and Lin examined the guest's luggage.

He was very organised, Robin concluded. 'He's got rich parents,' she said. 'Even the underwear's designer.'

'Parents?' Lin said, raising one eyebrow. 'Because he turned up with Grace? Because he acts like a puppy? I don't think he's as young as he's acting.'

'No dirty laundry,' Robin observed. 'No. Categorically, postively, he isn't as immature as he seems. What're we going to do with his stash?'

'Turn it into something he'll throw away,' Lin said. She slid her hand between two T-shirts and drew out a tobacco tin.

'Kitchen,' she said. 'Something noxious and smelly – like lighter fluid or turpentine.'

They went down to the kitchen. Lin opened the tobacco tin. Tidy young Alec kept his pills in an airtight polythene sachet and his grass wrapped in tin foil.

'I want just enough turps to grind these pills into a semi paste. They've got to stink so badly no one'd dream of putting any of it in his mouth. It's got to look like he was sold total shit and it degraded. Maybe a little green or yellow colour to ram the message home.'

'Are you sure?' Robin asked. 'What if he gives some to Grace?'

'Well,' Lin said, working with speed and delicacy, 'I'm sorry to say this, but if Grace lets some strange guy put this stinking mess in her mouth she deserves to die.'

'Lin!'

'Sorry, sweetie, but it's true. Oh, have a bit of faith in her. She's *your* daughter. *You* brought her up.'

'Ok, but think what you took when you were her age.'

'I never took anything that looked or smelled like this. Nor will she. And my bet is that Alec won't be offering it.'

'What're you going to do with the grass?'

'Smoke some,' Lin said, 'while you go and piss on the rest. We want it so wet it won't light, and smelly enough to make their little eyes water.'

'You're kidding?'

'You're a creative old broad,' Lin said. 'Think of something. Mother-love comes in strange shapes, I'm told.'

'Amen,' Robin said. The thread of her life looped and folded back on itself, intersecting at the point where two pre-adolescent girls took revenge on King Leer, the local dirty old man. King Leer was a retired major who lived on the route between school and home. He was in the Rotary Club, the Lions. A pillar of the community, their father said, making both girls collapse with stifled giggles.

For reasons neither of them understood, Lin was his number-one target. And for reasons Robin didn't understand even now, they never told their parents. Perhaps it was because *all* adults seemed to be malign, ranged like a cohesive army against children. Adult behaviour was incomprehensible at the best of times. So a nasty old man waving his genitals at Lin, or squashing them against the glass of his front window whenever she walked by, might have been just another unpleasant manifestation of the power all grown-ups wielded against children.

Whatever. Lin, the rebel, rebelled. Scheming Lin planned. Thieving Lin stole a spray can of black enamel paint from their father's garage. Secretive Lin carried it hidden in her school bag for a week until the right opportunity came along. And, when the right opportunity presented itself, along with King Leer's exposed and swollen shaft, vengeful Lin sprayed him.

'Sorry?' she said, peaches and cream, 'what is it you want me to look at?' She stepped forward, her right hand hidden in her school bag. And then she whipped out the spray can and pressed the nozzle. Fired straight at King Leer's naked crotch.

Horrified, Robin watched the mauve pink flesh turn shiny black. Up until then she never thought Lin would actually fire. She thought the plan was just another giggling, childish fantasy – what I'd do if I had a hundred pounds, where we'd go if we could fly. Not so. Quite deliberately, Lin sprayed the major's cock, his balls, his trousers, his shirt front and his horn-rim spectacles. Then she threw the can in his face.

'*Run!*' she screamed, and the girls tore away up the street, running, until they fell in an exhausted heap in the park. Horror and fright made them laugh till they choked.

They were laughing now, Robin dizzy from the grass and wine. Two grown women, two little kids, taking action against someone who offended them.

'I wonder what happened to King Leer,' she said aloud.

'What on earth made you think of him?'

'Don't know,' Robin said. 'There were no repercussions, were there? And we were astonished. We thought Mum and Dad were going to come down on us like a ton of bricks. We thought that dirty old bastard would tell the police. We didn't realise that he couldn't. Unless he incriminated himself. I guess we're applying the same principle to Alec.'

'Mmm,' said Lin. 'Good lesson, wasn't it?'.

When the kids came home from the movies they were horsing around as if they'd known each other all their lives. They made Robin wonder if she'd ever been capable of such instant, easy intimacy. Trust, she thought, based on the same taste in music, liking the same movie. How deceptive. What if one of you is lying? She was excluded. She had excluded herself by not trusting them. Betraying them again, she made lasagna and left the king prawns on the middle shelf of the fridge. Grace didn't notice.

Robin's secret was that she was keeping a secret. She was silenced by it, constrained, hiding her guilt behind pasta and salad. And Grace didn't notice. It was so simple. Robin felt a sick lurch of triumph.

Lin, more sinuous and supple, wove her way through the casual conversations and then went up with Grace to decide on party gear. Smooth Lin. Robin was still stoned but fighting it.

She sent Alec away to watch TV. She'd doctored his dope so she didn't want him helping her in the kitchen. She'd smoked some. She was light-headed, light-fingered, at his expense.

'What a rotten thing to do,' she said out loud, wiping the counter in meticulous spirals long after it was perfectly clean. 'Led astray – that's me. Lin, you're a bad influence – that's you.'

But it wasn't true. Lin was helping her. Because she was anxious about Grace. And now she was helping Grace dress.

'I could help Grace,' she said. 'I'm good at clothes too. I *am*. Different, but just as good. Why didn't she ask *me*?'

''Cos I'm just a boring old mum,' she answered herself. She nodded seriously at her reflection in the kitchen window and her boring old reflection nodded back.

Depressed she turned away and went upstairs to her bedroom, past the row of closed doors. She threw herself on the bed and bounced a couple of times. Then suddenly, almost violently, she dropped like a stone off a cliff, crashing into sleep.

★　　★　　★

The piano woke her. She rolled over, dry-mouthed, and looked at the clock. The big hand was on the seven, the little hand was halfway between the two and the three. She was fully clothed and the light was on.

The same phrase was repeated over and over: Der-*lang* lang lang, ta-ta-ta *dum,* der-*lang* lang lang, ta-ta-ta *dum.* That was the bass line. It was accompanied by short bursts of trills and descending chords in the treble.

Twenty-five minutes to three. Morning or afternoon? *Shit.* She flopped off the bed and stumbled downstairs.

In the living room, Lin was coiled around the piano. She didn't look up. Der-lang lang lang . . .

Robin felt that if she didn't pour a cup of hot sweet tea down her throat straight away she'd die. She staggered to the kitchen.

She returned with the teapot and two mugs on a tray, feeling a lot better. Not bumping into furniture, she noted with relief.

'Tea, Lin?'

Der-lang lang lang . . .

Robin poured tea into the mugs and went over to the piano. She said, 'What're you playing?'

Der-*lang* . . . ' "Eddie's Big Wheel" by Eddie Bo. Can't do it.'

'Sounds all right to me.'

'Well, it would,' Lin said morosely. ''Cos you don't know – he's one of those old piano players with a bit of God in every finger.' Der-lang lang lang . . . She still wouldn't look at Robin.

'Are the kids back yet?'

'No.'

'It's *three o'clock,* for Christ's sake.'

'It's a *party,* for Christ's sake.' Der *lang.*

'What's up, Lin?'

Ta-ta-ta *DUM.* Lin snapped the piano lid shut and leaned her elbows on it, still not meeting Robin's eyes. 'Your daughter,' she said, 'and slick little Alec met on one of Jack's web-sites. Out there in cyber-space, with no one watching, everyone anonymous, everyone *communicating*, spilling their poxy guts out, thinking there'll be no come-back. It's OK, see, because they're all just a bunch of cyber-space cadets. You're *free*, like, you can be who you wannabe. You can be Jack and Birdie's niece, if you wannabe. Not Lin's, you notice. Birdie's.'

'She told you this?' Robin asked with a cold draughty prickle starting at her ankles. 'But, Lin, you know she's so proud of you.'

'Why? What's to be proud of?'

'Well, you're glamorous. You're fun.'

'She didn't spill her little guts to Alec 'cos I'm fun. Grow *up*, Robin. And he didn't bring his state-of-the-art recording equipment into this house 'cos I'm good ol' Auntie Lin.'

'Oh, Lin, *no*.'

'Oh, Robin, yes. Plus a full set of burglary tools and a miniature spy camera. The only thing I didn't find was his press pass or PI licence. Whatever he is.'

'You unlocked his case thing? Oh Lin, I'm sure Grace doesn't know. She wouldn't let us down like that.'

'I don't know what she knows. It was, "Oh Lin, Alec thinks you're *fascinating*. Do talk to him. He's so sweet. You'll love him when you get to know him." Did you tell her what I was up to? Who I'm working for? Where I go?'

'I don't know.' Robin felt queasy. 'She asks about you. I wasn't keeping any secrets. It's *Grace*.'

'Yes it's Grace, all right. And I'm blown.'

'Blown? Lin, we're talking about Grace. She knows well enough not to gossip. She's been told.'

'And now she's doing the telling. g.ace. Start counting the spoons, Robin, and nail down anything you don't want stolen. Above all, don't open your mouth unless you want to see your tonsils in the tabloids.'

# III

## Sold for a Song

If love is a bitch, young love is a bastard. You follow your heart, you follow your hormones, you follow a man. You don't lead. You trail around, helplessly doing and saying things that'd either bore you or make you blush if you were in your right mind. In other words, love is bloody inconvenient. I wish I could have back even half the time I've wasted on love.

Now Grace is in love. She was courted by computer, and within three hours of meeting the little worm she fell in love – at the movies, while he stroked the palm of her hand with his warm thumb. Someone was dying on the screen. Giant images of ragged, bleeding humanity failed to move her. But the touch of warm skin sent her heart tumbling all the way to Idiotsville. *C'est l'amour.*

Poor little g.ace @ *et cetera* slash *et cetera*: she's not to be trusted. Her young love is bloody inconvenient for me.

But what I have to ask myself is this: who sent the little worm, and what does he want? If I can answer those questions without him rumbling me I'll be ahead of the game. Keep the enemy in view but don't let him know you're watching.

Sometimes, what you want simply falls into your hands. You walk into a small office to make an enquiry, for instance, and someone mistakes you for a secretary. By the end of the week you have the keys to the safe, the use of the computer, a network of private detectives a phonecall away and a weekly wage. The wage, of course, is tragic, but the facilities are a goldmine. In effect, I can do my own research, and be paid for the privilege, with no one any the wiser.

No, I didn't lose this job. I lied. Bad Birdie – lying to her own sister. But Robin talks to Grace, and Grace talks to Alec. And I do not yet know who Alec talks to. I'll find out eventually, but in the meantime, whoever he's talking to, he won't be telling the truth. I'll see to that.

I returned to a saviour's welcome. Sweet old George brought me coffee and Tina, gruffly, put a jar of Japanese anemones on my desk. I noticed that a mere ten-day absence had put the strain back into their partnership. They were like a married couple who sorely missed their child's nanny. They should have built a third person into the structure from the beginning. I blame Tina: she takes independence and self-sufficiency way too seriously. But she is competent. It's lucky for me that she hasn't had time in the last ten days to become familiar with her own software.

I opened the mail and logged all the overnight phonecalls. Then I sat in on their morning meeting to find out what I'd missed. There was nothing new – or rather there was more of the familiar. They asked me to make a new work schedule.

It's so easy. I'm like an air traffic controller deciding what can take off, what can land and what should go into a holding pattern. They do the work. The clients pay. They order equipment and pay the bills. There's a direct relationship between service, goods and money. You can see at a glance what's going on.

How very unlike the music business.

I should know – a few weeks ago I thought I would need a private detective to follow the paper trail, the corporate maze, the legal knots which are my financial history. Who would imagine that a bunch of ideas worked out on a piano and guitar could cause so much trouble, heartache and frustration.

We'd sit in a room, Jack and I, and just noodle with chords. Hmm, sounds nice, yeah, try the diminished seventh in there, oh yeah. Got a tune? Got any words to go with that? How about this for a beat?

No equipment to speak of – two heads, four ears, four hands, a piano, a guitar, a little tape recorder in case we were too stoned to remember, and a pad and pencil for the same reason. We made something out of nothing, golden Jack and I. Just ideas – those things in your head; things which simply wouldn't exist if you didn't give them a voice. How can anything so nebulous be the foundation of an industry so complicated, so twisted and vicious, that I needed a private detective to explain my small part in it?

I need an accountant and a lawyer too, but I don't trust them. Accountants and lawyers made me bankrupt for years and I still owe the taxman several hundred thousand.

Those nebulous, airy-fairy, arty-farty ideas took hundreds of people to produce, record, press, publish, promote, market and sell them. They turned Jack into a god and a paper millionaire. They turned me into a bitch and a pauper. The god did not even own his own house. No wonder he burnt it down.

If a guy thinks he must be very rich, and everyone treats him as if he's very rich, he spends a lot of money. It's natural. And, make no mistake, there was a lot of money. But it wasn't his. The millions weren't his earnings, as it turned out, they were only advances against earnings. Big difference. It means you don't know what you're actually worth, and worse, you don't know what you owe. That's what happens when there's no straightforward relationship between services, goods and money. The difference between songs and security windows is a big one.

At midday I logged in two new enquiries: a background search and a missing person. I thought my bosses would enjoy the change – their steadiest customers all want security advice and that's boring. Then I rang Ozzy Ireland on his mobile. It's no good ringing an A&R man before midday, and if he's any good you'll never catch him in the office.

'Hey, Oz,' I said. 'Word?'

'Hey Miz Bird,' he said, 'when did you get back?' He sounded tired and I could hear a baby crying in the background. He'd never mentioned having a family. Not surprising: A&R doesn't mix comfortably with family life – certainly not for long.

'Did I wake you?' I asked nastily. 'I could ring back.'

'No, no,' he said. 'You're so hard to get hold of, now I've got you I'll hang on. I'm glad you called today. InnerVersions are trying out the new material at that club in Oxford tonight and some of the brass are coming.'

'Who?'

'God, Birdie, I don't know what you said to Mr Freel, but there's been some action around here.'

'Yeah?'

'Someone from production came down and gave the guys a talking-to. The result of which is that Dapper Sapper's agreed to voice coaching – a quantum leap there, by the way – *and* they've got proper studio time booked. They're really putting some muscle into rehearsals now – not just hanging around beefing because we don't tell them they're geniuses every two minutes.'

'Now I *know* they aren't musicians.'

'Mee-*ow*,' Ozzy said. 'They're a nice little band, Birdie, and they come up lovely with a bit of polish.'

'I told *you* that,' I said. 'But only if they gave Karen more of everything. Without her you might as well call them Send In The Clones.'

'The trouble with her is she just isn't . . .'

'Forceful enough?'

'Sexy.'

'Silly me.'

'No,' Ozzy said, 'I know what you mean. But to do her credit, she gave Flambo the push.'

'Good girl.'

'But that might mean we'll have to help them find another drummer. He still isn't happy, only now the others aren't happy with him either. Pity, 'cos he's quite solid.'

'Between the ears,' I said.

'Anyway, the people on the top floor are paying some attention at last. So thanks.'

'Don't mention it,' I said. Although I was surprised; I'd been quite prepared to find out that my meeting with Sasson had gone the other way entirely.

'It's good to have someone like you in my camp,' Ozzy went on. 'To tell you the truth, I was beginning to think I was turning into yesterday's man. Glamour by association, that's what I needed. Still,

I don't suppose you'll be working with the likes of me for much longer.'

'Won't I?'

'Well not if what I'm guessing is true.'

'And what're you guessing, Ozzy Ireland?'

'Well,' he said, 'the Jack stuff.'

'What Jack stuff?'

'Fair enough. I know it's still under wraps, but I tapped into Dog's projected catalogue the other day and I couldn't help noticing.'

'Mmm?' I said cautiously.

'Well, I found a dummy promotion page. It presented ten new tracks and you were down for a production credit. I was really excited for you. Where did they find ten new Jack tracks?'

'Didn't you ask?'

'I don't think anyone's supposed to know. I only look at the future releases to see what's happening to my new acts. No one actually tells me anything.'

'Is this item there for anyone to see?' I asked. 'Or have you been steaming letters open – in a hi-tech sort of way?'

'Shit,' he said. 'You mean it's not a done deal?'

'You might say that.'

'Me and my big mouth,' he said, sounding pleasingly anxious.

'Oh, it's fine from my point of view,' I told him. 'I'm happy to know how they're thinking on the top floor. It'll give me more negotiating clout, but . . .'

'Me and my very big flapping mouth. For God's sake, Birdie, don't tell them where the information came from.'

I laughed. He was saying exactly what I was wanting to hear.

He said, 'Please, Birdie. I'm on a knife edge as it is. Wrong accent, wrong era. Dog's dumping people right, left and centre. I'm fucked in the long run. I know that.'

Oh yes, the music business is a greasy pole all right – hard to climb, terrifyingly easy to slide down.

'I think I'm only kept on the payroll because of this retro thing,' Ozzy said.

'Why don't you get out?' I asked. I could ask myself the same question.

'It's what I know,' he said.

Good safe answer, and I suppose I could say the same thing. 'Or move sideways? Management? Work for yourself. Publishing?'

'Too much paper in publishing.'

Amen, I said silently.

'I've thought about managing though. I'm well-placed to make a go of that. But I do need the old salary for a while yet.'

'Well,' I said, 'InnerVersions needs a good manager. All they've got is a so-so drummer who thinks he's way more together than he is.'

'It's a thought,' he said.

'So think about it.' But I could hear the baby crying again in the background and I wondered if he'd have the balls to jump before someone pushed him. And maybe he was too honest and too trusting. Look what he told me! He hasn't a clue how important that piece of information is.

I say, 'Ozzy, I think maybe InnerVersions could be part of my negotiations with Dog. It looks like they're bending over backwards to sweeten me up for that deal which you know nothing about and about which you kept your very big flapping mouth shut.'

'You won't let on? Birdie, you're a princess.' Some people are so easy to reassure.

I say, 'But Ozzy, think about it. If Dog are trying to keep me sweet, and I want them to make a deal with InnerVersions, then chances are, InnerVersions could have a deal. How nice a deal depends on who's representing them. If it's Flambo, they'll be fucked-over twice before breakfast. However, if a guy with several years of experiences in the business and a good working knowledge of Dog took a hand in it . . .'

'See what you mean.'

'Well, your first clients could be *paying* clients. Wouldn't that be a good start?'

'It needs thinking about,' he says. Disappointing.

I say, 'Hey, why don't I do it myself?'

'Hold on, Birdie, I said I was thinking about it.' Better.

'I'm not management material,' I say, as if I haven't heard him, 'but I *know* I could cut a stronger deal than Flambo.'

'I'd have to start my own business. It's expensive.' Wimp.

'All I'd need is phone, fax and p.c. And lots of contacts,' I say thoughtfully. 'I could do it from home to begin with.'

Jack and I had a company once. We set it up to protect his publishing rights and to buy back his old catalogue. It was called Jackdaw Corps. There were four shares. He had three and I had one.

Ah, well, who cares? It became Jackdaw Corpse soon enough, and the liquidator sold it for a song to the very people from whom we'd bought back Jack's old list. Great idea, that one, *great* protection.

'Everyone needs protection,' I say to Ozzy.

'I just had a thought,' he says. 'Maybe you're going to need representation too – with this thing I know nothing about.'

In your dreams, Ozzy Ireland.

'That's a thought,' I say. 'Except obviously there's nothing to talk about.'

'Obviously.'

'On the other hand, if someone were representing me, perhaps I could get off wages and back on points for songs I write or co-write.'

'Actually, I've never understood that about you, Birdie. Other people who deserve it less get way more credit than you do. Why?'

'Don't ask,' I say. 'You *know* what happens when you're in no position to bargain.'

Like when all your earnings in the UK are already garnished because you owe an unimaginable sum to the taxman, and if you want to keep any at all you have to be paid in cash under the table.

'So you *might* need an agent or a manager?' Ozzy says. 'Because it'd be a whole lot more attractive going into business for two clients than just for one.'

'Are you hustling me?' I ask with a breathless, defenceless laugh.

'I'm offering to hustle *for* you,' he says bravely. I listen carefully, but I can't hear the baby any more.

'Best offer I've had all day,' I say. 'Looks like we've both got a bit to think about.'

'See you tonight?' he says.

Oh yes. Got to see if my baby band has learned to crawl while I was away. Has Karen acquired the balls to use her new voice in front of a crowd? Will Sapper support her on her songs the way she supports him on his? Has Dram brought a little more discipline and a little less arty-axeman attitude to his technique? Might Corky have, just once, played against a metronome and checked to see if his instinctive sense of time is quite as brilliant as he thinks it is? And Flambo? Will he ever come to the sad conclusion that he is not Mick Fleetwood or Keith Moon and stop being the playground bully?

Oh, yeah, the continuing saga of a baby band. Less a musical than a soap. Tune in this evening at a scruffy club near you for tonight's thrilling episode.

Meanwhile, I must cover my footprints and wipe away all traces of the private work I've been doing in this office – including the draft of an anonymous communication sent to Barry Stears about the existence of at least ten unreleased tracks by the great Jack. It was sent from LA and it told of how greedy, thieving Birdie Walker attached her sticky little fingers to materials that were rightfully the property of Square Hole Records and spirited them out of the country.

George and Tina marvel at my efficiency and the way I take care of every little detail, so that when they're out in the field, they never have to think about what's happening back at the shop. I make sure they never forget a piece of equipment or paper, and they never have to interrupt a job or a meeting.

I organise the shit out of them so that when they're gone they stay bloody gone and don't come back to find me trying to work out what happened to Cutz UK or where Cutz Cayman's considerable assets went. Or I might be following the path that Square Hole took after it was bought by XY, which was in turn subsumed by Mo'Zee, which may, in the near future, eat a Dog. It's a big project, because it's also useful to learn what happened to the personnel at each stage. Which MD turned up on which board? Who was paid off? Who died? Who's pulling all those tangled strings now?

It's a dog-eat-dog world out there in the music business. But the funny thing is that it isn't all music. Cutz Cayman, for instance, wasn't about music at all. It was about money. And the money from an odd little Latin number called 'Dance for Daddy' didn't sit in a bank for twenty years gathering dust and interest. No, it was used to develop hotels and holiday villages all around the Caribbean. 'Dance for Daddy' was a nice little earner. For someone.

Big dogs eat little dogs. Little dogs eat lesser dogs, and so on – down to the fleas on their backs. Poor fleas, hopping around, looking for a mouthful, writing their songs, hoping for a starring role in the flea circus – chomp-slurp, and you're history.

At the time, I never knew how small I was. I was courted and fêted, illuminated by flashbulbs. So was Jack. We were protected, transported, interviewed. Jack played to stadia. He was seen on TV by millions of people at a time. He was loved, sought after, waited for by heads of state. Nobody knew he was a flea. Except at the end, maybe Jack guessed it himself.

We were at a celebrity charity auction once – the sort of glittering bun-fight where nobs and moguls are shamed by their wives into buying one of Lee Marvin's paintings or one of Barbra Streisand's fingernails or a denim jacket Marlon Brando wore once upon a time. Not our scene at all. In fact, so very not our scene that we ignored the invitation. But the organiser was a fan, and she needed yoof and live entertainment to jazz up her middle-aged freak show. And Jack was the happening thing. So she put the arm on the top banana of a TV station who owed her husband a favour. The top banana put the arm on the head honcho of Jack's US label. And the head honcho put the arm on Jack.

The deal was that Jack had to do a short acoustic set and then sell one song to the highest bidder and sing it especially for him or her. And me? I was the hottest chick in town so what did I have to auction? Well, it was a kiss. Oh my! A true reflection of my talent.

It didn't matter that we were in a Bel Air studio at the time doing the overdubs for a record which was already over-schedule and over-budget. We were dusted off and wheeled out to be auctioned for charity.

'We're just meat on the hoof,' Jack said, in the limo. 'They might as well cut us up for the finger buffet and serve us with asparagus tips.'

There was a sweet corollary to this incident which I never told Jack: the plump and powerful pig who bought my kiss enjoyed it so much that he offered me five thousand dollars to spend the night with him. When it finally got through to him that I was insulted he gave me a list of singers and film stars he'd bought for the same amount. Eventually he upped the offer to twenty thousand. At least when you play the whore you have a say in how much you're sold for. There's a very direct relationship between goods, services and money in that business. I might have been a flea, but I was a flea who knew her price.

What I didn't know was that the pig videoed his night of passion. I found out years later when his son tried to sell the video back to me after the pig died of fatty heart disease. By that time I had no money and no reputation anyway, so I just laughed. Who knows what happened to the video.

Today, a delivery man brought in a box of assorted stationery which needed to be signed for. While I was checking the contents against the invoice he said, 'What a way to spend your life, eh? Stuck in here counting envelopes and paper clips. At least I'm out driving around and meeting people.'

He'd looked at me and thought I was someone who'd spent her whole life checking invoices. No twenty-thousand-dollar nights for a middle-aged office manager apparently. No champagne adventures. I am what a delivery man expects to see. Perhaps I should start wearing lipstick to work.

That night, wearing lipstick, I took Grace and Alec to listen to InnerVersions. Oh, I'm so cool, I always know where the next band is coming from. What a rave! They know I'm working but I include them. How kind. Party time.

The band was already playing when we walked in. They were

playing what used to be an endless, shapeless number called 'More and More'. Now it's four minutes long and called 'Gimme More'. And it's tight. It's so tight that the dance floor is packed, and Grace heads straight for it towing Alec by the hand.

I stood for a minute and watched the dancers. Clearly, they trusted the band. They got up and moved because it was easier to dance than to sit still and drink. The band carried them there and they knew they were in safe hands. It was a good sight to see – a visible sign of progress.

I was waiting particularly for the end of the break between two choruses, because if the band was going to lose its nerve and blow it, that's where they'd do it. There were two linking bars which could lose them all the trust they'd built. They had trouble with them because they were so spare and simple it made them nervous.

Here we go, hiatus time. The band stops playing. The solid mass of sound is suspended. Karen peels away with a lonely electric sound. She climbs into the sudden silence with an ascending run – a modified minor pentatonic scale, sixteen beats to the bar. Half way up, she meets Corky coming down – a punched-out bass line, one and two, three, four and . . . wait for it now, hold your breath, we're coming home . . . and *bang*, everyone hits the key chord together. And it's *loud*. Tension released. Whoosh. Oh yeah, let's *dance*!

Excellent. Well done, babes, mama's proud of you. Wasn't that worth a little work?

Karen is almost laughing, triumphant. Go for it, girl.

It was such a small thing – just two bars – but it depended on precision. The people from Dog probably wouldn't even notice.

They were sitting at a table in a central position, giving nothing away. I slid through the crowd and sat at the edge of the group, nodding hello to Sasson and Ozzy. Sasson was watching Sapper. I half closed my eyes and tried to see Sapper for the first time too, ignoring the fact that he was an arrogant little shit who still took his laundry home to his mother. Can he make me believe in him? Because, in this game, it doesn't matter a dry fart who does your laundry. It's the illusion that counts.

# IV

## Dance the Night Away

Helen and Petra stood side by side in front of the mirror, their slippery strappy dresses almost touching. They looked like sisters, but they were best friends.

Helen said, 'Try it up.'

Petra lifted her hair off her neck and turned slowly from left to right.

'You should wear it up,' Helen said.

'It makes my face look too long,' Petra said, staring at her own neck. A boyfriend once told her that she had a neck like a model. She loved her neck.

Helen, too, looked at Petra's slender neck. 'You're right,' she said. Petra had too many advantages already.

'No, be honest,' Petra said.

'I was being.'

'Oh I don't know,' Petra said. 'I want him to notice us, that's all. Do you really think my face is too long?'

They were brimful of optimism and self-doubt. They knew which was the band's table. They knew exactly the spot on the dance floor they should occupy when the disco took over from the band. They had practised cool moves and body-rolls in Helen's bedroom until they looked like a pair of sophisticated clubbers. Their dresses had caused rows with their parents. But was it enough to make Sapper look at them? And if he looked, what would he see?

'Oh God,' said Helen. 'I think I've started to bloat.' She turned sideways in the mirror. 'Do you think I'm looking bloated?'

'It doesn't notice,' Petra said. She let her hair fall to her shoulders. A million magazines, a million pop videos, had shown her what the perfect face looked like. Surely hers was only a little too long.

'Oh God,' they said in unison, and attacked their make-up again.

Sapper comes off stage, his skin vibrating, applause acting on him like a cocaine body-rub.

Someone presses a beer into his hand, says, 'Good set, man. Wow.'

Dram and Corky stumble towards him. What are they doing here? Surely he's alone. Two minutes ago he'd owned the stage, the music. He'd been in sole command. The applause was his.

Dram says, 'Fuck! We're shooting 'em dead tonight.'

Stay cool. 'It went okay,' Sapper says.

'Get *you*!' Corky says. 'Mr Ice. You can't kid me. I saw you lapping it up.'

Sapper tips his head back and lets a mouthful of beer slide down his throat. His throat feels like a polished, oiled tube, infinitely supple. Could be those vocal exercises mean something. Could be they're worth more than Flambo says.

He searches through the crowd, looking for Birdie. She's been so focused on his faults. Where is she when he's showing his strengths?

There she is, on the other side of the room at a table with the record company suits. She's languid, keeping her distance, making the hard club chair look comfortable. Before Sapper can decide to risk Corky's barbed comments about arse-licking and go over to talk to her, she rises and follows Karen to the women's room.

'Typical,' Flambo mutters. 'I always thought Karen was a closet dyke.'

'She wasn't before she started shagging you,' jeers Corky.

Karen began the set with shaking hands and her heart in her mouth. She ended it on an unaccustomed spasm of triumph. Is this what confidence is? she asked herself, this feeling that you have what you're doing under your own control.

The bit she never told the others in InnerVersions was that the weeks in the rehearsal room, the writing, arranging and practising were a pleasure to her. They bitched and complained. They said, 'This is a farce and a waste of time: we should be out there playing live.'

She, on the other hand, felt for the first time that she was coming to grips with the material. In private.

Now they were testing the material and she still felt she'd kept a grip on it. Even in public.

The women's room is crowded. When she walked through, the other women turned to watch her and for once she didn't feel they would all start sniggering behind her back.

She takes several deep breaths to calm herself. Having tasted confidence, she is suddenly afraid of arrogance.

But Birdie hugs her and says, 'Good stuff, kid. Mama's proud of you.'

'You're just saying that,' Karen replies automatically.

'There's only you between prod and proud,' Birdie says. And Karen can't figure out what she means.

With the set finished Helen and Petra have to jostle to keep their places in front of the mirror. They see Karen come in and go straight to one of the bogs.

'That's Karen,' someone says.

Helen and Petra have seen her on-stage but they didn't know her name. She isn't Sapper, so she doesn't count.

'We could get to know her,' Petra whispers. 'It's a way to meet HIM.'

The old woman who came in with Karen is washing her hands.

'Do you think that's Karen's mum?' Helen whispers.

A tall girl pushes through the swing door, all hair and energy. She rushes up to the old woman and says, 'It's great, Lin. I wish I'd worn those other shoes.'

She's the student type, jeans and not enough make-up. Helen and Petra automatically decide to hate her.

'Are you going to introduce us to the band?' the student type says.

'Sure,' says the old woman.

Helen and Petra exchange an agonised glance in the mirror. They turn.

'Do you *know* them?' breathes Helen.

'Sure,' says the old woman, smiling.

'Do you know Sapper?' says Petra, gasping a little at saying HIS name out loud. 'Only, me and my friend think he's . . .' Helen jabs an elbow in her ribs.

'You know, the best way to meet a band is to ask for their autographs,' the old woman says. 'They'd like that.'

'Really? I'd feel . . .'

'Yes,' the old woman says. 'If you say you really like their music and you think they're great – that's what they want to hear. How're they going to know unless you tell them?'

'I couldn't,' Helen says.

'We'd die,' Petra says.

'Could we?' Helen asks.

'Got any paper?' the old woman says. 'And you'll need a pen.'

Sapper suddenly finds himself surrounded by girls. At first it was just two little honeys who hung back shyly and then plucked up enough courage to approach him.

'We think you're great,' they said in a rush. 'Can we have your autograph?'

'We really like the music,' one of them said.

'Could you make it out to Helen?' said the other.

'And Petra.'

Now he has a pen in his hand and he's modestly signing scraps of paper, beer mats, cocktail napkins, whatever they put in front of him.

He looks past the eager young bodies and sees Birdie watching.

Now she knows, he thinks. Now she'll see me for who I am.

He lifts his chin and turns his head, meeting her gaze from beneath lazy eyelids. It feels like a classic rock-star expression. It feels good. He knows he's imitating something he's seen before but he can't help it. He's starring in his own video. He sees himself from a distance, in a smoky club – somewhere blue-collar in the States. He is the tough outsider – the working boy genius – who catches the eye of the cool, unresponsive broad. In the next scene, he's on-stage singing to her, back-lit, lonely, but so irresistible. She begins to dance. In the next scene he's dancing with her. Final scene: he walks away down a wet, lamplit street, carrying his guitar case. On the other side of the road is a white limo with darkened glass windows. One of the rear windows rolls down and the cool but melting woman watches him walk away. There is just the beginning of a smile twitching at the corner of her mouth. She has plans for the tough, lonely genius. Oh yes, she does.

And it's all true. It's as if he's at last seen himself on MTV.

The thing that bewilders Ozzy Ireland the most about this gig is that he has recognised three scouts from other labels lurking in the crowd. Two come from little indie companies. But one is from MCA.

He points this out to Mr Freel who merely grunts in reply.

Later though, at the end of the first set, when the band is at the centre of a surprising rush of female attention, he hears Mr Freel ask the guy from production, 'Just what have we signed this band for?'

The answer he hears is, 'Interim contract. One of those suck-it-and-see things.'

'How long?'

'I think three months.'

Mr Freel grunts again.

Ozzy catches Birdie's eye. She winks, long and slow.

He's beginning to feel he's associated with something which might not be an instant success but which is certainly not a failure either.

'Enthusiastic local fan-base,' he says to Mr Freel.

'Mmm,' says Mr Freel.

Whenever Lin introduced Grace to anyone she never said, 'This is my niece,' or 'Meet Grace, she's my niece.' She always said, 'This is Grace,' as if Grace needed no explanation, no reason for being with Lin except as good company. It was one of the things Grace loved her for. She wasn't an add-on, or defined by her relationship. She could be an individual.

Tonight, she's meeting a lot of people: the band, the honchos from the record company. She's at the centre of things. She's excited.

And she's lucky: she's with a guy who isn't afraid to dance. That makes him perfect. When she looks around the floor she sees so many girls dancing on their own or in all-girl groups, while *she's* out there dancing with Alec. He isn't a particularly good dancer, but he's there. He doesn't show her up or drink too much or take the piss out of dancing like some guys do.

Grace doesn't know a lot of men who enjoy dancing. Check out any dance floor and you'll see what makes Alec special.

She's glad Lin likes him enough to invite him here tonight. And she's glad he likes Lin too. Somehow it makes Grace feel more attractive if one member of her family, at least, is warm, welcoming and with it. Unlike her mother whose suspicion is almost tactile.

Perhaps I shouldn't have brought him home unannounced, she thinks. But I thought Mum was flexible. She used to be nicer to my friends. Perhaps she doesn't want me to grow up. Perhaps she's getting too old.

Grace takes a drink out of Alec's glass and feels his arm around her shoulder. They're waiting for the band to go on-stage again.

Lin comes over and says, 'Can I leave the car keys with you, sweetie? You haven't been drinking too much, have you?'

'Aren't you staying to the end?' Grace says, disappointed.

'I've got to talk to some people. But if you've drunk too much to drive, call a cab.'

'I'll drive,' Alec says. 'I've only had a couple of beers. I won't drink any more.'

'Isn't he perfect?' Grace blurts out.

Lin laughs and says, 'Whaddya think, sweetie? Shall we ask him to leave his name with the booking agent? Give him a call when we need a good roadie?'

'Why not?' Grace says, recovering.

Alec throws back his head and snorts with laughter. Grace feels she's been saved from her own obviousness.

★   ★   ★

The second set begins with 'Thirty-nine Stitches'. Sapper hits it with everything he's got. He *is* the guy in the restaurant and he's the waitress too. He's begun to describe the song to anyone who'll listen as a character song, and tonight, for the first time, he feels the characters inhabiting him.

Bathed in white light, speeding, he picks Birdie out of the shadows in front of him. This is partly her song too. They wrote it together. A song about a young man and an older woman. He's giving it back to her – exactly how she wants it – hot and hard.

There's a heaving mass of dancers between him and her – girls, like snakes, are just about wriggling out of their skins. But he can feel her eyes. She's watching.

Next on the set list is 'Back in the Sweatshop'. 'Two nights with my baby – then back in the sweatshop again. Don't go, don't go, baby doncha leave me. Don't go, don't go, don't go.'

He looks for her, but she's gone. Her shadowy chair is empty. She doesn't come back.

Well, fuck her – who needs her anyway? Plenty more where that came from. Look at 'em all! Booty by the ton. All hot for me. 'But don't go, don't go, don't go. At least, my honey, stay with me until I've finished with you.'

Right at the bitter end, in the alley behind the club, when his muscles are aching and his skin is chill with drying sweat, he tastes the sourness of partially metabolised adrenaline and amphetamine. He has gorged on live flesh, so how come he's still hungry?

Sated and wanting more, he sees two girls in strappy, slippery dresses hanging out near the van.

'Pudding?' Dram suggests. 'Ours?'

'Aren't they a bit young?' says Karen.

'They're never too young to be up for it,' Flambo says. 'You go on home like a good girl. Unless you fancy some too.'

'Which one is yours?' says Dram.

'Don't fuckin' care,' says Sapper, edging forward. 'The one with the neck. You two can fight about the other.'

# V

## A Weird Little Man

The back of the Bentley was upholstered in blond suede. It was as big as a poor boy's double bed – not that I know a lot about poor boys' double beds. I leaned into the softness, closing my eyes. The ride was smooth enough to be sickening.

I wished I was alone. I wanted to empty my mind. But Sasson, who had been monosyllabic earlier, wasn't going to let that happen. The false intimacy in the back of a chauffeur-driven car was working on him.

'I hope you didn't think I was completely unresponsive back there,' he said. 'In fact, I think you're right – that's a nice little band you've got there. It's the commercial possibilities I have to consider.'

I sat tight behind closed eyes and didn't answer.

He continued, 'The singer seemed to be giving it a lot of top-spin.'

What did Sasson know about top-spin? It was a silly metaphor. What everyone's looking for is a lead singer you can't drag your eyes away from, and that isn't something you can work on the way a tennis player works on a stroke. A singer's got it or he ain't – it's one of life's mysteries.

'What's the matter, Birdie? Nothing to say? I thought you'd be pitching for him.'

'No. I've already told you what I think would be sensible and fair.'

'You must have a personal opinion though. I mean, think of the singers you've known. How does he stack against them?'

Sasson could answer that himself. He was goading me.

When I didn't reply, he said, 'Well, he's no Jack. That's for sure.'
Comparisons, comparisons. Poor Sapper.

I said, 'If you only signed bands who stacked up against the stars you'd only sign one every seven years and you'd be out of a job. You gotta have something new to sell. That's what you're in business for.'

'True,' he said. 'There aren't many Jacks around. It's just that I don't have your knack for talent-spotting. I sometimes wonder, if I hadn't grown up with Jack, if I'd first come across him in a club like tonight, would I have spotted him for what he was?'

'Did you have a tin ear, Sasson?' I asked with mild curiosity. 'Were you blind? Because you would've had to have been blind and deaf to fail to spot Jack.'

'Yes.' He sighed and mercifully shut up for a few more miles.

We rolled on west at a steady eighty miles an hour, he in his corner, me in mine; he with his thoughts, me with mine.

We were going to Dorset – not Sasson's county. It wasn't his house we were driving to, and we weren't in his car. The man behind the wheel wasn't his driver. In short, the trip was not Sasson's idea.

It wasn't my idea either – except that it is what I've been walking towards for years. So many little steps, one at a time, bring me to Nash Zalisky's doorstep.

Once, years ago, when he was still more or less a social creature, I met Nash Zalisky at a reception. Even then he was a formidable character. His own independent label had just been bought out by Columbia and he had been transformed from a music industry maverick into a rich, rich maverick with a three-year exclusion clause in his contract.

I was being stealthily pursued by a man with a telephoto lens, and I escaped up a flight of stairs to a shadowy gallery overlooking the reception area. Nash was the only other person up there – watching the party from above as if it were his personal bull-ring.

He said, quietly, 'Birdie, would you please go elsewhere. You attract too much attention.'

'Where?' I asked, because I was looking for a private way out and couldn't find one. I looked down and saw Jack at the centre of a crush of women.

He said, 'You know, I always wanted Jack on my label, but I couldn't afford him. Now I can afford him but I'm not allowed to work.'

'Money has a price,' I said.

He nodded seriously and we both watched the photographer look up and catch sight of us. With military precision, we took one pace back into the shadows.

He said, 'I would like to go to the movies now. Would you allow me to take you to the movies?'

'If you know a discreet way out of here,' I said, 'I'll allow you to take me anywhere.' At that moment I was sick to death of being a peep show at a circus. I was sick of the hype and fuss and flattery, the grabbing and groping. If a quiet man wanted to take me to fantasy-land and a darkened space I wasn't going to stop him.

'Only I must warn you,' he said, 'I won't tolerate talking at the cinema. And afterwards I do not want to discuss the film. Half-digested opinions drive me nuts. But I might want to hold your hand.'

'Fair enough,' I said. 'My side of the contract stipulates no groping and you pay for the tickets. Deal?' I thought he was joking.

'Deal,' he said. He wasn't joking.

We went to a Marx Brothers double bill at the Curzon, and we didn't exchange another word from the time we left the reception until he put me in a cab at the end of the second film. Then he kissed the hand he'd held all through *Horse Feathers* and said, 'Thank you for your company. It was surprisingly restful.'

I never saw him again from that day to this. But it wasn't the last time I heard of him. Quite apart from becoming a card-carrying eccentric and something of a recluse, when his exclusion clause ran out he came back on to the scene as a major player. Only this time he didn't let any of the big sharks buy him out. He was the shark.

Which, if my research tells me no lies, is why he can send a car for Dog's most important suit well after midnight, and Sasson will meekly hop in and drive away to Dorset when he'd much rather be home in bed. Better yet, he can send me a perfect gold and green orchid, packed in ice, and a handwritten invitation to a late supper. Oh my! Further, he can make Sasson very nervous indeed.

'I've never been invited to Badlands before,' Sasson confessed, shifting uneasily.

'Invited or summoned?' I said. I was uneasy myself. The flower was exquisite, and I wondered if that meant Nash might think I was still exquisite too. Being a recluse sometimes means that a man doesn't keep a grip on time.

'So, you haven't seen him recently,' I said.

'Who has? Well, he does come to town once in a blue moon – he hasn't completely cut himself off.'

'What does he do with himself?'

'Well, I suppose you might say he's become the *éminence grise* behind all sorts of ventures.'

'Which ventures?' I asked. 'Dog, for instance?'

'One thing I know for certain', Sasson said, glancing nervously at the back of the driver's head, 'is that almost everything you hear is wildly exaggerated.'

'So there's no truth in the rumour that he heads a multi-media consortium which has its own cable company?'

'Where did you hear that one, Birdie?'

'Just gossip,' I said, grinning in the dark.

'Nash doesn't like gossip.'

'Tough,' I said. 'Non-disclosure invites speculation.'

'You should know,' Sasson said bitchily.

'Indeed I do. Is he your boss, Sasson? Are you obeying orders? Who are you dancing for?'

'Actually, Birdie, I don't have a boss as such.'

'Right,' I said, 'and that's why you're dogging around in the wee small hours with a bitch you've resented for years.'

'I don't resent you, Birdie,' Sasson said in a voice you could pour from a cream jug. 'I just wish I could get a line on you – you're so wayward.'

I laughed and retreated. For the time being, fishing was a waste of energy.

We approached the house through iron gates set in a high wall. After about half a mile on gravel the drive became stone-paved, and at exactly that point the chauffeur switched the engine off and allowed the Bentley to coast silently around the last bend. We had just enough momentum to bring us to the base of a flight of stone steps. The house was enormous.

I said, 'Who's the king of the castle?'

'Shut up,' Sasson said, sounding distinctly uncomfortable. 'Birdie, please don't . . .'

'What?'

But I didn't find out. We were ushered out of the car and pointed up the steps to a pair of colossal doors. The doors opened without any prompting from us and we entered a sort of baronial hall. The floor should have been tiled with marble, but instead it was covered in deep-pile green carpet – acres of it.

'Aha,' I said. 'The rule of silence persists.'

'You remember,' said Nash, appearing from behind a thick oak door like a leprechaun popping out from between the pages of a book.

'I didn't know you knew each other,' Sasson said.

'Nobody meets for the first time,' Nash told him seriously, 'they only think they do. In fact, everyone has met everyone. It's just that they don't *know* anyone.'

'I see,' said Sasson.

'No you don't,' said Nash. 'Would you like some supper? I'm cooking *carciofi ripieni di mortadella*.'

'Er, wonderful,' said Sasson, looking blank.

'Well, I know Birdie loves globe artichokes,' Nash said. 'Come along.'

Miles of silent corridor led to a kitchen. The billionaire, it seemed, was doing his own cooking. Sasson and I sat at the kitchen table drinking Cuvée Dom Perignon while we watched Nash carefully brown his artichokes. It was a sight to see: he was dressed in black except for a white collarless shirt, which looked like a priest's dog collar under his black sweater – a billionaire vicar cooking supper. He was still very slight and boyish and his buck teeth gave him the appearance of class nerd – the boy who would be surrounded and kicked to shit in the playground. But, up close, his skin was as dry and lined as a man of seventy's and his hair had been dyed an improbable chestnut colour. A cook-book was open on the counter beside him and he studied it at every stage of the operation.

Nothing was said until the artichokes had been placed in a heavy metal casserole. He put damp kitchen paper between the lid and the pan – I didn't know if that was to muffle the sound of metal on metal or because it was what the cook-book told him to do.

This man, I thought, has been responsible for some of the loudest recordings in the history of rock music. I grinned and remembered how he'd sat through the Marx Brothers double bill with an earnest, anxious expression on his face, without once cracking a smile.

Nash sat down with us and poured himself a glass of champagne. He said, 'Forgive me if I seem blunt, but I abhor small-talk. I've heard that you are in possession of a quantity of Jack's recordings and a film which no one else has had sight of.'

'I expect you've heard about all sorts of things including artichokes.'

Sasson said, 'Birdie, please, no games.'

'What a shame,' I said. 'I'm feeling playful.'

Sasson looked at Nash and spread his hands in a helpless gesture. Nash looked at his watch and ignored us both.

Sasson said, 'Do the materials exist? A simple yes or no. Is that so hard?'

I smiled at him.

'Look,' Sasson said, 'I know you want to be the centre of attention and to be courted and all that, but I must point out to you that under the terms of Jack's contract at the time he died, all the outstanding materials . . .'

'Just a minute,' Nash said. He got up, opened the casserole, poked the artichokes with a fork, and then came back to the table.

'Where was I?' Sasson asked, thrown off his stride.

I said, 'You were about to explain to the egocentric airhead that, whatever she may or may not have, she has no legal claim to it.'

'Yes,' agreed Nash, 'and I was trying to divert you from that course. It isn't profitable.'

'Not to me,' I said. 'But Sasson's right. Never mind the contract – Jack's estate was bankrupt and I went down with it. All his assets, *all* of them, Sasson, were sold to Square Hole Records to pay off the debts. And that included publishing rights in which I had an interest.'

'Debatable,' Sasson said.

'Then debate it with Inland Revenue. I am still liable for tax on earnings which, according to you, are not rightfully mine.'

'You see,' said Nash to Sasson, 'I think Birdie's ahead of you. And if I may say so, it's contradictory to tell her that she doesn't own that which you are attempting to purchase.'

'To take it a step further,' I added, '*all* of Jack's existing assets were declared for estate reasons, bankruptcy reasons and tax reasons. Any new material, therefore, cannot exist. Which is a pity.'

'Are you saying that new materials do exist but you can't admit to them?' Sasson asked.

'Ding-dong,' said Nash, without a trace of humour.

I said, 'I'm not saying anything. Especially while this conversation is being recorded.'

There was a moment of electric silence and then Nash said, 'Sasson, I think you'd better leave. It's most discourteous of you to record a conversation between friends.'

'But . . .'

'I must insist. And please give Birdie the tape.'

Sasson's face was dark with embarrassment and rage. He fumbled in his inside pocket and drew out a little dictaphone.

'I wasn't recording you, Birdie,' he said. 'I was recording the band earlier.'

'Good explanation,' I said, 'when you already have access to the demo tapes.'

'You're so tricky and paranoid, Birdie.'

'Is that an apology?' Nash asked mildly.

'No,' said Sasson. 'Look Nash, if I've overstepped I apologise.'

'You'll find the car about a quarter of a mile down the drive.'

The speed with which Nash dismissed Sasson left me open-mouthed. Metaphorically, of course – a hanging jaw is not an attractive sight. I rested my chin in my hand and watched with a sleepy expression that masked my shock. For one thing, it was such an abrupt change of pace. For another, it only happened because I'd been trying it on. I didn't actually know Sasson was recording the conversation. It was always a possibility – given the way he was trying to pin me down, and given the way Dog was already floating the notion of an album with ten previously unreleased numbers on it. In those circumstances Sasson was simply doing his job. Of course, I was doing mine too by refusing to be pinned down and creating diversions when the talk got too tight.

Another interpretation might be that I engineered Sasson's departure in order to get my hands on an extra artichoke. That alone would have been worth doing: supper was delicious. Some say seize the moment. I say savour every bite. Especially when you don't know what's going to happen next and you're in the company of a man who, for the last thirty years, has always been on the winning team.

True to form, Nash didn't speak while eating, and afterwards he simply beckoned. I followed him along the padded corridor, through the hall and into a room furnished sparsely with sofas and books. He sat, leaning forward with his elbows on his knees. I slipped my shoes off and curled up in the corner of one of the chairs, massaging my feet.

'You're like a cat licking her paws,' he said unexpectedly. 'You have a cat's ability to take what's going and move on. I noticed that before. I hypothesised that feeding you might be a pleasure, and so it was.'

'I'm glad it was good for you too,' I said. 'I imagine that you're rarely wrong in your hypotheses.'

'There's a pattern to human behaviour, and as such it's predictable in the same way that animal behaviour is.'

'So when you say no one meets anyone for the first time, are you talking in the animal sense? Like when a horse meets another horse it's merely meeting itself in strange form. It should be already familiar with the stranger's horseness.'

'Most people think I'm talking about the transmigration of souls.'

'Is it useful to have people think you're dippy?'

'Yes,' he said. 'Is it useful to have people think you're stupid and greedy?'

'Sometimes. Sometimes it's annoying and a waste of time. Sometimes,' I added, 'it's entirely accurate.'

'I don't think it would be profitable to proceed in negotiations with you on the premise that you are stupid.'

I laughed at that. He blinked solemnly and paused. During the pause, the door opened and a man came in with a tray. He served me with a cup of espresso and glided out of the room leaving Nash still poised on the edge of the sofa looking earnest and anxious. While I, I hope, looked like a relaxed cat. It's always better to conform to your enemy's delusions about you.

Eventually he said, 'So, you have money troubles.'

I said, 'You know I do.'

He nodded. 'I could handle those.'

'With ease.'

'But that's not all?'

'No. I have a beef with the labels and the publishers. They ripped me off. And before that they ripped Jack off.'

He nodded again.

'And insofar as you are involved with the labels and the publishers,' I went on, 'you've ripped us off too.'

'You believe I'm involved?'

'Yes.'

'Then for the purposes of this conversation we'll accept that as true.'

For once I say exactly what I'm thinking: 'Well, Nash, that removes a whole layer of tedious accusation, denial and justification.'

'I told you, I abhor small-talk.'

'It wasn't going to be small,' I say. 'I have a stack of dodgy royalty statements which go back years.'

'Let me have copies.'

'You can handle that too?'

'It all depends on what you have to offer in exchange.'

'Nothing,' I say. I'm looking him straight in the eye when I say it, and he looks straight back. He's very difficult to read.

'Nothing?' he says, blinking slowly.

'Not while this conversation is being recorded.' Well, it worked once so it might again.

'I see,' he says. No confirmation, denial or justification.

We sit for a while in silence and I sip my coffee with apparent contentment. He looks perplexed but I don't for one moment buy it. I recall Sasson's unease in the car: maybe he was aware he could be overheard by someone other than the driver. And I remember how quickly Nash kicked him out and how outraged Sasson was. Like someone carrying the can for someone else. Maybe Nash has a reputation for bugging his own house.

Nash begins tentatively, 'If, for purposes of this conversation, we accept that as true, would you be more comfortable walking in the garden?'

'No,' I say. 'It's very late. There will be dew on the lawn. I don't want to spoil my shoes.'

'Well, Birdie,' he says with a helpless shrug, 'it seems that we have met twice and I have silenced you twice. I'm devastated. The first time it was because I thought your conversation would be inane.'

'Why did you want my company then?'

'You were beautiful and I was lonely. Why did you come?'

'I was fed up and lonely.'

'With Jack?' This time he looked genuinely perplexed.

'At the time Jack was in the full flood of narcissism. Life is lonely with a narcissist.'

'Why did you stay?'

'For the music.' I sighed. 'Besides, it's only a phase most rock-stars go through. With any luck they come out the other side.'

Nash said, 'Do you know how much courage it took to ask you out that time?'

'No,' I said. 'I've never asked anyone out.'

'Then you've never been refused.'

'That's a different question entirely. Of course I've been refused.'

'I mean sexually.'

'You didn't ask for sex. You asked for company.'

'But if I had asked for sex, Birdie?'

'You didn't, Nash. That's what distinguished you.'

'Did it? I always thought you wrote "Walks Like a Spider" about me.'

'You accept that I wrote it?'

'For the purposes of this conversation I accept that you had a hand in it.'

'It wasn't remotely about you,' I say, lying through my teeth.

'You see, you were so sweet in person, but the songs were napalm.'

'So much for being an inane conversationalist,' I say lightly. The turn he has taken gives me the creeps.

'I thought about it a lot in the intervening years,' he says. 'Yes, I thought you were uninteresting. You said two things: the first was that money has a price, which is a truism. The way you said it made it sound trite rather than apposite. That, I now believe, was the effect of your appearance and a light girlish voice. Your voice has strengthened over the years and your delivery has more impact.'

'It was still a truism,' I say. 'Even a cliché.'

'The second thing,' he goes on, ignoring me, 'was, "if you know a discreet way out of here, I'll allow you to take me anywhere." I should have paid more attention. You were selling yourself very cheaply in those days. You held my hand for the price of a cinema ticket.'

'When you say you abhor small-talk,' I say, 'it's because you haven't a clue how it works. Did you record all your conversations even back then? And replay them, searching for hidden meaning? Nash, you don't get out enough.'

'You are reputed to have a good memory,' he retorted. 'It's the same thing.'

'No it isn't,' I say. 'Memory is a reconstruction, of context as well as words.' I'm beginning to feel as if I'm trapped in an elevator with someone I don't trust.

'Memory distorts and degrades more quickly than tape,' Nash says. 'Tape is accurate and absolute.'

'Only if you take what's said at face-value,' I say. 'Nash, I'm getting tired and I've an appointment at nine.'

'Face-value?' he says. 'I thought you were accusing me of searching for hidden meaning.'

'What if there was no meaning at all?' I say. 'That's what small-talk is.'

'Of course there was meaning. I *knew* a discreet way out and you *came* to the movies with me. You didn't talk. I paid for the tickets. I did not grope, but I held your hand. The words were not without meaning; they were the basis of a deal.'

'OK. There was a deal. But it was a long time ago.'

'Nevertheless, what haunts me is that I missed something important – a clear equation between physical contact and money. If there was no meaning, why was the innuendo sexual? Why is it still sexual?'

'Still?'

'You said, only a short while ago: "I'm glad it was good for you too." Of course you were talking about the food, Birdie, but the reference was to that sordid question asked after carnal encounters.'

'It was a bloody *joke*, Nash.'

'No,' Nash says. 'The words mean something. They bring images to mind. Why do you conjure those particular images, Birdie?'

'Why do you receive them in that particular way? You're talking like one of those people who worry endlessly about song lyrics – even play them backwards.' As I say this, I realise with horror that Nash Zalisky, the *éminence grise* behind some of the loudest, weirdest recordings in rock history, is exactly such a person.

'Yes, lyrics,' Nash says, 'I was coming to that.' He's still sitting on the edge of the sofa, his hands clasped anxiously between his knees.

I've had enough. I uncoil myself and get up. 'Nash,' I say, 'don't start. This is a mistake. I'm playful with words. You aren't. Leave it at that. I'm going now.'

'Please don't go,' he says. 'Nothing's resolved.'

'There's nothing to resolve.'

'You keep saying that, but you're wrong. I should have offered you my protection years ago – for more than just a few hours. I'm offering it to you now. There's a room prepared for you upstairs. If you're tired, sleep. We can talk again when you wake up.'

'Thank you,' I say. But I'd rather die. 'I want to go home.'

He doesn't move, an anxious boy with an un-dead face. I'm in *Dorset*, for Christ's sake. I want to be in London.

I say, 'I need transport, Nash.' I've been careless. Now I'm carless.

'Yes, yes,' Nash says impatiently. 'But you'll have to wait.'

'You must have more than one car.'

'But only one driver.'

'I don't need a driver.'

'Oh,' he says. 'You can drive?' He sounds astonished.

'Can't you?'

'I never learned.'

We stare at each other. Impasse.

I say, 'Please will you lend me one of your cars?'

'As a matter of fact,' Nash says, 'I don't even know where they're kept.'

'I'll look.' I walk away from him. I'm almost expecting the door to be locked, but it isn't. I leave him sitting like a decaying child and find my way through the hall to the front door.

The front door, however, *is* locked and I can't find any way to open it. The only other place I know how to get to is the kitchen. The back door is impassable too. I wander in and out of every room I can get into and find no way out. It's a huge house with many rooms. Some of them are empty of everything but books, some are completely empty. There is a small cinema and an indoor pool. There's a banqueting hall, a ballroom, a lot of suffocating silence but no exit.

I stood in the middle of the ballroom feeling silly and angry. It was the one room Nash hadn't carpeted to death. The floor was a beautiful polished dancing surface. I tapped out an inaccurate paradiddle with my feet. There were two things going on, I thought. One of them has to do with what I want. The other is what Nash wants. Nash is a man and men are normally written in such big print that they're easy to read even by candlelight. But I don't know what Nash wants, and that is an unusual predicament for me.

If I didn't understand him I wouldn't be able to bargain with him. I *have* to know what a man wants. I have to be able to give him at least the illusion that he's won before he'll give me what I want. All my experience tells me that.

I twirled on the beautifully sprung floor. I swung my hips and boogied by the light of the moon streaming in through the long windows. Then I said aloud, 'Nash, in case you're listening, I'm in the ballroom. I hate being destructive, so please come along with a key before I break one of your elegant windows.'

He appeared so quickly that I thought he must have been waiting just outside.

He said, 'Why are you so desperate to leave me, Birdie?'

'Because I don't like the feeling of confinement.'

'It's protection I'm offering you, not confinement.'

'Thank you,' I say carefully. 'But sometimes the two can feel pretty similar.'

He sat down cross-legged on the floor. 'Did Jack feel that way too?'

'Yes.'

'But it's a brutal world.'

'All the same, I don't want to be cut off from it. Nor did he.'

'He would have been torn to pieces without protection and so would you.'

'That was a long time ago. Nobody's interested any more.'

'You're wrong,' Nash said. 'You're causing a lot of interest at the moment.'

'Not really. It's Jack. Some things don't change.'

'Do the new tracks exist?'

I smile in the moonlight and shake my head. I say, 'I'd love to talk to you properly. But I can't do it here.'

'It's safe here.'

'Where's your phone, Nash?' I say. 'I'd like to call a taxi.'

'Oh Birdie, Birdie,' he says. 'Have you any idea how much I could do for you?'

'If you want to do something for me,' I say, 'you could start by calling a taxi.'

'Is that all you want from me?'

Yes it is, no it isn't, you lunatic prick. If you hadn't put the wind up me so badly I'd have you tied up like a pet poodle by now.

I say, 'I want a taxi and I want a fair deal for Jack. I think you can provide those. I don't know what your relationship is with Dog Records or Barry Stears but I'm very wary of them. Once bitten, twice shy, and all that malarky. I have no cause to mistrust you personally, Nash, but you did once say you always wanted Jack on your label. If Dog's your label now, you've already got him, because Dog bought out both Cutz and Square Hole. If I'm reading the runes correctly, Mo'Zee is about to merge with Dog and that would give you the whole catalogue. And Jack's list is still doing nicely. Why can't everyone be satisfied with what they've got?'

'I only wanted to talk to you, as a friend,' Nash says plaintively. 'I wanted us to get to know each other.'

'We can do that,' I say. 'But not in a bugged house.'

For a moment, Nash stops staring at me and looks at the moon instead.

He says, 'Maybe I've always been a secretive man. Maybe I've always been self-protective. Great wealth, Birdie, allows one to take natural inclinations to great extremes. But you shouldn't mistrust me for that.'

'I don't,' I say. 'But men have been telling me to trust them for years. And people have been using me to get to Jack for years too. It takes time to make friends, Nash, especially when you don't know what they've got on their shopping list.'

'Ah,' he says painfully. 'Maybe I understand you better than you think I do. Wealth and power are like talent and beauty. You ask yourself: do they want me or do they want *it*?'

'Exactly.'

'Do you want me to give you something for nothing, Birdie? As proof of my sincerity?'

'Yes,' I say. 'A taxi.'

'Very well,' he says. 'But you must promise that we'll meet again soon.'

'A promise isn't nothing,' I say.

'Oh,' he says. 'I thought you meant nothing material.'

'Nothing is nothing, Nash.'

'You know,' he says, scrambling to his feet, 'you may not have wealth but you do have power. I'll make a call for you. Wait here.'

He skipped out of the ballroom in his tiny soft-soled shoes, and left me with a huge dance floor to prowl alone. I was glad the lights were off. I didn't want to see any reflection of myself. It's too late for bright lights, I thought, and I'm too old to stand them.

Nash comes out at sundown like Dracula, I thought, to suck the life and energy out of ageing rock chicks. Exactly the opposite to rock musicians who come out at sundown to give you all their life and energy.

Softly, almost under my breath, I sang 'Love Lies Bleeding' to remind myself that I was alive. I danced flexuous steps to go with the sinuous melody line, reminding my feet that they'd soon be far away.

As I completed the circuit I saw Nash almost hidden behind the door. A voyeur and an eavesdropper. If I ever agree to sleep in one of his beds, take me out and shoot me – I'll have become too gullible to be allowed to live.

'Don't stop,' he said. 'That was a great song. Did you write it?'

'No,' I said. 'That was pure, unadulterated Jack. And don't read anything into the word "adulterated" – it was a slip of the tongue.'

'There's no such thing.'

I shook my head. 'Do you remember that other song: "Sliding Widows"?'

'No,' he said. 'Remind me.'

'Well, that came from Jack misreading the side of a van belonging to the Sliding Window Company. He was charmed by his mistake, Nash. Mistakes make art.'

'I didn't know that,' Nash said, looking as if he'd like to take notes. 'I wish I could remember the song.'

'It would never have been written except for a slip of the brain.'

We stared at each other for a moment, and then he said, 'I'll walk you to the car – unless you've changed your mind.'

This time, the front door opened at the merest touch of Nash's hand and we walked out into the setting moon. The black sky was beginning to fray at its eastern edge and he screwed up his eyes as if it were the brightest glare.

As we walked towards the car, he said, 'I'll need some sort of tape or show reel. I'll need to be convinced you have something to sell.'

'Did I say I had something to sell?'

'No.'

'Anyway, I have no incentive. I mean, supposing I was to look through a trunk of old belongings forgotten in an attic or a cellar somewhere, and I happened to find a handful of Jack's demos or an old movie? Why would I tell you about them? If I did, you or

Sasson or some tax inspector would immediately claim them and say I should've given them up years ago.'

'There are ways round that.'

'What ways?'

'Let me think about it.'

'If there are "ways" you can ensure that I benefit from what I own – that I own what I own – then I might be encouraged to look.'

'Perhaps, sometime in the future, we could arrange an exchange of proofs.'

'But Nash, I have no incentive to look for anything. Proof would only become an issue if I found something.'

'What sort of incentive?'

'Cold cash,' I say. 'Something I don't have to declare.'

'I see.' He walks on a few paces. The car is in sight. It isn't a taxi – in fact it looks like the same Bentley that made the outward journey. I wonder what happened to Sasson.

'Here's my problem, Birdie,' Nash says. 'I think you're being disingenuous when you say you need an incentive to look. Why should I pay you to look for something you've already found?'

'No reason,' I say. 'In any case, as you said, this was only a meeting between friends. So, thank you for supper, it was truly delicious. I'm delighted to have met you again.'

We are beside the car. The driver gets out and opens a door for me. Nash takes my hand. He turns it palm up and kisses the inside of my wrist. I lean into him and kiss his withered cheek. His grip tightens in a spasm around my hand, as if an electric current has passed through him.

'À bientôt,' I say airily as I wrench my hand out of his grasp and slide on to the car seat. I'm losing my mind: I can't tell if his reaction is desire or disgust.

I wave goodbye. That is one seriously fucked-up little man, I think, and I rub my wrist clean on the blond suede of the upholstery. Will he go back to the house now and furiously shower in boiling water the way I want to? Or will he search fruitlessly through Jack's catalogue trying to find a song called 'Sliding Widows'?

Good luck, Nash, and good night.

# VI

*Rolling Stone Magazine*

## 'Hit The Road, Jack'
### By David Palmer

<u>27 Years Ago – Brighton, England</u>
*As the car draws up to the curb, two girls in silver hotpants leap into action. They come together, pubic bones grinding, knees between thighs. They strike a faux lesbian pose. The big one massages the small one's breast. The uniformed doorman looks on, expressionless. He's seen it all before.*

*Wearily, Jack climbs out on to the sidewalk.*

*'Wotcha doin', girls?' he drawls in that casual flat delivery only the British can muster at five o'clock in the morning.*

*'You,' choruses the teen duo. The big one says, 'We'll do you – any time, any place, anywhere.'*

*Jack turns his back on them to help his companion out of the car. She is wearing a sunshine-coloured silk maxi coat and little else under it. She's beautiful enough to be a slap in the face to Jack's teenage fans. They groan with disappointment.*

*The couple sweeps past and out of sight.*

*'Sorry, girls,' the doorman says. 'As you can see, Jack's got his hands full.'*

*But the girls turn up again next morning at breakfast. Still in their silver hotpants and wobbling platform shoes, they teeter across the lobby to the cordoned-off area of the hotel restaurant where Jack's Pack, in varying states of hangover, are eating bacon and eggs.*

*'Who let them in?' Jack mutters to Connie McKenzie, tour publicist.*

*'I think they spent the night in Wills's room.'*

'Get 'em outta here. We got the bleedin' BBC coming. I don't want them around.' Jack returns to his coffee and a copy of the London Times.

On the road with one of the great killer bands of all time, I discovered that the two would-be groupies weren't the only ones finding it difficult to gain access to the tour's inner circle. It was a raw March evening ten days into his punishing schedule of British venues before I found myself in the presence of kick-ass Jack.

In the two years since he last toured England, he has made so much of a reputation through album sales and concert tours in Europe and America that he finds himself somewhat in exile in his own country. Venues like the Lyceum Ballroom in Brighton (two matinées and an evening thrash, all sold out in three hours) are no longer big enough to contain him, and the security arm of this traveling circus is stretched to its limit. Isolated behind bouncers, photographers, managers, drivers and business advisers, Jack has become inaccessible even to the members of his own band. Tempers fray. In the hiatus between sound-check and performance there is nothing to do but bitch.

All this will change in May when the tour hits the United States, and you feel that Jack's private army can't wait to stretch their wings and fly to open spaces where they'll have room to breathe.

'We'll be all right in Chicago,' says Wills, bassist and long-time associate of Jack's. 'They're used to people like us.'

'Yeah, Mayor Daley loves us,' croons lighting engineer Ken Castle. 'He's so cool – puts us up in all the best hotels.'

The room rocks with laughter. Last year in Chicago half the road crew were arrested for possession of controlled substances and the tour would have been aborted without the timely intervention of Capitol Studios.

'Everyone wants us,' says Wills, dragging on an untidy handrolled cigarette of dubious provenance. 'Number-one attraction everywhere – that's us.'

Meanwhile Jack travels to the gig in a custom-built, heavily curtained bus. Inside, the bus is like a film set.

'In the style of a Tunisian bordello,' Jack explains when, credentials double-checked, I am ushered down the aisle and past the oriental rug that serves as a door.

He is sprawled, pasha-like, across black satin cushions with his head resting in his lady's lap.

'How many Tunisian bordellos have you visited, Jacko?' she asks, tapping his forehead lightly with one finger. She is dressed in cream shantung with a skirt split almost to the waist. Her legs go on for ever. Lack of access is not her problem; lack of privacy might be. In a decade when British rock stars are not in short supply, demand for this glamorous couple far outstrips their wish to meet it. Even during this short journey between hotel and hall, whenever we stop at lights or slow for an intersection, the drumming of hungry hands can be heard resonating through the reinforced panels of the bus.

'It's like Suddenly Last Summer,' remarks Jack. 'You wonder what they get out of it. Or rather, you sometimes wonder that they'd get out of it if they got in.'

'You're supposed to be thinking about the arrangement for "Adversarial Attitude",' his lady reminds him, showing an unexpectedly practical side to her nature. 'June's asking which musicians to book.'

## Cleveland, Ohio. 27 Years On.

I never did find out what musicians were required for 'Adversarial Attitude'. Search through the most complete discography and you won't discover a song of that title. As far as anyone knows it was never recorded. Twenty-five years ago the house that Jack built went up in flames and he with it. A three-month period of depression and spiralling drug-use ended in a blaze so hot and bright, they say it lit up the sky for most of the night. A casual remark made on a tour bus so many years ago serves only as a painful reminder of what might have been.

Today, at the conference preceding Jack's posthumous induction into The Rock And Roll Hall Of Fame, a panel analysed the myths, the songs and the influence of the music that is all that remains of Jack.

'We're interested in his cultural impact,' said Teddy Wright, gruff-voiced guitarist whose virtuoso licks adorned most of Jack's oeuvre.

Interest in the singer's life and times is still avid on both sides of the Atlantic. A docu-drama is slated for production next fall. Even more intriguing is a rumor that a collection of a dozen of Jack's previously unreleased tracks have turned up in the vaults of a London studio. They are to be cleaned up and digitally remastered for release in time for Christmas.

'This could be the most exciting discovery since the release of The Beatles' Anthology,' said Rocky Netzdorf, author of the brilliant quasi-fictional

Escape Into Fire *(reissued in paperback, Plume).* 'Facts are hard to come by, and spokespersons from Jack's record company are refusing to comment, but the vibe is there.'

Made conspicuous by her absence is Jack's last partner, Birdie Walker, she of the long legs and insolently beautiful face from the tour twenty-seven years ago.

'Of course we invited her,' said symposium head Richard Copeman, Rock Hall's Director of Education. 'We would have welcomed her input.'

The conference closed with a concert featuring, among others, Jack's Pack and Friends, a reunion of Jack's sidemen with guest appearances by singers from a later generation of bands influenced by him.

'We bought all the albums, growing up in Red Lodge, Montana,' said Skip Suskin of On-Line Animals. 'The first thing we did when we formed our own band was to cover some of Jack's numbers. It's a blast to be doing them again.'

'Adversarial Attitude' was not one of the numbers On-Line Animals would have been able to cover. But if the rumors prove true, maybe it is one of the songs that have been gathering cobwebs in a London vault. I hope so: twenty-seven years has been a long wait for the young reporter who first heard about the song in the back of Jack's own tour bus.

Sitting in a bar drinking a lonely toast to absent friends after the concert, I could almost hear Jack's flat London tones: 'Wotcher doin', Dave?' he might have asked.

Waiting for you, Jack. You're twenty-seven years late.

# VII

## Love and Other Stuff

Someone is turning up the heat. The voice at the other end of the line is pink and perky: 'Do you have a moment to chat?'

We were sitting around the kitchen table, Robin, Grace, Alec and I, finishing supper, when the phone rang.

'It's for you, Lin,' Grace said. 'Someone called Imogen.'

Imogen says she's a 'researcher' from Median Films. She's the third in five days. They aren't all from Median Films: one was from the BBC and the other said he was with *Mojo*.

'This is for the new bio on Jack,' Imogen says. 'I need to check a few facts.'

'Who gave you this number?' I ask.

'It's on file,' says perky Imo. 'I just wanted to ask you some background questions – like, how you met Jack, what he was like . . .'

'That must be on file too,' I say. 'Look, I'm sorry, I'm not going to talk about this.'

'If I've called at an inconvenient moment, can I leave you my number?'

'No,' I say, and I hang up.

'What?' Robin asks. 'What's the matter?'

'While we're all here,' I say, 'can I ask you a favour? If *anyone* from the media calls please would you say I'm not here and you don't know where to find me.'

'How do they get this number?' Robin's looking anxious, as she does so often these days.

'I don't know. And that's another thing. Please, if anyone asks you about anything to do with Jack or me, blow them off. I know you're already aware of this sort of thing, Grace, but Alec mightn't have come across it before.'

Grace blushes and Alec says, 'I don't understand. What's going on?'

Robin says tartly, 'They use anyone they can get their hands on to insinuate themselves into Lin's confidence.'

'But why now?'

'Oh, there's always some excuse – some anniversary or other.'

'But why don't you want to talk about it?' Alec asks. 'Wouldn't it keep Jack's . . .'

Grace interrupts, 'Lin finds it all too painful.'

'I'm sorry,' says Alec, looking as if this has never occurred to him before. 'But, if you talked to someone sympathetic, a friend, say, wouldn't it get the rest of them off your back?'

'No,' Robin says. 'It works the other way round. Talk to one and the rest think it's open season.'

'Say one word,' I put in, 'and it can come back to haunt you for the rest of your life.'

'Can't you put the record straight?'

'No. It's all like that question, "When did you stop beating your wife?" They start with a false assumption and you spend so much time and energy proving it false that everyone who doesn't say, "You protest too much," says, "There's no smoke without fire." Rumours and allegations stick, Alec. I'm sure you know that. You mess around on the Net. How much of what you've seen there would you say was true?'

Grace is blushing furiously now, but Alec says calmly, 'Not much, but I'm sure if people knew the truth they'd stop inventing the rubbish.'

'I don't think so. Which is the more interesting, Alec, Jack and Birdie met at a North London pub, or Jack met Birdie at a Tunisian brothel?'

Alec pauses for a moment and then says, 'Assuming it was neither of those, where did you and Jack actually meet?' Oh dear. The slick little prick is catching on.

I treat him to my saddest, most open smile and say, 'Yes, that's exactly my point. The truth, whether it's mundane or exotic, is the only thing I've got left that hasn't been thumbed through and fucked over by strangers. See, when you're associated with the entertainment business everyone thinks that your whole life is there to entertain them. That's what you are – a living breathing soap – and they have the right to include themselves in your life. You aren't real. You're just something to watch on telly. Every little thing is up for grabs: what *actually* happened, Birdie? What did it *feel* like? There's always someone who thinks they have the right to know the deepest, most sensitive details. Why? Because you're entertainment and entertainment is for everyone. It's like you made a contract to share every last thing with anyone who wants it. But you didn't.'

If you prevent yourself from blinking long enough, your eyes will start to sting and a tear will form. If you're lucky it will swell and roll gently over your lower eyelid and down your cheek.

Robin says, 'It's all right, darling. Here, let me fill your glass. You'll feel better in a minute.'

'Sorry,' mumbles Alec looking mortified. Even Grace is staring accusingly at him.

I've shared my deepest feelings with him. Yes I have. But I haven't told him where I met Jack.

Meeting someone new is the best, the wildest time. The air crackles and hums with promise and I can be reborn. I can reinvent myself to become the perfect lover again. I'm a stranger in a foreign country – learning the language, discovering unfamiliar pleasures. I'm newborn every time. Breathless, restless, greedy.

Dumping an old love is like dumping an old identity. It isn't only the old love you're tired of: it's also the old you – what you became after close proximity to the old love. I slough off my old skin and stretch out in a warm new one which is so thin and sensitive it tingles at the lightest touch.

I was with an American called Cy Fuentes. He came over to record because London was the place to be at the time. He was handsome, talented and jealous. We lived in a converted studio on Sydney Street. I was manifestly so uninterested in the domestic bit and he was so allergic to Bohemian squalor that he asked his sister, Gabriella, to come and keep house. Gabriella was responsible for my meeting Jack.

She was thrilled to be in London, thrilled to be on the music scene. English musicians were so cool. English boys were peachy and Gabriella couldn't wait to gobble one up. She came across Jack while trawling the King's Road one evening.

Normally, her taste was for clean-cut kids in mod uniform so she was afraid Jack would be as rude as he was scruffy. On top of that, she couldn't trust her own taste in music. Cy was always making fun of her bubblegum boys. So she took me along for a second opinion.

'Whaddya think, Birdie?' she said. 'I mean, if he got his hair styled and wore a suit?'

'No,' I said.

'But he could be gorgeous.'

'Shhh!' I hissed. The hair on the back of my head seemed to shiver. Goose-bumps came up on my arms. Because sometimes you hear a voice which you *know* can never be imitated or stolen. And then there's the rarest of all rarities – the unique voice with something to say. The real thing.

'He's got the cutest eyes,' Gabriella jabbered. 'Is he any good, do you think? He sounds kinda rough to me. I guess if he was any good he wouldn't be playing in a dim little club like this.'

She wouldn't shut up so I left her there and went home. I'd have to check him out when I was alone.

But the very next night Cy was playing at the Round House and at the end Gabriella brought Jack backstage to meet him. She wasn't showing him off so much as establishing her own credentials. She was saying, 'Look at me – my brother's famous, he gets the prestigious gigs – I'm someone to know. If you're nice to me maybe I'll do you a bit of good, introduce you to the big league.'

Now Cy was one of those hypochondriac musicians who go on endlessly about their health. His speciality was muscular aches and pains.

When Jack came in, Cy was surrounded by admirers and I was giving him a very public massage. Because that was another thing about Cy: he wanted to appear like a boxer after a fight, with a towel around his shoulders and his trainer – or in this case his handmaiden – in attendance.

Cy was saying, 'For fuck's sake, girl – it's where the Infraspinatus and the Teres major tuck under the deltoid – don't you know anything?'

Performers can be a real pain in the arse. But there were at least three hopefuls in the admiring crowd who would have cheerfully flattened me to get their hands on Cy's muscles.

I was in any case beginning to think Cy was too old for me. Too set in his ways. Too addicted to over-the-counter medicines. It was all becoming stifling and predictable. The world seemed full of older men who got their kicks from training young girls to be their own personal handmaidens.

That was the scene Gabriella dragged Jack into. She was saying, 'Hey, Jack, meet my brother, Cy.'

And Cy was coming over all anatomical about a kink in his shoulder. And the admirers were trying to show everyone their tits.

I wiped my hands on a towel and said, 'I was never any good at geography. Find your own Teres major.'

One of the admirers said, 'Let *me* – I studied shiatsu in Wales.'

'Go right ahead,' I told her. 'I was taught never to shiatsu on my own doorstep.'

No one laughed except Jack. I looked up and saw him sniggering behind Gabriella.

He said, 'Hi. Didn't I see you in the club a couple of nights ago? You walked out on me.'

Gabriella didn't even bother to give me a name. She said, 'This is my brother's girlfriend.'

'Not any more,' I snapped. 'Sorry Jack, I'm walking out on you again.' And I grabbed my jacket and marched towards the door.

'Honey!' Cy protested, 'come back. You know I think you've got great hands.'

But I kept on walking until I hit the street where an undignified little scene developed. Cy was half naked, trying to mollify me. Gabriella was saying snotty stuff like, 'This isn't the time for one of your sulks.' The admirer was saying to Cy, 'Take my coat – you'll catch your death.' About a dozen fans were clamouring for Cy's autograph. And Jack was laughing his head off.

Eventually one of the admirer's admirers passed a big fat joint around and things calmed down enough for all of us to climb into cars and go to a party in Hampstead.

But the damage was done. Golden, laughing Jack made Cy look like a crotchety old man. The air hummed when I looked at him, and the walls shook when he looked at me. He danced with me once that night, slipping his arm round my waist and pulling me on to his lean hard body as if he was trying me on for size. The heat was almost unbearable and I had to push him away before we melted and became glued together, belly to belly, thigh to thigh.

He said, 'You're not going home with him tonight.'

I said nothing, but I knew it was simply a statement of fact.

'Because', he said, 'that would be a shame and a crime, and a horrible waste.'

So that's how Jack stole me from under Cy's nose. And that's how I stole Jack from under Gabriella's nose – depending on who's telling what to whom.

The Tunisian brothel story is much better because it's a direct steal from a tale about Messalina and it contains all the elements of hubris and come-uppance you could possibly want.

They say I took a bet with a famous whore as to which of us could service the more johns. Points were awarded for artistic merit and degree of difficulty. They say I was winning by a country mile when Jack turned up with his guitar. Then two things happened: I captivated him with my venerean artistry and he captivated me with his music. I pulled out of the contest and he paid my debt of dishonour to the famous whore.

They say this was where I caught the syphilis with which I infected Jack, driving him mad and causing his death and my own downfall at a single swipe. Yep, that's how the story goes. Whores and heroes, venality and venery, pride and fall. Great ingredients, and if they're still telling it about Messalina two thousand years later, what chance have I got?

At the time, running away with Jack was seen as a bad career move. He wasn't rich and famous, like Cy. He didn't have the *trappings*. People suddenly talked about me as if I were a groupie and as if there were a recognised career structure for groupies. How unbelievably stupid.

Of course, what emerged, what neither Jack nor I recognised in his tiny shared flat with mattresses on the floor was that, as soon as Jack got me, he acquired the trappings. We became the subject of in-house, music-biz gossip. He became something other than just another young rocker. We were polluted from the very beginning, so to speak.

But I was only eighteen and Jack was only twenty-three. Babies. We didn't give a toss. When you don't know if you'll even last a single night together, when you don't know if you'll be having lunch with the one you went to bed with, how can you be accused of career moves? I could have blagged my way back into Cy's favour if I'd been interested in *trappings*. I'd done it before and I've done it since. Having my cake and eating it too was my speciality.

The miracle to me was that, at twenty-three, Jack was the youngest man I'd been with. His skin was as tight and supple as mine. He was someone I could *play* with. We could roll around like puppies. We could invent and shout nonsense at each other. We could dress up in freaky costume and hit the streets. We could tell secrets and giggle at grown-ups. We never did anything the same way twice.

Unlike all the others, Jack didn't have a ready-made world he wanted to slot me into. He didn't have a rigid attitude to music and life any more than I did. We could make it up as we went along.

I was astonished. I hadn't realised that even after leaving home and being kicked out of school I'd been hogtied. I'd been moulded and shaped to fit into the adult world. Even the so-called anarchists of rock'n'roll had some sort of master plan I was being groomed for.

Jack, at the beginning, was a *true* anarchist. If he didn't like something he changed it. If he didn't like what was expected of him he didn't do it. On-stage, he didn't play the entertainer. He sang what he wanted to sing in no particular order. He talked to the audience, fought with them sometimes. He quarrelled with the band. He changed songs in mid-flight leaving everyone else in disarray and scrambling to catch up. He wasn't afraid to fuck up.

It was undisciplined. It was irresponsible. It was irresistible.

Oh, and oh he smelled so sweet. He didn't smell like an adult. Even when his hair was unwashed, you could bury your face in it and swear he was a cat asleep in new grass. I didn't want a shower after I'd been with Jack – I liked the smell of his skin on mine. It was the smell of innocence. Beginnings are beautiful.

Now look what we're left with! Tonight, Grace comes into my room just as I'm turning out the light. She's weeping and she can hardly breathe for snot and tears.

'Oh Auntie Lin,' she says.

I hold the duvet back so that she can slide into bed beside me the way she used to when she was smaller than me.

'What's he done?' I say. Because no woman cries this way except for love. But Grace just cries and snuffles on my shoulder like an infant while I wait, getting wet and bored.

I wonder if Robin brought her kids up right. With our mother and father, howling achieved nothing but a slap and a period of isolation in our room. But Robin tried to make her kids' childhood a time of excitement and pleasure; above all, a guilt-free zone. She said she was crippled by the feeling that she was, in every way, unsatisfactory. Which, I suppose, was the burden a whole generation of English kids had to bear. So she gave her own children applause and encouragement and the sense that they were as important and valuable as the adults. It wasn't exactly that they could do no wrong, but wrong, once done, could easily be admitted to and just as easily forgiven. Which, as it turns out, is almost the same thing, because here is Grace who clearly feels it is OK to come howling to my room after midnight. Not only is it OK, but she's confident that she will be welcomed and comforted. Even if the wrong she's done is to me.

'Don't make him leave,' she gasps at last.

'Alec?' I say. 'Why?' Because, for the time being, I don't want her to know what I know; at least, not until I know what she knows.

'Well, I knew he liked the music,' she says, 'and I knew he wanted to meet you. But I thought it was *me*. I thought he came here for *me*.'

See what a sense of self-worth does? It's so much more of a bummer when you find out you aren't as important as you thought you were. Poor little Grace. I break out the tissues and pass a handful to her.

'Tell me about it,' I say – comforting, neutral Auntie Lin.

'You'll never forgive me,' she wails. She's never been unforgiven in her life – she's simply giving me notice that I must forgive her.

'He left his laptop in my room,' she says eventually. 'He was writing a letter but he wouldn't let me see it. I thought it might be to an old girlfriend. He swore there was no one else – but, Lin, he's so special. Other women must want him too, mustn't they?'

'Sure,' I say. That's another subject I have first-class honours in. 'So you read his letter, did you?'

'He was different tonight,' she tells me. 'Not cold, but like he was thinking about something else. So when he went back to Jimmy's room I started thinking, what if it's some*one* else? But it wasn't. It was you. He was writing a report about you.'

'Oh.' Extraordinary – at last the little sod has been careless with his security, but the wrong woman booted up the information.

'He's been following you,' Grace says. 'He's been recording your conversations. And I thought he loved *me*.'

'He isn't following me because he loves me,' I assure her.

'No-o,' she says. 'But he's fascinated with you.'

'No he isn't. He's doing a job.'

'Oh Lin,' she cries, 'I thought you'd be furious with me.'

'Why, sweetie? Because someone made a patsy of you?'

'Because I was indiscreet. I knew he wanted to meet you. I thought he was doing his doctorate on music journalism of the late sixties. That's why he was so interested in you and Jack. I should have told you, but I just wanted to help him. But I've let you down,' she says, weeping more comfortably. 'Can you ever forgive me?'

'I don't know,' I say.

She looks at me, shocked. I was supposed to tell her she was my little Grace and everything she does is peachy and not her fault.

'How much damage is done?' I ask instead.

She pulls herself away from my comforting-auntie arm, and for a moment I think she's going to say, 'I've apologised, what else do you want?'

But she's better than that. She says, 'How much damage can he do?'

'Who was he writing to?'

'Mr Sasson Freel,' she says, 'with a copy to a Mr B. Stears.'

'Ah.' I sigh. 'He can do quite a lot of damage.'

She sags. 'You're going to send him away, I know you are.'

'Well, what would you do, Grace?'

'I ought to kick him out. I ought to wake him up right now and throw him out. But I can't. I love him, Auntie Lin. I really do. And I don't want him to know I messed around with his laptop.'

So yet another generation of my family betrays itself for Jack's bright youth.

# Part 3

# THE MOVABLE MAN
# AND THE MOVIE

'He's drunk, he tastes like candy, he's so beautiful.
He's so deep, like dirty water. God, he's awful.'

Courtney Love

# I

## Peanuts and Promises

Alec Parry wasn't a bad man – he liked dogs and he tolerated children – but he loved the stories of young men who started out in the mail room and went on to own the company. Which was a good thing because a post-graduate course in Media Studies opened the world of mail rooms to him.

He knew that the film and music business was a world where thousands of over-qualified young people applied for every menial job. The lucky ones were then brutally exploited by a system of internships where you worked like a dog for less than a living wage in the hope that, if you distinguished yourself, you'd be taken on as permanent staff.

Memo Movies was an independent music film company. It dealt in archive footage and classic videos, and every two or three years it made a film of its own based on the history of jazz, blues, rock or the development of trip-hop. These productions depended heavily on Memo Movies' archive catalogue because, when tracing the roots of any new movement in music, it's illuminating to show the influences on it with film clips of music history. Memo Movies' archive went back as far as an old film of Bessie Smith, made in 1927. It was a diamond mine for anyone interested in that sort of thing.

Before joining Memo Movies Alec had never heard of Bessie Smith or Son House or Bill Broonzy or Howlin' Wolf or any of those legends who went back before the 60s. But he did like the music of the 60s and 70s – a fact he leant on in his interview. After joining, he made it his business to become as knowledgeable as he could about the seminal bands of that era. And he was surprised how far back into history his research took him. He hadn't realised that even revolutionaries have a spiritual lineage, that they, too, inherit a tradition.

To do him credit, Alec made an honest stab at filling in the gaps in his knowledge. His motto might have been, 'Blag your way in, become indispensable and then stick like glue.'

The problem was in sticking like glue. If history was anything to go by, when his six-month internship was up, Memo Movies would decide he was too expensive to take on full wages. They'd let him go and employ instead another monkey to whom they could pay the usual mixture of peanuts and promises. They would do this without appreciating Alec's potential. He was hard-working, ambitious, smart, well-educated and resourceful, but he couldn't prove it in a menial job. If he wanted to be recognised, he first needed to be noticed.

So Alec became the helpful young guy who made himself useful to anyone who had a permanent staff job. If a consignment of videos went missing, he'd stay on the phone and track it down. If the coffee machine or the copier broke down he was the one who badgered the repairman to have it fixed before the end of the day. If Production wanted to view material from Archives he took it personally to the editing suite and made sure he stayed long enough to try to find out what the project was about.

A month into his internship, after he'd found out how jealous and close-mouthed all the people on the production side were, he discovered that Memo Movies' current project was Jack. So Jack became Alec's project too. He bought the CDs, he read the books, he watched all the film and video he could lay his hands on, and he trawled the Internet for references which the dinosaurs in Production mightn't have come across.

Then he had a stroke of luck: in a Jack chat-room he met g.ace. To begin with, he only monitored conversations, not wishing to join in. Then one day he came in on an exchange which ended:

metalman: to say hardcandy is not nosecandy, naïve.

g.ace: to say what u say, banal.

metalman: what, then?

g.ace: sex with minors – h–c ref to taking candy from babies.

metalman: b***ox.

At this point Alec, who had himself been struck by the intimations of dirty sex in 'Hard Candy' which, as Metalman clearly thought, ought to have been a song about drugs, interjected.

cela5 to g.ace: yes. thought so too – but ambiguous.

g.ace to cela5: all jax birdie songs ambiguous.

After a while Alec concluded that g.ace was something of an expert and gave out his e-mail number. The conversation continued in private over the next week. He liked g.ace's style. There was wit and intelligence, and what looked to Alec like an inside track.

One day he delivered a folder of video cover designs to the Managing Director's secretary and found the great man himself leaning over her desk. He'd never met the MD before and he couldn't let the opportunity go by.

He took a deep breath and said, 'Good morning, Mr Stears. I'm Alec Parry, an intern here. Sir, as I'll probably never get to meet you again, please may I ask you one question?'

Mr Stears straightened, looking at first irritated and then indulgent.

Alec said, 'Sir, they say downstairs that you and Jack were actually friends, so I wondered if you knew: is it true that Jack was a football fan, that he followed Tottenham Hotspur and he had a cockerel tat on the inside of his left knee?'

Mr Stears's indulgent smile left his face. He said, quite sharply, 'Where did you hear that?'

'Well, sir, I've been looking on the Internet for stuff about Jack which might enrich the current project.'

'Who told you to do that?'

'No one, sir. I've been doing it for my own interest, in my own time.'

'Then I must ask you to stop,' Mr Stears said. 'Everything we do here is confidential. You must *not* discuss ongoing projects outside this building. Don't you know anything?'

'I'd never discuss a project,' Alec said indignantly. 'I was getting information, not giving it.'

'Idle gossip could give rival documentary makers a head start.'

'I don't gossip,' Alec said. 'I was simply encouraging someone else to. And I thought you might be the only one around I could check a *recherché* fact with.'

Mr Stears pushed his spectacles up his nose and gave Alec a hard stare. '*Recherché*, huh?' he said, 'I think you'd better come through to my office and tell me what you've been up to.'

Alec admired Mr Stears's office. He admired the stripped maple floor, the Sheraton desk, the gothic windows and the river view. But he promised himself that if – no, when – he ever made an office like this his own, he wouldn't spoil the effect by letting himself go to seed and getting overweight like Mr Stears. He'd keep the Wurlitzer jukebox though. That looked like a fun toy.

'OK,' said Mr Stears from behind the Sheraton desk. 'Who gave you your *recherché* fact?'

Alec explained why he didn't know who his informant was, and he went on briefly to recount the conversation. He was encouraged by Mr Stears's interest. If he wanted to be noticed, he thought, he'd lucked into exactly the way to do it.

'Let me tell you something,' Mr Stears said, after listening attentively for several minutes. 'This correspondence could be dangerous. Do you want to know why?'

'Why?'

'Because the *recherché* fact in question is probably known only to a very few people. Intimates. Family.'

'I didn't think Jack had a family.'

'He didn't. I'm talking about Birdie Walker and *her* family. You must have formed an opinion about Birdie if you've been doing your research properly.'

In truth, Alec had been keeping his eyes so firmly on Jack that, so far, Birdie was only the glorious appendage anyone would expect to see in the company of a rock god.

'Mmm,' he said, in what he hoped was a judicious tone of voice, 'tricky one, that.'

'Tricky isn't the half of it,' Mr Stears said. 'My concern is that if she gains even an inkling of what we're up to here, she'll block it any way she can.'

'Why would she do that, sir?'

'Jealousy,' Mr Stears said. 'Jealousy was always her problem. Jealous about Jack, jealous of Jack. Do you know, she even claims to have collaborated on some of the classic songs?'

'I didn't know that.'

'Well, I suggest you find out about her before you resume your cosy little correspondence. You might be writing to a snake in the grass.'

'I'll terminate the connection,' Alec said. 'I wouldn't want to compromise your production – that was the last thing on my mind. I had no idea it was so sensitive.'

'Now you know,' Mr Stears said dismissively. 'If you want to get on in this business you have to learn that although networking is a tool of our trade, blabbing foolishly to anyone who seems to share your interest is one of the easiest methods of having your ideas stolen or blocked.'

'I'm really sorry, sir,' Alec said, thinking, maybe coming to the attention of the MD wasn't such a great idea after all. 'But I promise you, I never said who I was or who I worked for or why I was interested. I was only coming off as a fan.'

'I hope you're right,' Mr Stears said and turned away towards the river view.

Pudgy creepo, Alec thought as he left the room, four-eyed twat. Why did the wrinkly fat twats get the good jobs? Why did being a pompous prat get you the sharpest office? Everyone says, show them how keen you are. That's supposed to win you points, not lose them. I'll be fired before the day's over, and all because I used a bit of initiative. I'll have to dust off the fucking CV. Again.

But later, after lunch, he was summoned back to the river-view office.

'Sit down, my boy,' Mr Stears said. 'Alec?'

'Alec Parry, sir.'

'Well, Alec, I've been thinking – maybe you shouldn't terminate your connection. Maybe you're overlooking an obvious strategy.'

'I am, sir?'

Mr Stears took a couple of seconds to straighten his silk tie. He said, 'Do you like working here?'

'Yes sir,' Alec said cautiously. He was no longer certain how clever it was to show keenness.

'Would you like to work on a special project?'

'I really would,' Alec said. This was more like it. This was *way* more cool.

'Then, perhaps you'd like to reconsider. If you were to continue this correspondence, in your own time of course, until you find out who you're writing to, you might have something to contribute.'

'I'd like that, sir.'

'But I can't stress strongly enough how cautious you must be. You must remember that you may be in touch with a member of Birdie Walker's family and it's impossible to overestimate how paranoid she is about media attention, how jealously she guards even those things of Jack's which should be in the public domain. Really, Alec, she's like the cobra coiled round the treasure chest.'

'I'll be super-careful.'

'And report back to me at every stage.'

'To you?' Alec said, gleefully. 'Personally?'

'I'll give you the number of my private line. And I'd like copies of the correspondence.'

'That may be a bit inhibiting, sir.'

'Why?'

'Well, I'll have to tell my informant a bit about myself if I'm going to personalise things. Sometimes you have to come on a bit strong if you want to intrigue people. I don't even know if I'm talking to a man or a woman.'

'All right then, a *précis* will do. But be careful. Expose yourself, Alec, and we could all be shot.'

War games, Alec thought, infiltrators. Spies on Level Four. And a foot in the door of the river-view office. When he left this time he thought maybe Mr Stears wasn't such a bad old fart after all – a bit slow, but he got there in the end.

A few days later he found out who g.ace was. He called Mr Stears immediately. 'Grace Emerson,' he said.

'Good God,' said Mr Stears. 'The niece.'

'Should I have recognised the name?'

'No. Better that you don't. At least . . . no, let me think about it. I'll talk to you later.' He hung up.

Alec was elated. He was really making an impression now, on all fronts. He was Mr Stears's blue-eyed boy, and Grace thought he was perceptive and sensitive. The dialogue with her quickly opened up to include books, movies and politics. But not sport. Sport, he'd learned the hard way, could be a chick repellent. On the other hand he confessed to a liking for sci-fi, because she would've expected something of the sort.

'dont give me a hard time on that,' he wrote.

'nobody perfect,' she replied. 'ursulaleguin ok.'

He liked her for knowing Ursula Le Guin.

'perfectwoman,' he wrote, 'dont tell me u married, 68, need walking frame.'

'how did u guess?' she wrote back.

'u breakin my heart.'

'got one? wow.'

Sassy, good fun, he decided. She didn't immediately ask for his phone number when he flirted. He awarded her points for that. It kept the game alive.

The game picked up speed. Mr Stears took him, in his chauffeur-driven car, to a Vietnamese restaurant in Soho to meet a man who was introduced as Mr Freel.

'This is Alec,' Mr Stears said, 'the bright young man I've been telling you about.'

Mr Freel looked the part: tall, weighty without flab, intent, grave. Impressive. Alec tried to sit straighter. He found himself playing to Mr Freel. Mr Stears seemed to recede into the shadows.

Yes, Alec thought, the secret to being in charge was to look as if you're in charge.

Mr Freel said, 'It seems to me that you've used your imagination. You saw the potential and acted on it. I congratulate you. How happy would you be to continue?'

Alec gave himself a moment to look as if he was weighing up his answer. 'To tell you the truth, Mr Freel,' he said with what he hoped was a thoughtful smile, 'I'm enjoying myself. The Jack production is great and I'm glad to be involved. My own part in it is tangential, I know. But it makes me feel involved.'

'It sounds to me as if this young man's a natural, Barry.'

'Well, he's with us on an internship,' Mr Stears said, 'so he's learning all aspects of the business. But he lacks experience.'

'I should think, by the time this project's in the can, he'll have gained plenty of experience. You ought to take him under your wing, Barry. Or maybe someone else will snap him up.'

'This is a slightly unusual situation, though,' Mr Stears said. 'Most projects don't require this degree of subterfuge.'

'Most projects, thank the Lord, don't require the co-operation of Birdie Walker. I expect you've included her in your research, Alec?'

'Yes, sir.' Alec raised his brows and flicked his eyes to the ceiling. Both older men smiled.

'So are you willing to beard the she-wolf in her lair?' Mr Freel asked, still smiling. 'Because it might come to that. Somehow we have to find out, first, does the Antigua Movie really exist? Then, if it does, and we're pretty sure it does, it becomes a matter of persuading Birdie to let us have it. No small problem, I might add. I don't know how far you're able to go with the niece, but it could be very useful to have a line on a member of that family.'

Alec waited, almost holding his breath. In fact, he'd already begun an absorbing fantasy starring himself as the subduer of the famous bitch-goddess. He was waiting for Mr Freel to order him into the front line. But apparently that wasn't his style. So eventually Alec asked, 'Is Grace anything like Birdie, do you think?'

'I only met her when she was a little girl,' said Mr Freel. 'What do you make of her?'

'I like her so far,' Alec said. 'Which is to say, I like the persona she's sending.'

'And does she like the persona you're sending?'

'We're still talking. If you don't like someone it's easy to sign off.'

'Tell me about her.'

'Well, I think she's bright, funny and sort of her own woman.

It's hard to say. We talk about a lot of things. I didn't want her to think that Jack was the only reason I was interested.'

'Very wise,' Mr Freel said. 'Barry, it looks like you picked a winner here.'

Being called a winner by someone like Mr Freel gave Alec the sort of confidence he hadn't tasted since he left college. The real world, for him, had been a series of rejections. It was a place where nobody recognised him and nobody took the time to get to know him. Ultimately nobody would remember his name because nobody gave him the chance to be memorable. Now he was turning it around.

He gave Grace his phone number that night. She rang and they talked for two hours. He wasn't nervous about talking to her; encouragingly, she seemed much more nervous than he was.

'Well,' she explained, 'you meet a lot of weirdos on Jack's sites. Not you of course.'

She really wants to make a good impression on me, he thought, surprised and pleased. It's supposed to be the other way round, but she doesn't know that. It's me who's taking the risk, not her.

So he relaxed, and let her do the work. It's almost like a real relationship, he thought. Once started, the women take over and make all the moves.

Meeting was her idea. Going to her mother's house was her suggestion. Absolved of responsibility, Alec went along for the ride. It was during that period – of suggestions and possible arrangements – that she told him about her connection with Jack and Birdie.

'It's just a family thing,' she said. 'I didn't want you to think I was showing off.'

'Why would I think that?' he asked, tense with excitement, staring down at the telephone as if it might be possible to *see* her at the other end of the line.

'Dunno,' she said. 'Some people get funny when they know you've got famous relations.'

'Got me,' he said. 'I'm turning into a monster. You'd better call off our date – oh-oh – I'm turning green – oh, my fangs and claws . . .'

'Shut up,' she said, laughing. 'I didn't mean you. You're different.'

Weird, he thought, how much more interesting listening to a woman was when you were waiting for her to say something important. He'd always found listening difficult, but learned how to fake it. With Grace he was forced to listen properly. And the more he listened, the more details she gave him. It was quite a discovery.

She told him for instance that Jack was a major influence on her life. Not because of the music, but because of the damage drugs had done to him. 'Everyone indulged him,' she said, 'but no one helped him. Birdie was the only one who tried, but she was too close to the problem. She just wasn't qualified. It damaged her almost as much as it did him.'

'Grace is biased, of course,' Mr Stears said when Alec reported the conversation. 'If you ask me it was Birdie's extravagance and infidelity that tipped Jack over the edge. She led him a terrible dance.'

Nevertheless it was the story of Jack's fatal instability that led Grace to study psychology at university. Now she was working for a rehab unit in Bristol. She wanted eventually to become a therapist, but that would be a long way in the future.

'I don't even understand my own past,' she said. 'The family dynamic is dominated by a tragedy Birdie won't talk about.'

'Why won't she talk about it?'

'At first it was all too painful. Then she internalised, and now the wound has been left to fester for so long it would take a really skilled therapist to help her.'

'Psychobabble,' commented Mr Stears. 'If you want my opinion the poor girl's had the wool well and truly pulled over her eyes. But that's Birdie – wool-puller *extraordinaire*. She doesn't want to talk about it because she won't admit to her part in the tragedy.'

Mr Freel, as Alec might have expected, took a more practical view. 'Grace is confiding in you,' he said. 'Good work. Keep her talking.'

By the time he met her, he felt he had the situation completely under his thumb. By that time too, he knew what his assignment was.

He cleared the decks. He told his mother and his girlfriend that he was being sent away on a junior management course and he wouldn't be in touch for a couple of weeks. He suffered an instruction session with Mr Stears, and two much more enjoyable afternoons, organised by Mr Freel, when he learned to operate the miniature equipment and tools he might need. Mr Freel, he reckoned, was The Guy.

Yes! he thought, as he watched Grace walk through the barrier at Paddington Station, game on!

He stepped forward, smiling easily. She was kind of cute – he wouldn't even have to pretend.

'Hi, Grace,' he said quietly, and watched her face relax and her lips part. She likes me, he thought, instantly. Oh you little angel, you like me. And she did.

If the watchful expression on her face had changed to disappointment or hostility he would've been, in the first nanosecond, blasted to stardust. He would have had to say – to Mr Freel of all people – 'She didn't like me. I don't know why. She just never gave me a chance.'

It wasn't something he could plan for or avert. The groundwork was perfect but, with girls, groundwork counted for nothing. They either went for you or they didn't.

But she did. Her face relaxed, her eyes widened and her soft lips parted.

'Hi, Cela Five,' she said, and held out her hand.

Game *on*!

It was suddenly as if there had never been a doubt in his mind – like watching the ball sail into the back of the goal: ball, goal, destiny. What was intended happened.

He wasn't even surprised to find Birdie at Grace's house. Him, Birdie, destiny. The stars themselves were playing into his hands. The goal was huge, the ball needed no persuasion. Alec was on a roll.

What did surprise him though was Birdie herself. He was expecting a towering figure. It wasn't that he'd imagined her to be unchanged from how she looked in the pictures he'd seen in Archives. It was more that he expected her to be . . . well, bigger – more imposing. When he saw Grace dancing with her, his first reaction was that Grace was the aunt and Birdie was the niece. No aunt he'd ever known danced like that.

He watched her, listened to her conversation with Grace and couldn't believe she was of the same generation as his own mother. The talk was quick and spicy, peppered with laughter.

The mother was more what he expected: slower, vaguer, more out of it. He had to work at remembering she was in the room and including her. Grace had described her as a bit of an old hippie and she hadn't misled him. He felt he could safely leave the mother out of the equation.

'What d'you think?' Grace said, breezing into his room, her brother's room.

'We-ell,' he began hesitantly, 'kind of amazing for her age.'

'Age?' Grace laughed indignantly. 'Typical ageist orientation.'

'OK, she's just amazing,' he said. 'And so are you. It's an amazing family.'

'Amazing Grace,' she said, striking a pose. 'And don't you forget it.'

Alec envied Grace her status with her aunt and her mother. If they never spoke of Jack, it was the only subject which wasn't acceptable in free-range conversation.

He liked Jimmy's room with its posters and the anarchy-coloured quilt. Lying on his single bed, either alone or with Grace tucked into his armpit, he'd stare at the posters as if they were his private portrait gallery. All were emblematic figures and Jimmy had arranged them like a football team. Wittgenstein was in goal behind a defensive line-up of Stephen Hawking, Puff Daddy, Karl Popper and Orson Welles. He wasn't afraid to put Mother Teresa in the midfield or to be childish and have Batman on the left wing.

Alec pictured himself among the strikers. Any team with him in attack would score. No argument. He had the juice.

Almost as proof, Jimmy had gone to Italy without coming home for the summer. I've never met the guy but he's doing me favours, Alec thought. Now he could settle in and take his time. Only the mother missed Jimmy, turning quiet and sombre.

Meanwhile he spent his time gaining points with Grace and covertly studying Birdie.

She came and went without explanation. He followed her once while Grace was washing her hair, leaving early and, unbelievably, catching a bus. Alec noted the number but didn't get on. It was odd to see her, mythic traumatised bitch goddess, in a bus queue. He searched her room, opened her laptop, found notes for lyrics, chords and arrangements filed under song titles, not in alphabetical order. He found accounts which seemed to make no sense at all. He couldn't find private letters – her filing system seemed random. Her clothes too ranged from massively expensive designer gear to scruffy jeans, all maintained with equal carelessness. She smoked sometimes, even in the kitchen, but at other times she didn't smoke at all. There seemed to be no pattern.

Alec didn't feel baulked or thwarted. Submerged somewhere at the base of his spine was an absolute confidence that all he had to do was be there. She would come to him. Like Grace, like Mr Freel, she would spin into his field of gravity.

She liked him. He would walk into the sitting room while she was playing the piano, and she'd turn and smile. She would play a few lines especially for him and sing in a lilting tone, 'Don't worry, be happy, every little thing gonna be all right.' She thought, as Grace did, that he was anxious about finding a job. They thought he was looking for a job and a place to live so that he could stay in London and not go back to his home town. Cleverly, he'd consigned his family to Hull – far enough away to be no threat.

He would drag a chair close to the piano and say, 'Go on, play something else. It's amazing – no one in my family has any talent at all.'

It wasn't flattery, he didn't have to fake an admiration he didn't feel. Truthfully, he felt that his own family would look lumpen beside Grace's.

'What d'you think?' she said. 'Bass going, da di da dum–dum da-dum; drums going, pa-*tum tum* ti-tum; melody like this; harmony here; and a little descant line up here? What d'you think, Alec?'

'Sounds great,' he said, in total ignorance, loving it.

'You must come to the club and see this band,' she said. 'You and Grace. I'd like to hear your opinion. You're the right age.'

'Honestly,' he said, 'I don't know anything about music.'

'Gut reaction – that's what I'm after – intelligent, sensitive first impressions. I *know* you can do that.'

Yes! he thought. She *likes* me. 'I'd love to,' he said. And was rewarded by the smile. The intimate smile, brilliant blue eyes crinkling, the deep corners of her mouth stretching. He couldn't help smiling back. The laugh was even better. It was throaty and husky. It seemed to bubble up like soda in a bottle neck.

He could make her laugh, that was the wonder. He might come across her alone, sitting in the kitchen late at night, maybe with a glass of wine in her hand. She'd have that dreamy-sad expression she wore when she was solitary. He found she enjoyed it if he said something a little cheeky like, 'My dad always told me to beware of secret drinkers.'

She wouldn't reply with something boring like: 'What're you doing up at this hour?' She'd offer him the bottle and say, 'Insomniacs of the world unite. Where do they keep the sleep in this house? I've searched everywhere.'

And he said, 'It's always on the top shelf, out of reach,' surprising himself and making him glad to have his own imaginative riposte secretly recorded. Bit by bit he was assembling a journal of her thoughts and memories, her comings and goings. Eventually it would be sent to Mr Freel, and he didn't want his own part in the dialogue to sound lumpen. He wanted his part to be as light and kaleidoscopic as hers. He wanted to sound like the right man for the job. He wanted Mr Freel to hear how Birdie was beginning to trust him.

'Don't let her seduce you,' Mr Freel had said. 'She can charm the snakes out from under stones.'

Well, listen and learn, Mr Freel, Alec thought, and then tell me who's seducing whom.

# II

## Excerpts from the Antigua Movie

If you succumb to heat and magnetism and fuck someone you've only just met, sometimes you can find yourself irretrievably attached without sufficient information. You commit the grossest intimacies with a total stranger and then the wind changes, and you're stuck with it. No one with even a modicum of sense would buy a house or a car on such a basis. A puppy? Yes. Exactly the same lack of logic controls your choice of pet – especially if you're the soft-hearted type who chooses from an animal shelter. Unless luck is as blind as love you'll find yourself devoted to a creature, riddled with ringworm, tape worm and ear mites, who snaps your thumb off when you offer the healing hand.

Jack stirs the heavy air with an alien finger. He says, 'Ripples.' After a pause he says, 'I wonder how long before these ripples reach London.' A longer pause, 'I hope, by then, they'll be a cyclone. They'll blow the roofs off houses and tear the arms and legs off the spidermen.'

The blonde chick sharing his hammock says, 'Assassination by cyclamen air.'

From this great distance, in time as well as space, the ripple touches my cheek like a snowflake. This time, however, I can't actually *see* the disc-shaped whirlpool of rainbow molecules. I'm not stoned. But the picture is pretty: there is turquoise sea, cerulean sky, ochre sand, indigo shadows. There are two fallen angels tangled in a single hammock.

I stop the Steenbeck and say, 'Can you lift a still photograph of this image?'

The technician says, 'OK,' and makes a note.

We go on, plodding frame by frame, into the past, illuminated by the dim light of an editing desk.

Some of the elements – 'tearing the legs off the spidermen', the 'cyclamen air', and the 'cyclone' – found their way into 'Walks Like a Spider', one of the cruellest songs Jack and I ever wrote – and, by the way, one of his most unlikely, melodic tunes. It took people a long time to recognise what a nasty song it was.

From this distance his instability and his paranoia are obvious. But so is his beauty. From this distance I say, 'Don't touch him. Call an ambulance.' I say, 'Could you really see only the beauty? Did you really think you could heal this lost creature?'

But, when he found me, how was he lost? He wasn't lost. He was found. And so was I. Foundlings, both of us, and delirious with joy at the discovery.

Wouldn't it be ironic if I left this tedious editing room believing in arranged marriages? The belief tucked into the same envelope as half a dozen still photographs of pretty young lovers in an idyllic setting. The photographs will be strategically placed where another young lover can find them. Will the belief touch him too? He'll know what to do with the stills. But common sense in the matter of his personal affairs . . . ? Oh no, that's still years and miles away.

Jack borrowed a small estate called South Winds. The house came complete with staff and groundsmen. But we never stayed in the house. We took first one, then two of the guest bungalows on the beach. Friends, hangers-on, the band, when they arrived, stayed in the house. It became crowded and the usual sniping and jealousy broke out.

To begin with, of course, we were alone. A sudden, mysterious departure caught everyone by surprise and we were gone before anyone could ask where we were going. We were gone, in fact, before we could ask *ourselves* what we thought we were doing.

'Got to get away,' Jack said. Get away from what exactly? From the attention? Yes. But we'd courted that. We'd expended time and ingenuity on making Jack famous. He wanted success with every cell in his body and he couldn't be successful without being famous. He was a *performer*, for Christ's sake.

When a performer rejects attention, he rejects a large part of himself. The greedy, look-at-me shadow of the man goes hungry. Then the shadow wages war against the man and tears him up, searching for food.

'Got to get away,' Jack said. 'Gotta chill. We can talk and play. It'll be like it was: maybe we can *write*, y'know, like we used to when we were alone.'

After only ten days, however, his hungry shadow found a bunch of American film students bumming around on the beach and employed them to watch us be alone.

Does it sound contrary? It sounded deeply contrary to me. But in those days I believed all the hype about simplicity and integrity. I hadn't accepted that nearly all men, women and children are at war with themselves to some degree or another.

It wasn't that Jack's hungry shadow won the war. That would be too simple. But the fight became more personal and way more bitter.

Here is a nice little piece of film: here is Jack at table. It's dark, he's lit by a couple of fat candles, surrounded by plates, bottles, wine glasses. A roach smoulders in the ashtray. His eyes are empty and sleepy. Hippie heaven. The simple life. The simple man with his simple wife.

'Yeah,' he says, 'tomorrow . . .' But he doesn't go on. He looks up, directly into the lens. From here, from this distance, his slow candle-lit blink looks surprised. 'Are you still here?' his bemused half-smile seems to say. 'Gimme a break.'

He dips his finger in the wine and begins to write on the table top. The drifty blonde wraith at his side reads what's written in wine. She gets up slowly and wafts away.

The next shot is from outside. It shows the silhouette of palm fronds blowing in front of the lit window. In the shot after that it is indeed tomorrow. And in between? The camera, this footage, implies that there was sleepy stoned love between the two shots, between the simple man and his drifty blonde. The appearance of two people, hand in hand, stepping off the porch into the warm sand in the morning confirms it. What you see is what you get.

What you don't get is what was written on the table top.

Jack wrote, 'I am the eye. The eye is watching me. The camera is eating my eyes.'

When the beaded blonde wraith read that, she got up, alarmed, and asked the Americans to stop shooting. Jack stayed where he was. He was literally paralysed with fear.

Look at the drifty little wraith, so sweet, so young, and from this distance so ridiculous in muslin and feathers. Someone substantial, a down-to-earth woman, would have packed up then and there. She would've checked Jack into a private clinic and let the experts help him.

What in God's name did the wraith think was going on?

I can't remember. I know I was alarmed. And I know I thought in my simple-wife way that what Jack wrote was a metaphor. I thought he meant that the camera was destroying his ability to see himself as he really was, and he'd chosen a macabre way of saying so. I suppose I agreed vaguely with what he wrote, so I saw it as a sign of sanity. His fear was what frightened me.

In spite of what you see in those ninety seconds of film, stoned love was the last thing on Jack's mind that night. It took four and a half hours and five tabs of Mandrax to persuade him even to lie down. He was rigid and gibbering with terror.

What did the wraith think? That it was an echo trip, or something? An incomplete metabolite of the previous day's acid? Oh yes, all that underground pharmacology – I remember *that*. We drank gallons of freshly squeezed orange juice next morning. How *very* effective.

But the sound-track to this excerpt is interesting. A single acoustic guitar is playing the twelve-bar blues riff which was eventually elaborated and became the underlying theme for 'Black Blonde' on the *Hard Candy* album.

I stop the film and turn to the technician. I say, 'I want to change the sound-track.'

'OK,' he says, making a note. 'Give me what you want in and I'll see what I can do.'

I hand him some old-fashioned reel-to-reel audio tape. He threads it on to the machine, and now the wraith is Jack's voice because this time there are vocals. This time the single guitar picks out a sixteen-bar pattern. Half hummed, half sung, Jack's voice rasps, 'In the morning she holds me, she folds me, she opens the drawer by her bed. She breaks me, she makes me, the widow mistakes me for the man she keeps wrapped in her head . . .'

'Yes,' I say. 'Fade up there . . . fade out here. Yeah, that'll do.'

The technician glances at me, puzzled. After all, 'Black Blonde' was perfect for the job. Why would I want to cut it out?

'Both versions,' I say. 'I'd like a copy of both versions. On film. But I'd like the original version transferred to video.'

# III

## Losing the Juice

It began to go wrong at the InnerVersions gig when Birdie led Grace to Dog Records' table to introduce her to Mr Freel. Alec couldn't duck out because he was with Grace. He was sweating from the dance floor and not feeling at all like bright young executive material. Mr Freel greeted him with a forbidding glare. Alec handled it rather well, he thought, by backing out and going to the bar to buy Grace a lager and lime. From then on, he avoided the record company table.

Avoidance meant dancing rather more often than he'd intended – which pleased Grace inordinately. Her pleasure was irritating, and worrying in case Mr Freel thought he was a lightweight who couldn't keep his mind on the job. But he didn't have a choice.

Birdie, unnaturally it seemed to Alec, was keeping company with Mr Freel and the bunch of guys who were clearly his subordinates. They were all easily distinguishable from the club crowd and, obviously, that was the way they wanted it. They were not there to have a good time. This was work.

Alec couldn't think of a way to signal to Mr Freel that he was working too. The best he could do was to be unobtrusive. It was annoying. He wanted to be closer to the action. How could he shine and be unobtrusive at the same time? Not by dancing with Grace, that was for sure. Dancing with Grace defeated both objects. He tried to look cool, but her bounce and zest called for some sort of response, and he began to feel disconnected.

What kept him going was Birdie's amused encouraging smile which he caught every now and then when he felt he was flagging.

'Keep at it,' her smile said, 'you're doing fine.' The problem was, he was forced to admit, that as she didn't know *what* he was doing she couldn't know whether he was doing it fine or not. All the same, he felt he had her approval.

She could, it seemed, move with ease between her family, the band and the company men. With Mr Freel she appeared to be polite but distant. She doesn't know he hates her, Alec thought once, standing on the edge of the crush at the bar, waiting to be served. The thought surprised him because, of course, Mr Freel didn't hate her. He only wanted something she was unwilling to hand over. Mr Stears was the one who hated her.

The music pounded into him like a jack-hammer, making him light-headed and glad he'd decided early on to go easy on the booze. He wished he could hear what Mr Freel was saying to the guy who'd pushed his way through the crowd to deliver a note. Mr Freel read the note, folded it and slipped it into his inside pocket. He leaned towards Birdie. Birdie nodded slowly.

'Isn't this great?' Grace said, taking a drink from his glass. 'Let's dance.'

But Birdie appeared in front of them holding out the Volvo keys.

'Aren't you staying to the end?' Grace said, disappointed.

'I've got to talk to some people. Will you be all right on your own?'

'Don't worry,' Alec said. 'I'll look after her.' He wanted to add, Unless there's something better I can do to help *you*. But he didn't.

'Isn't he perfect?' Birdie asked Grace. She gave Alec the keys.

A few minutes later he saw Mr Freel escort her through the club and Alec suddenly felt left behind. Mr Freel's hand was on her elbow, urging her forward, and she looked small, almost fragile, beside him. Not a fair contest, he thought, unexpectedly. And with a pang, he realised that Mr Freel, with his height, tailoring and power, might charm, bludgeon, cajole Birdie into co-operating with him. Then he wouldn't need Alec any more, and Alec would be demoted back to office gofer at Memo Movies.

'Dance?' Grace shouted over the din. But now there was no one to watch, no one to avoid and no one to approve or disapprove, and dancing lost its point. After a while he feigned a twisted knee, and after that, there was no reason to stay.

'Are you OK?' Grace asked, a lot later.

'A bit tired.'

'Is the knee still hurting?'

'A bit,' he said and remembered to limp as he left her bed and went back to Jimmy's room.

He wedged his door ajar so that he could listen for Birdie's key in the lock. Maybe he could meet her on the stairs and suggest a nightcap. But the hours slid away and she didn't come home.

What the hell is she doing? he thought. She said she was going to talk to some people, but nobody talks all night. He could still see her walking away with Mr Freel – Mr Freel urging her, Birdie small and reluctant. I'm sure she didn't want to go, he thought. Leave her alone, Mr Freel, she doesn't want to go and you're upsetting my game-plan. She doesn't trust you. She doesn't even like you. I can tell. She never smiled at you once. You'll come on too strong. I know how to handle her. You don't.

The worst thing about that night was that he could sense the juice draining out of him. He was slowly being expelled from the zone – left unprotected outside the palace gate. What he realised, as the time dragged by, was that he was vulnerable.

He lay, scratchy-eyed, his ears ringing with the tinnitus that comes from dancing too close to big speakers, and realised that he'd invested too much in her. Birdie was way more vivid in his mind than Grace. Grace was Birdie's shadow, her echo. The correspondence on the Net, the sassyness and invention, was a correspondence with Birdie through the medium of Grace – Grace's mimicry of Birdie's style. As soon as he met the original, Grace receded. The most vivid thing about Grace had been the correspondence. Grace in person was only Birdie's niece.

But that was what was supposed to happen, he told himself, get to Grace through Jack; get to Birdie through Grace; get back to Jack through Birdie. Circle complete. Game over. But something got distorted. It wasn't a clean simple circle any more. Maybe it never was. He should have added a tangent: get to Mr Freel through Jack; get the pretty office, the Wurlitzer, the Beamer through Mr Freel. But only if Mr Freel doesn't take over and award all the prizes to himself.

Insomnia was not in the game-plan. Anger, anxiety and bewilderment weren't either. Feelings were a pain in the arse. Alec saw them as blocks, chasms, snipers and hidden explosives on his screen. His game hero was weakened and in danger.

Shut down, he thought. But instead he waited all night for the sound of a middle-aged woman's feet on the stairs, and it didn't come.

'What's up?' asked Grace, clear-eyed, glossy-haired. 'You look dreadful.' She plunked a bowl of muesli in front of him.

'Why, thank you,' he said. 'You look enchantingly dreadful yourself.' But banter took too much out of him. He hadn't the heart for it.

'He's all worn out,' Grace explained to her mother. 'He's a maniac dancer but he just can't take the Grace pace.'

'Where's Lin?' Mrs Emerson asked.

'Didn't she come home?' Grace said. 'Dirty stop-out. These old people, staying out all night, worrying their children . . .'

She was interrupted by the sound of the front door opening.

'Lin?' Mrs Emerson called.

'Can't stop, sweetie,' Birdie called back. 'Got to shower, change and be gone.'

'At least have some breakfast.'

'No time.' Birdie's voice floated down from the top of the stairs. Doors opened and closed, water gushed and twenty minutes later she vanished again without Alec seeing her.

'She'll wear herself out,' Mrs Emerson sighed. And then with unusual vehemence she said, 'Sometimes I really hate rock'n'roll.'

'What do you mean?' Alec asked.

'I don't know,' Mrs Emerson said more vaguely. 'The way it builds you up and up till there's nothing left to do but crash. The way everything happens at night . . . I don't know. How does she think she can survive if she stays up all night with one of her bands and then rushes off to an interview in the morning?'

'Has Auntie Lin got another interview?' Grace asked.

'I think so.'

'You can't expect her to give up the music, Mum. She wouldn't be Lin if she didn't racket around at night. Can you *really* see her with a normal nine-to-fiver?'

'She'd be safer.'

'Give it up, Mum,' Grace said. 'Besides, she's my role model whenever I think of growing old disgracefully.'

'You don't know what you're talking about,' Mrs Emerson said. 'And I hope you never do.' She got up and drifted out of the room, leaving Grace biting her lip.

'Me and my mouth,' Grace said.

'Why?' Alec asked.

'Because Mum thinks Auntie Lin's one of the tragic casualties of the rock'n'roll holocaust. Whereas I think she's a survivor.'

'I thought you said she was traumatised.'

'Of course. Aren't we all?'

Alec couldn't disagree with her that morning. So unaccustomed was he to fatigue that he placed himself in the front rank of the traumatised hoard. But after breakfast he went back to bed and slept till lunch.

In the afternoon, feeling better, he began to compose a communication to Mr Freel.

'To Mr Freel,' he wrote. 'The subject has, since I last wrote, been in touch with – 1: BBC. 2: *Mojo* Magazine. 3: Virgin Records. 4: Mr Ireland at your own company. 5: Sheeney Tele-Cine. 6: Inland Revenue. 7: Paul and Dahl Hair Salon . . .'

Grace swung the door open. 'What're you doing? Let's go out.'

'Where?'

'Anywhere. Who're you writing to?'

'Just a friend.' Alec closed his laptop.

'You've got *friends*?' She stroked his hair and slid his hand under his shirt. 'What on earth do they see in you?'

'Rat!' he said, grabbing her hand.

Insults and terms of endearment: Alec was grateful, and congratulated himself on the interchangeability of the two. There was no commitment implied in calling someone a rat. If it was interpreted as affectionate no blame could be attached to him. Between him and Grace lay a shallow, frothy layer of jokes, puns and innuendo. It was what they floated on. Underneath, he felt, was nothing at all.

Birdie blew in at dinner time but before she'd settled down there was a phonecall from a film company called Median Films. Alec knew about Median – it wasn't as big a company as Memo Movies, but it was a competitor. The call upset Birdie.

At first, Alec was glad because it meant that if Median was making a film about Jack too, and Birdie was upset, she wouldn't co-operate with them. But it made him aware of the urgency of his mission.

Then, she explained for the first time why she was so allergic to media attention. And for the first time, Alec understood that what seemed to Mr Freel and Mr Stears like a dog-in-the-manger attitude was self-protection.

The conversation, unlike most of the conversations at that kitchen table, was serious. And, suddenly, Alec felt the force of all three women ranged against him. Even Grace let him down. She, who had previously advocated the healing power of talking, turned tail and left him on his own – left him with a serious enquiry on his hands and what should have been her lines in his mouth: 'Wouldn't you feel better if you put the record straight, if you talked to a sympathetic friend?'

And Birdie turned him down flat. If rejection wasn't bad enough, she made him feel that even his offer was wounding.

He'd been pushed into showing his hand too early by Mr Freel's interference and Median Film's intrusion. The result was appalling: Birdie cried. Tears hung suspended from her long lashes, and he had to look away because he didn't want to see them fall. That was what happened when you got serious – you left yourself open to attack. Tears were sharp, raking weapons to be avoided if at all possible.

'Oh, don't worry,' Grace said. 'She'll come round. She's tired, that's all. She didn't get any sleep last night, remember.'

He took refuge in the acid froth of their exchanges but later, when she went down to watch TV, he stayed in her room to finish his letter to Mr Freel.

How do you tell the Big Boss-man to butt out? 'I do think,' he wrote, 'in view of the subject's reaction to Median Film's approach (tape to follow), that anything that might be interpreted as intrusion or digging should be discouraged. It only serves to harden her attitude . . .' He was rather proud of that. It took him a long time to compose, but it sounded sophisticated and respectful while saying, 'Fuck off, you're ruining my game.'

Again, he didn't have time to finish. Grace said, 'Still at it? Well, you'll be happy to know that Lin went to sleep in her chair. It might be because what's on telly's so boring, but I think, personally, it's because tears are cathartic.'

# IV

## Excerpts from the Antigua Movie

Junior Moline sits like Buddha at the sound desk. On his right is a young beach bum with a lot of talent and attitude. On his left is The Widow Oats. Change focus and you'll see what they see: the band – Jack, Teddy and Wills, all with acoustic guitars – are sitting on the floor, working something out. Goff is tucked away behind a barricade of cardboard boxes to stop the drum sounds bleeding on to everyone else's tracks. A few more beach bums are building another baffle. What for? I can't remember. Over against the peeling back wall is an upright piano. Jack's blonde chick has her back to everyone and she's playing the piano but you can't hear her. All the mikes are in the middle with the boys. The electrical gear – guitars, amps, etc. – is strung together like charms on a giant black cable bracelet.

It's *ad hoc*, it's messy. It's like a nursery school with all the toys on the floor. Lyric sheets flutter and fall whenever anyone walks by.

Everyone, it seems, is playing trains. They're stoking the engine, building up steam to drive the sixteen-beats-to-a-bar locomotive rhythm which propels the title song, 'Hard Candy' – uh *huh* huh-hunh . . . Heads nod, feet pedal, knees pump, sweat rolls.

It's hot in there. The boys are stripped to the waist. The blonde chick's Indian shirt clings to her back.

Pull focus again and you see the way Junior's shorts cut into his meaty thighs. The beach bum's frayed cut-offs sag low on his narrow hips. The Widow's bikini top supports nothing. It clings perilously to the unbelievable cantilever of her astonishing bosom – crimson on bronze. A tiny gold cross winks slyly, heliography from the foothills.

She calls herself Stella Splendens. The blonde chick calls her Offences Against The Senses – Oats for short. Her perfume is too heavy, her make-up too thick, her colours too strong, her voice too brassy, her breasts way too improbable. She strikes me, even now from light years' distance, more as a billboard than a woman. Constructed like a mantrap by the roadside.

What was she doing there? She looks all wrong in that ragged company. Someone brought her. Someone was doing a favour for the rich Widow Oats. But she was out of place on the island. She was a hanger-on, not a hanger-out. A bit of a joke, I thought.

'Out of it,' Jack said. 'Uncool.' Then.

Later, when we came across her backstage, when Jack was touring *Hard Candy*, it was a different story. She didn't look so out of place in LA. She was built for LA. Built *in* LA, probably.

Never mind. She carried Jack away to her eyrie in the Hollywood Hills to sample her jacuzzi. Yeah, right! Which wouldn't have been too bad in itself, because shit like that happens on the road. Except that they were both such narcissists that they had to invite the paparazzi along to record the coupling. 'Rock Rebel In Hot Water.' Good headline.

'Birdie Flies' followed that, and 'Sauce For The Goose' – yes, that was the banner caption to a picture of me and Homer Webb on a converted trawler off the Adriatic coast. Homer was lovely. He taught me to fish and he made revenge truly sweet. He didn't deserve what Jack said about him, either in the papers or in 'Adversarial Attitude'.

Widow Oats, on the other hand, deserved every word of what I said about *her* in 'Sliding Widows'. And, do you know? – Jack didn't even *like* her. He certainly never defended her and some of the unkindest lines in the song are his.

'I'll tell you how I feel about her,' he said. 'It's the way you feel about turkey the week after Christmas.'

I would never have said a thing like that about Homer. In fact I could've stayed with him a lot longer if Jack hadn't come to find me. He was sweet. His voice was too obedient and MOR for blues or rock, but it was nice, just right for his material – a ballad voice.

I go to see him sometimes, even now, and he's still sweet. Widow Oats got what she deserved: she married a Hollywood producer.

'Fast forward,' I say to the technician, interested to note, in spite of this chasm of time between then and now, that The Widow still has the power to irritate the shit out of me. Actually, she didn't amount to anything in herself – it was the sight of Jack holing himself below the waterline on those titanic tits. It was so obvious, so show-biz. So disappointing.

Long ago, I believed that rock'n'roll wasn't show-biz. It was a way of life. It was somehow pure and exempt. I thought Jack and I were expressing real emotions – feelings which rejected show-biz bosoms as falsities, fallacies, falsies, false titties.

Maybe it wasn't fallible Jack who foundered on those improbable breasts, maybe it was me. There's no one so cynical as a disappointed believer.

It was Widow Oats who showed me the rock-rebel falling, not for the best, but for the biggest.

To be touched, to screw someone in heat or passion, is one thing – that happens – it isn't wonderful but it's understandable. To fall for such a trite caricature of sexual attributes and to exploit it for publicity isn't understandable at all. Or rather, it's only understandable in show-biz terms.

In the next sequence, 'Hard Candy' is coming together nicely. Jack is sitting on a stool. He still has the acoustic guitar strapped across his chest. Teddy and Wills have gone electric. Jack's chick is now playing a small organ.

Singer and organist are facing each other. There is intense eye contact between them. You might think that he is singing to her, that this is a moment of high romance. Don't be fooled by two beautiful kids' beautiful eyes locked together. They aren't romancing, they're counting. They're counting the vocals in so that stressed words fall on stressed beats. Complicated lyrics are being welded to driving rhythms.

Their slender young bodies sway and they look as though they're dancing. But they aren't. In each movement are the silent signals they're giving each other. Every swing of the shoulders, every dip of the head is a count or a signal. Nothing is done for effect. It's concentration, not show-biz.

It's Jack and his chick at their best. But, ah *but*, I say now in this dim editing room, it *was* being filmed. Doesn't that fact alone make show-biz out of concentration and a fallacy out of the notion of pure rock'n'roll?

I say to the technician, 'Transfer this sequence to video, please.'

I don't want to give the spidermen anything, but I'm forced to. If you want people to be jealous and acquisitive they must have some inkling of what they've been excluded from. This sequence, at least, shows Jack and his drifty blonde chick acting like people who can be more than enigmatic and decorative. Even if the chick is only being used as a human metronome, at least she is being used for something – she isn't just floating around looking edible. Ah, vanity. Even now.


I love islands. But now, the sandy, scruffy wildernesses are mostly tamed and thatched. The dusty dirt paths are metalled, the miniature jungles and mangrove swamps are cut back until they're little more than herbaceous borders, and all the tattered, unruly kids are groomed to be desk clerks. We're running out of islands. Maybe there were too many movies showing sexy glamorous people like Jack and me getting away, cooling it, on undiscovered dots in the ocean. Eventually everyone wanted a piece of one.

I bet the shack we used as a studio was torn down to be a tiny part of a huge hotel, and tourist money destroyed what it existed to share in.

Jack and Teddy sit in the shade outside, leaning against the crumbling wall. Occasional sea breezes lift their hair away from young, strong necks. They are on a break. The kids have a desultory football game going with Wills and Goff. Now and then the ball thumps against the wall. Nearby, an exhausted dog shares the meagre shade, its emaciated ribs rising and falling in starved sleep.

With nothing better on offer, the cameramen film the band doing bugger-all while the soundman tries his hand at interviewing Jack. What was his name? Chip? Cookie? The credits will tell me, for unfinished, ragged, unruly as this film is the guys who made it stuck their names, big and bold, at the end.

Chip says, 'What's your message, Jack? I mean, what's the point, man?'

Jack grins at him and raises a bottle of some local brew to his lips. He blows a long hollow note across the neck and says, 'Hear that lonesome whistle blow?'

'B-flat, I reckon,' Teddy says, cupping one ear.

'That's our message,' Jack says. 'Be sharp.'

'Yeah, man,' says Chip. 'But what're you telling the kids? Y'know, with the bomb and Agent Orange and shit?'

'Nothin' they don't already know,' Jack says.

'Like what?'

'Live, love and be happy,' Teddy says, ''cos tomorrow ker-boom.'

'Keep changing the light bulb at the top of the stairs,' Jack says with infinite wisdom. 'That's the one you need.'

Jack has made mincemeat of professional interviewers, and Chip would give up right now if he wasn't too stoned to realise that Jack is being neither friendly nor gnostic.

'Yeah, man,' Chip says in a wondering tone of voice, 'the light bulb . . . Like, ah, don't be left in the dark?'

Oh, this is wonderful. I turn to the technician and say, 'This bit. Let's transfer this bit to video.'

'OK,' says the technician. 'What the fuck're they on about?'

'Nothing,' I say. 'The message is that there's no message.'

But Chip isn't ready to throw in the towel. He says, 'But Jack, man, some of those songs are, like, so far out . . . There's that one line, y'know, you were doing it over and over just now . . . "Hold me down when the hot wind shatters time . . ." I can't get my head around it.'

'Don't ask me,' Teddy says. 'I only play guitar.'

'Jack?'

'I'll tell you,' Jack says slowly and thoughtfully.

Chip waits. Teddy waits. And Jack gets up to retrieve the ball a kid has kicked at his legs. He doesn't come back. Teddy sits in silence for a few seconds. Then he says, 'Yeah, lyrics, man. They're the things they use to break up the guitar solo, aren't they? Yeah, I thought so. Not much use otherwise.'

Chip says nothing. Jack's gone. There's nothing left to say. Teddy knows this – it's why he hates Jack – but he sits there stubbornly until his wife, Christy, crouches down beside him and gives him a slice of pineapple. End of sequence.

That is the first and only time you'll see Christy in this movie. She's doing what she did many, many times – rescuing Teddy from the small, intolerable humiliations which are a second fiddler's lot. Nice woman. Good cook. Fiercely loyal until Teddy dumped her. I would have liked her if she'd liked me. But she didn't. Naturally.

I didn't have any girlfriends then – except Robin. Sisterhood as a universal concept rather than a family connection was a thing of the future. Suspicion was much more prevalent than support. Nowadays, I could have all the girlfriends I ever missed when I was Jack's blonde piece. Oh yes – a drop in your oestrogen level does wonders for your popularity rating with other women. But nowadays it is I who am suspicious. Where were these sisters when I was edible and supple? They were out spreading the whorey rumours and telling naughty stories about me to journalists. The *zeitgeist* was whispering a different message in those days from the one it whispers now, and women are very sensitive listeners to the *zeitgeist*.

'Let's take a break,' I say to the technician. 'Is there a decent pub within walking distance? I'll buy you a drink.'

'OK,' he says. 'I'd better ring the girlfriend, tell her I'm going to be late.'

She won't mind if an old broad buys her feller a drink, will she? Old broads aren't any threat. Oestrogen and the *zeitgeist* are walking hand in hand a long, long way from island breezes and leggy, drifty chicks. No one will be betrayed tonight. Or will they?

# V

## Game Over

Alec dreamed he was in a playground surrounded by bright red and yellow swings and slides. Someone – his mother? – gave him something to hold. He carried the bundle up the ladder to the top of the tallest slide and let it go, intending to follow it down. But for some reason he didn't. He climbed up to a higher level and from there he saw, far below, a tiny baby rocketing, accelerating, towards the ground. The shawl it had been bundled up in blew away leaving the baby naked and tumbling, skidding uncontrollably, down the glittering steel slope.

'She didn't tell me,' he said, jerking upright in bed and seeing two giant female forms looming over him.

'Didn't tell you what?' Grace asked. The ceiling light was on, blinding him.

'Get dressed,' Birdie said. 'And be quiet. Don't disturb Robin. We'll be in the kitchen.'

'Wha' . . .' Alec mumbled, knuckling his eyes.

'The kitchen,' Grace said, 'and be quick.'

He peered at his bedside clock. 03.18. He looked back at the door. The women were gone.

He was awake, sort of. He dressed in T-shirt and track bottoms, and stumbled as quietly as he could down to the kitchen.

Birdie was sitting at her usual place at the table. She was wearing a long red robe of some kind. Grace was making tea.

As he entered, Grace put the lid on the teapot and then came over to him.

He said, 'What's up?'

For a second she said nothing, and then she hauled off and hit him a stunning smack around the ear. As his face swung away from the blow, his other ear met her other hand. Whack, whack. He staggered back. She pursued him and kicked him very hard on the shin.

He howled once and from his position, kneeling on the floor, he saw the hem of a red robe sweep around him and heard the kitchen door snap shut.

'Shut up,' Grace said. 'You'll wake Mum.'

'What're you *doing*?' he gasped, crouching, trying to protect himself from the next stinging slap.

'That's *my* question,' Grace said, delivering another one, two, three.

'Enough,' Birdie said quietly. 'I think the tea might be ready to pour.'

When he looked up Birdie was back in her place, calmly holding out a cup, and Grace just as calmly was pouring tea.

'You're mad,' Alec said. His shin was throbbing and aching. His face was hot and stinging. His teeth felt loose. His ears rang.

'Too right I'm mad,' Grace said. 'You used me, you bastard.'

'You're rumbled,' Birdie said. 'Take it like a man.'

'If that's what you are,' said Grace.

He stared at them, his mind running like a dog trying to catch its own tail. What did they know?

'I don't understand,' he said. 'What am I supposed to have done?'

'Oh dear,' Birdie said. 'This is going to take for ever. We've got an asshole on our hands.'

'No, really,' he pleaded. 'I don't understand.'

'What don't you understand?' Grace said. 'That cheating and lying and screwing a girl just to get into her house to spy on her aunt might upset me? Why should a tiny detail like Grade-A treachery spoil a beautiful friendship?'

'Look who's talking.' Alec was short of breath and his eyes and nose seemed to be running but he could still defend himself. He appealed to Birdie: 'She was the one who started talking about you.'

'Don't go down that road,' Birdie said, sipping her tea. 'That's between her and me. Concentrate on what's between you and her. You've got one chance and one chance only. Blow it and you're out.'

'What chance?' Alec said.

'Don't talk to me. Talk to Grace.'

'That's right Alec,' Grace said. 'Explain yourself to *me*. And don't lie. You left your laptop switched on so I know about Mr Freel and Mr Stears and "the subject". I know about your cameras and tape recorders. I know all that. Explain what you did to *me*. Tell me just who the fuck you think you are.'

She was sitting very straight and tall. Her face was pale and as hard as china.

There was only one thing left to lie about. Alec said, 'Oh Jesus Christ, Grace. I'm only a guy who wanted a job. I had no idea I'd feel this way.' That was true – he'd had no idea he'd be standing on the rim of a chasm with his teeth wobbling and his leg half broken.

'I've had ten jobs since I left college,' he said, 'and it's been hard. I wound up at Memo Movies on a trial. They're making a film about Jack. I was just trying to get myself noticed. I was visiting all the Jack web-sites when I met you. You seemed to know everything so I hung on to you. I didn't know who you were. I didn't know I'd feel this way about you.'

'And how's that exactly?'

'Grace, I . . . ' Maybe this was the question he'd been avoiding all his life. His head felt like a toybox: he was scrabbling about, looking for something at the bottom, couldn't find it.

'Well?'

'Grace, I . . . I just want to be close to you,' he said desperately. 'I want to be part of your life.'

Miracle. For a split second it looked as if the china mask might melt.

'What about your girlfriend?' she said, bone-hard again.

This time, his mind, like anxious hands, searched his hard disc. What had she seen? What had he written?

He shrugged hopelessly.

Grace and Birdie exchanged one of those terrifying, wordless female glances.

'I don't know what to say,' he cried. 'I lied to her too. I said I was on a management course. I'll have to tell her, whatever happens here. I can't go on with her any more. Not since you.'

It felt true and untrue. His girlfriend was safe, and part of him would've given anything to be safe right now. Another part of him knew that she was from the lumpen past.

He fastened on to the bit that felt true. He said, 'I've never met anyone like you before. I didn't know I could feel . . . this way. I think you've . . . changed me.'

Grace looked at Birdie again. She said, 'Do you believe him?'

Birdie, in her red robe, detached and almost judicial, said, 'Hard to say, sugar. You must make up your own mind. Sometimes they luck into the right words. Sometimes they believe them – that's what makes it so hard. He seems to believe himself, but Grace, that doesn't mean that what he says is true.'

'Well, I think I believe him.'

'But remember, he came into this house like a spy. He courted you, cultivated you with *his own ambition* in mind. You were a convenience, a means to an end.'

'It's true,' Alec blurted out, 'but I . . .'

'He kept it going,' Birdie went on, implacable. 'You have to ask yourself, would he *ever* have come clean if you hadn't rumbled him?'

'I've been going crazy,' Alec said, to Birdie. 'In the last few days I felt I was splitting apart. I didn't know what to do. But, Grace, you've read my last e to Mr Freel – you can see I was trying to find a way to make him back off.'

Grace looked at Birdie again. '*That's* true, isn't it?' she said.

'Yes, but why, baby?'

'Why, Alec?'

'Because . . . ' This was the big one, this was where you were expected to expose your throat. 'Because what I was doing was wrong. Not just to you, Grace, although that was the worst. I was doing wrong to all of you.' He turned to Birdie again. 'They said you were a bitch . . . a sort of monster. Like you aren't really human. So, at first I thought it was a sort of game. But they were wrong, and I'm so, so sorry.'

Grace said, 'Don't you believe him?'

'Believe what? That Sasson and Barry told him I was a bitch? Yes, I believe that. That he thought it was all a game? Yes, that too. That he's so, so sorry? Grace, honey, you have to think very carefully before you believe a guy who says he's sorry.'

God, she was hard. Alec felt his eyes and nose running again. That's what always happens when you apologise, he thought. They throw it back in your teeth. He tried to wipe his nose on his T-shirt.

Grace said, 'Well, I've thought about it and I believe him. I'm going to give him a cup of tea.'

Oh you little angel, Alec thought. You *do* like me. You really do.

'Get him an ice pack while you're about it,' Birdie said languidly. 'Unless you'd still prefer to give him an ice *pick*.'

'I *am* doing the right thing, aren't I?'

'Only you can say,' Birdie said. 'Only time will tell. It's a hung jury, but it's your vote which counts.'

Blag your way in, Alec thought, and then . . .

'One piece of advice,' Birdie said to Grace, '*before* you give him anything more than a cup of tea, if you want to know where he's coming from, make him take you to Hull to see his mother.'

Oh shit, shit, shit, Alec thought. He could feel himself blushing. 'Stanmore, actually,' he said.

'You see,' Birdie said, as if he hadn't spoken, 'with relationships, you take things on faith which no way would you take on faith in business. If you don't want to get burned again, check his references. It's only fair. He's already checked yours – in fucking spades.'

Grace looked at Alec.

'OK,' he said reluctantly.

'Tomorrow? I mean today?'

'I suppose.'

'*Now* you can give him an ice pack,' Birdie said. 'And Grace, if you're satisfied and you still want him after you've seen his mum, between us we might be able to come up with a plan to rescue his job. Because, as of this moment, he's lost all his points with Sasson and Barry, as well as with you. He's an embarrassment, and they won't be as kind as you when they find out.'

'You're not going to make me quit?' Alec said in surprise. Mentally, he was already on his way to the job centre.

'Do you want to?' Grace asked.

Key question. 'Yes,' he said. 'They lied to me . . . about your aunt.'

'They manipulated you,' Birdie said, looking directly at him, the dazzling blue eyes almost pinning him to the wall. 'What do you expect in show business? But if you have a choice, my advice to *you* would be don't quit from a position of weakness. Wait till you're strong and then flounce. Whether you have a choice or not depends on Grace. I'm going to bed.'

It was as if the spotlight had been switched off and he was left in the warmer, dimmer glow of Grace's hazel eyes. He sat down, carefully, and buried his face in his hands.

Now what? Exposed, humiliated, hurt. He should be toast. Why wasn't he toast? Because Grace saved him? No. Birdie *allowed* Grace to save his ass. Why? What for?

Ah. Alec saw a glimmer of light flicker across his screen. Game over? I don't think so – there's the double game to consider, the double infiltrator, the double agent. There's information and then there's misinformation. She *must* have thought of that.

And if she hasn't, Alec thought, I'll score points by suggesting it myself.

# VI

## Here Today Gone Tomorrow

Blackened redfish with some étouffée and jambalaya on the side, complementing the sweet potato – hog heaven. Junior gazed at his plate in ecstasy. On stage were Eddie LeJeune and the Morse Playboys – another rare treat. On the dance-floor some of the best Cajun dancers in the city were executing the fancy foot-work and controlled mayhem which went with the music. Traditional Cajun alive and kickin', Junior thought. Alive and cookin', he added, piling a little of everything on to his fork.

'You can't do better than Mulate's,' he said, through the starburst of flavours.

Barry Stears nodded. 'Perhaps a little spicy,' he said, cautiously prodding the bulging area under his rib-cage, preparing it for invading enemies.

Junior did the arithmetic: good music to listen to, plus good food to taste, plus good dancers to watch, minus Barry to deal with, equals . . . Well, even with Barry alongside, he still came out ahead. Especially when Barry was picking up the tab.

'Where were we?' Barry asked.

'You're making a TV programme about Jack and you want to interview me. For a fee.'

'Right,' Barry said, mashing étouffée into his potato. 'How does that sound?'

'Fair enough,' Junior said. 'As long as it's here in N.O. – I don't want to travel, man. They're making the planes too small and they won't let you smoke. And as long as we talk about the music – I won't do the gossip. And as long as the fee's cool. I'll have to ask Sandrine.'

'I'm particularly interested in *Hard Candy*.'

'Yeah?'

'Not just the album,' Barry said. 'You went to the Caribbean, didn't you, when they were doing the demos?'

'Yeah, six weeks. We worked most nights and slept most days. I didn't come home with much of a tan.'

'What do you remember about it?'

For a moment Junior held his loaded fork suspended between plate and mouth. 'Making do,' he said. 'It wasn't a proper studio – we had to build a lot of it ourselves. There were people everywhere – wives, friends, girlfriends, kids off the beach. Sometimes they'd have the kids singing and playing too. Dustbin lids and spoons. Nice stuff, lots of fire and invention.'

'And a film crew?'

'Yeah, a handful of young guys. It was a mess, but we got the job done.'

Barry reached into his inside pocket and pulled out an envelope which he placed next to Junior's plate.

'What's this?' Junior asked.

'Photographs. I wonder if you'd look at them and tell me if you think they were taken then.'

Reluctantly, Junior put down his fork and examined eight rather sludgy colour stills – Jack and Birdie playing in the surf, Jack and Birdie sharing a hammock, Jack on a shady veranda rolling a joint.

'Yes, look – that's the studio,' he said. 'See what it was like? Jerry-built. No proper sound-proofing. Where did you get these?'

'They're stills from the movie,' Barry said.

'What movie? Oh, *that* movie. Is this the thing Teddy came to see me about?'

'It might be,' Barry said, collecting up the photographs and restoring them to his pocket. 'For a long time I thought it'd been destroyed.'

Junior looked at Barry, taking in his tailoring and trendy tie, so tight-assed and out of place among the jeans and epigrammatic T-shirts. He realised for the first time that Barry wasn't drinking. Uh-oh, hassle. He said, 'Look, I told Teddy – I never saw the movie, and Birdie never stored anything with me.'

'No, no, old man,' Barry said. 'I know that. We're a few steps further on now. I'm only here to persuade you to participate. You were pivotal to the most important recordings.'

'Yeah, I was, wasn't I?' Junior said, taking a long swig of beer.

'It's a serious programme we're making – an evaluation – about the times, the innovations, influences. How that unique sound came about, its impact on the present day.'

'Sounds OK to me,' Junior said. 'Just as long as it doesn't turn into a hatchet job. There's been too much said . . . y'know, personally.'

'Absolutely not,' Barry said. 'I know you've remained friends with Birdie, and I respect that. I wish I could say the same – after all Jack was my very best friend and I would've liked to have stayed in touch with her after his death. Maybe if things had been different I could have helped her – stopped her going off the rails.'

Junior took refuge in the food. Good food represented comfort in times of stress.

'I'm still hoping I can prevail upon her to contribute. But I'm not holding my breath. And I'm not asking you to use your influence either.'

'That's good,' Junior said, ''cos I ain't got none to use.' He was relieved to see that even if Barry wasn't emptying his glass, at least he was clearing his plate.

'I was wondering,' Barry said, 'it's a long shot, I know, but did you keep any of the production notes?'

'For *Hard Candy*?'

'For instance.'

'The record company kept all those.'

'I mean what you did in Antigua. For the demo. There was stuff on the demo which didn't appear on the album, wasn't there?'

'Sure. Some of it came out on the next album. But I wasn't involved with that.'

'I know,' Barry said, 'and I've never understood why.'

'Lots of reasons. Everyone fighting. Anyway, Jack wanted to produce himself. He'd got so's he thought everyone was trying to take things away from him, bend him out of shape. I couldn't deal with it. I came here.'

Barry nodded in approval. 'I can see why. But it'd be useful, for the purposes of our programme, if you could remember what was on the Antigua tapes. We'd like to be able to reconstruct the decision-making process – why certain songs were on *Hard Candy*, why others were held over for *Hard Time*. If you kept production notes it'd be a great help.'

'Mmm,' Junior said. 'I don't know, man. I could go through my records, see what I still got.'

'Good,' Barry said. 'That's all I ask.'

'It was a long time ago.'

'Don't I know it,' Barry said, petulance creeping into his voice. 'I've been talking to the guys – Teddy, Wills, Goff – trying to reconstruct what you all did in Antigua. Do you know, none of them remembers the same things.'

'I'm not surprised, man,' Junior said. 'There was a bucket-load of mood-enhancing substances floatin' around.'

Barry sighed. 'God, I wish I'd been there. *I'd* have kept accurate records. Stoned musos are a historian's worst nightmare. That's why notes would be a godsend – anything you've got in black and white. I'd be prepared to pay generously for them.' He leaned towards Junior, suddenly confidential. 'There's something else,' he said. 'There are other film companies on the prowl and I don't want anyone but Memo Movies to talk to you. As I say, I'll pay very generously for any help you can give me, but it must be exclusive help. Is that clear?'

'OK,' Junior said. Barry's breath was tickling his ear, making him uncomfortable. 'But exclusive ain't cheap.'

'It will be built into your fee.'

'That'd be useful,' Junior admitted, noticing with regret that his plate was empty. Production notes. What you did. When. Who was playing which instrument. How you achieved any particular sound on which numbers. Levels. Keeping track of tracks. Very organised. In theory. He said, 'I never thought what we did would have any significance two weeks later, let alone two decades plus. It was a here-today-gone-tomorrow thing.'

'Except it wasn't gone tomorrow,' Barry said. 'Or the day after that. It just went on and on, gathering significance and value as time passed. Even the out-takes – the tracks Jack rejected at the time – if we could lay our hands on those, they'd be worth a fortune now.'

'What tracks?'

'That's why we need production notes. To see if there were any numbers which didn't make it into either *Hard Time* or *Hard Candy*.'

'Right,' Junior said. 'Well, I don't remember any off-hand. You should ask Birdie. She's the one with the memory.'

'And she's the one with the negative attitude. But her loss is your gain, if you see what I mean.'

'No,' Junior said.

'Well, if she was co-operating, your contribution wouldn't be half as valuable.'

'Oh.'

'Damn right,' Barry said. 'Think about it.'

'It's a pity you can't lay your hands on any of the working tapes,' Junior said. 'Jack used to come to the studio with some really fizzin' guide tracks they'd put together themselves. But I guess that was the sort of stuff which went up in flames. That really *was* here-today-gone-tomorrow.'

He looked at the dancers – watching with pleasure the intricate couple movements, one configuration leading to another, speedy precise footwork. When the number closed, everyone clapped and went back to their beer. All gone, all the activity and artistry disappearing into silence. No reminder of their skill remaining unless you counted sore feet. Live music, live performance, existing one time and one time only. God bless 'em all, Junior thought, anything else is like pinning butterflies to corkboards – you got a dead butterfly, but you ain't got what moves you.

# Part 4

## GOING DOWN

' 'Cos you paid the price to come this far – Just to wind up where you are . . .'

Ry Cooder

# I

## The Blues

Hard cash, cold cash, cash on the nail. Nash Zalisky came through with a finely judged amount. He hadn't lost his touch: his judgment was so admirable it made me laugh. It was banknotes of a number a hard-working person would save for the trip of a lifetime – the sum needed to travel halfway round the world in comfort, stay somewhere comfortable for three weeks and then come home. Comfort is the key word, not luxury. If you travelled first-class you'd blow it all in two days.

It was an amount which wouldn't pay off the mortgage or buy a new car or put the kids through school. You couldn't go mad on it except for a very short time. But it wasn't insulting either. It was perfect windfall cash.

I packed a bag and told Robin I was going to the States for a couple of weeks. Modestly I took the shuttle to Heathrow, Terminal Four. It was a long way to go to use a telephone but details matter in this game.

When Nash came on the line I said, 'Thanks, Nash. I hope I'll have some good news for you soon.'

'Good, Birdie, good,' said his fussy little voice. 'Where are you?'

'On my way.' At the same time an announcer said, BA flight blah to Boston and blah . . .

I said quickly, 'Listen, Nash, I wanted to ask, if I run out of time or money, can you . . . ?'

Bing-bong. 'This is a security announcement . . .'

'I can wire you a reasonable amount any time, anywhere in the world,' Nash said. 'But Birdie . . .'

'My phone card's running out,' I said. 'I'll be in touch.'

'Birdie . . .'

I cut the connection and yanked my card. Then I took the shuttle back to London and went to Maida Vale. Call me paranoid if you like but from now on I don't want Nash to know my mobile number or which phone company I use. A weasel like Nash can insert himself into the smallest gap in your security system. Communications are his speciality.

Years ago, there was only one phone company and it was relatively easy to buy your target's number. I know, because Jack had to change his every two weeks or so. Now there's a whole tangle of land lines and satellite junk. More ways to communicate, but more opportunities for people like Nash to eavesdrop or tap into revealing little items like your telephone bills. I wonder how long it takes these days for the freaks to buy the stars' phone numbers?

There's no phone at Maida Vale. It's a wretched little flat and it isn't mine. But it's free and I have the key. Narrow dark stairs lead to a narrow dark hall and then this wretched dark space. I can put up with it for a short while when necessary but, oh, it dampens my spirit and cramps my style. The worst of it is that I know it's the only place I could afford if I were ever to consent to living within my means and having my means determined by the spidermen.

The place is filled with boxes and, again, most of them don't belong to me. They belong to a woman called Marielle who used to dress a glittery-glam guy I knew years ago. She ran the wardrobe and the laundry for him when he went on tour. I refused to go on tour with him after the first time. But I liked her, and while she was away I watered her plants and fed her cats. Now, many miles down the pike for all of us, her cats and plants are dead and she is in an old folks' home with premature Alzheimer's, as alone and scared as a body can be. One day she'll die, alone and scared, unable to remember her own name. Everyone's a stranger to her and every step she takes is into the unknown. At the mercy of badly paid professionals, she is allowed only four fresh incontinence pads a day. Soon, resenting even this extravagance, they'll strap her to a commode. You'd think the glitter-glam guy would help her out.

But he's driving a cab in Manchester and can't even pay his own kid's maintenance. It's just another rock-biz story playing itself out. And meanwhile I still have the key and a place to hide in.

If it all goes wrong I could end up living here permanently with nothing much to do except reflect on how cruel life is to insane, incontinent old women, and how the older you grow the harder it is to pick up the pieces and start again.

The beautifully judged mad money Nash has bestowed upon me, if it's all I make out of this, will not see me into a comfortable old age. It won't protect me from being scared and alone, nor will it buy a lifetime's supply of incontinence pads. Because, walking through this narrow doorway, that's what I think I'll need – one step into this wretched little world, and already I'm shitting myself.

I look at Marielle's cardboard boxes and I think: is this all there is? She started packing, unpacking, packing, long before anyone knew something was going wrong. Bundling up her life into smaller and smaller boxes for the trip of a lifetime to a foreign country where she would be a perpetual stranger even to herself. Her life is in these boxes, not in her head. There's more of her life in my memory than there is in hers. I can tell stories about her. She can't. It's all wiped off her screen. Blanked.

Terror-struck, I realise that the process began when she was only a couple of years older than I am today.

I jam Taj Mahal's *Natch'l Blues* into my personal CD player and clamp the earphones around my head. I press, crush, the cans against my ears as if the strength of my arms will ram music into my brain. I close my eyes tight and wait for the moment when music becomes thought and thought becomes music, when my hips move of their own accord, when pulse equalises with beat and kick-starts the heart.

It's what the Blues are for. Courage. When circumstances are crap, when you can't face life, when you can't face yourself, when you're sinking, the Blues give you grit.

Without music and money you might as well fade away and die.

# II

## Soft Touch

These days, when George Adler walked into the office in the morning, he walked with the lightest step a heavy man is capable of. He enjoyed seeing fresh flowers on the reception desk. When he came in early, arriving before Tina, he would find that although Linnet was absent, the overnight calls had already been logged and the coffee machine was primed and ready to switch on. Then he could sit alone with a steaming mug in his hand and recover from commuting, mulling over what was to be done that day, even reading the morning paper.

George was good in the early morning. Tina wasn't, she built up steam as midday approached. And Linnet was best in the afternoon and evening. As a team, he thought, the three of them worked an eighteen-hour day in shifts. He went home early, Tina a couple of hours later, and Linnet would clear everyone's desk, organise the next day and lock up.

Today though, when he arrived, he found the office already open for business and the coffee ready to pour.

'Hello?' he called, and went to his room to unpack his brief-case. These days he rarely had to take work home so his briefcase usually only held the morning paper and a lovingly prepared packed lunch.

'Morning, Linnet,' he said when she came in with his coffee. 'You're early. Something special on today?'

'I couldn't sleep.'

Her smile was so warm that he nearly missed the pallor and the shaky hand.

When she came back half an hour later with the opened mail, he said, 'Anything urgent in that?'

'No,' she said. 'Routine. There are a couple of things waiting for signature but otherwise . . .'

'Are you feeling all right?' he asked, because although she was as quick as usual he sensed an uncertainty about her.

'Yes,' she said. She turned to go and then stopped in the doorway. 'Yes,' she said more slowly, 'but I do have a problem. George, would you mind if I took off my employee's hat and signed on as a client for a moment?'

'A client?' he said, surprised. 'What's up?'

She sat opposite him on the client's chair and said, 'I'm afraid it's one of those stories where past and present collide. But the immediate difficulty is that I'm being followed and I've been forced to move out of my house. Also, I've had some things stolen.'

Later that afternoon, talking to Tina, George said, 'I could scarcely believe what I was hearing. I mean, I knew she was different. I said from the first, didn't I, that she was a bit special?'

'At length,' said Tina.

'Please,' said George, 'don't mock. I'm only saying I'd never've guessed that our wonderful Ms Walker had a story like that up her sleeve. Even *I* have heard of Jack.'

'Gosh,' Tina said. 'And I bet you've heard of Elvis and the Beatles too, you trendy old raver.'

'All right already.'

'Well, me old dear, you *are* coming over a bit star-struck all of a sudden. However glamorous the setting is, she's our Ms Walker, a middle-aged woman with a problem, needing a bit of advice. *Pro bono*, unfortunately.'

'She did offer to pay, of course.'

'And of course you declined.'

'You're giving me that look,' George said. 'I am *not* a soft touch.'

'But you do have a soft spot for Linnet. Admit it.'

'The point is,' George said, huffing gently, 'are we going to help her? Or are you prejudiced against her because she's had a racy past and a lot of people have said bad things about her?'

'Racy's putting it a bit mildly,' Tina said. 'But no. Handsome is as handsome does, and I've got to admit that she's done handsomely by us.'

'So?'

'So, all I'm asking is that you look at it coolly. Break it down. Take the drama and emotion out of it and what've you got? Just an ordinary middle-aged woman who's afraid she'll be ripped off.'

But George was having difficulty seeing Linnet as an ordinary middle-aged woman. Had he ever? If he was brutally honest with himself he'd have to say that he'd never seen her as ordinary. There was a part of him that had always felt that they were using a Rolls-Royce to deliver the milk.

'Tina doesn't seem to see that this is both qualitatively and quantitatively different,' he told Fay over dinner that night.

'Maybe Tina resents having employed someone under false pretences,' Fay suggested. 'More pie?'

'Ah, but where were the false pretences?' George asked, holding out his plate. 'She told us her name. If I was of a generation too old for it to mean something, and Tina was too young, that's our look-out, surely.'

'She gave you her proper name,' Fay pointed out, 'not the name she's known by.'

'How long can a grown woman live with a sobriquet like "Birdie"?'

'A linnet is a bird too,' Fay said, as if it were highly significant.

'The point is,' George said, irritated, 'there's something rather gallant about a woman trying, all by herself, to protect a dead lover from powerful, acquisitive forces.'

'Isn't that a rather romantic way of seeing it?'

'Romantic?' George said, startled. He stared at Fay, but she was looking back at him with nothing more than amusement in her eyes.

'Maybe it's the thought of a *pro bono* case,' he said, recovering quickly. 'Tina's very hard-headed about expenditure. The business is only just beginning to turn the corner, after all.'

'What does Linnet actually need?' Fay asked.

'I don't know yet. I'm still thinking about it.'

'You like her a lot, don't you,' Fay said musingly.

'Yes I do. So does Tina.'

'Does she?'

'Of course.' He watched Fay covering the pie dish with foil, carefully tucking down the edges. Did Tina like Linnet? Why was it important for him to tell Fay that she did? Why was he asking himself these questions? It was because of a curious expression that Tina and Fay shared. It reminded him of his mother. The saying, 'There's no fool like an old fool' popped, unbidden and unwelcome, into his head.

'Oh for God's sake,' he exclaimed, and stumped away crossly to watch tennis on TV.

Ten minutes later Fay came in with two cups of peppermint tea. She settled beside him on the sofa and asked him the question he'd been asking himself. 'Dear,' she said, 'why are you being so defensive about this? It's most unlike you.'

'I don't know,' he said with a sigh. 'I think it's because both you and Tina seem to be implying that I'm emotionally involved.'

'What's so bad about that? After all, Linnet has made your working life bearable – if not a pleasure – so it's understandable that you wouldn't want her threatened.'

'Exactly,' he said with relief. He sank back into the cushions, prepared to let the matter rest. But Fay was still waiting.

'What?' he said.

'Maybe,' she said gently, 'Tina and I are wondering about the woman who gave you some rather iffy references and yet can still make you act out of character.'

'I'm not acting out of character,' George said, annoyed. 'Do you know, Tina accused me of being star-struck.'

'No!' Fay said. 'How very insulting!'

'This isn't a joke.' He got up and stamped away to bed leaving his peppermint tea untouched.

# III

## Sex and Suicide

'The lady's a spring chicken,' Jack sings. 'No meat on her bones, slim pickings. Sleeping on my dirty floor, she says to me, she says, "no more" . . .'

I look at Marielle's dusty carpet. I couldn't bear to sleep in her bed so I laid a mattress on the floor.

In the beginning Jack and I slept on a dirty floor next to the kitchen with its creeping detritus and dripping taps. The others had to step over us to get to the cornflakes. We didn't give a toss. But we wanted to be alone so we rented a flat a couple of blocks away and we bought a bed. No chairs, no tables, just a big second-hand bed. We didn't care who'd been born, who'd died, who'd lain sleepless in it. Quite soon we bought the Camden Hill house.

Jack's graph was on the rise. Slowly at first and then steeply, up, up, and with it we rose through the lower strata of property – a sort of rake's or rock's progress – until we reached the big house in the home counties with its protective wall and gate. If the graph had continued in the same trajectory the next step would've been to the big house in a tax haven – France, Switzerland or the Caribbean, and apartments in all the cool cities. But it didn't. The trajectory ended in tragedy and here I am back on a dirty floor. Oh yes – the yo-yo motion of real estate in rock-biz – nine times out of ten you'll find yourself at the end of your string.

Blackwood Park was the house that Jack burned down. The protective wall and gate prevented the fire brigade from getting straight to it. Precious minutes were lost while panicking grounds-men searched for the spare key. The housekeeper and her husband ran around in their night-wear like headless hens trying to save their own valuables. Outside the gate, with the fire brigade stalled, the little group of fans who had set up a semi-permanent campsite on the verge cried and wailed and tried to scramble over the wall. To do what? To save Jack? Or to ask him for his autograph?

I don't know. I wasn't there so I only saw the pictures like everyone else. And everyone else saw pictures of me a day later gazing, stunned, at the wreckage. 'Ladybird, ladybird, fly away home', jeered the caption. 'Your house is on fire and your meal ticket's gone.' There's nothing so cuddly and comforting as the British press.

At the inquest, the housekeeper inaccurately said Jack had been drinking. She told the coroner that she'd served supper at ten-thirty but that Jack had eaten very little. She said he'd been 'down in the dumps'. She prepared a tray of sandwiches and snacks with a thermos of hot coffee which she left in the sitting room. She went to bed at eleven-thirty and heard nothing till the smoke alarm woke her and her husband at four in the morning.

Her husband said that after supper Jack went down to his studio in the basement. Jack was working, he said, and seemed vague, 'not quite himself'.

The chief officer of the fire service said that the blaze had been started in the basement with some sort of accelerant like lighter fluid or kerosene. He said that the beams and joists burned away and that by the time his crew got to the scene the ground floor and an upper storey had collapsed into the basement. It took them several hours to control the fire and a further two days to recover the body.

Jack's doctor said that three weeks previously he'd prescribed Valium for Jack because he appeared to be suffering from depression and stress following an arduous tour of the United States. As far as he knew Jack seemed to be a sensible sort of chap who could be trusted with prescription drugs. Laughter from the press gallery was quickly silenced by the coroner.

Jack's shrink said that Jack was experiencing paranoid delusions and that he had prescribed Mandrax because of stress and fatigue. He had been seeing Jack for six months on a regular basis – when he was in the country and when he remembered to turn up for his appointments.

No one asked for my unqualified opinion about the state of Jack's mind. All they wanted to know was why I'd left him alone, why I hadn't burned to death too – keeping him company like a good wifey. It was, by that time, already well known that I'd been at a party on board a launch on the Thames. There were pictures of me dancing with a couple of minor aristos, James Coburn and Björn Borg. Ho-ho.

I said that we'd both been invited, we'd both planned to go, but Jack pulled out at the last moment. I went because it would have been impolite for us both to bail. I didn't hear about the fire until the boat docked and we disembarked for breakfast.

The crowd outside the court booed and threw flour, eggs and vegetables when I came and went, telling me clearly that the wrong one died. It was a bad mistake to shack up with the man everyone else loves, and it was worse than a mistake not to throw myself on his funeral pyre.

A journalist once asked me what it was like to be hated by just about everyone, and I didn't answer. What could I say? It's a way of life? It's a cherished facet of my complex identity? Or should I have asked in return: what should I do to make everyone love me? Dump Jack? Mutilate my face? Go on a chocolate binge? Have two-thirds of my brain surgically removed? Die?

Actually, the question is more interesting than it appears to be, especially in the UK where brains and beauty are commodities you're supposed to conceal and apologise for. You can get away with beauty if you turn yourself into a joke blonde with big boobs and a generous heart. And you can get away with brains if you can dilute them with large helpings of the common touch and humility. But if for any reason you lead a public life and you don't butcher your natural attributes you'll face tremendous hostility. Simply by being who you are, you'll antagonise the majority of the general public.

People need to feel sorry for you or superior to you or they won't accept you as one of their own. If they don't accept you and you commit further crimes, like shacking up with the sexiest man in the country and being seen to live a glamorous life, you will be treated like a thief. You are seen to be stealing something which rightfully belongs, not to you, but to them.

So Jack died horribly in a fire and left his arrogant blonde piece alone without protection – tally-ho, open season.

Unfortunately, the people who came to help Jack's arrogant blonde piece were the people who understood and had themselves suffered from the boom and bust cycles of media attention – those who were themselves very rich, very famous or very both. Thus the blonde piece was seen to be *profiting* from Jack's horrible death – double scoop of tally-ho, open season.

I wonder, if they saw me now, on a little camp bed, with my nose six inches from a dirty floor in a dark and wretched flat, would they forgive me? Nah, probably not. They'd say I was getting my come-uppance. And who knows – they might be right. Distinction deserves punishment. We all strive for equality.

Why couldn't they wait? Age and Alzheimer's, after all, do the same job pretty completely. We all end up in a similar place. Where will the dangerous distinction be then?

So much for my problems, such as they were. What of Jack's? Did he have any? He was beautiful, talented, rich and famous – obviously no problems there. On top of that, he was loved. No one hated him. He had the most efficient lightning conductor money could buy to divert hatred. He had me. I protected him from being struck by jealousy and hatred. He was safe while he walked under my umbrella.

Lucky Jack – all those gifts, all that unconditional love and approval. That's what everyone wants. Well, maybe, but it destroyed Lucky Jack.

After all Lucky Jack started out as a rebel rocker. His hair, his clothes, his demeanour were, at that time, an outsider's slap in the face for the establishment. His songs had some hard things to say about the narrow constraints of England, about po-faced, joyless morality, about the land of hope and glory with its impotent militarism and xenophobia. His very existence was predicated on opposition.

He didn't see himself as speaking for a generation. He was speaking for himself, and then he was adopted by a generation.

When that happened he found himself in a position of leadership, bearing the weight of millions of hopes and fears. He couldn't speak for himself any more. He was representing his generation. And he found he didn't have the freedom any more to fuck up.

He was loved, and it's a lot harder to dismiss love than hatred. I at least had the freedom to despise and fight against the people who hated me. He was not allowed to show the slightest contempt for the people who loved him. Slowly but surely he was suffocated by love and approval.

The night he blew it all away we were both supposed to be on the launch chugging around Marlowe, Cliveden and other significant landmarks on old father Thames. We were supposed to make merry with the hereditary hoorays and their henriettas, with safely selected elements of show-biz and sport. I could go. I could take what they had to offer in a spirit of detachment like a thief at their table, well aware of their contempt.

He couldn't. They were offering him a place at their table without irony or contempt. We love you, Jack, you're one of us.

He wasn't one of them. But they loved him so they were adopting him too. Lucky Jack.

I went to the party and he went out of his mind.

He thought they were stealing his soul. Along with the trinkets, the clothes, records, ideas, photographs, time, which everyone was already pinching with impunity, now they were stealing his beliefs and appropriating his rebellion.

Even now they're still at it: the tele-cine lab I was secretly working at was broken into, and a reel of film – images of Jack, sounds of Jack – was stolen. Someone believes that what belongs to Jack, Jack himself, is their own property. He's loved and desired, even now. So many years later he must still give himself freely. Lucky Jack.

The last thing he said to me before I left for the party was, 'You smell of sex and suicide.'

And I said nothing because I was pissed off with him.

Sex and suicide are not concepts you talk about in a coroner's court unless you want them aired and analysed in public for weeks afterwards. I kept Jack's last words to myself.

The coroner asked, but I told him that Jack simply said, 'Good-bye, have a ball.'

I tried to imagine what would've happened had I told him the truth: 'He said, "You smell of sex and suicide," but that was normal. Jack was always coming out with stuff like that. That's the way drug-crazed rock stars talk.'

And yet I could've said that. Sex and suicide are two good s-words. They sound well together. Who knows, maybe Jack was trying out a line – they have an end-of-chorus ring to them. I wouldn't have been surprised to come home to find Jack asleep with a partially completed song called 'Sex and Suicide' crumpled next to his elbow. Waiting for me to finish it for him. Certainly I'd have been less surprised to find a song than to find the smoking wreckage of his mansion on the hill.

Speaking of mansions on the hill, I've given that soul-snatching spiderman enough time. I'll ring him from a public call box in the West End tonight after work.

'Nash,' I say. 'I might have something for you.'

'Have you, Birdie?' he says. 'Why am I not surprised? What've you found?'

'What have you arranged?'

'Ah, Birdie, Birdie, why won't you trust me? Haven't I already sent you ample proof of my good will?'

'Not ample, no,' I say. 'Sufficient but not ample.'

'Sufficient is ample,' Nash says fussily.

'Trust is expensive.'

'No, Birdie – trust is free. *You* are expensive.'

I laugh and wait.

Nash says, 'I want to see what you've got.'

'A sample,' I say. 'I could arrange to show you a sample – pay per view. Maybe.'

'I've been giving your problems a lot of thought,' he says. 'I'd like to be able to clear up one small matter for you.'

'How kind,' I say. 'Which small matter is that?'

'Tax,' he says. 'A representative of mine has been talking to the Inland Revenue. He says that they'd be willing to do a deal. You could start again from scratch for seventy-five per cent of the total bill if it were paid in a lump sum.'

'That's sweet of you, Nash. But I couldn't pay it if it were seven per cent.'

'Well, of course not. That's why you're in such a mess. It's so sad, Birdie. I wish you'd come to me before. I can sort this out for you with a single phonecall. Think about it – you could come back to the UK to live, you wouldn't have to wander like a gypsy and work for gangsters.'

'Are you calling Sasson a gangster?'

'I'm talking about a Malaysian gentleman who owns a chain of night clubs. I understand you were reduced to booking acts for him.'

'He wasn't a gangster as far as I was concerned,' I say. 'He paid me well and he kept all his promises. How do you know about him anyway?'

'I'm *interested* in you, Birdie. I wish you'd believe that. I want to help you. And to prove it, the minute you show me whatever it is you've found, I'll make that call to the Inland Revenue. There should be no more secrets between us.'

'You're going too fast for me, Nash,' I say. 'It's unnerving.' It's true, I am unnerved. He's been talking about my affairs to some bastard in the tax office. He's been checking up on my contacts. I can feel him crawling all over my life.

'Let me think about it,' I say. 'It's true that the tax bill has been an impossible burden, but it doesn't solve the problem of future earnings and . . .'

'Come here,' Nash says impatiently. 'Bring your sample or whatever you call it. Show it to me and I'll make the call.'

'No,' I say. 'Wait. I'll make the arrangements.' I will not go back to his house unprotected and I'll be damned if I'll show him so much as a nail clipping on the mere promise of a phonecall. I hang up.

# IV

## Show Time

'Who's paying for this hotel room?' Tina asked.

'Linnet,' George said. 'She gave me cash.'

'This is weird. She should be here.' Tina twitched the curtains and looked down over London rooftops and half-hidden streets. 'Cash payments,' she said, 'fingers on phone buttons. It's like buying back kidnapped children, or extortion or something.'

'Well,' George said, 'I advised her not to be here, and you wanted someone in the office.' He turned the TV round so that it faced one of the easy chairs while Tina tested the video.

'A poncey hotel room!' she said. 'We could've done this in the office.'

'Not if Linnet wants to keep her place of work confidential.'

'It won't be confidential for long,' Tina said. 'This bloke's going to check us out quick as a fox.'

'But not before this meeting.'

'And we'll be a bleeding sight easier to check out than he is,' Tina continued, looking at her watch. 'He's big-time.'

'Exactly,' George said. 'This makes sense. Don't tell him the venue till the last minute and don't tell him the room number till he arrives.'

'It makes sense,' Tina agreed, 'but only if you're totally paranoid about him bugging the room and re-routing phone calls. Bloody hell, George. I feel silly. It's only a bloody video.'

George sighed. He'd made up his mind not to defend Linnet or any of the decisions they'd made jointly but already he was acting like her advocate. 'Look,' he said, 'we all agreed. So let's just stick to the plan and get it over with.'

'Amen,' said Tina, and the phone rang. She picked up the receiver, listened and said, 'Thanks. Would you send them up.'

'Them?'

'Visitors,' Tina said. 'Didn't say how many. Come on, George, don't look so anxious. It's show time.'

A few minutes later there was a tap on the door. Tina opened it and admitted a short, stocky man in a pale raincoat.

He said, 'Good afternoon. I'm Mr Zalisky's assistant. Would you mind if I look round? It's only a formality – just a routine we go through whenever he goes anywhere.'

'Be our guest,' Tina said, standing aside and glancing at George.

George watched. The stocky man was practised and thorough. Bugs, bombs or bandits would've stood no chance.

'Amazing,' Tina muttered. 'Looks like we've got paranoia on both sides.'

It was real, George thought. Up till now, a secret part of his brain had thought he might be indulging Linnet.

He was pleased to see Tina follow their unexpected guest to the bathroom. They both watched while he closed the window and the curtains, cutting all the daylight out of the room.

'OK,' the stocky man said. 'Thank you.' He punched a button on his walkie-talkie and said, 'Everything's fine.' Then he stood in the middle of the room. 'Terrible summer we're having,' he remarked pleasantly. 'I like to play a round of golf myself but I've hardly had the chance. Oh, by the way, by all means send down for coffee for yourselves – Mr Zalisky always brings his own.'

'I don't think we'll bother,' Tina said.

'Don't blame you,' the stocky man said. 'Who do you work for, if you don't mind my asking?'

'Whoever the client is,' George said. 'In this case Ms Walker.'

'I mean, what's your outfit? What's the name of the firm?'

'Oh, I see,' said George. 'It's a small South London firm. You wouldn't have heard of it. Why? You looking for a job?'

'You never know these days,' the man said. 'Got a card?'

George patted his pockets. 'Somewhere,' he said. 'Tina?'

'Tell you what,' Tina said, 'I'll look one out and give it to you before you leave.'

'OK,' the man said. 'I must say, I don't think Mr Zalisky was expecting professionals. He thought he'd be . . .' He broke off as a knock sounded at the door.

Tina opened it to a little man dressed all in black. He blinked at her nervously through thick steel-rimmed spectacles as if his mother had sent him next door to borrow a cup of sugar and he wasn't at all sure of his reception.

'Where's Birdie?' he asked plaintively.

George said, 'I'm George Adler and this is my colleague, Ms Cole. Are you Mr Zalisky?'

The little man nodded, and George went on, 'Ms Walker sends her apologies. She's asked me and my colleague to represent her in this matter.'

'Oh dear,' the little man said, opening his hands helplessly. 'I don't know . . . I was expecting to see her. This is most disappointing.'

Tina said soothingly, 'Ms Walker has given us detailed instructions and a video to show you.'

Her tone was so maternal that for one moment George thought she was going to pat the little man on the head. He said, 'Would you like to take a seat, Mr Zalisky? Shall we get on?'

But Nash Zalisky dithered in the doorway until the stocky man opened his bag and brought out two pillows and a handful of clean white napkins. One pillow went on the seat of the chair opposite the TV. The other rested against the back. Napkins were spread over the arms and back like antimacassars. Only then did the fussy, anxious little man consent to sit down. The stocky minder stood behind the chair like a soldier at ease.

'The tape, the tape,' Nash Zalisky said, fluttering his hand.

Tina picked up the remote and pressed the play button. The screen lit up to a picture of sun and sea. Surf was rolling in, small black kids were playing beach soccer. In the background a guitar played. The camera scanned the horizon, turned and came to rest on a hammock strung between palm trees. Two young people were sharing the hammock. They looked like a pair of film stars. The camera crept closer. The man had one arm round the girl. His other hand made circles in the air.

'Ripples,' he said. 'I wonder how long before these ripples reach London.'

Tina touched the pause button and the image of the handsome man stuck trembling to the screen.

George said, 'Is this the video you want to see, Mr Zalisky?'

'Maybe,' Nash Zalisky said. 'But how do I know this isn't all there is?'

'Shall I fast-forward?' Tina asked. 'You can tell me when to stop.'

Images raced silently across the screen. 'It's all here,' Tina said. 'We haven't substituted Tom and Jerry.'

But on the screen people scampered and chased each other through the sunshine, speeding through dawn to dusk like cartoon characters.

'Stop!' Zalisky cried, and the headlong rush halted suddenly in a candle-lit room. The shuddering picture showed George a close-up of a heartbreakingly young Linnet with dim light gleaming off unruly fair hair.

'Can you go back?' Zalisky said. 'I want to see this bit.'

'I'm sorry,' Tina said. 'George?'

George dragged his eyes away from the screen and said, 'I'm afraid, at this stage, we're only authorised to confirm to you that the footage exists.'

'Just a couple of minutes,' Zalisky pleaded. 'Surely there's no harm in that?'

'I'm sorry,' Tina said. 'Our instructions are explicit: we can only go on when the money's been transferred.'

'What absolute nonsense,' Zalisky said. 'Why doesn't she trust me?' He was staring at the screen as if he thought he could persuade the blonde child to change her mind. Still staring, he held out his hand and the thickset man placed a mobile in it.

He punched a number, and said, 'Yes, this is he. Would you call Mr XYZ and confirm the arrangement we made this morning.' He snapped the phone down and turned to George. 'I'm here to *help* her,' he said. 'Has her life been *so* full of betrayal that she can no longer tell who her real friends are?'

George found himself disliking the little man so intensely that he couldn't answer. He picked up his own mobile and called the office. 'Hello there. Just to tell you Mr Zalisky has made his call.'

Linnet's soft voice replied, 'Thanks, George. I'll check that and ring you back.'

Zalisky said, 'Is that her? I'd like to speak to her.'

'I'm sorry,' George said, 'but she hung up.' He cut Linnet off.

'Now we'll have to wait,' Tina explained. 'Ms Walker wants to make sure all your arrangements are to her satisfaction.'

'This is ridiculous,' Zalisky said. 'I hope you can see how unnecessary all this is.'

'I'm sure you're right,' Tina said.

'Then . . . ?'

For a moment, George thought the little man was going to make them a counter-offer. His eyes flicked between the two of them with something like hope, but then he shrugged helplessly. The thickset man rummaged in his bag and produced a flask from which he poured a single cup of black coffee. Zalisky accepted the cup and returned to his scrutiny of the face on the screen.

The face on the screen, George thought, was extraordinary: eyes lowered, shadowed by long lashes, lips parted as if she were about to speak, luminous skin, the whole framed by gleaming, coiling hair. She seemed to be emitting light. She could have had a career in the movies, he thought, and wondered why she hadn't.

Electronic interference slashed jagged lines across the immobile face. But the horizontal lightning was powerless against such a potent image of perfect, dewy youth. The youth, the sheer lack of years, got to George and made him feel he was protecting a child, any child, his own child, from whatever harm life had in store for her.

Whatever was in store for that face had already happened. He knew that, and it almost brought a lump to his old, experienced throat. But he wondered, suddenly, if it was the same illogical emotion which was driving Linnet. Wasn't she trying to protect Jack, the young handsome subject of the film, from further harm?

After the call came through and Tina rewound the tape to the beginning, he watched Linnet the child wander through ten minutes of excerpts, barely saying a thing. She was clearly Jack's adornment, Jack's medal, first prize for simply being Jack. There was little to see of the Linnet George knew, and he wanted to stop the film and lecture the child as if she were his own daughter.

'Say something,' he might have said. 'You're worth more than this. Be yourself. If they don't like it – tough; that's their problem, not yours.'

But the only time he saw the real Linnet break through the blank mask of beauty was in a short scene near the end where she was playing a keyboard and Jack was singing. Then he saw the astonishing eyes focus, concentrate and communicate the way they did every day years later in the office. That was the only time, though, and when the scene came up he was surprised because he didn't know she could play piano. In fact, with only the film as evidence, it was surprising to find out she could do anything useful at all.

At the end, when the screen went black and Nash Zalisky said, 'What a loss, what a waste,' George had to make an effort to realise that he was talking about Jack. The film was about Jack, not Linnet – Jack, Jack, Jack, all the way. George's inner dialogue with the child Linnet was irrelevant.

Tina rewound the tape but left the cassette in the machine. She said, 'The next step is to ask you if you wish to buy the cassette with no transmission, publication or reproduction rights attached. It would be for your own personal use only.'

'It's a sample,' Zalisky said. 'A sample of what?'

'Of a film of about ninety minutes' length,' Tina said, 'and some unedited footage which survived after the film was edited.'

'Do you know for a fact that the film and the extra footage exist?'

'Yes,' said George, carefully avoiding Tina's eyes. Neither of them had seen it.

'Have I your word on that?'

'Yes.'

'You see,' Zalisky said, 'we have a problem. Of course I want the cassette. I want to examine it at leisure and I need to show it to my consortium of backers. But the consortium feels that the price we discussed prior to this meeting is too high. I've already paid heavily just to view it here.'

'The price,' Tina said, 'is not negotiable. Neither Mr Adler nor I are authorised to negotiate. We're simply here to carry out Ms Walker's instructions.'

'What the consortium has in mind', Zalisky said, as if Tina hadn't spoken, 'is an exchange.' He turned to look at George. 'This is difficult,' he went on, clasping his hands between his knees. 'As you know, I'm trying to be a friend to Birdie. I'm trying to protect her – to safeguard her future. But my backers have other ideas. I too have instructions to carry out. You must understand that I'm representing money and interests that are not my own. This, unfortunately, is business.'

'Even so,' Tina persisted, 'we can't negotiate with you.'

'What the consortium proposes is a simple exchange – one cassette, plus those reproduction and transmission rights which Birdie wants withheld, in exchange for another cassette.' Zalisky held out his hand and the stocky man behind his chair gave him a video cassette of his own. 'I'm afraid', he said, 'that when Birdie finds out about *this* piece of tape she'll want to rethink her strategy. As I say, this is not my idea, and I'm quite devastated about it. But you'll have to see it so that you can make Birdie understand that the consortium means business.'

'Hold on,' Tina said. She looked at George. 'We should discuss this.'

'What's on the tape?' George asked.

'I haven't seen it,' Zalisky said, licking his dry lips fastidiously. 'But I am assured that it's unpleasant. Birdie won't want it in circulation.'

'I'll ring her.' George punched his radial button and a moment later heard Linnet saying, 'Hi, how's it going?'

'There's a snag,' George said, keeping his voice neutral. 'Mr Zalisky wants the cassette, plus all the rights, in exchange for something you won't want to see in circulation. It's another video cassette.'

There was a short silence and then she said, 'Have you seen it?'

'Not yet. He wants to show it to us.'

More silence. George looked at Tina for help but she was watching Nash Zalisky with narrowed eyes.

Linnet said in a small voice, 'George, do you think he's bluffing?'

Without warning, George felt his knees begin to tremble. He said, 'Talk to Tina, maybe she knows.'

Tina took the phone and George sat down on the edge of the bed, staring at the blank TV screen.

He heard Tina say, 'I think it would be wise to find out. OK, talk to you later.' She turned to Zalisky and said, 'We'd better see what we're dealing with.'

She took Linnet's cassette out of the VCR and substituted Zalisky's.

Zalisky accepted the remote and said, 'I think I'll use your fast-forward technique. I don't think any of us will want to view this in real time.'

What followed ripped through George's brain like an express train. It was black and white footage shot from a fixed camera position. The location was a hotel room with the bed in the centre of the screen. A man and a girl trotted jerkily in, dancing to and fro, tossing drinks down their throats, tossing clothes on to chairs, their bodies emerging rapidly from their colourless garb like trees stripped of leaves by a strong wind. A brief scene of jolting coupling was followed with barely a pause by another in a different position.

Zalisky stopped the film at a place where both faces were turned towards the camera. The man was at least three times the girl's age. He was heavy and balding. His meaty hands gripped the girl's slender hips holding her immobile on her knees. There was no expression whatsoever on her face. It was the same blank mask of immaculate young beauty she had shown George on the previous tape.

Zalisky said, 'Sadly, I think we can all agree that we're looking at Birdie. What a shame. It really does undercut her bargaining power.'

George crossed to the window and opened the curtains. Outside, the sky was as grey as the picture on the screen. Behind him, he heard Tina clear her throat.

'Let me get this straight,' she said. 'What are you proposing to do with this tape?'

'Nothing,' Zalisky said. 'For myself, I'd burn it and all the existing copies. Unfortunately it isn't within my power to do so, and the owner of the tape has already received an interesting offer for it from a multi-media group. He would, of course, reject the offer and destroy the tape if we can come to a sensible agreement with Birdie regarding the Antigua Movie and the audio material she claims to possess.'

'I see,' Tina said. 'So you'd like us to relay this offer to Ms Walker? She should give up all materials and rights to them in return for a promise to suppress a few minutes of pornographic film. Is that the deal?'

Zalisky replied, 'I'm sorry to say that it isn't simply a question of pornography. If you force me to continue I'm told that we'll see the ingesting of cocaine, and at the end there is clear evidence that this was a commercial transaction.'

'I should bloody well hope so,' Tina said. 'No one goes with a pig like that for the fun of it.'

George turned to face the room again just in time to see Zalisky blinking in surprise. He said quickly, 'You'd better call Ms Walker again, Tina, and see how she wants us to proceed.' The anger in Tina's voice calmed him, made him feel that his own emotional reaction was not entirely foolish.

While Tina was making the call Zalisky said, 'This pains me. It really does. Please, please, assure Birdie that I'm doing everything I can to protect her. If only she'd *talk* to me I think she'd realise that I'm the only friend she's got. I do urge you to explain to her that where Jack's image and recordings are concerned we are the only game in town. No other record company will touch them once the contractual situation has been disclosed. And with this . . . er . . . pornography extant, I don't think anyone else will take her claims to title or copyright at all seriously. I would so much like to shield her from inevitable rejection and disappointment.'

George considered picking the fussy little man up by the scruff of his neck and dangling him out of the ninth-storey window until he shut up. Instead, he clasped his hands behind his back and rocked gently on his heels. The stocky man, who was still standing at Nash Zalisky's elbow, seemed to be transfixed by the dirty grey image that was still shuddering on the TV screen.

Tina put down the phone, stepped across the three men and switched the TV off. She said, 'Well, Mr Zalisky, you've given our client a lot to think about. In the meantime, thank you for coming. We'll be in touch.'

Zalisky said, 'Is that all? Doesn't Birdie at least want to exchange tapes? I wish you'd let me talk to her.'

'Our client is very disappointed with your counter-offer.' Tina sounded as if she were reciting lines. 'She instructs me to say that she needs time to think it over.'

'She has forty-eight hours,' the little man snapped. 'Even I can run out of patience. She'll have to learn to take the hand of friendship and not to scratch it.' He rose to his feet and darted waspishly out of the room leaving his minder to scuffle around collecting pillows and napkins. The minder's last act was to snatch the video out of the machine and stuff it in his pocket before hurrying into the corridor.

'Well, cheerio and *hasta la vista* to you too,' Tina said to the closing door. 'Jesus Christ, George, what a bust! I apologise. Paranoia, in this case, is entirely justified.'

George sighed and sat down on the bed. 'What did she really say?' he asked.

'She was pretty upset. But what the hell – she got all her back tax paid. That's not bad going for letting that little prat watch a ten-minute video.'

'We've still got it, haven't we?'

Tina patted her shoulder bag. 'Right here,' she said. 'I wouldn't give that extortionate little pile of parts a kick in the pants, let alone something he really wants.'

George allowed himself to smile at last. The afternoon had gone very badly, but at least he felt Tina was on the team. 'I thought you were going to have one of your famous lapses of good nature,' he said.

'Did you see his face?' Tina asked indignantly. 'I thought he was going to lick the screen. You know what's really pornographic, George? It's men's expressions when they're watching it. Not yours though. You looked as if you were watching a tragedy. Which maybe you were. Oh, fuck it. Let's pack up the VCR and get out of here.'

'I wonder what she'll do now,' George said, watching Tina fiddle with plugs and cables.

'Mr Zalisky's one hungry little bastard,' Tina said from behind the TV set. 'He'll be in touch again. Linnet's got something he wants. He isn't going to leave it there.'

# V

## Serenity

There's a rock'n'roll cliché which goes, 'If you screw up really badly on stage, pretend it's part of the act and carry on.' I tell all my baby bands that one. I also tell them not to be afraid of rock'n'roll clichés – they're there for a reason: they work.

Carrying on isn't always easy, especially if you need to carry on *con brio*. You can't buy *brio* in a supermarket. You can, however, buy it from a dealer who might call it by another name – like amphetamine sulphate or cocaine. That's another rock'n'roll cliché – one I tell my baby bands to handle with care. I'm in no position to advise not handling it at all, and besides it'd be a waste of breath. Bands do drugs or they don't. They pig out on them or they don't. It all depends on availability, personality and peer pressure. It does not depend on sensible advice from a woman old enough to be their mother.

A little white candy gives you time and space. It clears your head and returns all the *brio* you lost during the course of a horrible day. A sensible woman knows better than to take more than a little. A sensible woman knows the difference between *brio* and bouncing off walls. Besides, this particular woman only had a little. It was in her first-aid kit and it was there for emergencies.

I thought I could go home to Robin's house, to warmth and light and company. But after the way Nash turned my plans upside-down a sensible woman would keep her bolt-hole a secret and her family out of the firing line.

I am a sensible woman so here I am, back in the wretched dark place Marielle used to call home, with only my first-aid kit for company.

Like cocaine, loud dirty music is a good antidote to a busted day. It courses through the veins, racing from hips to fingertips, chasing frustration and depression out of your system.

I look in the trade papers, I search through *Time Out*, but I can't find the music I'm looking for. So I go to see InnerVersions play upstairs at the Fleece and Firkin instead.

I'm late and the first set is almost over. There's something wrong with the band – they're all isolated from one another, heads down, not communicating. The silly, baby-bastards have been fighting again. This band does not know how to use its negative energy. Great bands do. Great bands do not go into sulks and take it out on their audience. Great bands explode from inner tensions – they do not implode with a sad farty sigh. However bad a great band is on any particular night it does not depress its fans, bring them down or send them home cold.

InnerVersions piss me off. I leave in disgust, but on the way out I have an idea – an old idea, but it makes me laugh. I walk down the street till I find what I want at an all-night deli. I buy a packet of trickery and half a pound of film-flam – the fixings for a bitch-brew.

Back at the Fleece and Firkin I make sure the band has seen me but I don't join them. They're doing what they do best – which is avoiding each other in a collective huddle like a dysfunctional family on holiday. They see me and clearly they think I should come over. What do they expect me to do? Give them a pep talk? Use all *my* charge to top up their batteries while they bring me down? No thank you, I'd prefer to sit in a dark corner and work any magic I still possess for my own benefit.

After a few minutes Sapper comes over. I knew it would be him. He begins with some tedious complaint against Flambo and Dram. I smile at him – warm, affectionate, amused. It's a good smile and it puzzles him because it's such an inappropriate response to his whinging. Mysteriously, while smiling, I'm cutting slits in sultanas with my little silver penknife and I'm doing it secretively under the table.

'What're you doing?' he says, craning his neck, trying to see.

'Shhh,' I say. 'Don't be uncool.'

'Oh,' he says as if he understands, and while he's watching I slice a fragment from a small shapeless cake of a grey-brown substance. I stuff the fragment carefully into the slit in the sultana and then surreptitiously I put it in my mouth. I chew slowly and sip a little dark rum. My splendid smile becomes heavenly.

'What is it?' Sapper asks.

'Shh,' I say again. 'Serenity. Haven't you heard of it?' A good question to ask a young man who's both arrogant and ignorant.

'Isn't that something they took in the 60s?' he asks.

I say vaguely, 'It went out of style when the heavy chemists took over.'

'What does it do?' he asks.

'What is it called?' I counter. 'That's what it does. Nothing spectacular. It's a natural substance. It just makes you feel better.'

'Well then, lay some on me,' he says. 'I'm ready.'

'Sure?'

'Bloody Flambo,' he says. 'He really gets up my nose . . .'

While he's complaining and watching like a hawk I repeat the procedure with the tiny brown fragment and the sultana.

'Chew it very slowly,' I say. 'Keep it in your mouth as long as you can – especially under your tongue. A sip of rum helps bring the sweetness out.'

It's truly amazing what people will put in their mouths if someone tells them it will make them feel good. Sapper only has my word for it but he takes his medicine like a lamb. I have expertise on my side, a little silver knife, a dexterous way with a sultana, and a sliver of substance X. It looks like 60s arcana, it tastes good and by golly it'll do him good.

'Now shoo,' I say, waving him away like a child I've indulged with a treat, 'and don't come back till you're in a better mood.' I send him off, an advertisement on two legs.

Sure enough, after only five minutes, first Corky, then Karen, Dram and Flambo drop casually by for a taste of mama's little helper. Not only them but also their friends and their friends' friends. Word is out. Everyone wants a hit.

The band excepted, I make them pay. No one appreciates what they get for free. Besides, magic never comes cheap.

I do very good business. It cheers me up no end. The very novelty of it! I mean, whoever heard of a middle-aged lady dealing? It just isn't done. There's a dance in the old dame yet, and that's no lie.

The real joke of it is that when the band got up for the second set they were relaxed, grinning like lunatics and playing their tiny hearts out. They gelled, they yelled and clearly, from the audience's reaction, they hit the sweet spot. Oh yeah, I'll have them singing 'All You Need Is Love' if they don't watch out.

Drugs do what you expect them to do. You are told what you're going to feel. Everyone else tells you what *they* are feeling, so you wait for it with suspense and anticipation. Hope and expectation make you feel what you think you should feel. In this case it's serenity.

Do you know that in the 20s and 30s they referred to the effects of good ol' peace'n'love marijuana as 'reefer madness'? Who knows why. Maybe people just acted the way they thought they should act. Reefers were marketed as go-crazy stimulants so people dutifully went crazy. Nowadays Sweet Mary Jane is a chill-out soporific. Same drug, opposite effect. It all depends on marketing. So if you want a mellow evening, invest in a packet of sultanas, stuff them with scraps of diced shitake mushroom, and call your product Serenity. It's all in the name. No wonder Ecstasy took off like a rocket.

I wish I could have pulled the trick on Jack. But he knew me too well. Or maybe it only works on recreational users because, in the main, they're inexperienced and highly suggestible. Heavy users are neither.

But I don't want to think about failures tonight so I put Jack out of my mind and concentrate on the band. They're doing a song called 'Half Empty', and something nice is happening. Usually, Karen does the harmony, almost unnoticed, from behind the keyboard. Tonight, under the influence of Serenity, her voice melds with Sapper's in almost mystical exactitude. The most surprising thing of all is that Sapper – for once – is listening.

He turns towards her and then goes over to the keyboard. They sing together, breathe together, and their voices make a perfect chord.

Ozzy Ireland appears and comes over to my table. There's rain on the peak of his baseball cap and an inquisitive look in his eye. 'Staff meeting at Dog,' he explains. 'What's going on? Have you signed? They are talking *openly* about a Jack retrospective with ten new songs. There's a huge buzz on the top floor.'

'Listen,' I say, pointing to Sapper and Karen. 'Sounds good, eh? Maybe, when InnerVersions fragments, you could build a new band around just those two.'

While he's engaged, I slip away. The last thing I want to talk about is Dog and how confident Nash, Sasson and their cronies are feeling.

# VI

## A Grotesque Suggestion

'And this,' Barry Stears said, 'is Alec Parry who's done such sterling work for us. Alec, meet Mr Zalisky.'

Alec stepped forward ready to shake hands but Mr Stears blocked him. Mr Zalisky, it appeared, did not want any physical contact.

'Alec has been our eyes and ears,' Mr Freel murmured.

Both men, Alec thought, seemed buttoned-up. Breath was being held. He was excited by the tension in the room. The whole huge house seemed to be whispering, Hush, let's have a respectful silence for the concept of wealth.

Brought up on magazine articles and TV programmes about lifestyles of the rich and famous, Alec felt he should be more blasé, but now he was here what overwhelmed him was the simple fact that one man owned so much space. Here, the notion of conspicuous consumption was turned on its head: trophy possessions like antiques and Wurlitzers were booted out like so much catalogue junk. The real prize was space and other men's time. While apparently doing nothing and being nobody, Mr Zalisky commanded and received, at a moment's notice, the presence of two important, busy men. How the hell, Alec wondered, did a wizened runt manage a trick like that? It wasn't as if Alec was the only one who had been left to cool his heels for an hour in the cavernous hall. Mr Stears and Mr Freel had to wait their turn too. Astonishingly, neither man complained.

Of course Alec was the last one in and would probably be the first out, but in the meantime, here he was at the centre of the cabal. Birdie called them 'the troika'.

Alec sat in the only vacant chair, completing a square around a glass coffee table. The meeting wasn't even taking place in a proper office. They were in a vast, bare room with a deep, deep carpet and thick brocade curtains which shimmered in dim light.

Mr Freel began by saying, 'Well, Alec, my boy, Mr Zalisky wants to ask you a few questions.' He then went on to ask them all himself, with a few interjections from Mr Stears. Sir, it seemed, didn't even have to use his own vocal chords.

'I wonder if you'd go through the events leading up to our acquisition of a small can of film,' Mr Freel said.

'Well, as you know,' Alec said, 'I'd been monitoring phone calls made to and from Mrs Emerson's house, and I noticed quite a cluster for Sheeny TeleCine. I reported the fact.'

'This was before Birdie left the country?' Mr Freel asked.

'Yes, sir. So I went there. It's a scruffy place in Brook Green. They specialise in transferring film to video. I think most of their business comes from people who want to look at their old home movies on TV. They do titles and graphics and other odds and ends. Anyway, Mr Stears was looking for a film, so a tele-cine lab rang a few bells.'

'Could Birdie have known you'd found the place?' Mr Freel asked.

'I don't see how, sir. It wasn't as if I followed her there, or as if I talked to anyone who could have told her. I just had a look at the building and reported back to Mr Stears.'

'Now, the photographs you brought us,' Mr Freel said. 'The ones you thought might be stills from a movie. Has anyone noticed they're missing?'

'No one's said a word. They came from a shoebox at the bottom of Mrs Emerson's wardrobe. She . . . I don't know, sir, she collects things. There's all sorts of stuff that looks as if, well, as if she'd only keep it because it had something to do with Jack. It's a real jumble. I only noticed because the envelope had 'Antigua' written on it.'

Mr Stears turned to Mr Zalisky and said, 'Apparently Birdie's sister carried a torch for Jack. Her bedroom's something of a shrine to him.'

'I'm sure she would be really upset if she knew anything was missing,' Alec said, 'and she hasn't been upset.'

'Fair enough,' Mr Freel said. 'We're simply trying to establish whether or not you've aroused suspicion.'

'I don't think so, sir.' Alec carefully prevented himself from blinking. 'But the, er, burglary happened after Birdie went away so I don't know how she reacted when she heard about that.'

'Right. She packed up quite suddenly one night and left the next morning?'

'Yes and I don't know why. A hand-delivered package arrived. It seemed to be something she was waiting for. It might've been money, but I don't know.'

Mr Freel and Mr Stears glanced at sir, but sir remained silent.

'Where did she go?' Mr Freel asked.

'I don't know. Nor do Grace or Mrs Emerson. That's what she does – just blows without saying where. It's a bit of a joke in the family. I've looked at her passport, of course. There are immigration stamps from airports all over the world. But if she went abroad, she's back now. She called Mrs Emerson from a public phone in Maidenhead last night.'

The troika nodded. They already know that, Alec thought, disappointed.

They already knew a lot, Alec told Birdie later that night. 'What they seemed most interested in was where you go. Where are you now, by the way?'

'In Devon,' she said, the husky laugh making his ears tingle, 'but don't tell anyone.' Their secret.

'They speculated for a long time about whether you knew that I knew about the lab. And there was a lot about if the lab could manipulate sound and images. Which I couldn't really answer. Mr Stears knows more about that than anyone.'

'What conclusion did they come to?' Birdie asked.

'Well, Mr Stears said he couldn't tell without seeing the video. He said the film he had was clearly made from the original negative, but obviously anyone could switch sound-tracks if they had the original material. He said he'd have a better chance of diagnosing it if he could compare the film with the video. Mr Freel said that obviously it was the video which was manipulated because that was the one they were intended to see. But he said that ultimately it didn't matter.' Alec paused, then he said, 'I'm muddled, Birdie. *Did* you manipulate the video?'

'There were two versions,' she said, 'with different sound-tracks. They stole one – with your help. I showed Nash the other. Don't worry about it, Alec. I'm just keeping them on their toes. What did Nash say?'

'He didn't say anything. He just sat there fidgeting and making everyone really nervous.'

Birdie laughed again.

'So there was a lot of talk about what you might have done in the lab and, especially, how much time you'd had to do it.' Alec was wondering how to tell her the rest. He didn't want to upset her even if she was in Devon. But he had to warn her.

It had come unexpectedly after Mr Freel said, 'Does it really make any difference if the video was doctored? That's Jack's voice we heard on the sound-track. We're all in agreement about that, aren't we? So we have concrete proof there is at least one brand-new song – and it's unbelievably good.'

Mr Stears said, 'I know you'd be satisfied with a few extra tracks, but I've got a far more exciting idea in mind. I went over it again and again with Junior Moline. He looked up all his old notes – such as they are – and nowhere can he find any reference to a song called "Sliding Widows". He doesn't remember anything like it. Nor does Teddy.'

'That doesn't mean a thing,' Mr Freel said. 'We know Jack was planning a new album several months before he died. David Palmer mentions it in that *Rolling Stone* article. Jack kept writing up to his death.'

'But that doesn't explain the quality of the sound – especially if Jack was recording himself at home,' Mr Stears argued. 'Junior couldn't explain it either. He thought at first that it was a *digital* recording. He was convinced. But then he said it couldn't possibly be because digital recording simply wasn't around then. But he kept saying the quality of the sound was too good to be analogue. Digital didn't exist then, Sasson. But it does *now*.'

'You're crazy, Barry,' Mr Freel said. 'This is a complete red herring. This is where those "Elvis is alive and well and living on Mars" stories come from. The important thing is that we now have evidence that previously unreleased recordings do actually exist. Besides, Junior had nothing to do with any of Jack's production after *Hard Candy*. Jack produced *Hard Time* himself, working with other engineers. Maybe Birdie had the sound-track digitally re-mastered. That's done all the time.'

It was as if they'd forgotten Alec's presence and were continuing an old argument. The only one to remember was Mr Zalisky. He spoke up for the first time saying timorously, 'Maybe this isn't the time or place for such a discussion?'

It was comical to Alec that an interruption as weak and uncertain as this made Mr Freel and Mr Stears shut up like school kids caught shouting in chapel. That was real power, Alec thought, when you didn't even have to raise your voice or sound halfway confident but you could still make grown men stand to attention.

Reluctantly, he reported what Mr Stears had said. There was a moment of silence. Then Birdie said, 'Oh Alec, that's grotesque.' Just four words from a long way away but he could hear a lifetime of sadness in her voice. They continued to speak for a while longer but when at last he rang off, Alec felt heavy with her distress. He looked across the room at Grace who was curled up in a chair pretending to read *The God of Small Things* but actually listening to his side of the conversation.

'What did she say?' Grace asked.

'She said, "That's grotesque",' he told her, imitating Birdie's tone of voice.

'Well it *is*,' Grace said angrily, 'really stupid and cruel. Lin's right – whatever you give them they always want more.'

'I know,' Alec said. He was hiding his exhilaration, even from himself. He wished he still had the piece of film Mr Stears was so excited about. He wished he could use his own ears to compare the quality of the sound against a digitally remastered copy of *Hard Candy* or *Hard Time*. There must be some way, he thought, of distinguishing a track which was digitally recorded from an analogue track which had been digitally remastered. If anyone could say for sure that it was a digital recording then Mr Stears's 'bigger prize' would be within his grasp. What if Mr Stears was right? What if that was Birdie's big secret? She'd go to any length to protect Jack if he were still alive.

'It's so absolutely dumb and off the wall,' Grace said, as if she could read his thoughts. 'If Mr Stears is hinting Jack's still alive he's out of his mind. Wouldn't I know about it? Wouldn't Mum? I hope he keeps shit like that to himself. Poor Auntie Lin.'

'Don't you get sad too,' Alec said. He went over to her and sat on the arm of her chair. 'It's all right. Mr Stears is an idiot.'

Grace nestled against him. She was, he thought, both harder and softer than she had been before the night of the big bust. He never quite knew what to expect.

She said, 'If it wasn't so tough on Mum and Auntie Lin, I'd say I wish he'd say it out loud and get so much egg on his face he'd never be able to show himself in public again.'

'May he die of lingering humiliation,' Alec said.

'Then we'd appoint you Managing Director of Memo Movies in his place.' Barry Stears, since the big bust, had become the scapegoat, the author of Alec's corruption. Grace in particular seemed to find Barry Stears a useful excuse for all his wrong-doing. Long may it last, Alec thought, grateful that she needed an excuse as much as he did. She likes me, he thought for the hundredth time.

'What does your Auntie Lin do in Devon?' he asked, stroking Grace's hair.

'She goes fishing,' Grace said. Her cheek was resting on his thigh. 'She's got an old friend down there. An old boyfriend, Mum says.'

'Fishing? I can't imagine Lin up to her thighs in cold water.'

'You'd be surprised,' Grace said. 'She says it's the most fascinating occupation in the world. She's quite zen about it.'

'Is she zen about the old boyfriend too?' Alec coiled a lock of Grace's hair round his forefinger and held his breath.

'She never says a word about him. You know what they say about old flames, don't you? They never die – they just cool off. But all you have to do, if you want to revive them, is to blow on them. Shall I show you?'

'Ooh yeah,' he said, 'go on then.'

Devon, Alec thought as he tumbled on to the floor.

# VII

## Thank God for Lipstick

Every song has to come to an end. While you're recording, if you can't think of a proper ending the fade will save your ass – repeat to fade. On stage live, however, you need to find a way out and hit it with conviction. Give the audience something to applaud. Of course that can cut both ways: you might be giving an audience the perfect chance to boo and chase you off-stage with flying beer cans and other messy missiles. You can find yourself after a gig, cowering in your dressing room, swearing to give up music for ever. If you don't like risk, I tell my baby bands, get a job in a dry cleaner's. It's much, much safer.

Real life, sometimes, is like playing live. There's no graceful fade when you run out of steam. You either have to carry on carrying on or you have to come to a dramatic conclusion. For all the planning you put into a certain phase of your life it's hard to see how it will end. Will you be taking encores, or will you be shivering in your dressing room? It all depends on whether or not you've made your audience dance to your tune. Have you been able to please a hostile crowd? Or have you not?

I knew when I began this phase of my life that I was facing a very hostile crowd. Now, it doesn't look as if I'll be able to get off-stage without beer in my hair. There was a message on my voice mail from Tina Cole which said, 'Linnet, sorry to ring you so late. I don't know how he got my home number, but I've just had a call from Mr Zalisky. He wants to remind you that you only have twenty-four hours left to come to an arrangement with him. He says that you should present yourself and *all* the materials, both audio and visual, at his home. You may bring representatives, but you must come in person. I said I thought it was unlikely that you'd agree to an arrangement like that, but he ignored me completely. He said if you don't deliver, you will get nothing but grief. That's all.'

I lay down on the canvas lounger and wondered what smart-as-a-whip Tina Cole would do now? No advice from her. She thinks he's just saying put up or shut up, when actually he's saying, Birdie Walker, I've got *your* number. You're nailed.

It's interesting that Nash picks Tina's home number, not George's, to demonstrate his infallibility. I bet he had a choice. I bet he thought about it and decided she'd be the more objective conduit for his message.

Karen tells me she has dreams sometimes of standing on-stage in front of a packed house playing a number she doesn't know on a keyboard which is slowly turning into a tablecloth. Every time she moves her hands another couple of keys have become useless and she'll soon be reduced to playing with one finger. Maybe Karen is dreaming for me.

I slide headphones over my ears and listen to one of the great rock'n'roll dreamers until I find enough consolation to think about sleep. It's five in the morning and dawn's breaking. For most of my life I've gone to bed with the lark. Take that how you will – I'll take it lying down.

I remove the headphones just in time to hear someone hammering on the door downstairs. Hammer away, I think, there's no one at home. Marielle's not here, and nor am I.

Then, as the knocking continues, a lifetime of training kicks in. I get up and flush the contents of my first-aid kit down the toilet. I brush my hair, powder my nose and put on a good pair of shoes. Trapped in Marielle's wretched apartment, if someone comes in, I can neither fight nor bolt. In any case, as the song says, I'm a lover not a fighter. If someone comes in and I am, as Nash hinted, nailed, I want to greet the intruders looking good.

I won't make it easy. I won't open the door for them. But whatever weapons I have I'll use. Unfortunately my best weapons are useless against brute force. A smile, wit, charm and good shoes only work against those who are vulnerable to them.

The hammering increases in volume and ends with a splintering crash. Heavy footsteps on the narrow stairs come to a halt at my door. Then the cry: 'Police. Open up.'

Police? Unbelievable – pull the other one.

But it is indeed the police. 'We have a warrant to search these premises.'

'What on earth for?'

'Illegal substances.'

'Please tell me this is a joke,' I say. 'What illegal substances?'

'We must ask you to accompany an officer to the police station.'

I am stunned. I refuse. But, as the song goes, 'When the Lord says "Get ready", you gotta go.' So I went.

Here is the kicker – as I went out on to the early-morning street with a policeman on either side of me two flashguns went off in my face. I wasn't expecting them and I didn't have time to turn my head. I was, as Nash implied, nailed. When the police and the press are in cahoots there's nowhere to run, nowhere to hide.

The story broke in the first edition of the evening paper the very same day. There was a picture of me on the front page. I'm flanked by two smug cops and I'm looking straight into the lens with a defiant expression on my face. Thank God for lipstick, I say, because, cruelly, the picture editor also inset an old photo of me dancing with Jack from over twenty-five years ago. There we were, supple and slender, bright hair flying, without a care in the world. And here she is now, old superbitch in a raincoat, allegedly caught dealing drugs to school kids at a nightclub – the woman the British public most loves to hate.

Yes, yes, they rifled the archives and resurrected my history. They reprinted bowdlerised versions of the worst stories. They said that my fight for control of Jack's fortune had ended in failure and that after my looks faded I'd been reduced to prostitution and drug-dealing to make ends meet.

I shouldn't have been surprised. When they really want to hurt a woman the media always accuses her of faded looks, sexual depravity and vice against children. No, I really shouldn't be shocked or upset. It is, after all, only more of what I was so accustomed to when I was young.

The funny thing was that when I saw the pictures and read the article I was tucked up in Tina Cole's spare bed with a glass of her best Scotch to calm me down. Free. The police didn't charge me with anything, because of course there was nothing to charge me with. They couldn't put me in jail for sharing a packet of sultanas with a bunch of kids.

Eventually, they admitted that they'd been misinformed. But they didn't apologise. They said that they did not alert the press. I pretended not to believe them, but I do. That piece of planning has someone else's fingerprints all over it.

The police never apologise; they simply release you into an indifferent world without a stain on your character. The world is indifferent because it is only interested in stains. Clean is boring. Clean does not get your picture on the front page.

'It's not such a bad picture,' Tina says. 'You don't look like a criminal.'

What does she know about good or bad pictures? She's never had photographers hiding at the bottom of her stairs or under gratings trying to see up her skirt. She's never had to use kitchen doors, fire exits or lavatory windows when she wants a little privacy. I can't imagine her covered by a blanket on the floor of a car because she's had a little too much to drink at a party and doesn't want it splashed all over the papers the next day.

She's still trying to come to terms with the notion that her reliable, organised Ms Walker is a woman with a past and a debatable reputation. She is, herself, a straightforward person. What you see is what you get. She can't quite appreciate that in me she got unimaginably more than what she saw. She wanted efficiency and know-how. Well, be grateful, Tina Cole – that's exactly what I gave you. Don't blame me because you saw only what you wanted to see.

She says, 'I don't understand why the police thought you were dealing drugs.'

'Because they were told. Someone must've seen me with the band. But this has nothing to do with drugs, Tina. It's about searching the place where I was staying. It's about reducing my bargaining power. It's about what's done to notorious women.'

It's so strange, isn't it, Tina Cole, to find out that your quiet Ms Walker, with her respectful manner, mixes with rock musicians and kids in clubs. It isn't dignified in a woman her age. OK, so maybe we all went a bit crazy when we were young, but most of us grew up and hid the Strat in the cupboard under the stairs. Most of us got married, bred and paid mortgages. Most middle-aged women would rather stay home and watch *Love Story* than racket around in clubs after midnight. Or would they, Tina Cole? Maybe older women do what's expected of their age group rather than what they'd like to do.

Which is worse, Tina Cole, a woman suspected of dealing drugs or an *older* woman suspected of dealing drugs? A woman racketing around by herself in a club or an older woman doing the same thing? It's a fine point, but a telling one. If you want the question answered, read the evening papers – they'll tell you exactly what to think about your oh-so-respectable Ms Walker.

My two worlds have collided in a way I never intended.

She says, 'These new songs, materials, whatever it is Mr Zalisky wants – what's happened to them?'

I sigh, and tell her simply that they're safe. But she's read the article. She's read the paragraph which said, 'A leopard does not change its spots and it seems that Birdie, after so many years in the wilderness, is still trying to feather her nest at a rock legend's expense. A spokesperson for a well-known record company today said, "She approached us several weeks ago with tapes of dubious provenance that she claims are Jack's last work. If true, this would be of inestimable interest to the record-buying public. But as no one has yet been allowed to verify the quality, or indeed the existence, of these songs we cannot comment." With the twenty-fifth anniversary of Jack's death coming up we shouldn't be too surprised if many such claims surface. There is still a fortune to be made from the sales of records by dead rock-stars.' The article then went on to evaluate the posthumous worth of everyone from Elvis to Kurt Cobain, giving them marks out of five and using little money-bag symbols as counters.

Without a doubt this article is killing several birds with one stone, and I am the least of them. I don't have to rack my brains to decide who gave the journalist this information. Or why.

Tina says, 'Why does the record company spokesman say the tapes may be bogus?'

'Because he wants to say that I'm bogus. He wants to say that my ownership is bogus. He wants to create a buzz and drum up controversy – is this the real Jack or is it a clever fake? One way or another it's great advertising for the record company and terrible publicity for me.'

'It's sneaky,' she says, nodding.

' "She approached us",' I quote. 'Doesn't that sound shady? Isn't it a wonderful choice of words? "With tapes of dubious provenance." Peddling dodgy bootlegs in car-parks. You'd never guess from that who's been importuning whom, would you?' I sigh again.

'Well, look, why don't you get some rest?' she says awkwardly. 'We'll sort something out later.'

'I'm not asking you to sort it out,' I say. 'It's way too murky. Besides I know what you charge. I work for you, remember. Or I used to work for you before I got my picture in the paper as a drug dealer. That won't look too cool, will it, in your line of business?'

'Oh, bugger that,' she says. But she's thought about it. She'd be a fool not to think about it, and she's no fool. She leaves, closing the door softly as if I'm an invalid – an unemployed invalid.

I sit on her spare bed and massage my feet with hand cream. The good shoes, which made my legs look long and slim in the photograph and which caught the eye of a detective inspector, have crippled me. They were never designed to be worn for fourteen hours straight. They're impress-the-punters pumps which should be removed before your feet swell and you need a can opener.

Someone ratted on me. I think about lines of communication and who is in touch with whom. I think about my baby band. My mind settles on Flambo: not only is he a piss-poor drummer but he blames me for rearranging InnerVersions, rearranging their sound and consequently for marginalising him. He got high on Serenity. Therefore Serenity, for him, is a real drug and I am a drug dealer. If he wants to get rid of me, ratting on me to Sasson might be the way to do it.

I noodle on it sleepily. If Flambo were not such a piss-poor drummer, would I be so quick to call him a rat? Even now, after all these years, I'm still liable to believe that good musicians will be better human beings than bad musicians. It's been proved to me a thousand times in a thousand ways that good art does not, *per se*, come from good people. And yet, and yet . . . Maybe I will always be susceptible. If Flambo were a shit-hot drummer I would not automatically suspect him of being a rat.

And anyway, it doesn't fuckin' signify who ratted on me. The only person to blame is myself. I disobeyed the first law of bunko – which is never, never, never pull a stunt on your own doorstep.

On the other hand, maybe that doesn't signify worth a damn either – if the troika wanted to hang me out to dry they'd have found a way without Serenity.

# Part 5

## AIN'T GOIN' DOWN

'She's sweet – does she mean it? . . . She's mean – I think she
means it.'

Jack

# I

## Patchwork

In a drawer beside Robin's bed was a rose-coloured silk sachet. The rose silk was shot through with gold and silver thread. It came from a Kashmiri scarf which Jack once gave Lin and which Lin once left behind after a flying visit. Robin appropriated the scarf. It was her favourite, she wore it all the time. But small children who experiment with paint and scissors are very hard on favourite garments. The scarf retired, injured. Robin was never a woman to give up on beautiful favourites, so pieces of it appeared in one of her layered hippie skirts, in a tiny waistcoat she made for Grace, and a sachet she made to hold pot-pourri.

Now, as well as pot-pourri, it held an ugly shapeless lump of metal – a gift, again inadvertent, from Lin. She came home in the dead of the night, after that dreadful, empty day, her face scraped bare with shock and grief, her clothes smelling of charcoal and her hands balled into fists. Robin, utterly bereft herself, badly needing comfort herself, with no words, no consolation to offer, simply opened her door, her arms, to her widowed sister. And Lin opened her clenched fist to show the ugly fragment hidden there.

'The Egyptian ring,' she said. 'He was wearing it. Oh Robin, there was nothing else. Keep it for me. I've held it for hours. I know it's insane because it's been through fire but I've been trying to keep it warm. And I can't. It used to be lovely. Now it's hideous, but it's all I've got.'

So Robin kept it. And with it she kept the smell of charcoal and ashes, of killing smoke, of soot and smuts, trapped in a misshapen lump which had once been bright Egyptian gold. Every so often she changed the pot-pourri because, even now, she sometimes woke up with tears in her eyes, certain that she could smell smoke. Lin never asked for it back.

Robin was sure she hadn't forgotten – how could anyone forget a thing like that? But that end had been the beginning of a rootless, drifting existence for Lin, with never a place to call her own, never a place to settle down and gather treasures around her. Because a week later she disappeared, chased out of Robin's house by door-steppers, unceasing phonecalls and envelopes dropped through the letter box.

Twenty-five years ago, Robin thought, and it seemed like yesterday. Especially now. She peered through a crack in the curtains and could identify at least half a dozen strange cars in the street outside. She couldn't answer the phone and finally Grace unplugged it.

'They're mad,' Grace said. 'Auntie Lin pushing drugs? Why are they saying these things?'

All Robin could do was shrug helplessly. 'They've always said terrible things about her. I don't know why.'

'I bet there are whole chapters about it in feminist psych books,' Grace said. 'Punishing famous women or something like that. If there aren't there should be. Maybe I'll write one if I stick to psychology.'

'Why wouldn't you stick to psychology?' Robin asked anxiously. 'Is it Alec? Is he telling you to give up your job?'

'Don't be silly, Mum. But women's lives seem to go where the wind blows and it might be more fun to blow back to London. Maybe I'm tired of serious subjects. A job in film or TV . . .'

'I thought you liked psychology.'

'I did. I do. But at the moment all I'm doing is helping no-hopers. I'm like a junior social worker. You can't expect me to stick with a career I've grown out of.'

'Have you grown out of it?' Robin asked quite tartly. 'I'd have thought a little understanding of human behaviour might be pretty useful to you.'

'It's Alec, isn't it? You've never liked him, have you?'

'I never said that. But I do think he could've been more honest with us.'

'Well he's being honest now,' Grace said, 'and if that isn't good enough for you we can both leave.'

Why did everyone always leave her or threaten to leave? It seemed to be everyone's ultimate weapon. And it worked. The thought of the people she loved dropping out of her life frightened Robin and made her obedient. It caused no end of trouble too. Even the threat of putting her crazy old mother in a home where Robin couldn't keep an eye on her had driven her into an action which exasperated her husband. Me or your mother, he said. Choose. She couldn't choose, and her husband left.

She wanted everyone. She knew what it was like to live with a gaping hole in her heart where a loved someone had been, and she didn't ever want to repeat the experience. Even if it means a lifetime of . . . of what? Servitude? The word 'blackmail' fell with a thud into the back of her mind.

Without thinking she reached out her hand and plucked a white Venetian mask from the top of her chest of drawers. She held it in front of her face and said in hollow, theatrical tones, 'Go, my child. If you have learned all I have to teach you, then go. A strong woman has no need of her mother. My work here is done. Go, and,' she added, running out of invention, 'may the force be with you.'

'You're a nutter, Mum,' Grace said, laughing uncertainly.

Robin tied the mask securely on to her head and opened the curtains. All at once, a man with a camera popped up from behind the hedge and took her picture.

'Come away,' Grace said. 'They'll think you're Auntie Lin.'

'Tough,' Robin said. But she stood back from the window. She kept the mask on because she didn't want Grace to see the beads of sweat on her lip or the fear in her eyes. Even joking she couldn't tell Grace to leave without paying a heavy fine.

'We're going stir-crazy,' Grace said. 'When's Alec going to come back with the bread? Where's Auntie Lin?'

'I don't know,' Robin said. 'She can't phone 'cos she knows I won't answer and she won't come here with all these idiots on the doorstep.'

'Maybe she's gone back to Devon.'

'Maybe.'

Twenty-five years ago there had been islands and villas and yachts to escape to, Robin thought. Where were they now? She couldn't imagine any of those rich stars, made respectable by longevity, swooping down like knights in shining armour to scoop Lin up and spirit her away this time. Not after this latest sleazy, seedy, slimy smear. Which no one was bothering to retract. Lin no longer looked the part, no longer looked like the child princess in distress. All the ageing knights and princes had grown-up families and supermodel brides to support. This latest slur cast Lin as the wicked old witch. Princes don't gallop up on white horses to rescue wicked old witches. Wicked old witches burn in their own ovens, Robin thought. Only the young and lovely are fit to be rescued. Even ageing princes knew that. Especially ageing princes. The old and the wicked must, perforce, rescue themselves, if they could. Or burn if they couldn't.

The smell of charcoal and smoke mixed with pot-pourri drove Robin out of her bedroom and up to the attic to work on a garment fashioned from a thousand pieces of silk remnants. Somewhere, she thought, there was still a square of the old rose-coloured scarf. She searched through her boxes.

If I find it, shall I use it? she wondered. No. Or only if I make this into a dress for Lin. Lin's scarf was Lin's past. No one else deserved it. However much a private client was prepared to pay, Robin knew she couldn't sew a remnant of Lin's story into a garment which Lin wouldn't wear.

Bugger that, Robin thought. And bugger the rich private client. I'll make this silk patchwork into a dress for Lin. I'll clothe her in her own beautiful youth, in her fairy-tale past.

Robin paused for a moment, picturing Lin swishing into a room wearing the riot of glowing colours. She nodded, and Lin smiled back at her. Yes.

Swirling Lin morphed into spinning Jack, strutting in front of thousands of screaming fans in a coat of many colours. Robin made the coat for him and he wore it on his last tour. Perfectly cut to swing and shimmer under spotlights, to be seen from the back rows of theatres and stadia, to let his fair skin breathe in the heat and

264

frenzy of performance – it was Robin's best work. And like Jack it went up in flames twenty-five years ago. Gone.

Time tangled itself in a knot and Robin sewed, pinned and cut till lunchtime. A shape was forming in her mind, a queenly shape, a garment to be worn with pride. It must have a high collar, she thought. Lin, you won't hang your head in this frock, no way.

Downstairs, in the kitchen, she found that Grace and Alec were making toast. Some of yesterday's chicken soup was simmering on the stove.

'Sit down, Mum,' Grace said. 'Alec wants to tell you something.'

# II

## Negative Energy

'No,' I say, 'no, no, no.' Oh I have power – the power of refusal. I can't make stuff happen the way I want it to, but I can stop it happening.

'Your forty-eight hours,' Tina reminds me.

'Not mine,' I say. 'Forty-eight hours was arbitrarily and unilaterally imposed by Nash.'

'Haven't you taken enough stick?' she asks reasonably.

'Yes,' I say, equally reasonably.

We're sitting in her living room. Three of us. The curtains are closed. Outside, lurking, is a handful of reporters. Someone whose name we can only take a wild guess at knows I'm here and has leaked Tina's address. She, in spite of her reasonable tone, is angry. George is worried. He sits in a deep armchair, his fingers playing nervous scales on his ample shirt front.

'But if you talk to Nash,' she says, 'won't he call the dogs off?'

'He can try,' I say. 'But I think his understanding of dogs is incomplete. They're harder to stop than to start. Please take my word on that one.'

'Isn't it worth a try?'

'From your point of view it is, from mine it isn't. I can solve your problem by finding somewhere else to stay – which I will do; this is no way to thank you for rescuing me from the police station.'

'Stay with me,' George says.

I smile at him – he's very sweet. 'Thank you, but that'd only transfer this gig to another venue.'

'I don't think Fay would exactly rejoice,' Tina says.

'She wouldn't,' I agree, 'and I'm not going to do it.'

'Well, what *are* you going to do?' she asks. 'It seems to me that there are two ways to go: one is talk to Nash Zalisky, and the other is talk to the press.'

'The third is leave the country,' I say. 'That's what I usually do in these circumstances.'

'You'll lose everything,' George points out. 'Plus you risk having that pornography released on the Internet or whatever Mr Z plans to do with it.' He shifts uncomfortably. 'I wish that damn lawyer would pull his finger out and get here.'

That damn lawyer is someone he and Tina trust. Their in-experience is most obvious here. The lawyer is not a music-biz lawyer – he has that in his favour, but he has that against him too. Talk to a lawyer. Talk to Nash. Talk to the press. All reasonable suggestions – if you don't know lawyers, Nash and the press like I do.

I am tired. I drank too much Scotch last night hoping it would help me sleep. Fatigue and hangover are sitting between my ears like twin incubi, jabbing my brain and giving me visions of other times when it all went wrong. They winkle out the memories of loss and theft, of impotence and humiliation. They speak through my mouth and say 'no' to every suggestion. They have hidden all my chutzpah in their deep dark pockets.

'I'll make some coffee,' I say, and I leave Tina and George to make their naïve suggestions to each other. I go to the kitchen pretending to be quiet efficient Ms Walker. She may be in a jam, she may be causing a jam, but she's ever so helpful and she uses real beans. Her mask is perfect: she's useful, tidy, organised. She expends her energy in the service of others. And she doesn't cost much.

Birdie grimaces behind Ms Walker's tidy mask.

The phone rings and is answered. A moment later, George comes through to the kitchen. He says, 'It's Mr Z. Tina's talking to him.'

I let him carry the tray and follow him.

Tina shields the mouthpiece with her hand and says, 'Mr Zalisky is summoning you to Badlands. He's sending a car.'

Tidy Ms Walker says nothing. She begins to pour the coffee.

'Linnet?' Tina says. 'You don't have to go alone. I'll come with you.'

'So will I,' says George. 'So will that damn lawyer when he bloody gets here.'

'Mr Zalisky says that you'll have all the protection you need from the media at Badlands.'

Ms Walker hands George a cup. Black, no sugar. She knows what he likes. She places a cup on the table beside Tina. White, one sugar. She considers Mr Zalisky and his summons. She knows what he'd like, too.

'Linnet?'

I say, 'Tell Nash thanks but no thanks. Tell him that Ms Walker will be making a statement to the press – the sort of statement which will have the media camping on *his* doorstep within half an hour of its release. And press helicopters flying over his house. Tell him especially about the helicopters and how noisy they are. If he can lie about me, I can lie about him. And I'm *way* more inventive than he is. Tell him further that I've put up with shit before and I can do it again. He isn't hurting me, he's just raising my price.'

'But he *is* hurting you,' George says.

'As for his forty-eight-hour deadline,' I say, smiling pleasantly at George, 'here's one of my own: tell Nash that unless he comes up with an acceptable offer within forty-eight hours I will call a press conference in Hyde Park, at the site of Jack's last free concert, and I will explain the situation and then publicly burn all the materials, both audio and visual. If I can't do one last honest deal for Jack the whole lot goes up in smoke. The symbolism will be very clear.'

'For God's sake, Linnet,' Tina says. 'You won't do that.'

'Try me,' I say. 'What have I got to lose? Money? If Nash has his way I'll be robbed blind anyway. My reputation? I never had one. Tell Nash it's cash or conflagration. His choice.'

Tina looks at me as if I'm a child having a tantrum. Mature women negotiate reasonably. I walk away and go to the spare bedroom before she can talk me down. That was my message, Tina Cole. Deliver it.

Ten minutes later they come to find me, and by that time my

bag is packed. I say, 'The usual procedure is a decoy car at the front door and a greengrocer's van at the back – in the absence of which, I'll call a cab. I'll contact you at the office later.'

'Stop it,' Tina says. 'Let's talk about this.'

'All right, but there isn't much alternative. I know you think I'm being destructive and unreasonable, but this is an unreasonable situation. Mature, reasonable folk with mature, reasonable aspirations don't succeed in rock'n'roll.'

'So you put a gun to your own head and say, "If you don't give me what I want I'll pull the trigger", is that it?'

'Sounds pretty much like it,' I say, and start to laugh. 'What did Nash say?'

'He said you were wilful and cutting off your nose to spite your face. Then he hung up on me.' She thought about it for a moment and then said, 'Wilful? I haven't heard that one since I was about five years old. He really does think you're a moron, doesn't he?'

'Well,' I say, 'he thinks I'm a hysterical greedy woman. Same thing maybe.'

George says, 'Did you mean any of what you said?'

'Oh yes.'

'Then start with the press release,' he says. 'I wouldn't mind seeing Mr Z take a dose of his own medicine.'

'Right away, Mr Adler,' I say, 'as soon as I get settled. It's top of the list.'

'Where are you going?' Tina asks. 'Look, I know I'm pissed off with the twats outside but I think you'd better stay. George won't forgive me if I let you go.'

The phone rings and she goes to answer it. George looks at me and says, 'She's right – I won't. She isn't asking you to leave, you know. I know you think you should but it isn't necessary.' He has a relieved, twinkly look in his eyes. I know that look. I've done something which pleases him. What is it?

He says, 'The thing about Tina is that she's very concerned with fairness. Unfairness makes her angry. She isn't angry with you.'

Ah, that's it. Efficient Ms Walker has behaved like a child throwing a wobbler, which you'd think was a great big turn-off. But in fact sweet George digs it. It allows him safely to hold my hand, protect me and explain the world to me. Essentially, it has allowed him to become parental in his relationship with me. He can act in the mask which suits him best – the Good Father's mask. Yes, sweet Mr Adler is at his most comfortable as the Good Father.

'Tell me about the tapes,' he says. 'Are they really so valuable?'

'Yes. And no. They're just songs taped on a little four-track. They were only meant to be guide tracks. But death and age have given them enormous value. There's a mystique too. It's all part of the unfairness. Why does one singer gather mystique and value and another drop out of sight? Why is fame and success splashed so liberally on a few and not on others? It's neither fair to the famous nor to the forgotten. Value doesn't necessarily have anything to do with quality. Jack's tapes are extremely valuable because so many people want them.'

'And for no other reason?'

'They're good songs,' I say. 'But that's not what's causing all the fuss, is it?'

'No,' he says. 'Fame and notoriety are causing all the fuss. What I want to know is how valuable are they to you?'

'I can't say.' I think about it. 'If your house was on fire, and all the people you loved were already safe, what would you rescue?'

'Ah yes, that question,' he says. 'But you say you'll destroy them.'

'Yes.'

'Wait a minute,' he says, 'something's coming back to me. In olden times, some parents would murder their own children rather than let them be taken into slavery. I don't agree with it but you can see their point.'

If you let a man answer his own question he will find an answer he understands. He may not understand *you*, but an answer is generally a satisfactory substitute for understanding.

Fortunately Tina returns before the dear man's answers become even more absurd. 'Well, well, well,' she says, 'your lousy reputation's working in your favour for a change. Mr Zalisky seems to think you're capable of acts of vandalism and self-destruction beyond my wildest dreams. What a way to do business!'

'He believes her?' George asked.

'We-ell, maybe he thinks he can't afford to disbelieve her. Linnet, what did you ever do to the man? He's very, very weird about you.'

'I went to the movies with him once a long time ago,' I say. 'But it isn't me. He's weird about Jack. It's that old mystique again. Jack had it in truckloads.'

'No,' Tina says. 'he's weird about you. Why do I think he's a pervert?'

'A pervert?' says Good Father George.

'I want to send myself to the laundry after talking to him. Why?'

I just smile and shake my head.

'And how did he get to be so rich and powerful? He's such a warty little shrimp.'

'He does challenge evolutionary theory, doesn't he?' I say.

'It really frightens me when two women discuss a man they don't like,' George says. 'So would you mind sticking to the point. What did the warty little shrimp agree to?'

Tina consults her phone pad. 'Well, subject to Linnet's approval, the suggestion is that we send our lawyer over to talk to his lawyer.'

'Lawyers,' I say. 'He's got them in football teams. We've got to discuss that.'

# III

**Q** *BIRDIE WALKER: As mad and bad as ever. 'Jack did what Jack did. Shit happens.' Now the face that launched a thousand hits takes on Super Spider. Who's your money on?*

Words: Ty Casparo
Photographs: Roy O'Brien

*It is one of those soft late summer days and the overgrown garden behind the Chelsea Arts Club is suspended for a moment between sunshine and showers. Ms Walker sits on the terrace with a glass of wine in her hand treating the aging hipsters to a rare glimpse of Birdie unbuttoning.*

*'Rule number one,' wannabe music scribes were taught back in the bad old days, 'Birdie walks, but she doesn't talk.' Those were the days when rockchicks were mad, bad and dangerous to know. So how's she feeling today? Bad? Not so's you'd notice. Dangerous? Well you might want to avoid those Ibiza-trash heels. Mad? Ah, now you're talking! 'Mad as hell,' she steams.*

*She is not, as you might suppose, referring to her recent arrest for allegedly dealing mind-altering substances to minors. 'If it weren't so stupid it would be funny,' she says loftily. 'It's not my fault if someone can't tell the difference between a handful of sultanas and Class-A drugs.' Not something you could accuse Birdie herself of. 'History,' she retorts with a flick of the once-famous golden mane. 'I'm not apologising for the past.'*

*But wasn't it the excesses of yesteryear that added her legendary lover Jack to the list of drug fatalities? 'Jack did what Jack did, and he didn't do anything by halves. Fame, drugs and paranoia can be a destructive cocktail.*

*Shit happens.'* Shit happening seems to be on the Bird brain today and that's what's making her so mad. *'Jack was convinced the record companies were ripping him off and, surprise, surprise, they still are. More than ever now with Jack's anniversary coming up – all the old stuff repackaged, prepackaged, your usual multimedia T-shirt, Jack-on-the-rack culture – co-ordinated by Super Spider.'*

Super Spider, it seems, is Birdie-speak for Nash Zalisky, the eccentric, reclusive mogul behind many of the pipelined Jack projects. *'He always wanted to lure us into his web,'* Birdie shudders. *'If Jack hadn't died, Super Spider would've sucked him dry. Not many people know that Nash was totally obsessed. He still is. He's been searching basements and rubbish bins for anything to do with Jack: photos, nail clippings – you name it. So he comes to me and says, "What've you got?" And I'm like, Whoa! I'm not into the necrophilia thing. Besides, why should I give him anything of Jack's? New stuff, new deal – or no deal.'*

Hold on a minute! New stuff? Can the original Rock Widow mean that there's a secret legacy snatched from the grave? It seems she can. A forgotten stash of demo tapes and some unique sought-after movie footage have miraculously surfaced just in time for the eagerly anticipated Jack-fest. But we aren't talking about mere nail clippings now, are we? *'We are not. Dog spokesmen want to downgrade what's been discovered but that's for the usual exploitative reason: they want to own it but they don't want to pay.'*

Almost from the start, Birdie claims, corporate double-dealings left Jack with the lifestyle of a megastar but practically zilch in his pockets. *'It's a rockbiz cliché,'* she seethes. *'The people who take the profits aren't responsible for the losses. They take the bread and the people who make the music live on the crumbs. Jack didn't even own his house or his car. What's worse, he didn't own his music.'*

So who does? *'I do.'* The brilliant blue eyes gaze out defiantly. *'It's something the record companies never accepted. But I worked with Jack and I can prove it.'*

Quite a claim. True or false? Someone who worked extensively with Jack, and witnessed relations between the glamorous couple, told **Q**: *'He'd start a song; she'd finish it. She'd come up with a line; he'd construct a whole theme from it. Being in the same studio as those two was like watching a game of ping-pong. They were almost inside each other's heads.*

But of course Jack was the star so Jack got all the credit. That's the way it was in those days.'

Not everyone interpreted the relationship in quite the same way. 'She was riding on his back,' one source close to Jack's band informed **Q**. 'He was the golden goose and she had a taste for foie gras.'

The face who reportedly launched a thousand hits doesn't deny it. 'Sure I enjoyed the high life,' she admits. 'Who doesn't?'

It's a lifestyle that she may enjoy again if the contractual mare's-nest of the past twenty-five years can be resolved. But without a new deal, she insists, there will be no new music. 'It's great stuff but I'd rather burn the lot than sell Jack into slavery again.'

Birdie, if anyone cares to remember, is no stranger to the tragic results of fire, so you're forced to the conclusion that she means what she says. Behind the blonde hair and innocent blue eyes there's a core of pure steel. 'No, it's not an idle threat,' she chirps. 'I haven't come all this way just to make things easy for someone I think of as a prime case for natural deselection.'

Ouch! Watch out, Super Spider, Birdie Walker sharpened her talons long ago, when rockchicks really knew how to be mad and bad. She wrote the book on dangerous-to-know back in the days when such things mattered. Today, it seems, she's going by the book.

# IV

## Feel Like Shit and Ashamed

My sister has made me a dress. And what a dress! There's nothing else like it in the world. It is unique and when I put it on I am unique too. There are no designer labels and it cost her nothing but time – by which I mean that it cost her the whole of her life and experience, her hands and her eyes.

Years ago, I took her gift for granted. 'Oh, Robin will make you something,' I said to Jack when he wanted a certain kind of stage costume. Anyone can sew if they've got the patience and nothing better to do. Robin's patient and she's got nothing better to do than run you up what you want. I knew she'd make him something marvellous because she adored him. Adored him but bored him. There was always something abject in her devotion. Sugar and no spice.

Oh but there's spice in this dress. And wit. Look at the collar – it rears up and then curls gracefully over below the ears. It's a collar which forces me to hold my head high and stare into the mirror-mirror-on-the-wall. This is a dress for me *now*. Today. It is not feathers for a bird-brained chicky-babe.

Tina taps on the door and comes in. Her eyes say, 'Wow!' when she sees what I'm wearing, but her mouth says, 'Are you ready? I was going to call a cab, but someone's sent a car.'

'Call a cab,' I tell her through the mirror. 'Send the car away.'

'But it's a Rolls,' she says wistfully.

'Nash bugs his cars. But keep it outside your door if you want to look good.'

'I'll get rid of it,' says puritan Tina. No ostentation without good reason. 'But we ought to get a move on or we'll be late.'

'Exactly,' I say. 'We're going to be late. Relax. Make a cup of tea and chill.'

I have my reputation to consider. Am I the type to turn up dutifully, on the dot, and then wait patiently for the honchos to get their act together? I am not. Nor is this dress. Robin has made a garment worth waiting for. Nash sent his car, but it is not, as Tina thinks, a mark of respect. He wants to know where I am, and when I will arrive. It is a symbol of control. Go suck your tiny thumb, Nash. I'll come when I'm good and ready.

Tina is uneasy. In her world they're punctual and reliable. They prove their worth by doing what they say they're going to do when they've said they're going to do it. In my world you prove your worth by winning the status games. Hurry-up-and-wait is a losing gambit. All it will do is prove to the opposition how easy you are to control. If I showed up on time I'd be telling Nash he'd got me beat, that I'd been frightened and brought down by public exposure, that my own threats had no sting. Whereas what I want to tell him is that time's on my side. I've got Jack in my pocket, the way I always had, and if he wants Jack he'll have to deal with me. I am Rainbow Woman, Nash Zalisky, fuck with me and you'll never see your pot of gold. What a difference a great frock makes!

I sit in the cab while George pays the driver, then I get out and sweep into Dog Records' lobby in one fluid swoop. I leave my briefcase in the cab, forcing Tina to retrieve it and hurry after me carrying it. We meet our two lawyers.

I have four in my entourage. Not as many as I'd like, not as many as I used to have, but four more than I've had for ages. Two lawyers, one security man and one PA to carry the bag. That's how it will look. Tina tries to return the bag to me, but I ignore her. Silly woman – whatever is she thinking? Rainbow Woman doesn't carry her own bags.

We go up in the lift to the top floor and find Sasson waiting to greet us. Good – that's more like it.

Now here is a strange thing: Sasson takes my hand and kisses my cheek. 'God, Birdie,' he says, 'you look stunning.'

He waves my party of four into the boardroom but he delays me.

Now we will have to enter the meeting together – which will indicate, to those present, an alliance or friendship. Sasson cannot be ignorant of the visual language of meetings.

He says, 'Birdie, whatever happens, please believe that I was not responsible for the smear campaign. I wouldn't do that.'

' "Whatever happens"? What *is* going to happen, Sasson? Any more tricks up that midget sleeve?'

'Not that I know of. I think your legal team's done a good job – a better job than I'd personally like.'

'You mean it's a straight deal?'

'I mean, Birdie, you don't want to make the pips squeak over every damn percentage point. There's such a thing as being *too* tough, you know.'

'I just regret not getting tough years ago when Jack was alive.'

'Ah yes,' he says, just for a split second looking like young Sasson.

I wonder how much he allows himself to remember. Is there a tiny corner of his memory which makes him feel that he let Jack down? Or has he armoured that tiny corner and remembered only the fiction: that I drove a wedge between him and Jack.

He says, 'Birdie, before we go in, is there anything I should know?'

'Like what?'

'I don't know – anything else you're hiding, another ace in the hole that'll up the ante again. I've got a lot riding on this deal. I'd like to think, now we've got the finance sorted out, we could work together.'

I don't get a chance to answer because Nash bustles out of the elevator with his bodyguard. However late I was, he wanted to be later. I laugh. I look at Sasson and he can't resist it. He laughs too.

'What? What?' Nash asks, suspicion flaring behind his glasses.

Sasson straightens up first. He says, 'Nash, good of you to come. Shall we go in now?'

'I don't know,' Nash says warily. 'I had a terrible dream. I nearly didn't come. I nearly didn't get out of bed. Birdie, have you ever had a dream so bad that you feel the whole day will be cursed?

Remind me to tell you about it. What a beautiful dress, Birdie. Did I buy that for you?'

'Not a chance,' I say, letting the old laughter linger in my voice. 'This is a dress no mere money can buy.'

'Oh,' he says to Sasson, 'we've been paying her too much.'

'We'll see,' Sasson says. 'I can't wait to hear the new tracks.'

'Why are we standing out here?' Nash says plaintively, and Sasson leads us into the boardroom.

I slip into a chair between George and the more savvy of the two lawyers. Nash sits at the centre of an army. Sasson, as host, sits at the head of the table with an array of board members and advisors. The only one not present is Barry Stears, which is strange because the deal involving the movie is with him.

Everyone turns and watches me sit down. I am the show, the girl in the spangled tights. Roll up, roll up, the notorious scarlet woman has just made her entrance. Watch her balance on the wire – soar or floor – it doesn't matter as long as there's a spectacle.

I lean towards the savvy lawyer and whisper, 'Where's Barry Stears?'

'I'm told he had to go to the US suddenly. That's his proxy over there.' He indicates another grey spidery man with the smallest flick of one finger. The savvy lawyer has played this game before: he knows the value of *sotto voce* conferences with his client. Nothing important is said. Sometimes, at a strategic point, he leans towards me and says something idiotic like, 'Bit warm in here, isn't it? I wish they'd turn the air-conditioner up.' And I look down at his unreadable notes nodding sagely. The secret agenda: you've got to have one even if you haven't got one. Otherwise, I sit back, nonchalant, relaxed, legs crossed, shimmering in my rainbow garb.

The main deals are these: first, the new Dog album; sub-clauses, my participation in arranging and producing it, publishing, copyright, the videos, reproduction and mechanical rights. Second, Memo Movies' film; sub-clauses, visual material to be supplied by Ms Walker, sound-track and rights thereto, interview fees etc. Third, the authorised biography; sub-clauses, Ms Walker's agreement to be interviewed and supply previously unpublished photographs.

Hanging over all this is Nash's deal with Dog and Memo, giving him TV, Radio and CD-ROM/e-commerce rights. In other words, Nash wants the world première on everything, because he is number-one spider, and he can afford it.

Most of this was thrashed out by grey men, including *my* grey men, over the previous few days. From my point of view the offers are now adequate and the payment schedule is satisfactory. Even better, my lawyers have set up a private bank account for me with a subsidiary account in . . . wait for it . . . yes, in the Cayman Islands.

With this account in place and the knowledge that I've forced all three parties to do separate deals rather than allow myself to be bundled tidily into one all-encompassing contract, I can afford to sit back.

In fact, I am secretly jubilant. I have brought us to this stage without ever letting the opposition have a proper sight of what they're buying. The old-fashioned method of seduction has a lot to recommend it. Do not display your wares because to do so would cheapen them. Conceal and hint. Build hunger, and then in a carefully contrived accident, flash a little flesh. Ooh yeah – I've gone back to long skirts and petticoats for this deal.

From across the table I catch Nash staring at me. I lower my eyes shyly and think, yep, attempted rape only drives the bride price up, I wonder if he understands that now. I hope not. Let him think he's forced me to this table. Let him think that my counter-threat began as a tantrum and ended with one mildly snide article in **Q** magazine. Now he thinks there's a chink in the wall – I've broken my silence once, so I'll be easy meat for any interviewer he chooses to feed me to. I have all the stories, the essence of Jack, locked in my head; let him think he's found the key and I'll spill my precious load into his waiting hands. Well, Nash, we'll have to see about that.

But eventually, the time comes when even Rainbow Woman has to show and tell. All parties, including mine, are satisfied so far. Now they want to see the bride's face.

I ask Tina for the tape cassette and the video cassette. She gives them to me with a rather sour look. I expect that while this meeting has been grinding on, she sat there silently wondering what the hell she's doing. Good Father George isn't wondering. He knows he's here to protect me. But Tina, being rather more sceptical, has probably come to the conclusion that her only purpose is to look like a personal assistant and bag-carrier to the woman who used to tidy her office. Tough break, Tina, but that's show-biz.

'What do you want first?' I say, turning to Sasson, 'music or pictures?'

'Music,' he says. 'Do you mind if I ask my chief engineer in to hear this? I know we won't be listening to the masters yet but I'd like him in on this as early as possible.'

I smile and say, 'Of course.' I'm pleased with Sasson. He's provided the dramatic pause. During it I get up and walk over to the sound equipment. I keep the tape and video in my hand. Even these simulacrums of the real deal are too valuable to give to anyone else.

I look at the sound system, the giant speakers, the Star Fleet control panel. Mooching, figuring out how the system works, I have separated myself from my team, from the ranks of suited spiders. I am music, they are business. Music versus money. Romance against finance.

The silk rainbow swirls against my thighs as I walk to the window, turning my back on the table, looking out over the Soho rooftops to the clouds beyond. There are faces and fungi in the clouds. It is a dreamer's sky, full of morphing images. No two people will see the same picture on the cloudy canvas. No two dreamers will dream the same dream. That is the art of clouds and dreams. Those are the clouds and dreams of the artist. And these are the thoughts I can't afford to be thinking in the company of spiders.

I turn back towards the room and find that every eye is upon me. Nash is getting out of his chair to join me at the window. Oh no, that'll never do. I let him commit himself and then I glide around the other side of the table and out through the door. Leaving the boardroom without explanation, carrying with me the cassette and video. I cause pandemonium. Unbelievably, several of them chase my skirt as it flicks out into the corridor.

In the open-plan office at the end I stop at the first desk and ask for the ladies' room. The chasing posse is there to be ignored. I sashay into the ladies room and lock the door.

It is extraordinary. Am I a rogue elephant or a psycho? No one, it seems, has the slightest idea of what I'm going to do next. Am I really so unpredictable that I cannot avoid Nash and go to the ladies room without being treated like an absconding prisoner?

In the mirror I look at my reflection and smile. Unpredictable, exotic Rainbow Woman is still, for the time being, in charge of the goldmine, the means of production, the wealth of the grey nation. No wonder they're scared shitless.

By the time I return, the grey nation has assumed some semblance of dignity, leaving just one scout by the elevator to make sure I 'don't get lost'. But I cannot sit at a table with them any more. I need the separation, especially if I am to listen to Jack's voice. After I've slotted the cassette into the deck I go back to the window and turn my back on the audience.

Jack's voice begins, husky with cigarette smoke, 'Gimme time, gimme one last chance . . . ' The opening line of 'Adversarial Attitude'. There is solid rich rhythm guitar under his voice and some honky-tonk piano providing the fills. It's the timeless song of the ill-treated man, his stone-hearted rival and the stolen woman. It's violent and insulting: 'She says he's steady, kind and sweet – I know the whoring, boring man who beats his meat . . .' Jack calling poor Homer a wanker in his own inimitable fashion. Anger stretches his voice and gives it the horn-like power which can cut through any rock'n'roll band, however loud, and dominate it. If you heard that voice only once, even if you never heard it again, you wouldn't forget it.

I stare out at the clouds remembering how the hair on the back of my head prickled when I first heard Jack. I remembered thinking that no one could possibly mistake that voice for any other. And how he stuttered on some of his consonants, 'My b-baby', partly playing for time if he came in a breath too early, partly the result of taking speed. Whatever. It was impossibly sexy. Standing alone, staring at clouds, remembering, I can feel even now the lurch I felt long, long ago.

The tape rolls on. I left a couple of false starts in. Jack says, 'Fuck it, babe. What're we doin' here?' And I say, 'G, A minor seven and G. Split bars, remember?' 'Yeah, right,' says Jack and begins 'Hopeless Case' again.

Another time he says, 'What's it say here, Birdie-bird? I can't read your writing. Whadya mean you don't know? It's your fuckin' song – I'm just the poor bleedin' singerman.'

Once he says, 'Take three, fuck it. This time, doll, skip the harmony except on last words and the last line of chorus.' And I say, '*Thank* you, Maestro', in a sarcastic tone as if that's what I'd been telling him all along.

Mostly though, I've been very kind to the grey nation – apart from three superficial interruptions, I've given them ten good takes of pure Jack. I do not want to belabour the point I'm making. Which is that they must not assume that Jack wrote alone or worked unaided. They must not assume, as they always used to, that little Birdie-bird was there simply to roll his joints and warm his chilly toes.

The tape rolls on until there's nothing but audio hiss to listen to. Nobody moves. Nobody says anything. I don't bother to look at their faces but I leave the window and eject the tape into my own hand. Then everyone starts talking at once.

This is a charade of my own making and I can't blame anyone but myself. I feel like shit and ashamed. That's one of Jack's lines in 'Coal Dirty Soul' – 'Feel like shit and ashamed, rode the roller 'til I went stone blind . . .'

Now is not the time to walk away. I should've done that years ago. But I didn't, and now I have to stand here like a huckster in the market place with my goods in my hand, peddling what can never be paid for.

Maybe you can't bridge the gap between art and money. Maybe you can't ever sell what's precious to you without feeling like shit.

Ah fuck it, I think. We've been here before. If you feel like a slut, make 'em pay through the nose. We all sell whatever we've got to sell – skill, muscle, time, sex. We don't have to respect the buyer, but we've all got to eat. Jack wasn't pure. Only his voice was pure.

Sasson comes over to where I'm standing, contemplating the

cleanliness of clouds. He lays his arm around my shoulders and says, 'Well, well, Birdie dear, you *did* have something to sell, didn't you? That was the real McCoy. Very good quality for cassette tape. But you do have the masters, don't you?'

'Of course.'

'I won't ask you where you found them.'

'No. Pointless.'

'But if there's any more . . .'

'It's never enough, is it, Sasson?' I shake off his arm and turn to face him. 'What more do you want?'

'Nothing,' he says quickly. 'Really, Birdie, nothing more. It's just that I didn't know anything about these songs. They aren't left-overs or make-weights. They're fresh and whole and alive.'

'Unlike the poor singerman,' I say. 'You don't have to sell them to me, Sasson. I'm selling them to you.'

'And I'm ready to sign,' he says. 'I don't mind telling you, Birdie, a couple of days ago I thought your agents were pushing too hard. But now I'm not so sure.'

Nash calls out from his side of the table, 'Are there cue-sheets?'

I say, 'Yes. I'll give them to Sasson with the masters.'

'I'd like to see them now,' he says waspishly.

'No can do,' I say. 'Besides, the music deal's with Dog.'

'Who do you think owns Dog?'

'I think you own the whole world, Nash, but you'll get the cue-sheets when you get the masters.'

My savvy lawyer butts in to remind Nash of the payment schedule: front money first, contract second, materials third. But Nash silences him. 'When were these songs written, Birdie? Before *Hard Candy*, after *Hard Time*?'

'Before, during and after,' I say vaguely.

'Aren't there any production notes?'

'There wasn't a producer, Nash. Just us. We didn't make notes. We didn't write a diary. And before you ask, there aren't any hand-written, dated, lyric sheets either. I made the cue-sheets when I transferred the masters to cassette.'

'And when was that?'

'After I found the masters. What's the matter, Nash? Are you afraid I'm holding out on you?'

He looks up at me like a worried gnome who's about to burst into tears. 'I don't know, Birdie. You never tell me anything.'

Sasson says, 'Shall we move on? We should take a look at the visuals now.'

Blinds are drawn, lights are dimmed, and I am denied the consolation of clouds. But I'm less in need of consolation for visual images. Images of young Jack and Birdie do not move me with anything like the force that Jack's voice does. I am hardened against pictures of myself, and pictures, in any case, have less power over me than music does. I'd give you my eyes to save my ears any day.

Pretty people in pretty places – so what? Picture postcards. Flick through, see Jack walk and talk. Amazing, huh?

Around the boardroom table the grey nation watches Jack turn his head to look out to sea, and yes, it's such a pretty profile. There's sun on his face and wind in his hair. Good ol' Jack – for ever young and beautiful – one of the world's most marketable men. He had it all in an age which wants it all. The singer's a genius: fine, yawn. The singer's a beautiful young genius with a lop-sided sexy smile: woh-yeah, *now* we're cookin'. Video did indeed kill the radio star. It gave birth to a whole generation who could only listen with their eyes.

The Memo Movie team are all leaning forward, watching intently, and again I'm surprised that Barry is absent. This was what he wanted. Sasson at the head of the table is taking notes. Nash, who has seen some of this before, is watching me.

I go back to my seat between George and the savvy lawyer. George whispers, 'How're you holding up?'

'OK,' I say. 'I wish it were over.'

The savvy lawyer says, 'Don't worry, everything's fine. We've covered all the bases.'

From across the table Nash's reptile eyes blink slowly and my hand, in response, closes tightly round the audio cassette. He will have recorded my recording – of course he will – in spite of the veto my lawyers put on copying. But a copy of a copy won't help him much. It will just join his collection of stolen property.

Soon, the lights are switched on and refreshments are brought in. There's tea and coffee, sweet and savoury nibbles. I notice, on the bottom tray of the caterers' trolley, ice buckets with bottles of a very good champagne in them. All you can eat and free champagne, just sign on the dotted line.

The Memo Movies men bat me questions about film stock, format and the condition of the materials. My savvy lawyer and his honest but inexperienced colleague field them. One of Nash's representatives asks for and receives a handful of photos. He asks if negatives are available. They are. My savvy lawyer shows them. He collects the video from the machine, he brings the photographs back to our side of the table. The small hoard still belongs to me. So far I have signed nothing away.

The lawyers buzz around in circles comparing amendments, inclusions and deletions, shaking crumbs off the contracts. We are almost ready.

Sasson says, 'I suggest we begin with the music.'

Everyone shuffles back to their places. Sasson is straining at his tether and chivvying.

I whisper to the savvy lawyer and he raises his hand. 'My client would like to begin with her agreement with Mr Zalisky.'

'Birdie, *please*,' Sasson says impatiently. 'Surely the music is at the top of the list.'

I shake my head and my savvy suave lawyer digs his heels in. Birdie is being capricious again. She won't budge.

Nash turns the pages of his copy of the contract as if he's never seen one before in his life. It's as if the decaying little boy is rummaging through birthday wrapping paper, searching for a present he might have missed.

'Nash?' Sasson says. 'Would you mind kicking off?'

Nash hands the contract to one of his lawyers to tidy. He looks at Sasson and me. The lawyer shows him where to sign and hands him a pen.

He puts the pen to the paper and waits for me to do the same. As I start to write he puts the pen down and sits back in his chair. His expression is sulky and dissatisfied. He says, 'I don't know. I'm still not sure.'

Sasson turns his impatience on Nash. 'What aren't you sure of, Nash? We've heard the tracks. Everything is as Birdie said it would be. Now, please, may we get on?'

'Oh, well, yes,' Nash says uncertainly. 'The tracks. Magnificent, of course, but I keep asking myself, are we contracting ourselves to the wrong party?'

'What on earth . . . ?' says my savvy lawyer. 'We've spent hours, days, establishing title.'

'Nash,' Sasson says warningly, 'you gave me your word.'

'Well, I suppose I did.' Nash dithers with pen and contract. Then he drops the pen again. 'It's no good,' he whines, 'I can't quite bring myself to do it. I'm sorry, Sasson, but what if Barry's right? Wouldn't we feel just awful if we signed this extortionate deal with Birdie when we should be signing with Jack?'

A thick silent fog drops on the room. People peer at each other, eyebrows raised. They look at me.

Sasson says, 'This is absurd. Birdie, I'm so sorry. This wasn't supposed to happen. Barry thinks Jack is still alive. He's gone to the States to look for him.'

I cannot think of a thing to say. I glance around the shrinking room. The walls are creeping towards me. The grey nation's grey faces sway in my direction like giant mushrooms.

Nash's slitty little mouth moves. His voice sounds like an owl hoot. 'I could've spared you this, Birdie, if only you'd come to me. I don't really understand Barry's reasoning and I'm sure neither Sasson nor I concur with him, but there you are. He's convinced. What could we do?'

'You could've tried harder to talk him out of it,' Sasson says disgustedly. 'You didn't have to lend him your plane. And you certainly didn't have to introduce the subject now.'

'Ah, but Sasson,' Nash hoots, 'keen as we all are, we cannot be party to a fraud.'

Only my sister's clever dressmaking keeps my head erect.

'Yes, Birdie,' Nash says, his frog-spawn eyes magnified behind his glasses. 'I'd love to sign, believe me. You know I have your best interest at heart. But Barry, well, he was always such a *fan*, don't you think? He's sure he'll find Jack alive on a small island off the

Florida coast. I hope you won't be too upset but we'll have to postpone the signing till after his return.'

My two lawyers are on their feet, arguing. Nash ignores them. He says, 'I wish you'd trusted me, Birdie. Mistrust, you see, breeds mistrust. And now look what's happened. Barry is utterly out of control. Do you know, he's so certain that he's found Jack's location that he's taken your sister, Robin, along to help him with the identification.'

'Catch her,' George's voice booms in my ear, 'I think she's going to faint.'

# V

## What's Done in the Dark
## Will Come to the Light

In the night, Robin listened to the roar of the engines. It filled her head, driving cotton wool thoughts into a stampede. Everything was too loud: jet planes, cars, baggage carts, human voices, all chewed up and blended in the air-conditioner.

Robin was not a good traveller. Nervous of flying, prone to air sickness, a martyr to jet lag, she always felt she'd left three-quarters of her brain at home with all the other essentials she'd forgotten to pack. And nowadays she could add swollen ankles to her list of miseries. Swollen ankles and disillusionment.

Flying in a private plane should exempt you from the discomforts of coach-class travel. There was a bathroom, with scented soap and face spritzers, so why did her skin feel oily and bloated? Why were her fingers puffy and clumsy? The food was freshly cooked in the galley and presented with an elegant vase of flowers, so why was her stomach bubbling with gas exactly the same way it did when she couldn't distinguish fish from foul fowl on normal flights. Surely millionaire moguls should have solved the problems of earache and flaky elbows in their private transport.

Oddly though, discomfort was a comfort to Robin. It filled her mind with small, pressing spikes and distracted her from a huge and terrible vertigo. If she opened her eyes and looked ahead she would certainly see where she was going, and she'd know that although the jet was flying, she was falling.

Without indigestion to concentrate on she would have felt like thieving Judas – stealing her sister's life. Lin's life was planes and travel. Lin always said, 'Gotta go,' and then hopped it without explaining. Robin was the one left behind. Lin rang up from Paris, LA, Bangkok. Robin was there to take the call. Strange men sent cars to carry Lin to strange places. Robin left a covered plate of food in the fridge for when she returned.

Robin still wore her ex-husband's ring years after he emigrated to New Zealand with his new family. Robin kept Jack's Egyptian ring in a sachet next to her bed for twenty-five years. She did not fling down her life, leave her daughter alone with a stranger, abandon her sister at a difficult time and whizz off to the other side of the world at the word of a fat man she didn't trust.

Barry Stears, the pickpocket of rock music, always trying to squeeze into the same frame as the talent, jealously eyeing his neighbour's plate, receiver of stolen images – he had told her a theory so unbelievably laughable, so laughably unbelievable that, if it were true, it would turn the last twenty-five years of her life into a mockery.

'You're insane,' she said. 'You're pathetic.'

'No, listen,' he said.

'Get out of my house,' she said.

And here she was unable to sleep or think. Because she was going to squash the cruel story flat. Laugh it into oblivion and save Lin the trouble. Really.

Really? Wasn't it just as likely that she was a pitiful straggler climbing up Glastonbury Tor on midsummer eve, hoping for a glimpse of King Arthur's ghost? Arthur lives and is watching over England. One day he will return to lead his people and all that crap. UFOs. Atlantis. The Second Coming. Pitiful.

But something sick and triumphant made Robin write a note to Grace: 'I'm off to the States. Shouldn't be gone for more than a couple of days. Look after yourself.' Borrowing Lin's attitude, Lin's handwriting almost. Gotta go. See you soon. Love.

Alec, furious, dropped a bottle of milk on the kitchen floor. Shattering glass, milk splashing on his shoes and trousers, allowed him to swear – fuck, fuck, fuck, fuck, fuck.

'Just mop it up,' Grace said, irritable too, but for a different reason.

There was no reason that Alec could see. So she had to make her own breakfast once in a while. Big fucking deal. It wasn't like she'd been kicked out of her own game, back to level one, after doing all the work, and having all the inspiration which should have taken him to level ten. To the airport. To the States. Grace wasn't the one who'd cooked up all the arguments that had allowed Mr Stears into the house and kept him and Mrs Emerson talking. All she did was look at him narrowly every now and then and say, 'Whose side are you on?'

'Yours,' he'd say every time. 'Yours, a hundred and twenty-five per cent. Don't you see? This is for you. It's like an abscess. It needs to be lanced.'

'If it's true,' she said. 'But it isn't true.'

'Then Barry needs to be zapped before it gets any further. One way or the other we've got to get involved. Don't you see? We can't let him run around like some renegade. We've got to know what he's up to.'

Playing both sides wasn't a game for amateurs, he decided. Make one little mistake and both teams would come down on you like a ton of rubble. And now, on hands and knees, sloshing around in spilled milk, he seriously considered packing it all in and heading for home.

Devon was my error, he thought. The old bloody boyfriend in Devon.

'Devon?' Mr Stears said, perking up. 'Are you sure? Why didn't you tell me before?'

'I didn't know what you were thinking,' Alec said. 'And besides I only just heard about it.'

'An old boyfriend? Does she go regularly? How long does she stay?' Mr Stears seemed excited. 'Good work Alec. See what else you can find out.'

But a day later he said, 'Absurd, what on earth made you think Devon was the target? Don't you know anything about Birdie yet? If she says south-west, the best place to start looking is north-east.'

I bet you didn't come up with that one all by yourself, Alec thought, annoyed. He said, 'But she does go to Devon, Mr Stears. Grace is sure of it.'

'Well, of course she does,' Mr Stears said tetchily. 'Homer Webb has a farm there.'

'Who's Homer Webb?'

'He's one of Birdie's old boyfriends,' Mr Stears explained with exaggerated patience. 'But he's the wrong old boyfriend.'

You might've remembered that yesterday, Alec thought.

'I know there are a lot to choose from,' Mr Stears said, 'but you'll have to do better than Homer Webb.'

Like this whole Jack-hunt was my idea, Alec thought. But he did come up with something better. And it was something that had been staring him in the face ever since he came to stay in Grace's house. Every morning. It was one of the things that was so different from his own lumpen family. Mrs Emerson made coffee with real beans and, here's the cruncher, she juiced real fresh oranges – the Produce of the State of Florida, USA.

'I'm glad you like it,' she said when he complimented her – as he was always careful to do. 'They're the best juice oranges in the world. Lin sends me crates of them.'

It was an unremarkable tit-bit of information which went unremarked for weeks while Alec was supposed to be tracking down old movies, film labs and sound-tracks. But suddenly bells rang when he began to search for traces of Jack.

Florida oranges. Crates of them sent by Birdie to her sister in England. Why would Birdie go to Florida? Not for Disney World, that was for sure. He wanted to ask her but she wasn't around to be asked. She'd abandoned him, got herself arrested and made him feel he'd picked the losing side.

One morning after breakfast, without any purpose in mind, Alec examined the box of oranges and discovered that the original order had come from an insignificant little island off the Gulf Coast of Florida. More to revive Mr Stears's flagging approval than anything else, Alec suggested the notion of a secret island hideaway. A really ace idea. It should've put Alec on Mr Zalisky's plane, not Mrs Emerson. A move like that deserved a better reward than milk-soaked trousers.

The car was huge. Alicia, the driver, was tiny. She sat on a cushion, but even so Robin worried that she couldn't see over the dashboard. Robin worried about a lot of things – the heat, the glare, not having dark glasses, Alicia driving with only one hand on the wheel. She didn't want to die on the Tamiami Trail in the company of a dwarf and a slug. Tiny people shouldn't be put in charge of outsize cars. Slugs with jet lag shouldn't be put in charge of conversations.

After a stop for coffee and doughnuts, Robin moved to the front of the car to get away from Barry. Alicia talked non-stop and Robin found her hard to follow. But she gathered that Alicia was the agent's wife. The agent was on the island and he worked real hard. There was this phonecall at three in the morning, and Guido had been workin' on it ever since. Alicia hadn't seen Guido for days. Presumably because he was on the island. A big agency in Tallahassee called Guido. Or was it a big legal firm who did stuff for Disney in Orlando? Anyways, with Guido on the island, there was no one else to hire the car and meet the non-scheduled flight in Tampa except Alicia. But, hey, that was cool, she liked driving, and they were going to the island, so, what the heck, she just put a coupla clean shirts for Guido in the trunk and here she was. Neat, huh? England was neat too. Alicia went there once when her older sister's husband, who was in the air force, was stationed in Essex.

Robin smiled. Barry had been under the impression that Nash would lay on a chauffeur-driven limo, and he couldn't come to grips with this tiny woman who insisted on eating her chocolate doughnut at his table and who talked a blue streak. He slumped in the back seat and tried to maintain a dignified silence.

'This glare's killing me,' Robin said. 'I forgot to bring dark glasses.'

'No problem,' Alicia said. 'There's a Wal-Mart in the next plaza. We'll do some shopping.'

Robin bought a black T-shirt which said 'Oh shit, sharks!' for Grace, and another one for Jimmy which said 'And now I'm going straight to hell' in gothic script. Then she bought a straw hat and dark glasses for herself. Buying presents for the kids made her feel more normal.

'What's the matter with you, Robin?' Barry snarled from the back seat. 'We aren't on holiday, you know.'

★   ★   ★

'You've got to come home,' Grace said to Jimmy on the phone. 'Everyone's gone crazy. Auntie Lin's in trouble. Mum's flipping out. She just ran off without telling me. Some stupid, stupid bastard's gone and convinced her that Jack might . . .'

'That's why I'm ringing,' Jimmy said through a lot of static. 'There was a picture of Auntie Lin being arrested in one of the Italian gossip mags. I couldn't believe it, sis. What's the old raver been up to now?'

'She was set up by a bunch of rock-biz dirt-bags. And she won't come home 'cos of the tabloids door-stepping this place. It's like the old days, Jimmy. It sucks, it really sucks.'

'Oh for God's sake, Grace,' Jimmy said. 'What're you talking about? You don't remember the old days – you were just a baby.'

'You'd be surprised,' Grace said loftily. But in spite of what she told Alec, Jimmy was right. She couldn't remember Jack at all. She didn't want to admit it, though. Jack was her one and only claim to glamour and she wouldn't let him go without a fight.

'Anyway,' she said, 'that's what Mum told me. She said history was repeating itself. And now she's freaked out and gone to the States to look for Jack . . .'

'She's done *what*?'

'I told you. This fat creepo Alec works for turned up and gave her a song and dance about Jack being alive and Auntie Lin hiding him out on an island, and she fell for it. She *fell* for it, Jimmy, and she pushed off to the States while Alec and I were at the movies. Please, Jimmy, you've got to come home.'

'Maybe I'd better,' Jimmy said. 'It sounds like you've all lost your marbles. Does Lin know what's happening? Or is she still in chokey?'

'She's undercover somewhere. I can't talk to her because the phones are all bugged.'

'Oh Grace,' Jimmy said wearily, 'please tell me you're joking.'

'They're bugged,' she said firmly. 'Alec did it himself.'

'Then tell him to undo it. Is this the guy Mum put in my room?'

'Sort of,' Grace said. She felt stupid and depressed. She shouldn't have mentioned the bugged phones, not on the phone. Things were falling apart.

'Where is he? I want to talk to him.'

'He's out.' Where? Alec was in a foul mood. That's why she was so glad Jimmy had called. She was in need of someone to talk to. She was feeling unusually insecure.

'This stinks,' Jimmy said with authority. 'Go out to a public phone box and try to get hold of Auntie Lin. She's a tough old bird – she'll know what to do.'

'She'll freak.'

'She's nowhere near as fragile and romantic as you think she is. She's survived all sorts of shit.'

'But they're trying to turn Jack into Elvis. It's horrible and grotesque.'

'They probably think it'll sell more records. I'm sorry they've sucked Mum in, though. She's the one who'll freak.'

'Are you coming home?'

'Hell, yes,' Jimmy said. 'You're making a right dog's dinner of this. Anyway, I only rang to see if Mum would send me some dosh. Italian campsites suck and I'm going broke.'

Thank God, Grace thought, someone's coming. It was only Jimmy, but it broke the isolation. It occurred to her that she'd never been alone in the house for more than an hour or two. It was her home and her mother was always there. Always. She worked in the attic and she rarely went out, except to go shopping or make deliveries. This was her mother's domain. She was never more than a yell away. Everyone else came and went, but Mum was a constant.

It never occurred to her that her mother might even own a suitcase. Now she was gone, and without her, oddly, Alec seemed to lose his charm. He suddenly became a stranger. Nice-looking, yes, but a bit self-centred and sort of unsafe. Like, she could trust him when Mum or Lin was there, but alone, she felt weird about him – like, she couldn't see the point any more.

The place was extraordinary, Robin thought. You drove down a long straight road behind all the slowly cruising Chevies and Buicks. On either side of you were golf courses and condominiums with names like The Beach Place, The Verandah, Buttonwood

Harbor, all sticking up clean and white like false teeth. Behind the false teeth, the Astro Turf grass and sprinklers, the sea winked and glared.

Then you turned right into Bowsprit Lane, past a line of tidy bungalows with mail boxes shooting laser beams of reflected sunlight straight into your eyes. The lane petered out into a turning circle and then became a sandy track which disappeared into dense dark undergrowth.

She was barely a hundred yards from the main road, scarcely five hundred feet from the twin rows of holiday bungalows and, without warning, she was about to step into a tangle of wild oak, unrecognisable tropical trees and vines.

The sun couldn't penetrate the twisted unrestrained greenery. It was dark. She took off her new sunglasses and peered into the gloom. She could just distinguish the outline of a screened porch. The timber was the same grey colour as the tree trunks, and thick exotic foliage pressed up against the mosquito netting, making it look like a forgotten, overgrown aviary.

'This can't be it,' she said out loud, almost making herself jump. 'Lin would never own a place like this. Not here. It's all wrong. Just not Lin at all.'

She turned back to Barry and Guido. 'Really,' she said, 'this just isn't Lin. There's been a mistake.'

Guido said, 'Yes, m'am.'

Barry said nothing. He was looking extremely unsure of himself.

Guido said, 'Shall we go sit in the car? I'll get a coupla cans from the cooler. I got beer, Diet Coke or Sprite.'

'Sprite,' said Barry.

'Beer, please,' said Robin. She needed a drink. There was something unnerving about the coiling distorted vines and trees – the unexpected darkness. It was a vestige of primeval forest, forgotten by the planners and architects and landscape designers. Forgotten by progress.

Guido was only an inch or so taller than his wife, but poking out from the sleeves of his crisp short-sleeved shirt was a pair of arms which would have made Popeye the Sailor Man proud. He and Alicia drank Diet Coke. After a pause he said, 'See, I was surprised as you. But I checked twice at the Land Registry *and* the post office.'

Alicia said, 'He always double-checks, Robin. He's known by it.'

'I didn't mean to be rude,' Robin said. 'It's just . . . well, I know my sister.'

'Sure you do,' Alicia said.

Guido cleared his throat politely. 'The property was purchased twenty-seven years ago and it's registered to the Eagle Holding Company, sole proprietor, Ms Linnet Walker.'

'Who pays the property tax?' Barry asked, sounding confident again.

'Eagle Holding.'

'No, no,' Robin said. Lin pay property tax? Surely not. Lin didn't *do* taxes. Lin wasn't a resident anywhere. She never even had a place to hang her hat unless it was Robin's house.

'Have you spoken to the neighbours?'

Neighbours? Robin looked round vaguely. Of course there were neighbours, close neighbours, on this tacky, *nouveau riche* playground of an island. But this corner of nightmare jungle seemed to have been picked up from the set of a film about mad swamp dwellers. The darkness, the silence, argued for total isolation.

'See, there's a problem,' Guido said. 'This part of the key ain't residential. People own property, sure, but, like, it's vacationers – they just come for the season to play tennis or golf or for the sailing. Hardly no one lives here all year round except the people who work here. And most of them come in daily from the mainland.'

'Regular folks wouldn't live here and raise families,' Alicia concurred. 'No regular folks, no regular neighbours.'

'But I talked to the Quaker lady at the post office,' Guido said, 'and a guy who's been at the pharmacy in the Avenue Mall for years. They say there's a guy here who was wounded in 'Nam. He don't never come off the property, never shows his face. He don't get no deliveries and he doesn't own an automobile. They say there used to be a black woman came a coupla times a week but nobody's seen her in years.'

'Are you listening, Robin?' Barry said pompously. 'Doesn't ever show his face. Maybe wounded in Vietnam. Or maybe suffered serious burns in a fire twenty-five years ago. It adds up.'

'But that's as far as I can go,' Guido said. 'I can't sit here and watch the house 'cos that's what the Sheriff's Department here don't like. You hang out here for a spell and just see if they don't slide on through to check out where you're at. People here dial 911 if they see a bicycle in a no-parking zone.'

'It's that kinda place,' Alicia confirmed. 'Exclusive.'

'Way I see it,' Guido went on, 'only thing you can do is walk on up to the door and talk to the guy straight up.'

'Oh dear,' Barry said.

Talking to people straight up was not one of Barry's strengths, Robin thought. She'd had twenty-four hours of his hints and sly rummagings for information.

'Only problem with that', Guido said, 'is the dogs. Guy got a coupla mean suckers in there. I saw 'em night before last. Pit bulls or something. Came out after racoons, I guess.'

'Pit bulls?' Barry said.

'What do you want to do?' Guido asked inexorably. ' 'Cos I suggest you don't wait till after dark. If the dogs don't get you the bugs will. This guy doesn't spray – he got mosquitos here big as dinner plates.'

Guido's getting a kick out of this, Robin decided. He's treating us like greenhorns in the wild west. She looked at Barry dithering, playing with his Sprite can, rolling the cold surface over his pink cheeks and between his plump palms.

She said, 'Well, Barry? This was your idea. What're you going to do?'

Barry's buttocks writhed against the car seat. He said, 'Robin, look, I mean, Jack was virtually your brother-in-law.'

'Yes. And I've been listening to twenty-four hours of you saying he was your best friend.'

'But if he's scarred, Robin? If he's mad . . .'

'If he's scarred and mad, he's still Jack.' Robin opened the car door and waves of wet heat rolled in. She said, 'Come on. We've got to find out, one way or the other.'

The picture of the bright angel on her wall, the one who greeted her every morning, beckoned. And summoned, Robin walked forward into the gloomy tangled jungle.

When I think of all those stories of people looking where they've been told not to look – Orpheus in the underworld, Pandora and her forbidden box, the foolish bride in Bluebeard's Castle – I see initiative poorly rewarded. Loss and death follow the curious. Don't look, they say. Don't be too clever. Don't ask too many questions. Death stalks the detective. But the human condition is to ignore warnings, to go where you're not welcome. That's how new worlds get populated. The naked ape isn't satisfied with the tree he was born under. 'Gimme more,' he says as soon as he learns to speak. Greedy little bastard.

Good. The globe is crawling with greedy little bastards. I know, because I proudly count myself as one of them. My gimme-more gene is highly developed, so in that respect I understand Nash, Sasson and Barry perfectly.

It should be simple: They want what I've got; I want what they've got. That's the basis of a great relationship. But nothing is simple in a relationship between art and commerce. For one thing, these days, the art is of secondary importance to the artist. Sometimes I think they don't want the art at all – they only want a marketable artist. And increasingly, of course, that is just what they're getting – kids so greedy for attention that they sell their pretty young images to front a product so banal that no one listens to it.

Which makes it tough when what you want to sell are songs to the greedy bastards who only want the singer.

And that is why, when Nash was staring at me from across the boardroom table with his little saurian eyes magnified by thick plastic lenses, even before he opened his greedy mouth to drop his bombshell, I wrote on my copy of the contract, 'Up your bum, Nash Zalisky.' Childish, undignified? Yes. Satisfying? Oh, absolutely.

'I always wanted Jack,' he told me once, not mentioning music at all. Well, I'm not selling Jack. I'm not loaning him, leasing him, or giving him away either. I have ten good songs and that was all I ever intended to sell. The rest? Well, call it my advertising campaign, if you like. It was never up for grabs.

The Antigua Movie? What was that but beautiful visual images packaged for a music industry which is willing to spend more on making a video than on cutting an album. It was beautiful visual images which got my back taxes paid, brought me to the bargaining table and gave me a bank account with money in it.

Nash will want it all back, of course. But he can't have it. He'll have to let it go – the way I've had to let go of all those past royalties, the way Jack had to let go of a little dance number that went platinum in Brazil.

Obviously Nash will say I scammed him. But he'll never be quite sure. Nor will Sasson, and nor will any of the other legal and financial advisors sitting at that table. After all, it was Nash who pulled out of the deal, Nash who said he didn't want to sign with me. Everyone at the table heard him. He said he'd prefer to sign with Jack. I was the innocent party in the rainbow dress who fainted from the shock.

He spent quite a lot of money on nothing. But even so, the price was small compared with what the industry owes Jack and me. He'll never pay that back. What he paid was the price for being a greedy little bastard who looked where he wasn't supposed to look – or rather, being Nash, sending his minions to look. It's the price he pays for looking when he should be listening, for listening when he has no right to listen, for stealing images I didn't want to show him, for corrupting kids like Alec who are primed from birth to want, want, want. But most of all, it's the price he pays for corrupting, with hope, innocent dreamers like my sister.

Her weakness was to love a man who didn't even see her. And Nash exploited her love. He said, 'You can have him, but only if you betray him.' You pay for that, Nash. I only wish I could've made you pay more.

Later, what Robin remembered most vividly of the horrible, frightening incident was teeth: the gleaming white teeth of snarling dogs and the yellow ochre teeth of a heavy smoker who mouthed the words 'Fuck off' at her through mosquito netting.

The frenzied dogs clawed at the screen, rattling it, threatening to hurl their lean muscular bodies through it. She did not back off or run away. She stood her ground and called through the din, 'Anyone at home?'

And then the face appeared at a window curtained only by mosquito netting. It was a nightmare face, bearded with wiry salt and pepper hair. Leathery skin hung in corrugations from sharp cheekbones. One eye was missing and the eyelid sank into an empty socket like a withered petal.

'Jack?' she said uncertainly. 'Is it you?' She tried in vain to make out the colour of the surviving eye – willing it, like a prayer, to be gloriously blue. But the surviving eye was so narrow, so screwed up with enmity and spite, that she couldn't identify a trace of colour in the hate-filled slit.

'Jack?' she said again, provoking the dogs to more insane rage. But the single slitty eye just poured cold contempt on her quaking heart. The ragged hair around the mouth parted, showing chipped yellow teeth, and the lips formed the words 'Fuck off' but not a sound could be heard above the barking and snarling of the dogs. Then the face disappeared, leaving the black square of window bare.

She stood in front of his porch for fully ten minutes, waiting. She stood with tears pouring down her face, waiting for a stranger to come out and tell her that he wasn't Jack, that however long she waited he never would be Jack. Jack was gone. But the disfigured stranger didn't even return to the window. He left her standing in front of his porch while his dogs screamed and roared.

After a while she wiped her eyes on the hem of her pretty summer dress and walked slowly back to the car.

'Well?' Barry asked, his cheeks wobbling with anticipation. 'Well?'

'It wasn't him,' Robin said, her throat sore from gulping tears.

'Wasn't? Wasn't?' Barry said. 'Then why are you crying?'

'Because it might have been,' she said, utterly defeated. 'It might have been but it wasn't.'

'Are you sure?'

'Absolutely sure.'

'Did you see his face? How can you be so certain? I don't know that I trust either of the Walker sisters.'

'Go and look for yourself.' Robin climbed wearily into the car. With silent sympathy, Alicia handed her a fistful of tissues and she buried her face in them, unable to prevent another wave of grief from shaking her drooping middle-aged body.

With the car door open they could all hear the hysterical barking of the dogs. Barry got out and took a couple of steps towards the dark secret house. Then he turned and got back in again.

'If you're absolutely sure,' he said.

To believe anything else, Robin would have had to accept that her bright angel had become an ugly monster. She would have accepted his ugliness. After all, she had kept the ugly blackened lump that had once been his gold ring. But she could not accept that the man who gave her barmy mother a house when he didn't have one himself could stare at her with such contempt and hatred. She couldn't believe the beautiful youth whose voice made her heart soar could set his dogs on her and stand there staring while she wept in front of his house. An ugly face and body she could accept as Jack's but not an ugly soul.

Therefore it was not Jack's face she saw at the window. Robin's bright angel was a charmed thing etched into eternity. She knew she might not recognise his face, but she could never be mistaken about his soul.

# CODA

'You left your mark on me, it's permanent, a tattoo.'

Lucinda Williams

# I

On a grey, drizzly hillside in north Oxfordshire the Hebbingdon Free Festival was in the middle of its noisy, gaudy first day. The damp grass was covered with groundsheets and polythene, and the groundsheets were covered by a sea of stoned kids, rocked into mindless paralysis by stacks of giant speakers from three stages.

Sheltering under the apron at the back of Stage Two were the five members of InnerVersions, Dram, Sapper, Corky, Karen and their new drummer, Patsi Noble. It was their first festival – their first time playing on an outdoor stage, and they were nervous as hell.

'So many people,' Sapper said. 'There must be thousands.'

There *were* thousands – the hillside was carpeted with kids. They weren't all waiting for InnerVersions though. They were simply hanging and waiting for whatever happened next.

'The sound's horrible,' Karen muttered. It *was* horrible – muddled and muddy. The only thing to be said for it was that it was loud. But no louder than the sounds from the other two stages which could be heard clearly from where the band shivered under the backstage. Every now and then the wind blew across the faces of the open mikes causing a thunderous roar.

InnerVersions was slotted in between The Rolling Clones and a club act called Doreen Doreen with only fifteen minutes for the stage crew to set up. There would be no time for a proper soundcheck.

They'd never played to such a large audience and to do so without a proper soundcheck reminded Karen of all those dreams of incompetence and unreadiness. Thousands and thousands of people, only a forty-minute set to make an impression on them, and no bleeding soundcheck.

Worse, the Clones were doing very well. They had the front of the crowd jumping and singing along to 'Brown Sugar'.

'If they like that,' Dram said gloomily, 'they'll fuckin' hate us. No one knows us. They want a singalong, fuck it, and no one knows our material.'

'They will after today,' Ozzy Ireland said. He was getting used to InnerVersions' pernicious habit of bringing each other down. 'Enjoy yourselves for once. Go up there and just belt it out.'

'Easy for you to say,' Corky said with a sly look at Patsi. 'This isn't your first outing with a new drummer.' He emphasised the word 'outing'. He still couldn't quite believe that Flambo had been replaced by a woman, a muscular woman who, it seemed, could count.

'Shut up and listen to this,' Ozzy said. He folded back the flapping pages of *Mojo* magazine and began to read aloud. ' "In the studio this month: Birdie, self-styled widow of the more famous Jack, is overseeing production and remastering of the eagerly awaited ten lost tracks. The Hyde Voodoo studio in New Orleans was picked for its proximity to ex-Jack producer, Junior Moline. 'We're going for a raw, live sound,' says Moline, 'something as close to the spirit of *Hard Candy* and *Hard Time* as we can get without too much overdubbing. We're calling the album *Hard On* at the moment but I expect the label will have something to say about it.

' "Surprisingly, the label is not Jack's old company, Dog Records, as was expected and indeed publicised. The prize, which is expected to go gold in its first week of release, has gone to Atlantic. After the aborted signing a spokesman for Dog was tight-lipped about the loss. 'We are releasing a Jack-In-The-Box set of our own in time for Christmas,' was his only comment. But a little Birdie tells us that the rift was caused when conglomerate boss, Nash Zalisky, flipped his lid and started to believe in Jack sightings from as far afield as Acapulco, Miami and Bali. 'The ghosts of dead rock stars are always haunting us,' she said with her familiar sexy laugh, 'but you don't expect multi-media moguls to want to sign contracts with them.' So, no *Hard On* for Dog this Christmas." '

'Well that explains why we haven't seen her,' Corky said, digging his elbow into Sapper's ribs. 'Nothing personal, old fruit – she was just feathering her own nest.'

# II

It is finished and I'm holding in my hand the slim plastic box with a cover-picture of sunlit, windblown Jack. His face emerges like a spectre's from a stormy sea. Or is it receding into the waves? Coming or going? Who knows – it's all down to individual interpretation, like everything else in rock music.

I'm holding in my hand the voice that can still make my loins ache. I haven't done it any harm. It rings out clear as a bell. It's warm and cold. It's angry, hard, sad and sexy. It's funny and sly. It takes you places you've never been. It finds secret longings, corners of your soul and memory you never knew existed. It makes you get down and boogie. That voice. Remember it?

If I'd had a voice like that . . . ah, but I didn't. It was a gift, and it was not given to me. It was given to Jack. Jack had it and Jack used it. May God bless him and keep him. Beautiful Jack.

I didn't have a voice, but I had some music and I had some words. What could I do but give them to Jack? People wanted to listen to him. They didn't want to listen to me. Even if I'd had a voice, no one would have wanted to hear it. My young life was a performance before an audience of millions. It was a role thrust upon me by nature and my own youthful stupidity. But it was a non-speaking, non-singing role – which I suppose you could see as something of a tragedy for a woman who thought she had something to say.

But never mind. It's all over now, and at least sometimes I had Jack's voice to speak for me. I would never, never, *ever*, have harmed that voice. No. Jack did that all by himself when he burned his throat out with boiling, choking smoke and lost it for ever. May God curse him for that. That voice could have lasted for decades if he'd taken care of it. But he didn't, and now all he has is fame – empty, resounding, eternal fame.

Here's another rock'n'roll story: this one's about the destructive power of fame. Lethal fame and lethal longing. One dark night a famous self-indulgent rock-star is prowling around his mansion under the influence of reds, greens, blues. He's a famous rock star so he has uppers and downers of all the colours of the rainbow. You name it, he's got it. He's got it so he takes it. That's what rock-stars are supposed to do. This rock-star is playing at being a rock-star, out of his skull in his lonely old mansion. He may be very famous but he can also be quite banal at times.

Outside his gate there's a hippie camp, a gathering of stoned kids who are playing at being besotted fans. They wait there, all day and all night, for a glimpse of the famous rock-star. Whenever he comes out they crowd around his car, screaming, 'Yeah, Jack! We love you, man.'

And then, into this tableau walks the real thing – the *truly* besotted fan, the one who, when he isn't thinking he owns Jack and all his work, thinks he *is* Jack and all his work. He looks at the hippie camp. He looks at the gate. He looks at the wall. He sees no barrier. It's only God's little mistake that Jack is inside and he is outside. He is mad enough to think that he can rectify God's mistake. He can climb walls. He can cross lawns. He can walk straight into a lonely mansion on the hill. And when Jack sees him, Jack will recognise him as his brother, his twin, his other self. Because that is what Jack is to this crazy fan – his other self. So Jack will have to recognise him. There's no other way.

Except, of course, Jack doesn't recognise him. Jack sees him as a trippy nightmare figure creeping down the basement stairs with a kerosene lamp in his hand, like the robed figure of Death with empty eye sockets. Jack freaks. The mad other self freaks. The angel wrestles frantically with Death. Hell-fire laps around his ankles. The mansion on the hill burns to a crisp.

All Jack had to do was talk the guy down. All he had to do was hit the panic button. Wait for help. Ah yes, but you're forgetting all those yellows, reds, greens and blues. And what about whatever the mad other self had dropped to help him on his crazy way?

We'll never know about that. He never even got the chance to tell Jack his name.

Anyway, I don't know how much of this is true. I'm making half of it up, and Jack couldn't remember properly the half I'm not making up. It was all a nightmare to him.

All I know for certain is that the charred bone fragments in the basement were not Jack's. And the ugly lump of gold which I wept such bitter tears over was not Jack's Egyptian ring.

When I saw Jack next it was a week later and I nearly didn't recognise him. He came in the night to Robin's kitchen door. The right side of his face and his right hand were a mass of healing burns. The fire had scorched away every beautiful hair on his head. He could only speak in a hoarse whisper. He couldn't remember where he'd been or how he got home. And he thought he was a murderer.

Technically speaking, I don't suppose anyone else would have even called him a killer, let alone a murderer. But the mad other self left an indelible calling card on Jack's mind as well as on his body.

'Hide me,' he whispered. 'Help me. Hide me.'

God help me, God hide me – that's exactly what I did. I thought I could heal him. Did I really think that? Did I really think at all? I know I thought I could help him find his voice again. I thought that when the burns closed, when his hair grew back, his mind would heal too. So much for the optimism of youth.

Youth and optimism faded together. Ah well – goodbye both. I was sorry to see you go, but you went – the way you always do.

And, fuck it, what was I supposed to do? Feed Jack – bald, burned, whispering Jack – to the tabloid vultures hanging around my sister's house? Are you insane?

No, I had a bolt-hole, a tiny cabin on a scruffy overgrown key on the Gulf Coast of Florida. I bought it with the proceeds from a shameful transaction in LA. Check out a certain pornographic web-site on your computer and you'll clearly see Birdie-the-whore accepting twenty-thousand dollars for unspeakable services rendered to a plump, powerful pig. You can check it out any time, night or day, courtesy of Nash Zalisky.

Unspeakable services, my arse! It was just a fuck, and it bought me a house. My house. Not the bank's, not the record company's, not Jack's. Mine. A little cedar shack on the beach. An old broken-down dock, just right for tying up an old broken-down outboard. My back door on to the mangroves – in the days when the mangroves were thick and plentiful.

In those days you could only get to the key by boat across the bay. And the bay was teeming with pompano, and the mangroves were teeming with herons, egrets and the elusive snook. Then, you could see ibis stalking the beach every morning and watch the sea eagles circling the trees. It was a safe place to hide out in.

Nowadays you're lucky ever to see an ibis, and the key is linked to three other keys and the mainland by concrete bridges which bring rivers, floods, of holiday-makers like some infernal aqueduct. The little spit of sand and greenery is groaning under the weight of condominiums and golf clubs. No, this island is no longer even an island. I could sell my few acres of it tomorrow. And believe me I've had some very tempting offers. I could sell up and move Jack to another island without a backward glance. Except that Jack won't let me because that would leave his only friend, Mekong Marty, without a home.

Mute Mekong Marty is the only man on the island uglier, madder and worse off than Jack. Jack is a peach compared to Marty, and maybe that's why Jack likes him. They built their houses together. Jack's house is right on the bay, Marty's is between Jack's house and the road. Marty and his dogs guard Jack from intruders. Marty will never leave. He'll shoot himself and his dogs – three bullets into three welcoming skulls – rather than be uprooted.

If I couldn't sell, I couldn't buy another place. The scruffy plot of land was the only thing I could call my own. So I had to watch while the road was paved, the bridges were built. More and more buildings went up and the water table went down. The ibis flew away.

Now, though, everything has changed. This slim box with Jack's bright picture on the cover has changed everything. I can move Jack and leave Mekong Marty where he wants to be. I can afford proper care for Jack and a good new outboard for me.

You'd think, wouldn't you, that I'd have told Robin. Who would be better to tell than her? She would've looked after Jack. She might have put our mother in a home for Jack's sake. Or she'd have brought her along with her two little children. She'd have lived in isolation and secret with her entire family just for the privilege of looking after Jack. Hooray for the selfless heroine, the woman who would beggar herself and die for love.

She does love him, she always has. She loved him better and much more faithfully than I ever could. It's her nature to love that way. The poor deluded cow even loves *me*.

Well, that's why I never told her. I could kid you and say I kept silent to protect her and her children from the consequences of her sweet love. But no one would believe that. So I'll tell you instead that the one I want to protect from sweet love is Jack.

Obsessive love nearly killed him. He's had too much love to cope with – no one should have to suffer so much love. And Robin's sweet love would soften him and rot him to the core like sugar rots a tooth. He doesn't get that kind of love from me. Never has, never will. And he's better off without it.

I'll be with him in time for Christmas, and he'll come to the edge of the dock. He'll whisper, 'Hey, babe. What's that you've got there? Have you brought me a present?'

And I'll say, 'I've brought your stupid voice back, take it or leave it.'

He'll take it. And maybe he'll laugh, or maybe he'll cry, you can never tell with Jack. But one thing's certain – he won't rot. And another thing's certain – he won't starve. Not now. And nor will I.

## A NOTE ON THE TYPE

The text of this book is set in Bembo, the original types of
which were cut by Francesco Griffo for the Venetian printer
Aldus Manutius, and were first used in 1495 for Cardinal
Bembo's *De Aetna*. Claude Garamond (1480–1561) used
Bembo as a model and so it became the forerunner of
standard European type for the following two centuries. Its
modern form was designed, following the original, for
Monotype in 1929 and is widely in use today.